Praise for Åsa Larsson's A

THE BLOC

Named Sweden's Best Crime Novel of the Year in 2004

Chosen as a Book Sense Notable Book

"Hugely atmospheric." —*Booknews* from The Poisoned Pen

"Psychological suspense with a refreshing twist . . . an excellent book."
—*Mystery Scene*

SUN STORM

Named Sweden's Best First Crime Novel of the Year in 2003

"Suspense builds." —*OK!* magazine

"*Sun Storm* won her Sweden's 'Best First Crime Novel' award, and the book is notable for its convincing evocation of the extreme cold and dark of winter in Sweden's rural north. . . . Larsson's strong writing (superbly translated by Marlaine Delargy) merits the positive attention *Sun Storm* has received." —*Houston Chronicle*

"If you like Karin Fossum and Henning Mankell, you are going to love Åsa Larsson, yet another brilliant new author from Scandinavia. This translation of her first novel, written in 2003, simply sizzles, and it promises more good novels to come." —*Toronto Globe and Mail*

"Complex characters and the setting in the dark and frigid northern winter distinguish this tale." —*Mystery Lovers Bookshop News*

"This is a chewy book, filled with betrayals, wrongs, emotional scars and a rich, all-too-human plot that's very strong for a debut effort."
—*Bookgasm Reviews*

"Larsson depicts her characters with mordant wit and describes their village with richly atmospheric details." —*Kirkus Reviews*

"The story builds to a thrillerlike ending." —*Publishers Weekly*

"A sure-handed thriller from a talented first novelist . . . Larsson builds suspense gradually but inexorably, and she is equally good at creating mood, using the frozen landscape and isolated location to evoke the icy inner lives of the church members and building the need for release. More like Ruth Rendell's psychological thrillers than the procedurals of Martinsson's fellow Swedes (Mankell and Thursten, for example), this impressive debut nevertheless heralds yet another striking voice from Scandinavia." —*Booklist*

"For those who eschew exotic travel in favor of the familiar hammock, there's nothing better than a well-written and well-translated story from someplace you'll probably never visit. *Sun Storm* is that story and more. . . . A fine tale." —*Rocky Mountain News*

Also by Åsa Larsson

Sun Storm

The Black Path

THE BLC

DELTA TRADE PAPERBACK

OD SPILT

TRANSLATED BY MARLAINE DELARGY

ÅSA LARSSON

THE BLOOD SPILT
A Delta Book

PUBLISHING HISTORY
First published in Sweden as *Det blod som spillts*
Delacorte Press edition / February 2007
Delta trade paperback edition / January 2008

Published by
Bantam Dell
A Division of Random House, Inc.
New York, New York

All rights reserved
Copyright © 2004 by Åsa Larsson
Translation copyright © 2007 by The Bantam Dell Publishing Group, a
division of Random House, Inc.
Cover photo © iofoto/Shutterstock
Cover design by Craig DeCamps

Book design by Glen Edelstein

Library of Congress Catalog Card Number: 2006048498

Delta is a registered trademark of Random House, Inc., and the colophon is
a trademark of Random House, Inc.

ISBN 978-0-385-34079-3

Printed in the United States of America
Published simultaneously in Canada

www.bantamdell.com

BVG 10 9 8 7 6

See, where the Lord comes out from his dwelling-place, holds

the nations of the world to account for their guilt! Earth shall

disclose the blood spilt on it, and no more cover its dead.

—Isaiah 26:21

Hold they shall not, your terms with death, your compact

with the grave; when the flood of ruin sweeps past, it

shall leave you prostrate.

It will carry you away as it passes; pass it will, suddenly,

in the space of a day and a night, and the very alarm of it

will make you understand the revelation at last.

—Isaiah 28:18–19

THE BLOOD SPILT

FRIDAY JUNE 21

I am lying on my side on the kitchen sofa. Impossible to sleep. At this time of year, in the middle of summer, the nights are so light they allow you no rest. The clock on the wall above me will soon strike one. The ticking of the pendulum grows louder in the silence. Smashes every sentence to pieces. Every attempt at rational thought. On the table lies the letter from that woman.

Lie still, I say to myself. Lie still and sleep.

My thoughts turn to Traja, a pointer bitch we had when I was little. She could never settle, walked round and round the kitchen like a restless soul, her claws clicking on the lacquered wooden floor. For the first few months we kept her in a cage indoors to force her to relax. The house was constantly filled with the sound of "sit" and "stay" and "lie down."

Now it's just the same. There's a dog in my breast who wants to jump up every time the clock ticks. Every time I take a breath. But it isn't Traja who's inside me ready to pounce. Traja just wanted to trot around. Get rid of the restlessness in her body. This dog turns her head away from me when I try to look at her. She is filled with evil intent.

I shall try to go to sleep. Somebody should lock me in. I ought to have a cage in the kitchen.

*   *   *

I get up and look out of the window. It's quarter past one. It's as light as day. The long shadows from the ancient pine trees along the edge of the yard extend toward the house. I think they look like arms. Hands stretching up out of their restless graves and reaching for me. The letter is lying there on the kitchen table.

*   *   *

I'm in the cellar. It's twenty-five to two. The dog who isn't Traja is on her feet. She's running around the edges of my mind. I try to call to her. Don't want to follow her into this untrodden territory. My head is empty on the inside. My hand takes things off the wall. Different objects. What do I want with them? The sledgehammer. The crowbar. The chain. The hammer.

*   *   *

My hands place everything in the trunk of the car. It's like a puzzle. I can't see what it's meant to represent. I get into the car and wait. I think about the woman and the letter. It's her fault. She's the one who's driven me out of my mind.

*   *   *

I'm driving the car. There's a clock on the instrument panel. Straight lines with no meaning. The road is carrying me out of time. My hands are clutching the wheel so tightly that my fingers are hurting. If I kill myself now they'll have to cut the steering wheel out of the car and bury it with me. But I'm not going to kill myself.

*   *   *

I stop the car a hundred meters from the shore where she keeps her boat. I walk down to the river. It's shining and quiet, waiting.

There's the faint sound of lapping water beneath the boat. The sun is dancing on the ripples caused by a salmon trout coming to the surface to eat flies. The mosquitoes are swarming around me. Whirring around my ears. Landing round my eyes and on the back of my neck and sucking blood. I don't take any notice of them. A sound makes me turn around. It's her. She is standing no more than ten meters from me.

*   *   *

Her mouth opens and forms itself around words. But I hear nothing. My ears are sealed up. Her eyes narrow. Irritation springs to life in them. I take two tentative steps forward. I still don't know what I want. I am in the territory beyond all sense and reason.

She catches sight of the crowbar in my hand. Her mouth stops moving. The narrow eyes widen once again. A second of surprise. Then fear.

I catch sight of the crowbar myself. My hand whitens around the steel. And suddenly the dog is back. Enormous. Paws like hooves. The hair is standing up from the back of its neck all the way down to its tail. Teeth bared. It's going to swallow me whole. And then it's going to swallow the woman.

*   *   *

I've reached her. She looks at the crowbar as if she were bewitched by it and so the first blow strikes her right on the temple. I kneel down beside her and lay my cheek against her mouth. A warm puff of air against my skin. I haven't finished with her yet. The dog rushes out like a mad thing, straight for everything in its way. Its claws rip the earth, leaving great wounds. I am rampaging. I am racing into the far country that is madness.

And now I am lengthening my stride.

Pia Svonni the churchwarden is standing in her garden smoking. She usually holds the cigarette the way girls are supposed to, between her index and middle fingers. But now she's holding it firmly between her thumb and her index and middle fingers. There's a hell of a difference. It's nearly midsummer, that's why. You get kind of crazy. Don't want to sleep. Don't need to either. The night whispers and entices and draws you in, so you just have to go outside.

The wood nymphs are putting on their new shoes, made of the finest birch bark. It's a real beauty competition. They forget themselves and dance and sway in the meadows, even though a car might pass by. They wear out their shoes while the little ones stand hidden among the trees, watching with huge eyes.

Pia Svonni stubs out the cigarette on the base of the upturned flowerpot that serves as an ashtray and drops the stub through the hole. She suddenly decides to cycle down to Jukkasjärvi church. Tomorrow there's a wedding there. She has already done the cleaning and made everything look nice, but now she has the idea of picking a big bunch of flowers for the altar. She'll go out into the meadow beyond the churchyard. Buttercups grow there, and globe flowers and purple cranesbill in a haze of cow parsley. And forget-me-nots whisper along the edge. She pushes her cell phone into her pocket and pulls on her tennis shoes.

The midnight sun casts its glow over the yard. The thin light falls through the fence and the long shadows from the slats make the lawn look like a homemade rag rug, woven in stripes of greenish yellow and dark green. A flock of thrushes is screeching and playing havoc in one of the birch trees.

* * *

The whole way down to Jukkasjärvi is one long downhill run. Pia pedals and changes gear. Her speed is lethal. And no helmet. Her hair streams out behind her. It's like when she was four years old and used to swing standing up on the old swing made out of a tire in the yard, until it felt as if it were going to swing right round. She cycles through Kauppinen where some horses gaze at her from under the trees. When she passes the bridge over the river Torne she can see two little boys fly-fishing a little way downstream.

The road runs parallel with the river. The village is sleeping. She passes the tourist area and the restaurant, the old Konsum supermarket and the ugly community center. The old folk museum's silvery timber walls and the white veils of mist on the meadow in front of the fence.

At the far end of the village, where the road runs out, is the wooden church, painted Falun red. A smell of fresh tar comes from the roof timbers.

The bell tower is part of the fence. To get into the church, you go in through the bell tower and walk along a stone path that leads to the church steps.

One of the blue doors to the bell tower is standing wide open. Pia clambers off her bicycle and leans it against the fence.

It should be closed, she thinks, walking slowly toward the door.

Something rustles among the small birch trees to the right of the path down to the rectory. Her heart races and she stops to listen. It was only a little rustle. Probably a squirrel or a shrew.

The back door of the bell tower is open as well. She can see straight through the tower. The door of the church is also open.

Now her heart is really thumping. Sune might forget the door of the bell tower if he's been celebrating—after all, it's the night before midsummer's eve. But not the door of the church. She thinks about those kids who smashed the windows of the church in town, and threw burning rags inside. That was a couple of years ago. What's happened now? Pictures flash across her mind. The altarpiece sprayed with graffiti and piss. Long slashes with a knife on the newly painted pews. Presumably they've got in through a window, then opened the door from the inside.

She moves toward the church door. Walks slowly. Listens carefully in every direction. How has it come to this? Little boys who ought to be too busy thinking about girls and fiddling with their mopeds. How have they turned into queer-bashers and thugs who set fire to churches?

When she passes the porch she stops. Stands beneath the organ loft where the ceiling is so low that tall people have to stoop down. It's silent and gloomy inside the church, but everything seems to be in order. Christ, Laestadius and the Sami maiden Maria glow from the altarpiece, unblemished. But still something makes her hesitate. Something isn't right in there.

There are eighty-six corpses beneath the floor of the church. Most of the time she doesn't think about them at all. They are resting in peace in their graves. But now she can feel their unease rising up through the floor, pricking like needles under her feet.

What's the matter with you? she thinks.

The aisle of the church is covered with a red woven carpet. Exactly where the organ loft ends and the ceiling opens upward, something is lying on the carpet. She bends down.

A stone, she thinks at first. A little white splinter from a stone.

She picks it up between her thumb and index finger and walks toward the sacristy.

But the door to the sacristy is locked, and she turns to go back down the aisle.

As she stands at the front by the altar, she can see the lower part of the organ. It is almost completely covered by a wooden partition that goes across the church from the ceiling, and hangs down one third of the height of the ceiling. But she can see the lower part of the organ. And she can see a pair of feet hanging down in front of the organ loft.

Her first lightning thought is that somebody has come into the church and hanged themselves. And in that very first split second she is angry. Feels it's inconsiderate. Then she thinks precisely nothing. Runs down the aisle and past the partition, then she sees the body hanging in front of the organ pipes and the Sami sun symbol.

The body is hanging from a rope, no, not a rope, a chain. A long iron chain.

Now she can see dark stains on the carpet, just where she found the splinter of stone.

Blood. Can it be blood? She crouches down.

Then she understands. The stone she is holding between her thumb and her index finger. It isn't a stone at all. It's a splinter from a tooth.

Up onto her feet. Her fingers lose their grip on the white shard, she almost flings it away from her.

Her hand fishes the phone out of her pocket, punches in 112.

The lad on the other end sounds so bloody young. While she's answering his questions, she tugs at the door to the organ loft. It's locked.

"It's locked," she says. "I can't get up there."

She races back to the sacristy. No key to the organ loft. Can she break down the door? What with?

The lad on the other end of the phone makes her listen to him. He tells her to wait outside. Help is on the way, he promises.

"It's Mildred!" she shouts. "It's Mildred Nilsson hanging there! She's our priest. God, she looks so terrible."

"Are you outside now?" he asks. "Is there anyone nearby?"

The boy on the phone talks her out onto the steps of the church. She tells him there isn't a soul in sight.

"Don't hang up," he says. "Stay with me. Help is on the way. Don't go back into the church."

"Is it okay if I have a cigarette?"

That's all right. It's all right to put the phone down.

Pia sits down on the steps of the church, the phone beside her. Smokes and notices how calm and collected she feels. But the cigarette isn't burning properly. She finally notices that she's lit the filter. After seven minutes she hears the sirens from a long way off.

They got her, she thinks.

Her hands begin to shake. The cigarette jerks out of her grip.

The bastards. They got her.

FRIDAY SEPTEMBER 1

Rebecka Martinsson climbed out of the taxi boat and looked up at Lidö country house hotel. The afternoon sun on the pale yellow facade with its white decorative carving. The big garden full of people. Some black-headed gulls from nowhere screeched above her head. Persistent and irritating.

Where do you get the energy, she thought.

She gave the taxi driver a tip that was much too big. Compensation for her monosyllabic answers when he'd attempted to talk.

"Big party," he said, nodding toward the hotel.

The whole law firm was assembled up there. Almost two hundred people milling around. Talking in groups. Detaching themselves and moving on. Handshakes and air kisses. A line of enormous barbecues had been set out. Members of staff dressed in white were laying out a barbecue buffet on a long table covered with a linen cloth. They scurried between the hotel kitchen and the table like white mice in their ridiculously tall chef's hats.

"Yes," replied Rebecka, and hoisted her crocodile skin bag onto her shoulder. "But I've got through worse things."

He laughed and pulled away, the prow lifting out of the water. A black cat slunk silently down from the jetty and disappeared into the tall grass.

Rebecka set off. The island looked tired after the summer. Well trodden, dried out, worn out.

This is where they've walked, she thought. All the families with children, carrying their picnic blankets, all the well dressed, tipsy people from the boats.

The grass was short and turning yellow. The trees dusty and thirsty. She could imagine what it would look like in the forest. No doubt there were heaps of bottles, cans, used condoms and human feces under the blueberry bushes and ferns.

The track up to the hotel was as hard as concrete. Like the cracked back of a prehistoric lizard. She was a lizard herself. Just landed in her spaceship. Wearing human clothing on her way into the trial by fire. Trying to imitate human behavior. Look at people around her and do the same. Hope the disguise wouldn't gape at the neck.

She had almost reached the gardens.

Come on, she said to herself. You can do this.

After she'd killed those men in Kiruna she'd carried on with her job at the law firm of Meijer & Ditzinger as usual. Things had gone well, she thought. In fact they'd gone completely to hell. She hadn't thought about the blood and the bodies. When she looked back now to the time before she was signed off on sick leave, she couldn't actually remember thinking at all. She'd thought she was working. But in the end all she was doing was moving paper from one pile to another. True, she was sleeping badly. And wasn't really there, somehow. It could take an eternity just to get ready in the morning and get to work. The catastrophe came from behind. She didn't see it before it landed right on top of her. It was just a simple merger and acquisition case. The client had been wondering about the period of notice on a local rental agreement. And she'd given completely the wrong answer. All the files with all the contracts right under her nose, but she hadn't understood what they said. The client, a French mail order company, had demanded compensation from the firm.

She remembered how Måns Wenngren, her boss, had looked at her. His face blood red behind the desk. She'd tried to resign, but he wouldn't agree.

"It would look terrible for the firm," he'd said. "Everybody would think you'd been pushed out. That we were letting down a colleague with psychological . . . who isn't very well."

She'd staggered out of the office that same afternoon. And when she stood on Birger Jarlsgatan in the autumn darkness with the lights of the expensive cars swishing past and the tastefully decorated shop windows and the pubs down on Stureplan, she was suddenly overcome by a strong feeling that she'd never be able to go back to Meijer & Ditzinger. She'd felt as though she wanted to get as far away from them as possible. But it didn't turn out like that.

She was signed off on sick leave. For a week at a time, first of all. Then for a month at a time. The doctor had told her to do whatever she enjoyed. If there was anything she liked about her job, she should carry on doing that.

The firm's criminal caseload had begun to increase significantly after Kiruna. Her name and picture had been kept out of the papers, but the name of the firm had appeared frequently in the media. And it had produced results. People got in touch and wanted to be represented by "that girl who was up in Kiruna." They got the standard response that the firm could provide a more experienced criminal lawyer, but that girl could sit in and assist. In this way the firm got a foothold in the big trials that were reported in the press. During that time there were two gang rapes, a murder with robbery and a complicated bribery and corruption case.

The partners suggested she should carry on sitting in on the cases while she was on sick leave. It didn't happen very often. And it was a good way of keeping in touch with the job. And she didn't need to do any preparation. Just sit in. But only if she wanted to, of course.

She'd agreed because she didn't think she had any choice. She'd embarrassed the firm, got them involved in a compensation claim and lost a client. It was impossible to say no. She owed them, and she nodded and smiled.

At least she managed to get herself out of bed on the days she was sitting in court. Usually it was the accused who drew the first glances from the jury and the judge, but now she was the main attraction in the circus. She kept her eyes fixed on the desk in front of her and let them look. Criminals, magistrates, prosecutors, jurors. She could almost hear them thinking: "so that's her . . ."

She'd arrived at the gardens in front of the hotel. Here the grass was suddenly fresh and green. They must have had the sprinklers going like mad during the dry summer. The scent of the last dog-roses of summer drifted inland on the evening breeze. The air was pleasantly warm. The younger women were wearing sleeveless linen dresses. The slightly older ones covered their upper arms with light cotton cardigans from I Blues and Max Mara. The men had left their ties at home. They trotted back and forth in their Gant trousers with drinks for the ladies. Checked out the charcoal in the barbecue and chatted knowledgeably with the kitchen staff.

She scanned the crowd. No Maria Taube. No Måns Wenngren.

And one of the partners was heading toward her—Erik Rydén. On with the smile. "Is that her?"

Petra Wilhelmsson watched Rebecka Martinsson coming up the track toward the hotel. Petra had only just started with the firm. She was leaning against the railing outside the entrance. On one side of her stood Johan Grill, also new to the firm, and on the other side stood Krister Ahlberg, a criminal lawyer in his thirties.

"Yes, that's her," confirmed Krister Ahlberg. "The firm's very own little Modesty Blaise."

He emptied his glass and placed it on the railing with a little bang. Petra shook her head slowly.

"To think she killed somebody," she said.

"Three people, actually," said Krister.

"God, it makes my hair stand on end! Look!" said Petra, holding her arm up to show the two gentlemen in her company.

Krister Ahlberg and Johan Grill looked carefully at her arm. It was brown and slender. A few very fine hairs had been bleached almost white by the summer sun.

"I don't mean because she's a girl," Petra went on, "but she just doesn't look the type to . . ."

"And she wasn't. She had a nervous breakdown in the end. And she can't cope with the job. Sits in on the big name criminal trials sometimes. And I'm the one that does all the work then gets left behind in the office with the cell phone switched on just in case something comes up. But she's the star."

"Is she a star?" asked Johan Grill. "They never wrote anything about her, did they?"

"No, but in legal circles everybody knows who she is. Sweden's legal circle isn't very big, as you'll soon find out."

Krister Ahlberg measured out a centimeter between the thumb and forefinger of his right hand. He noticed that Petra's glass was empty, and wondered if he ought to offer to get her a refill. But that would mean leaving little Petra alone with Johan.

"God," said Petra, "I wonder what it feels like to kill somebody."

"I'll introduce you," said Krister. "We don't work in the same department, but we went on a course together on commercial contract law. We'll just wait until Erik Rydén's let her out of his clutches."

*　　*　　*

Erik Rydén took Rebecka in his arms and welcomed her. He was a stocky man, and his duties as host were making him perspire. His body was steaming like a bog in August, surrounded by a miasma of Chanel Pour Monsieur and alcohol. Her right hand patted him several times on the back.

"Glad you could come," he said with his broadest smile.

He took her bag and gave her a glass of champagne and a room key in return. Rebecka looked at the key ring. It was a piece of wood painted red and white, attached to the key with a clever little knot.

For when the guests get drunk and drop them in the water, she thought.

They exchanged a few remarks. Gorgeous weather. Ordered it especially for you, Rebecka. She laughed, asked how things were going. Bloody great, just last week he'd landed a big client, something in biotechnology. And they were about to start negotiations on a merger with an American company, so it was all go at the moment. She listened and smiled. Then another latecomer arrived, and Erik had to carry on with his duties as host.

A lawyer from the criminal cases department came over to her. He greeted her as if they were old friends. She searched frantically through her mind for his name, but it had vanished into thin air. He had two new employees trailing after him, a girl and a boy. The boy had a tuft of blond hair above the kind of brown face you only get from sailing. He was a bit short, with broad shoulders. Square, jutting chin, two muscular arms protruding from the rolled-up sleeves of his expensive jumper.

Like Popeye the sailorman, styled by experts, she thought.

The girl was blonde as well. Her mane of hair firmly anchored by a pair of expensive sunglasses on top of her head. Dimples in her cheeks. A cardigan that matched her short-sleeved jumper was hanging over Popeye's arm. They said hello. The girl chirruped like a blackbird. Her name was Petra. Popeye was called Johan, and he had some sort of elegant surname, but Rebecka couldn't remember it. That's how things had been for the last year. Before, she'd had compartments in her head where she could file information. Now there were no compartments. Everything just tumbled in, and most of it tumbled straight out again. She smiled and managed a handshake that was just firm enough. Asked who they were working for at the office. How they were settling in. What they'd written their essays about and where they'd done their articles. Nobody asked her about anything.

She moved on between the groups. Everybody was standing there at the ready, a ruler in their pocket. Measuring each other. Comparing everybody else with themselves. Salary. Where they lived. Name. Who you knew. What you'd been doing during the summer. Somebody was building a house in Nacka. Somebody else was looking for a bigger flat now they'd had their second child, preferably on the right side of Östermalm.

"I'm a complete wreck," exclaimed the house builder with a cheerful smile.

Somebody who had just become single again turned to Rebecka.

"I was actually up around your home turf back in May," he said. "Went skiing from Abisko to Kebnekaise, had to get up at three in the morning while the snow was still firm enough. During the day it was so wet you just sank right through it. All you could do was lie in the spring sunshine and make the most of it."

The atmosphere was suddenly strained. Did he have to mention where she came from? Kiruna forced its way into the circle like a ghost. All at once everyone was gabbling the names of other places they'd been. Italy, Tuscany, parents in Jönköping, Legoland, but Kiruna just wouldn't disappear. Rebecka moved on, and everybody breathed a sigh of relief.

The older associates had been staying in their summer cottages on the west coast, or in Skåne, or out in the archipelago. Arne Eklöf had lost his mother, and told Rebecka quite candidly how he'd spent the summer quarrelling about her estate.

"It's bloody true," he said. "When the Lord turns up with death, the devil turns up with the heirs. Can I get you another?"

He nodded toward her glass. She refused. He gave her a look that was almost angry. As if she'd refused further confidences. Presumably that was exactly what she'd done. He stomped off toward the drinks table. Rebecka stayed where she was, gazing after him. It was a strain chatting to people, but it was a nightmare standing there on her own with an empty glass. Like a poor pot plant that can't even ask for water.

I could go to the bathroom, she thought, glancing at her watch. And I can stay in there for seven minutes if there isn't a queue. Three if somebody's waiting outside the door.

She looked around for somewhere to put her glass down. Just at that moment Maria Taube materialized at her side. She held out a little dish of Waldorf salad.

"Eat," she said. "Looking at you frightens me."

Rebecka took the salad. The memory of last spring flooded through her when she looked at Maria.

* * *

Harsh spring sunshine outside Rebecka's filthy windows. But she has the blinds pulled right down. In the middle of the week, on an ordinary morning, Maria comes to visit. Afterward Rebecka wonders how come she opened the door. She should have stayed under the covers and hidden.

But. She goes to the door. Hardly conscious of the doorbell ringing. Almost absentmindedly she undoes the security lock. Then she turns the catch of the lock with her left hand while her right hand pushes down the door handle. Her head isn't connected to anything. Just like when you find yourself standing in front of the refrigerator with the door open, wondering what you're doing in the kitchen anyway.

Afterward she thinks that maybe there's a sensible little person inside her. A little girl in red Wellingtons and a life jacket. A survivor. And that little girl had recognized those high heels tip-tapping along.

The girl says to Rebecka's hands and feet: "Ssh, it's Maria. Don't tell her. Just get her up and make sure she opens the door."

Maria and Rebecka are sitting in the kitchen. They are drinking coffee, just on its own. Rebecka doesn't say much. The pyramid of dirty dishes, the drifts of post and junk mail and newspapers on the hall floor, the crumpled sweaty clothes on her body say everything there is to say.

And in the middle of all this her hands begin to shake. She has to put her coffee cup down on the table. They are flailing about like mad things, like two headless chickens.

"No more coffee for me," she tries to joke.

She laughs, but it comes out more like a discordant hacking noise.

Maria looks her in the eyes. Rebecka feels as though she knows. How Rebecka sometimes stands out on the balcony looking down at the hard asphalt below. And how she sometimes can't make herself go out and down to the shops. But has to live on whatever she happens to have in. Drink tea and eat pickled gherkins straight from the jar.

"I'm no shrink," says Maria, "but I do know things get worse if you don't eat and sleep. And you have to get dressed in the mornings and go out."

Rebecka hides her hands under the kitchen table.

"You must think I've gone mad."

"Honey, my family is crawling with women who've got Nerves. They faint and swoon, have panic attacks and hypochondria the whole time. And my aunt, have I told you about her? One minute she's sitting in a psychiatric ward with somebody helping her get dressed, the next she's starting up a Montessori nursery. I've seen it all."

The following day one of the partners, Torsten Karlsson, offers to let Rebecka stay in his cottage. Maria used to work with Torsten in the business law section before she moved over and started working for Måns Wenngren with Rebecka.

"You'd be doing me a favor," says Torsten. "It would save me worrying whether somebody had broken in, and driving up there just to do the watering. I ought to sell the place really. But that's a load of hassle as well."

She should have said no, of course. It was so obvious. But the little girl in the red Wellingtons said yes before she'd even opened her mouth.

Rebecka ate some of the Waldorf salad dutifully. She started with half a walnut. As soon as she got it into her mouth, it grew to the size of a plum. She chewed and chewed. Got ready to swallow. Maria looked at her.

"So how are things?" she asked.

Rebecka smiled. Her tongue felt rough.

"Actually, I have absolutely no idea."

"But you're okay about being here this evening?"

Rebecka shrugged her shoulders.

No, she thought. But what can you do? Force yourself to go out. Otherwise you'll soon end up sitting in a cottage somewhere with the authorities after you, terrified of people, allergic to electricity and with a load of cats crapping indoors.

"I don't know," she said. "It feels as if people are checking me out when I look away. Talking about me when I'm not there. As soon as I come along, the conversation kind of starts afresh. You know what I mean? It seems as if it's 'Tennis, anyone?' in a mad panic as soon as they see me coming."

"Well, it is," smiled Maria. "You're the firm's very own Modesty Blaise. And now you've gone to stay out at Torsten's place and you're getting more and more isolated and peculiar. Of course everybody's talking about you."

Rebecka laughed.

"Oh, thanks, I feel much better now."

"I saw you talking to Johan Grill and Petra Wilhelmsson. What did you think of Miss Spin? I'm sure she's very nice, but I just can't take to somebody whose backside is up between her shoulder blades. Mine's like a teenager. It's kind of liberated itself from me and wants to stand on its own two feet."

"I thought I heard something dragging along the grass when you turned up."

They fell silent and gazed out over the channel where an old Fingal was chugging along.

"Don't worry," said Maria. "People will soon start to get really pissed. Then they'll come weaving over to you wanting to chat."

She turned to Rebecka, leaned in close and said in a slurring voice: "So how does it actually feel to kill somebody?"

*   *   *

Rebecka's and Maria's boss Måns Wenngren was standing a little way off, watching them.

Good, he thought. Nicely done.

He could see Maria Taube was making Rebecka Martinsson laugh. Maria's hands were waving in the air, twisting and turning. Her shoulders moved up and down. It was a wonder she could keep her glass under control. Years of training with upper-class families, presumably. And Rebecka's posture softened. She looked brown and strong, he noticed. Skinny as a rake, but then she always had been.

Torsten Karlsson was standing a little way to the side behind Måns studying the barbecue buffet. His mouth was watering. Indonesian lamb kebabs, kebabs of beef fillet or scampi with Cajun spices, Caribbean fish kebabs with ginger and pineapple, chicken kebabs with sage and lemon, or Asiatic style, marinated in yogurt with ginger, garam masala and chopped cucumber, along with lots of different sauces and salads. A selection of red and white wines, beer and cider. He knew they called him "Karlsson on the roof" at the office, after the character in Astrid Lindgren's books. Short and stocky, his black hair sticking up like a scrubbing brush on top of his head. Måns, on the other hand, always looked good in his clothes. There was no way women told him he was sweet, or that he made them laugh.

"I heard you'd got a new Jag," he said, pinching an olive from the bulgur wheat salad.

"Mmm, an E-type cabriolet, mint condition," answered Måns mechanically. "How's she getting on?"

For a split second Torsten Karlsson wondered whether Måns was asking how his own Jag was getting on. He looked up, followed the direction of Måns' gaze and landed on Rebecka Martinsson and Maria Taube.

"She's staying up at your place," Måns went on.

"She couldn't stay cooped up in that little one room apartment. She didn't seem to have anywhere to go. Why don't you ask her yourself? She's your assistant."

"Because I've just asked you," snapped Måns.

Torsten Karlsson held up his hands in a don't-shoot-I-surrender gesture.

"To be honest, I don't really know," he said. "I never go out there. And if I am there we talk about other things."

"Like what?"

"Well, about putting fresh tar on the steps, about the red Falun paint, about her plans to replace all the putty round the windows. She works all the time. For a while she seemed to be obsessed by the compost."

The expression on Måns' face encouraged him to go on. Interested, almost amused. Torsten Karlsson pushed his fingers through the black mop of hair on his head.

"Well," he said, "first of all she set about building. Three different compost bins for garden and household waste. Bought the rat proof kind. Then she built a rapid compost heap. She practically made me write down how you had to layer it all with grass and sand—pure science. And then, when she was supposed to go on that course on corporate taxation in Malmö, you remember?"

"I do, yes."

"Well, she rang me up and said she couldn't go, because the compost was, now how did she put it, there was something the matter with it, not enough nitrogen. So she'd fetched some household waste from a nursery nearby, and now it was too wet. So she'd have to stay at home and scatter and drill."

"Drill?"

"Yes, I had to promise to go out there during the week she was away and drill down through the compost with an old hand drill—the kind you use to make holes in the ice. Then she found the former owners' compost heap a little way into the forest."

"And?"

"There was all sorts in there. Old cat skeletons, broken bottles, all kinds of shit . . . so then she decided to clean it. She found an old bed behind the outhouse with a kind of mesh base. She used that as a huge sieve. Shoveled the stuff onto the bed and shook it so the clean compost fell through. I should have brought along some of our clients and introduced them to one of our promising young associates."

Måns stared at Torsten Karlsson. He could see Rebecka in his mind's eye, rosy cheeks, hair standing on end, frantically shaking an iron bed on top of a pile of earth. Torsten down below with wide-eyed clients dressed in dark suits.

They both burst out laughing at the same time and almost couldn't stop. Torsten wiped his eyes with the back of his hand.

"Although she has calmed down a bit now," he said. "She isn't so . . . I don't know . . . the last time I was there she was sitting out on the steps with a book and a cup of coffee."

"What book was it?" asked Måns.

Torsten Karlsson gave him an odd look.

"I didn't think to look," he said. "Talk to her."

Måns knocked back his glass of red wine.

"I'll go and say hello," he said. "But you know me. I'm crap at talking to people. And even worse at talking to women."

He tried to laugh, but Torsten wasn't smiling.

"You have to ask her how she is."

Måns blew air down his nose.

"I know, I know."

I'm better at short-term relationships, he thought. Clients. Cab drivers. The checkout girl in the local shop. No old conflicts and disappointments lurking just under the surface like tangled seaweed.

*   *   *

Late summer's afternoon on Lidö. The red evening sun settling over the gentle contours of the rocks like a golden bowl. One of the archipelago cruise boats slips by out in the channel. The reeds down by the water put their heads together and rustle and whisper to each other. The sound of the guests chatting and laughing is carried out over the water.

Dinner has progressed to the stage where cigarette packets have appeared on the tables. It was okay to stretch your legs before dessert, so it wasn't quite so crowded around the tables. Sweaters and cardigans that had been tied around waists or slung over shoulders were now slipped over arms chilled by the evening air. Some people were paying a third or fourth visit to the buffet, standing and chatting to the cooks who were turning the spitting kebabs over the glowing charcoal. Some were well on the way to being drunk. Had to hold on to the railings when they went up the steps to the toilets. Waving their arms about and spilling cigarette ash all over their clothes. Talking just a bit too loudly. One of the partners insisted on helping a waitress carry out the desserts. With great authority and a gentlemanly flourish he relieved her of a big tray of vanilla cream tartlets with glazed red currants. The tartlets slid alarmingly toward the edges of the tray. The waitress gave a somewhat strained smile and exchanged a look with the cooks who were busy at the barbecue. One of them dropped what he was doing and hurried to the kitchen with her to fetch the rest of the trays.

Rebecka and Maria were sitting down on the rocks. The stones were releasing the heat they'd stored up during the course of the day. Maria scratched a mosquito bite on the inside of her wrist.

"Torsten's going up to Kiruna next week," she said. "Did he tell you?"

"No."

"It's this project with the Jansson Group Auditors. Now that the Swedish church has separated from the state, it's an interesting client group to link up with. The idea is to sell a legal package, including accounting and auditing of the Swedish church assets all over the country. Offer help with just about everything, 'how do we get rid of Berit and her fibromyalgia,' 'how do we reach an economically sound deal with entrepreneurs,' the whole package. I don't really know, but I think there's a long-term plan to work together with a broker and grab the capital administration. Anyway, Torsten's going up to give the sales pitch to the church council in Kiruna."

"And?"

"You could go with him. You know what he's like. He'd think it was really nice to have some company."

"I can't go to Kiruna," exclaimed Rebecka.

"No, I know that's what you think. But I'm wondering why."

"I don't know, I . . ."

"What's the worst that could happen? I mean if you bumped into somebody who knows who you are? And what about your grandmother's house, you miss that, don't you?"

Rebecka clenched her teeth.

I can't go there, that's just the way it is, she thought.

Maria replied as if she'd read her mind.

"I'm going to ask Torsten to ask you anyway. If there are monsters under the bed it's just as well to put the light on and turn over onto your stomach and have a look at them."

*   *   *

Dancing on the hotel's stone terrace. Abba and Niklas Strömstedt pouring out of the loudspeakers. Through the open windows of the hotel kitchen comes the sound of porcelain crashing and the rush of water as the plates are rinsed before they go into the dishwasher. The sun has taken her red veils down into the water with her. Lanterns hang from the trees. A crush around the outdoor bar.

Rebecka walked down to the stone quay. She'd danced with her table companion then crept away. The darkness placed its arm around her and drew her close.

It went well, she thought. It went as well as anybody could expect.

She sat down on a wooden bench by the water. The sound of the waves lapping against the jetty. The smell of rotting seaweed, brine and diesel. A lamp was reflected in the shiny black water.

Måns had come over to say hello just as she was about to sit down at the table.

"How's things, Martinsson?" he'd asked.

What the hell am I supposed to say to that? she thought.

His wolfish grin and the way he called her by her surname was like a great big stop sign: No confidences, tears or honesty.

So it was head up, feet down and an account of how she'd painted the window frames out at Torsten's place with linseed oil. After Kiruna it had seemed as if he cared about her. But when she couldn't work any longer he'd completely disappeared.

You're just nothing then, she thought. When you can't work.

The sound of footsteps on the gravel path made her look up. At first she couldn't make out a face, but she recognized that high-pitched voice. It was that new girl, the blonde one. What was her name again? Petra.

"Hi Rebecka," said Petra, as if they knew each other.

She came and stood far too close. Rebecka suppressed the urge to get up, shove her out of the way and scurry off. You couldn't really do that sort of thing. So she stayed put. The foot on the end of the leg that was crossed over the other leg gave her away. Jiggled up and down in annoyance. Wanted to run away.

Petra sank down beside her with a sigh.

"God, I've just had three dances one after the other with Åke. You know what they're like. Just because you work with them they think they own you. I just had to get away for a bit."

Rebecka grunted some kind of acknowledgment. In a little while she'd say she needed the bathroom.

Petra twisted her upper body toward Rebecka and tilted her head to one side.

"I heard about what happened to you last year. It must have been terrible."

Rebecka didn't reply.

Wait for it, thought Rebecka nastily. When the quarry won't come out of its hole, you have to lure it out with something. It ought to be some little confidence of your own. You hold out your own little confession and swap it for the other person's secret like a bookmark.

"My sister had a terrible experience like that five years ago," Petra went on when Rebecka didn't speak. "She found their neighbor's son drowned in a ditch. He was only four. After that she went a bit . . ."

She finished the sentence with a vague hand movement.

"So this is where you are."

It was Popeye. He came over to them with a gin and tonic in each hand. He held one out to Petra, and after a microsecond's hesitation offered the other one to Rebecka. It was actually for himself.

A gentleman, thought Rebecka tiredly, putting the glass down beside her.

She looked at Popeye. Popeye was looking greedily at Petra. Petra was looking greedily at Rebecka. Popeye and Petra were going to feast on her. Then they'd go off and have sex.

Petra must have sensed that Rebecka was about to run away. That the opportunity would soon have passed her by. Under normal circumstances she would have let Rebecka go, and thought to herself that there'd be other times. But right now too many drinks from the bar and too many glasses of wine with the food had clouded her judgment.

She leaned over toward Rebecka. Her cheeks were shiny and rosy when she asked:

"So, how does it feel to kill a person?"

* * *

Rebecka marched straight through the middle of the crowd of drunken people. No, she didn't want to dance. No, thank you, she didn't want anything from the bar. She had her overnight bag over her shoulder and was on her way down to the jetty.

She'd managed to deal with Petra and Popeye. Assumed a thoughtful expression, gazed out over the dark water, and replied: "It feels terrible, of course."

What else? The truth? "I have no idea. I can't remember."

Maybe she should have told them about those totally pathetic conversations with the therapist. Rebecka sitting and smiling at every meeting and in the end nearly bursting out laughing. What can she do? She just doesn't remember. The therapist very definitely not smiling back, this is no laughing matter. And finally they decide to take a break. Rebecka is welcome to come back at some point in the future.

When she can't work anymore she doesn't get in touch with him. Can't bring herself to do it. Pictures the scene, sitting and weeping because she can't cope with life, and his face, just enough sympathy to cover the what-did-I-tell-you expression.

No, Rebecka had answered Petra like a normal person, it felt terrible but that life must go on, however banal that might sound. Then she'd made her excuses and left them. It had been fine, but five minutes later the rage hit her, and now . . . Now she was so angry she could have ripped a tree up by the roots. Or maybe she should lean against the wall of the hotel and push it over like a cardboard box.

Just as well for blondie and her little friend they weren't still down on the quay, because she'd have kicked them into the water.

Suddenly Måns was right behind her. Beside her.

"What's going on? Has something happened?"

Rebecka didn't slow down.

"I'm leaving. One of the boys in the kitchen said I could borrow the skiff. I'll row across."

Måns uttered a snort of disbelief.

"Are you crazy? You can't row across in the dark. And what are you going to do when you get to the other side? Come on, stop. What's the matter with you?"

She stopped just before the jetty. Spun around and growled.

"What the fuck do you think's the matter?" she asked. "People asking me what it feels like to kill a person. How the hell should I know? I didn't sit there writing a poem while it was going on, analyzing how I felt. I . . . it just happened!"

"Why are you angry with me? I didn't ask you, did I?"

Suddenly Rebecka was speaking very slowly.

"No, Måns, you don't ask me anything. Nobody could accuse you of that."

"What the hell," he replied, but Rebecka had already turned on her heel and stomped off onto the jetty.

He dashed after her. She'd thrown her bag into the skiff and was untying the mooring rope. Måns searched around for something to say.

"I was talking to Torsten," he said. "He told me he was thinking of asking you to go up to Kiruna with him. But I told him he shouldn't ask."

"Why?"

"Why? I thought it was the last thing you needed."

Rebecka didn't look at him as she answered.

"Perhaps you'd allow me to decide what I need and don't need."

She was beginning to become vaguely aware of the fact that people nearby were tuning in to her and Måns. They were pretending to be busy dancing and chatting, but hadn't the general murmur of conversation dropped a little? Maybe now they'd all have something to talk about next week at work.

Måns seemed to have noticed as well, and lowered his voice.

"I was only thinking of you, I do apologize."

Rebecka jumped down into the boat.

"Oh, you were thinking of me, were you? Is that why you've had me sitting in on all those criminal trials like some kind of tart?"

"Right, that's enough," snapped Måns. "You said yourself that you didn't mind. I thought it was a good way of keeping in touch with the job. Get out of that boat!"

"As if I had a choice! You could see that if you bothered to think about it!"

"Stop doing the bloody criminal cases, then. Get out of the boat and go upstairs and get some sleep, then we'll talk in the morning when you've sobered up."

Rebecka took a step forward in the boat. It rocked back and forth. For a moment the thought went through Måns' mind that she was going to clamber out onto the jetty and slap him. That would be just perfect.

"When I've sobered up? You . . . you're just unbelievable!"

She placed her foot against the jetty and pushed off. Måns considered grabbing hold of the boat, but that would cause a scene as well. Hanging on to the prow till he fell in the water. The office's very own comedy turn. The boat slipped away.

"Go to bloody Kiruna then!" he shouted, without paying any attention to who might hear him. "You can do what you bloody well like as far as I'm concerned."

The boat disappeared into the darkness. He heard the oars rattling in the rowlocks and the splash as the blades slid into the water.

But Rebecka's voice was still close by, and had gone up a pitch.

"Tell me what could possibly be worse than this."

He recognized the voice from those endless rows with Madelene. First of all Madelene's suppressed rage. Him without the faintest idea of what the hell he'd done wrong this time. Then the row, every time the storm of the century. And afterward that voice, a little bit higher pitched and about to splinter into tears. Then it might be time for the reconciliation. If you were prepared to pay the price: being the scapegoat. With Madelene he'd always trotted out the old story: said he was just a heap of shit. Madelene in his arms, sobbing like a little girl with her head leaning on his chest.

And Rebecka . . . His thoughts lumbered drunkenly through his head searching for the right words, but it was already too late. The sound of the oars was moving further and further away.

He wasn't bloody well going to shout after her. She could forget that.

Suddenly Ulla Carle, one of the firm's two female partners, was standing behind him wondering what was going on.

"So shoot me," he said, and walked off up toward the hotel. He headed for the outdoor bar under the garlands of colored lanterns.

TUESDAY SEPTEMBER 5

Inspector Sven-Erik Stålnacke was driving from Fjällnäs to Kiruna. The gravel clattered against the underside of the car and behind him the dust from the road swirled up in a great cloud. When he swung up toward Nikkavägen the massive ice blue bulk of Kebnekaise rose up against the sky on his left-hand side.

It's amazing how you never get tired of it, he thought.

Although he was over fifty he still loved the changing seasons. The thin cold mountain air of autumn, flowing down through the valleys from the highest mountains. The sun's return in the early spring. The first drips from the roof as the thaw began. And the ice breaking. He was almost getting worse with every passing year. He'd need to take a week's holiday just to sit and stare at the countryside.

Just like Dad, he thought.

During the last years of his life, must have been at least fifteen, his father had constantly repeated the same refrain: "This summer will be my last. This autumn was the last one I'll ever see."

It was as if that was the thing that had frightened him most about dying. Not being able to experience one more spring, a bright summer, a glowing autumn. That the seasons would continue to come and go without him.

Sven-Erik glanced at the time. Half one. Half an hour until the meeting with the prosecutor. He had time to call in at Annie's Grill for a burger.

He knew exactly what the prosecutor wanted. It was almost three months since the murder of Mildred Nilsson, the priest, and they'd got nowhere. The prosecutor had had enough. And who could blame him?

Unconsciously he stepped on the gas. He should have asked Anna-Maria for her advice, he realized that now. Anna-Maria Mella was his team leader. She was on maternity leave, and Sven-Erik was standing in for her. It just didn't seem right to disturb her at home. It was strange. When they were working together she felt so close. But outside work he couldn't think of anything to say. He missed her, but yet he'd only been to visit her once, just after the little boy had been born. She'd called in at the station to say hi once or twice, but then all the girls from the office were all over her, cackling like a flock of chickens, and it was best to keep out of the way. She was due back properly in the middle of January.

They'd knocked on enough doors. Somebody ought to have seen something. In Jukkasjärvi, where they'd found the priest hanging from the organ loft, and in Poikkijärvi, where she lived. Nothing. They'd gone round knocking a second time. Not a damned thing.

It was so odd. Somebody had killed her, on the folk museum land down by the river, quite openly. The murderer had carried her body to the church, quite openly. True, it had been the middle of the night, but it had been as light as day.

They'd found out that she was a controversial priest. When

Sven-Erik had asked if she had any enemies, several of the more active women in the church had answered "Pick any man you like." One
woman in the church office, with deep lines etched on either side of
her pursed mouth, had practically come out with it and said that the
priest had only herself to blame. She'd made the headlines in the local paper when she was alive as well. Trouble with the church council
when she arranged self-defense courses for women on church property. Trouble with the community when her women's Bible study
group, Magdalena, went out and demanded that a third of the time
available at the local ice rinks should be set aside for girls' ice hockey
teams and figure skating. And just lately she'd fallen out with some of
the hunters and reindeer farmers. It was all because of the she-wolf
who'd settled on church ground. Mildred Nilsson had said that it was
the responsibility of the church to protect the wolf. The local paper
had run a picture of her and one of her opponents on its center page
spread, under the headings "The Wolf Lover" and "The Wolf Hater."

And in Poikkijärvi vicarage on the other side of the river from
Jukkasjärvi sat her husband. On sick leave and in no condition to
make any sense of what she'd left behind. Sven-Erik felt once again
the pain that had filled him when he'd talked to the guy. "You again.
It's never enough for you lot, is it?" Every conversation had been like
smashing the ice that had formed overnight over a hole in the ice.
The grief welling up. The eyes wrecked by weeping. No children to
share the grief.

Sven-Erik did have a child, a daughter who lived in Luleå, but he
recognized that terrible bloody loneliness. He was divorced and
lived alone. Although of course he had the cat, and nobody had murdered his wife and hung her from a chain.

Every conversation and every letter from the assorted lunatics
confessing to the crime had been checked out. But of course nothing
had come of it. Just pathetic scraps of humanity who'd been temporarily fired up by the newspaper headlines.

Because there had certainly been headlines. The television and
the papers had gone completely mad. Mildred Nilsson had been

murdered right in the middle of the summer when the news more or less dries up, besides which it was less than two years since another religious leader had been murdered in Kiruna—Viktor Strandgård, a leading figure in the church of The Source of All Our Strength. There had been a good deal of speculation about similarities in the two cases, despite the fact that the person who had murdered Viktor Strandgård was dead. But that was the angle they took all the same: a man of the church, a woman of the church. Both found brutally murdered in their respective churches. Priests and pastors were interviewed in the national press. Did they feel threatened? Were they thinking of moving? Was fiery red Kiruna a dangerous place to live if you were a priest? The reporters standing in for the summer traveled up and examined the police's work. They were young and hungry and wouldn't be fobbed off with "for reasons connected with the investigation . . . no comment at this stage." The press had kept up a stubborn interest for two weeks.

"It's getting so you have to turn your damned shoes over and shake them before you put them on," Sven-Erik had said to the chief of police. "Just in case some bloody journalist comes tumbling out with his sting at the ready."

But as the police weren't getting anywhere, the news teams had eventually left the town. Two people who had been crushed to death at a festival took over the headlines.

The police had worked on the copycat theory all summer. Someone had been inspired by the murder of Viktor Strandgård. At first the national police had been very reluctant to do a profile of the perpetrator. There was no question of dealing with a serial killer, as far as anyone knew. And it wasn't at all certain that this was a copycat murder. But the similarities with the murder of Viktor Strandgård and the demands in the media had finally brought a psychiatrist from the national police profiling team up to Kiruna, interrupting her holiday to do so.

She'd had a meeting with the Kiruna police one morning at the beginning of July. There had been a dozen or so sitting and sweating in the conference room. They couldn't risk anyone outside hearing the discussion, so the windows were kept shut.

The psychiatrist was a woman in her forties. What struck Sven-Erik was the way she talked about lunatics, mass murderers and serial killers with such serenity and such understanding, almost with love. When she cited real-life examples she often said "that poor man" or "we had a young lad who . . ." or "luckily for him he was caught and convicted." And she talked about a man who'd been in a secure psychiatric unit for years, and had then been well enough to be released and was now on the right medication, living an orderly life, working part-time for a firm of decorators, and had a dog.

"I can't emphasize strongly enough," she'd said, "that it's up to the police to decide which theory you wish to work on. If the murderer is a copycat I can give you a plausible picture of him, but it's by no means certain."

She'd given a PowerPoint presentation and encouraged them to interrupt if they had questions.

"A man. Aged between fifteen and fifty. Sorry."

She added the last word when she noticed their smiles.

"We'd prefer 'twenty-seven years and three months, delivers newspapers, lives with his mother and drives a red Volvo.'" someone had joked.

She'd added:

"And wears size 42 shoes. Okay, imitators are notable in that they can start off with an extremely violent crime. He won't necessarily have been convicted of any kind of serious violent crime before. And that's backed up by the fact that you've got fingerprints but no match in the register."

Nods of agreement around the room.

"He might be on the register of suspects, or have been convicted of petty crimes typical of a person without limits. Harassment along the lines of stalking or hoax calls, or maybe petty theft. But if it is a copycat then he's been sitting in his room reading about the murder of Viktor Strandgård for a year and a half. That's a quiet occupation.

That was somebody else's murder. That's been enough for him up to now. But from now on he's going to want to read about himself."

"But the murders aren't really alike," somebody had interjected. "Viktor Strandgård was hit and stabbed, his eyes were gouged out and his hands were cut off."

She'd nodded.

"True. But that could be explained by the fact that this was his first. To stab, cut, gouge with a knife gives a more, how shall I put it, close contact than the longer weapon that appears to have been used here. It's a higher threshold to cross. Next time he might be ready to use a knife. Maybe he doesn't like close physical proximity."

"He did carry her up to the church."

"But by then he'd already finished with her. By then she was nothing, just a piece of meat. Okay, he lives alone, or he has access to a completely private space, for example a hobby room where nobody else is allowed to go, or a workshop, or maybe a locked outhouse. That's where he keeps his newspaper cuttings. He probably likes to have them on display, preferably pinned up. He's isolated, bad at social contacts. It's not impossible that he's using something physical to keep people at a distance. Poor hygiene, for example. Ask about that if you have a suspect, ask if he has any friends, because he won't have. But as I said. It doesn't have to be a copycat. It could be somebody who just flew into a temporary rage. If we are unfortunate enough to have another murder, we can talk again."

Sven-Erik's thoughts were interrupted as he passed a motorist exercising his dog by holding the lead through the open car window and making the dog run beside the car. He could see that it was an elkhound cross. The dog was galloping along with its tongue lolling out of its mouth.

"Cruel bastard," he muttered, looking in the rearview mirror.

Presumably he was an elk hunter who wanted the dog in top form for the hunt. He considered turning the car around and having a chat with the owner. People like that shouldn't be allowed to keep animals. It was probably shut in a run in the yard for the rest of the year.

But he didn't turn back. He'd recently been out to talk to a guy who'd broken an injunction banning him from going anywhere near his ex-wife, and was refusing to come in for an interview although he'd been sent for.

You spend day after day arguing, thought Sven-Erik. From the minute you get up until you go to bed. Where do you draw the line? One fine day you'll be standing there on your day off yelling at people for dropping their ice cream wrappers in the street.

But the image of the galloping dog and the thought of its torn pads haunted him all the way into town.

*   *   *

Twenty-five minutes later Sven-Erik walked into Chief Prosecutor Alf Björnfot's office. The sixty-year-old prosecutor was perched on the edge of his desk with a small child on his lap. The boy was tugging happily at the light cord dangling above the desk.

"Look!" exclaimed the prosecutor as Sven-Erik came in. "It's Uncle Sven-Erik. This is Gustav, Anna-Maria's boy."

The last remark was addressed to Sven-Erik with a myopic squint. Gustav had taken his glasses and was hitting the light cord with them so that it swung to and fro.

At the same moment Inspector Anna-Maria Mella came in. She greeted Sven-Erik by raising her eyebrows and allowing the hint of a wry smile to pass fleetingly across her horse face. Just as if they'd seen each other at morning briefing as usual. In fact it had been several months.

He was struck by how small she was. It had happened before when they'd been apart for a while, after holidays for example. It was obvious she'd had time off. She had the kind of deep suntan that wouldn't fade until well into the dark winter. Her freckles were no longer visible because they were the same color as the rest of her face. Her thick plait was almost white. Up by her hairline she had a row of bites that she'd obviously scratched, little brown dots of dried blood.

They sat down. The chief prosecutor behind his cluttered desk, Anna-Maria and Sven-Erik side by side on his sofa. The chief prosecutor kept it short. The investigation into the murder of Mildred Nilsson had come to a standstill. During the summer it had taken up virtually all the available police resources, but now it had to be given a lower priority.

"That's just the way it has to be," he said apologetically to Sven-Erik, who was gazing out of the window with a stubborn expression. "We can't tip the balance by abandoning other investigations and preliminary examinations. We'll end up with the ombudsman after us."

He paused briefly and looked at Gustav, who was removing the contents of the wastepaper basket and arranging his treasures neatly on the floor. An empty snuff tin. A banana skin. An empty box of cough sweets—Läkerol Special. Some screwed up paper. When the basket was empty Gustav pulled off his shoes and threw them down. The prosecutor smiled and went on.

He'd managed to persuade Anna-Maria to come back half-time until she went back up to working full time after Christmas. So the idea was that Sven-Erik should carry on as team leader and Anna-Maria devote her attention to the murder until it was time for her to go full time again.

He pushed his glasses firmly up to the bridge of his nose and scanned the table. He finally found Mildred Nilsson's file and pushed it over to Anna-Maria and Sven-Erik.

Anna-Maria flicked through the file. Sven-Erik looked over her shoulder. He had a heavy feeling inside. It was as if sorrow filled him when he looked at the pages.

The prosecutor asked him to summarize the investigation.

Sven-Erik worked his fingers through his bushy moustache for a few seconds while he thought things through, then he explained without digressions that the priest Mildred Nilsson had been killed on the night before midsummer's eve, June 21. She had held a mid-night service in Jukkasjärvi church which had finished at quarter to twelve. Eleven people had attended the service. Six of them were tourists staying in the local hotel. They had been dragged out of their beds at around four in the morning and had been interviewed by the police. The other people at the service had all belonged to Mildred Nilsson's old biddies' group, Magdalena.

"Old biddies' group?" asked Anna-Maria, looking up from the file.

"Yes, she had a Bible study group that consisted only of women. They called themselves Magdalena. One of those network things people go in for these days. They'd go to the church where Mildred Nilsson was holding a service. It's caused bad blood in certain circles. The expression was used both by their critics and by themselves."

Anna-Maria nodded and looked down at the file again. Her eyes narrowed when she came to the autopsy report and the remarks of the medical examiner, Pohjanen.

"She was certainly smashed up," she said. " 'Impact marks from a blow to the skull . . . fractured skull . . . crush damage to the brain at the points of impact . . . bleeding between the soft tissue of the brain and the hard outer layer . . .' "

She noticed fleeting expressions of distaste on the faces of both the prosecutor and Sven-Erik and carried on looking through the text in silence.

Pointless, uncharacteristic violence, then. Most injuries about three centimeters long, with connective tissue between the edges of the wound. The connective tissue had been shattered. But there was a long wound here: "Left temple straight reddish blue contusion and swelling . . . the furthest edge of the impression wound is three centimeters below and two centimeters in front of the auditory canal on the left-hand side . . ."

Impression wound? What did it say about that in the notes? She flicked through the file.

". . . the impression wound and the extended wound above the left temple with clear demarcation along its sides would suggest a crowbar-like weapon."

Sven-Erik continued his narrative:

"After the service the priest got changed in the sacristy, locked the church and walked past the folk museum down to the river where she kept her boat. That's where she was attacked. The murderer carried the priest back to the church. Unlocked the door and carried her up to the organ loft, put an iron chain around her neck, attached the chain to the organ and hung her from the organ loft.

"She was found not long afterward by one of the churchwardens who had cycled down to the village on an impulse to pick some flowers for the church."

Anna-Maria glanced at her son. He had discovered the box of papers waiting to be shredded. He was ripping one sheet after another to bits. Sheer bliss.

Anna-Maria read on quickly. A considerable number of fractures to the upper jaw and zygoma. One pupil blown. Left pupil six millimeters, right four millimeters. It was the swelling in the brain that caused it. "Upper lip extremely swollen. Right-hand side discolored, bluish purple, incision shows heavy bleeding, blackish red . . ." God! All teeth in upper jaw knocked out. "Considerable amount of blood and blood clots in the mouth cavity. Two socks pushed into the mouth and rammed against the back of the throat.

"Nearly all the blows directed just at the head," she said.

"Two chest wounds," said Sven-Erik.

" 'Crowbar-like object.' "

"Presumably a crowbar."

"Extended wound left temple. Do you think that was the first blow?"

"Yes. So we can assume he's right-handed."

"Or she."

"Yes. But the murderer carried her a fair way. From the river to the church."

"How do we know he carried her? Maybe he put her in a wheel-barrow or something."

"Well, there's knowing and knowing, you know what Pohjanen's like. But he pointed out which way her blood had flowed. First of all it flowed downward toward her back."

"So she was lying on the ground on her back."

"Yes. The technicians found the spot in the end. Just a little way from the shore where she kept her boat. She took the boat across sometimes. She lived on the other side. In Poikkijärvi. Her shoes were on the shore too, just by the boat."

"What else? About the bleeding, I mean."

"Then there are lesser bleeds from the injuries to her face and head, running down toward the crown of the head."

"Okay," said Anna-Maria. "The murderer carried her over his shoulder with her head hanging down."

"That could explain it. And it isn't exactly gymnastics for house-wives."

"I could carry her," said Anna-Maria. "And hang her from the or-gan. She was quite small, after all."

Especially if I was kind of . . . beside myself with rage, she thought.

Sven-Erik went on:

"The final signs of bleeding run toward the feet."

"When she was hung up."

Sven-Erik nodded.

"So she wasn't dead at that point?"

"Not quite. It's in the notes."

Anna-Maria skimmed through the notes. There was a small bleed in the skin where the neck injuries were. According to Pohjanen, the medical examiner, this indicated a dying person. Which meant that she was almost dead when she was hung up. Presumably not con-scious.

"These socks in her mouth . . ." Anna-Maria began.

"Her own," said Sven-Erik. "Her shoes were still down by the river, and she was barefoot when she was hung up."

"I've seen that before," said the prosecutor. "Often when somebody is killed in that particular way. The victim jerks and makes rattling noises. It's most unpleasant. And to stop the rattling . . ."

He broke off. He was thinking of a domestic abuse case that had ended with the wife being murdered. Half the bedroom curtains down her throat.

Anna-Maria looked at some of the photographs. The battered face. The mouth gaping open, black, no front teeth.

What about the hands, though? she thought. The side of the hand where the little finger is? The arms?

"No sign of self-defense," she said.

The prosecutor and Sven-Erik shook their heads.

"And no complete fingerprints?" asked Anna-Maria.

"No. We've got a partial print on one sock."

Gustav had now moved on to pulling every leaf he could reach off a large rubber plant that was in a pot on the floor topped with gravel. When Anna-Maria pulled him away he let out a howl of rage.

"No, and I mean no," said Anna-Maria when he tried to fight his way out of her arms to get back to the rubber plant.

The prosecutor attempted to say something, but Gustav was wailing like a siren. Anna-Maria tried to bribe him with her car keys and cell phone, but everything was sent crashing to the floor. He'd started stripping the rubber plant and he wanted to finish the job. Anna-Maria tucked him under her arm and stood up. The meeting was definitely over.

"I'm putting in an advert," she said through clenched teeth. "Free to good home. Or 'wanted: lawnmower in exchange for thriving boy aged eighteen months, anything considered.' "

*   *   *

Sven-Erik walked out to the car with Anna-Maria. Still the same old scruffy Ford Escort, he noticed. Gustav forgot his woes when she put him down so that he could walk by himself. First of all he wobbled recklessly toward a pigeon that was pecking at some scraps by a waste bin. The pigeon flew tiredly away, and Gustav turned his attention to the bin. Something pink had run over the edge; it looked like dried vomit from the previous Saturday. Anna-Maria grabbed Gustav just before he got there. He started to sob as if his life was over. She shoved him into his car seat and slammed the door. His muted sobs could be heard from inside.

She turned to Sven-Erik with a wry smile.

"I think I'll leave him there and walk home," she said.

"No wonder he's making a fuss when you've done him out of a snack," said Sven-Erik, nodding toward the disgusting bin.

Anna-Maria pretended to shrug her shoulders. There was a silence between them for a few seconds.

"So," said Sven-Erik with a grin, "I suppose I'll have to put up with you again."

"Poor you," she said. "That's the end of your peace and quiet."

Then she became serious.

"It said in the papers that she was a bluestocking, arranged courses in self-defense, that sort of thing. And yet there were no marks to indicate that she'd struggled!"

"I know," said Sven-Erik.

He twitched his moustache with a thoughtful expression.

"Maybe she wasn't expecting to be hit," he said. "Maybe she knew him."

He grinned.

"Or her!" he added.

Anna-Maria nodded pensively. Behind her Sven-Erik could see the wind farm on Peuravaara. It was one of their favorite things to squabble about. He thought it was beautiful. She thought it was ugly as sin.

"Maybe," she said.

"He might have had a dog," said Sven-Erik. "The technicians found two dog hairs on her clothes, and she didn't have one."

"What sort of dog?"

"Don't know. According to Helene in Hörby they've been trying to develop the technique. You can't tell what breed it is, but if you find a suspect with a dog, you can check whether the hairs came from that particular dog."

The screaming in the car increased in volume. Anna-Maria got in and started the engine. There must have been a hole in the exhaust pipe, because it sounded like a chainsaw in pain when she revved up. She set off with a jerk and scorched out on to Hjalmar Lundbohmvägen.

"I see your bloody driving hasn't got any better!" he yelled after her through the cloud of oily exhaust fumes.

Through the back window he saw her hand raised in a wave.

Rebecka Martinsson was sitting in the rented Saab on the way down to Jukkasjärvi. Torsten Karlsson was in the passenger seat with his head tilted back, eyes closed, relaxing before the meeting with the parish priests. From time to time he glanced out through the window.

"Tell me if we pass something worth looking at," he said to Rebecka.

Rebecka smiled wryly.

Everything, she thought. Everything's worth looking at. The evening sun between the pine trees. The damned flies buzzing over the fireweed at the side of the road. The places where the asphalt's split because of the frost. Dead things, squashed on the road.

The meeting with the church leaders in Kiruna wasn't due to take place until the following morning. But the parish priest in Kiruna had phoned Torsten.

"If you arrive on Tuesday evening, let me know," he'd said. "I can show you two of Sweden's most beautiful churches. Kiruna and Jukkasjärvi."

"We'll go on Tuesday, then!" Torsten had decided. "It's really important that he's on our side before Wednesday. Wear something nice."

"Wear something nice yourself!" Rebecka had replied.

On the plane they'd ended up next to a woman who immediately got into conversation with Torsten. She was tall, wearing a loose fitting linen jacket and a huge pendant from the Kalevala around her neck. When Torsten told her it was his first visit to Kiruna, she'd clapped her hands with delight. Then she'd given him tips on everything he just had to see.

"I've got my own guide with me," Torsten had said, nodding toward Rebecka.

The woman had smiled at Rebecka.

"Oh, so you've been here before?"

"I was born here."

The woman had looked her quickly up and down. A hint of disbelief in her eyes.

Rebecka had turned away to look out of the window, leaving the conversation to Torsten. It had upset her that she looked like a stranger. Neatly done up in her gray suit and Bruno Magli shoes.

This is my town, she'd thought, feeling defiant.

Just then the plane had turned. And the town lay below her. That clump of buildings that had attached itself to the mountain full of iron, and clung on tight. All around nothing but mountains and bogs, low growing forests and streams. She took a deep breath.

At the airport she'd felt like a stranger too. On the way out to the hire car she and Torsten had met a flock of tourists on their way home. They'd smelled of mosquito repellent and sweat. The mountain winds and the September sun had nipped at their skin. Brown faces with white crow's feet from screwing their eyes up.

Rebecka knew how they'd felt. Sore feet and aching muscles after a week in the mountains, contented and just a bit flat. They were wearing brightly colored anoraks and practical khaki colored trousers. She was wearing a coat and scarf.

Torsten straightened up and looked curiously at some people fly-fishing as they crossed the river.

"We'll just have to hope we can carry this off," he said.

"Of course you will," said Rebecka. "They're going to love you."

"Do you think so? It's not good that I've never been here before. I've never been further north than bloody Gävle."

"No, no, but you're incredibly pleased to be here. You've always wanted to come up here to see the magnificent mountains and visit the mine. Next time you come up on business you're thinking of taking some holiday to see the sights."

"Okay."

"And none of this 'how the hell do you cope with the long dark winter when the sun doesn't even rise' crap."

"Of course not."

"Even if they joke about it themselves."

"Yeah yeah."

Rebecka parked the car beside the bell tower. No priest. They strolled along the path toward the vicarage. Red wooden panels and white eaves. The river flowed along below the vicarage. The water was September-low. Torsten was doing the blackfly dance. No one opened when they rang the bell. They rang again and waited. In the end they turned to go.

A man was walking up toward the vicarage through the opening in the fence. He waved to them and shouted. When he got closer they could see he was wearing a clerical shirt.

"Hi there," he said when he got to them. "You must be from Meijer & Ditzinger."

He held his hand out to Torsten Karlsson first. Rebecka took up the secretary's position, half a pace behind Torsten.

"Stefan Wikström," said the clergyman.

Rebecka introduced herself without mentioning her job. He could believe whatever made him comfortable. She looked at the priest. He was in his forties. Jeans, tennis shoes, clerical shirt and white dog collar. He hadn't been conducting his official duties, then. Still had the shirt on, though.

One of those 24/7 priests, thought Rebecka.

"You'd arranged to meet Bertil Stensson, our parish priest," the clergyman continued. "Unfortunately he's been held up this evening, so he asked me to meet you and show you the church."

Rebecka and Torsten made polite noises and went up to the little red wooden church with him. There was a smell of tar from the wooden roof. Rebecka followed in the wake of the two men. The clergyman addressed himself almost exclusively to Torsten when he spoke. Torsten slipped smoothly into the game and didn't pay any attention to Rebecka either.

Of course it could be that the priest has actually been held up, thought Rebecka. But it could also mean that he's decided to oppose the firm's proposal.

It was gloomy inside the church. The air was still. Torsten was scratching twenty fresh blackfly bites.

Stefan Wikström told them about the eighteenth-century church. Rebecka allowed her thoughts to wander. She knew the story of the beautiful altarpiece and the dead resting beneath the floor. Then she realized they'd embarked on a new topic of conversation, and pricked up her ears.

"There. In front of the organ," said Stefan Wikström, pointing.

Torsten looked up at the shiny organ pipes and the Sami sun symbol in the center of the organ.

"It must have been a terrible shock for all of you."

"What must?" asked Rebecka.

The clergyman looked at her.

"This is where she was hanging," he said. "My colleague who was murdered in the summer."

Rebecka looked blankly at him.

"Murdered in the summer?" she repeated.

There was a confused pause.

"Yes, in the summer," ventured Stefan Wikström.

Torsten Karlsson was staring at Rebecka.

"Oh, come on," he said.

Rebecka looked at him and shook her head almost imperceptibly.

"A woman priest was murdered in Kiruna in the summer. In here. Didn't you know about it?"

"No."

He looked at her anxiously.

"You must be the only person in the whole of Sweden who . . . I assumed you knew. It was all over the papers. On every news broadcast . . ."

Stefan Wikström was following their conversation like a table tennis match.

"I haven't ready any papers all summer," said Rebecka. "And I haven't watched any television."

Torsten raised his hands, palms upward, in a helpless gesture.

"I really thought . . ." he began. "But obviously, nobody bloody . . ."

He broke off, glanced sheepishly at the clergyman, received a smile as an indication that his sin was forgiven, and went on:

". . . nobody had the nerve to speak to you about it. Maybe you'd like to wait outside? Or would you like a glass of water?"

Rebecka was on the verge of smiling. Then she changed her mind, couldn't decide which expression to adopt.

"It's fine. But I would like to wait outside."

She left the men inside the church and went out. Stopped on the steps.

I ought to feel something, of course, she thought. Maybe I ought to faint.

The afternoon sun was warming the walls of the bell tower. She had the urge to lean against it, but didn't because of her clothes. The smell of warm asphalt mingled with the smell of the newly tarred roof.

She wondered if Torsten was telling Stefan Wikström that she was the one who'd shot Viktor Strandgård's murderer. Maybe he was making something up. No doubt he'd do whatever he thought was best for business. At the moment she was in the social goody bag. Among the salted anecdotes and the sweet gossip. If Stefan Wikström had been a lawyer, Torsten would have told him how things were. Taken out the bag and offered him a Rebecka Martinsson. But maybe the clergy weren't quite so keen on gossip as the legal profession.

They came out to join her after ten minutes. The clergyman shook hands with them both. It felt as if he didn't really want to let go of their hands.

"It was unfortunate that Bertil had to go out. It was a car accident, and you can't say no. Hang on a minute and I'll try his cell phone."

While Stefan Wikström tried to ring the parish priest, Rebecka and Torsten exchanged a look. So he was genuinely busy. Rebecka wondered why Stefan Wikström was so keen for them to meet him before the meeting the following day.

He wants something, she thought. But what?

Stefan Wikström pushed the phone into his back pocket with an apologetic smile.

"No luck," he said. "Just voicemail. But we'll meet tomorrow."

Brief, casual farewells since it was only one night until they were due to meet again. Torsten asked Rebecka for a pen and made a note of the title of a book the clergyman had recommended. Showed genuine interest.

*   *   *

Rebecka and Torsten drove back into town. Rebecka talked about Jukkasjärvi. What the village had been like before the big tourist boom. Dozing by the river. The population trickling silently away like the sand in an hourglass. The Konsum shop looking like some sort of antiquated emporium. The odd tourist at the folk museum, burnt coffee and a chocolate eclair with the white bloom that suggests it's been around for a long time. It had been impossible to sell houses. They had stood there, silent and hollow-eyed, with leaking roofs and moss growing on the walls. The meadows overgrown with weeds.

And now: tourists came from all over the world to sleep between reindeer skins in the ice hotel, drive a snowmobile at minus thirty degrees, drive a dog team and get married in the ice church. And when it wasn't winter they came for saunas on board a boat or rode the rapids.

"Stop!" yelled Torsten all of a sudden. "We can eat there!"

He pointed to a sign by the side of the road. It consisted of two hand-painted planks of wood nailed together. They were sawn into the shape of arrows, and were pointing to the left. Green letters on a white background proclaimed **"ROOMS"** and **"Food till 11 p.m."**

"No, we can't," said Rebecka. "That's the road down to Poikkijärvi. There's nothing there."

"Oh, come on, Martinsson," said Torsten, looking expectantly along the road. "Where's your sense of adventure?"

Rebecka sighed like somebody's mother and turned on to the road to Poikkijärvi.

"There's nothing here," she said. "A churchyard and a chapel and a few houses. I promise you that whoever put that sign up a hundred years ago went bust a week later."

"When we know for certain we'll turn round and go into town to eat," said Torsten cheerfully.

The road became a gravel track. The river was on their left, and you could see Jukkasjärvi on the far side. The gravel crunched beneath the wheels of the car. Wooden houses stood on either side of the track, most of them painted red. Some gardens were adorned with miniature windmills and fading flowers in containers made out of tractor tires, others with swings and sand pits. Dogs galloped as far as they could in their runs, barking hoarsely after the passing car. Rebecka could feel the eyes from inside the houses. A car they didn't recognize. Who could it be? Torsten gazed around him like a happy child, commenting on the ugly extensions and waving to an old man who stopped raking up leaves to stare after them. They passed some small boys on bikes and a tall lad on a moped.

"There," Torsten pointed.

The restaurant was right on the edge of the village. It was an old car workshop that had been converted. The building looked like a whitish rectangular cardboard box; the dirty white plaster had come off in several places. Two big garage doors on the longer side of the box looked out over the road. The doors had been fitted with oblong windows to let the light in. On one end there was a normal sized door and a window with bars. On each side of the door stood a plastic urn filled with fiery yellow marigolds. The door and window frames were painted with flaking brown plastic paint. At the other end, the back of the restaurant, some pale red snowplows stood in the tall dry autumn grass.

Three chickens flapped their wings and disappeared around the corner when Rebecka drove into the gravel yard. A dusty neon sign that said **"LAST STOP DINER"** was leaning against the longer side of the building facing the river. A collapsible wooden sign next to the door proclaimed **"BAR open."** Three other cars were parked in the yard.

On the other side of the road stood five chalets. Rebecka presumed they were the rooms available for renting.

She switched off the engine. At that moment the moped they'd passed earlier arrived and parked by the wall of the building. A very big lad was sitting on the saddle. He stayed there for a while, looking as if he couldn't decide whether to get off or not. He peered at Rebecka and Torsten in the strange car from under his helmet and swayed backwards and forward toward the handlebars a few times. His powerful jaw was moving from side to side. Finally he got off the moped and went over to the door. He leaned forward slightly as he walked. Eyes down, arms bent at a ninety degree angle.

"The master chef has arrived for work," joked Torsten.

Rebecka forced out a "hm," the sound junior associates make when they don't want to laugh at rude jokes, but don't want to remain totally silent and risk offending a partner or a client.

The big lad was standing at the door.

Not unlike a great big bear in a green jacket, thought Rebecka.

He turned around and went back to the moped. He unbuttoned his green jacket, placed it carefully on the moped and folded it up. Then he undid his helmet and placed it in the middle of the folded jacket, as carefully as if it were made of delicate glass. He even took a step backwards to check, went forward again and moved the helmet a millimeter. Head still bent, held slightly on one side. He glanced toward Rebecka and Torsten and rubbed his big chin. Rebecka guessed he was just under twenty. But with the mind of a boy, obviously.

"What's he doing?" whispered Torsten.

Rebecka shook her head.

"I'll go in and ask if they've started serving dinner," she said.

She climbed out of the car. From the open window, covered with a green mosquito net, came the sound of some sports program on TV, low voices and the clatter of dishes. From the river she could hear the sound of an outboard motor. There was a smell of frying food. It had got cooler. The afternoon chill was passing like a hand over the moss and the blueberry bushes.

It's like home, thought Rebecka, looking into the forest on the other side of the track. A pillared hall, the slender pine trees rising from the poor sandy soil, the rays of the sun reaching far into the forest between the copper colored trunks above the low growing shrubs and moss covered stones.

Suddenly she could see herself. A little girl in a knitted synthetic sweater that made her hair crackle with static when she pulled it over her head. Corduroy jeans that had been made longer by adding an edging around the bottom of the legs. She's coming out of the forest. In her hand she has a china mug full of the blueberries she's picked. She's on her way to the summer barn. Her grandmother is sitting inside. A smoky little fire is burning on the cement floor to keep the mosquitoes away. It's just right, if you put too much grass on it the cows start to cough. Grandmother is milking Mansikka, the cow's tail clamped to Mansikka's flank with her forehead. The milk spurts into the pail. The chains clank as the cows stoop down for more hay.

"So, Pikku-piika," says Grandmother as her hands squeeze the udders rhythmically. "Where have you been all day?"

"In the forest," answers little Rebecka.

She pushes a few blueberries into her grandmother's mouth. It's only now she realizes how hungry she is.

Torsten knocked on the car window.

I want to stay here, thought Rebecka, and was surprised by how strongly she felt.

The tussocks in the forest looked like cushions. Covered with shiny dark green lingon with its thick leaves, and the fresh green of the blueberry leaves just starting to turn red.

Come and lie down, whispered the forest. Lay down your head and watch the wind swaying the tops of the trees to and fro.

There was another knock on the car window. She nodded a greeting to the big lad. He stayed out on the steps when she went in.

The two garages that made up the old workshop had been converted into an eating area and a bar. There were six pine tables, stained with a dark color and varnished, arranged along the walls, each with room for seven people if somebody sat at the corner. The plastic flooring of coral red imitation marble was matched by the pink fabric wall covering; a painted design ran right around the room and even continued straight across the swing doors leading into the kitchen. Someone had wound plastic greenery around the water pipes, also painted pink, in an attempt to cheer the place up. Behind the dark-stained bar on the left of the room stood a man in a blue apron, drying glasses and putting them on a shelf where they jostled for space with the drinks on offer. He said hello to Rebecka as she came in. He had a dark brown, neatly clipped beard and an earring in his right ear. The sleeves of his black T-shirt were pushed up his muscular arms. Three men were sitting at one of the tables with a basket of bread in front of them, waiting for their meal. The cutlery wrapped in wine-red paper serviettes. Their eyes firmly fixed on the football on TV. Fists in the bread basket. Work caps in a pile on one of the empty chairs. They were dressed in soft, faded flannel shirts worn over T-shirts with adverts printed on them, the necks well worn. One of them was wearing blue overalls with braces and some kind of company logo. The other two had unfastened their overalls so that the upper half trailed on the floor behind them.

A middle-aged woman on her own was dunking her bread in a bowl of soup. She gave Rebecka a quick smile then stuffed the piece of bread into her mouth quickly, before it fell apart. A black Labrador with the white stripes of age on his muzzle was sleeping at her feet. Over the chair beside her was an indescribably scruffy Barbie-pink padded coat. Her hair was cut very short in a style which could most charitably be described as practical.

"Anything I can help you with?" asked the earring behind the counter.

Rebecka turned toward him and had just about managed to say yes when the swing door from the kitchen flew open and a woman in her twenties hurtled out with three plates. Her long hair was dyed in stripes—blond, an unnatural pink and black. She had an eyebrow piercing and two sparkling stones in her nose.

What a pretty girl, thought Rebecka.

"Yes?" said the girl to Rebecka, a challenge in her voice.

She didn't wait for an answer, but put the plates down in front of the three men. Rebecka had been about to ask if they served food, but she could see that they did.

"It says 'rooms' on the sign," she heard herself asking instead, "how much are they?"

The earring looked at her in confusion.

"Mimmi," he said, "she's asking about rooms."

The woman with the striped hair turned to Rebecka, wiped her hands on her apron and pushed a strand of sweat-soaked hair off her face.

"We've got cottages," she said. "Sort of chalets. Two hundred and seventy kronor a night."

What am I doing? thought Rebecka.

And the next minute she thought:

I want to stay here. Just me.

"Okay," she said quietly. "I'll be in shortly having a meal with a man. If he asks about rooms, tell him you've only got space for me."

Mimmi frowned.

"Why should I do that?" she asked. "It's bloody awful business for us."

"Not at all. If you say you've got room for him as well, I'll change my mind and we'll both go and stay at the Winter Palace in town. So one overnight guest or none."

"Having trouble fighting him off, are you?" grinned the earring.

Rebecka shrugged. They could think what they liked. And what could she say?

Mimmi shrugged back.

"Okay then, " she said. "But you're both eating, are you? Or shall we say there's only enough food for you?"

*   *   *

Torsten was reading the menu. Rebecka was sitting opposite, looking at him. His rounded cheeks, pink with pleasure. His reading glasses balanced as far down his nose as possible without actually stopping him from breathing. Hair tousled, standing on end. Mimmi was leaning over his shoulder and pointing as she read it out. Like a teacher and pupil.

He loves this, thought Rebecka.

The men with their powerful arms, their sheath knives hanging from their belts. Who had mumbled a reply when Torsten swept in wearing his gray suit and greeted them cheerfully. Pretty Mimmi with her big boobs and her loud voice. About as far as you can get from the accommodating girls at the Sturecompagniet nightclub. Little anecdotes were already taking shape in his head.

"You can either have the dish of the day," said Mimmi, pointing to a blackboard on the wall where it said "Marinated elk steak with mushroom and vegetable risotto. Or you can have something out of the freezer. You can have anything that's listed there with potatoes or rice or pasta, whichever you want."

She pointed to the menu where a number of dishes were listed under the heading "From the freezer": lasagne, meatballs, blood pudding, Piteå potato cakes filled with mince, smoked reindeer fillet in a cream sauce and stew.

"Maybe I should try the blood pudding," he said excitedly to Rebecka.

The door opened and the tall lad who'd arrived on the moped came in. He stopped just inside the door. His massive body was encased in a beautifully ironed striped cotton shirt buttoned right up to the neck. He couldn't quite bring himself to look at the other customers. He kept his head twisted to one side so that his big chin was pointing out through the long narrow window. As if it were signposting an escape route.

"Nalle!" exclaimed Mimmi, abandoning Torsten to his deliberations. "Don't you look smart!"

The big lad gave her a shy smile and a quick glance.

"Come over here and let me have a proper look at you!" called the woman with the dog, pushing her soup bowl to one side.

Rebecka suddenly noticed how alike Mimmi and the woman with the dog were. They must be mother and daughter.

The dog at the woman's feet raised its head and gave two tired wags with its tail. Then it put its head down and went back to sleep.

The boy went over to the woman with the dog. She clapped her hands.

"Don't you look wonderful!" she said. "Happy birthday! What a smart shirt!"

Nalle smiled at her flattery and raised his chin toward the ceiling in an almost comical pose that made Rebecka think of Rudolph Valentino.

"New," he said.

"Well yes, we can see it's new," said Mimmi.

"Going dancing, Nalle?" called one of the men. "Mimmi, can you do us five takeaways from the freezer? Whatever you like."

Nalle pointed at his trousers.

"Too," he said.

He lifted up his arms and held them straight out from his body so that everybody could see his trousers properly. They were a pair of gray chinos held up with a military belt.

"Are they new as well? Very smart!" the two admiring women assured him.

"Here," said Mimmi, pulling out the chair opposite the woman with the dog. "Your dad hasn't arrived yet, but you can sit here with Lisa and wait."

"Cake," said Nalle, and sat down.

"Of course you can have some cake. Did you think I'd forgotten? But after your meal."

Mimmi's hand shot out and gave his hair a quick caress. Then she disappeared into the kitchen.

Rebecka leaned across the table to Torsten.

"I was thinking of staying the night here," said Rebecka. "You know I grew up by this river, just a few miles upstream, and it's made me feel a bit nostalgic. But I'll drive you into town and pick you up in the morning."

"No problem," said Torsten, the roses of adventure on his cheeks in full bloom. "I can stay here as well."

"The beds won't exactly be the height of luxury, I shouldn't think," said Rebecka.

Mimmi came out with five aluminum packages under her arm.

"We were thinking of staying here tonight," Torsten said to her. "Do you have any rooms free?"

"Sorry," replied Mimmi. "One cottage left. Ninety centimeter bed."

"That's okay," Rebecka said to Torsten. "I'll give you a lift."

He smiled at her. Beneath the smile and the well-paid successful partner was a fat little boy she didn't want to play with, trying to look as if he didn't mind. It gave her a pang.

* * *

When Rebecka got back from town it was almost completely dark. The forest was silhouetted against the blue black sky. She parked the car in front of the bar and locked it. There were several other cars parked there. The voices of burly men could be heard from inside, the sound of forks being pushed forcefully through meat and clattering on the plate underneath, the television providing a constant background noise, familiar advertising jingles. Nalle's moped was still standing there. She hoped he'd had a good birthday.

The cottage she was sleeping in was on the opposite side of the road on the edge of the forest. A small lamp above the door lit up the number five.

I'm at peace, she thought.

She went up to the cottage door, but suddenly turned and walked a few meters into the forest. The fir trees stood in silence, gazing up toward the stars which were just beginning to appear. Their long blue green velvet coats moved tentatively over the moss.

Rebecka lay down on the ground. The pine trees put their heads together and whispered reassuringly. The last mosquitoes and black-flies of the summer sang a deafening chorus, seeking out whatever parts of her they could reach. She could cope with that.

She didn't notice Mimmi, bringing out some rubbish.

Mimmi went into the kitchen.

"Okay," she said, "it's definitely wacko-warning time."

She told him that their overnight guest had gone to bed, not in her bed in the cottage, but on the ground outside.

"It does make you wonder," said Micke.

Mimmi rolled her eyes.

"Any minute now she'll decide she's a shaman or a witch, move out into the forest, start brewing up herbs over an open fire and dancing around an ancient Sami monolith."

YELLOW LEGS

It is Easter time. The she-wolf is three years old when a human be-ing sees her for the first time. It's in northern Karelia by the river Vodla. She herself has seen people many times. She recognizes their suffocating smell. And she understands what these men are doing. They're fishing. When she was a gangly one-year-old she often crept down to the river at dusk and devoured whatever the two-legged creatures had left behind, fish guts, dace and ide.

Volodja is laying ice nets with his brother. His brother has made four holes in the ice and they are going to lay three nets. Volodja is kneeling by the second hole ready to catch the cane his brother sends beneath the ice. His hands are wet, aching with the cold. And he doesn't trust the ice. All the time he makes sure his skis are close by. If the ice gives way he can lie on his stomach on the skis and pull himself ashore. Alexander wants to lay nets here because it's such a good spot. This is where the fish are. The water is fast flowing and Alexander has struck with his ice pick exactly where the bottom plunges down into the deep river channel.

But it's a dangerous place. If the water rises, the river eats up the ice from below. Volodja knows. The ice can be the thickness of three hand breadths one day and two fingers the next.

He has no choice. He's visiting his brother's family over Easter. Alexander, his wife and two daughters are crammed together on the ground floor. Alexander and Volodja's mother lives on the upper floor. Alexander is stuck with the responsibility for the women. Volodja himself travels all the time working for Transneft, the oil company. Last winter he was in Siberia. In the autumn in the gulf of Viborg. In recent months he's been stuck out in the forest on the Karelian isthmus. When his brother suggested they should go out and lay nets, he couldn't say no. If he'd refused Alexander would have gone out alone. And tomorrow evening Volodja would have been sitting at the dinner table eating fish he hadn't bothered to help catch.

Such is Alexander's rage, it makes him force himself and his younger brother out onto the perilous ice. Now they're here, the weight pressing down on Alexander's heart seems to have eased slightly. He is almost smiling as he kneels there with his hands in the water, blue with cold. Maybe that buttoned-up fury would lessen if he had a son, thinks Volodja.

And at that very moment, with a fleeting prayer to the Virgin that the child in the belly of his brother's wife shall be a son, he catches sight of the wolf. She is standing on the edge of the forest on the opposite side, watching them. Not far away at all. Slant-eyed and long-legged. Her coat is curly, thick for the winter. Long coarse silver strands sticking up among the curls. It feels as if their eyes meet. His brother sees nothing. He has his back to her. Her legs are really extremely long. And yellow. She looks like a queen. And Volodja is on his knees on the ice before her like the village boy he is, with wet gloves and his fur cap with the earflaps sitting askew on top of his sweat drenched hair.

Zjoltye nogi, he says. Yellow legs.

But only inside his head. His lips don't move.

He says nothing to his brother. Alexander might grab the rifle resting against his rucksack and fire off a shot.

So he is forced to release her from his gaze and take the net line off the pole. And when he looks up again she is gone.

By the time Yellow Legs has gone three hundred meters into the forest she has already forgotten the two men on the ice. She will never think of them again. After two kilometers she stops and howls. The other members of the pack answer her, they are just a few miles away and she sets off at a steady trot. That's the way she is. Frequently goes off on her own.

Volodja remembers her for the rest of his life. Every time he returns to the place where he saw her, he peers at the edge of the forest. Three years later he meets the woman who becomes his wife.

The first time she rests in his arms he tells her about the wolf with the long yellow legs.

WEDNESDAY SEPTEMBER 6

The meeting about involvement in a legal and economic umbrella organization was held in the home of Bertil Stensson, the parish priest. Present were Torsten Karlsson, partner in the legal firm of Meijer & Ditzinger, Stockholm; Rebecka Martinsson, a lawyer with the same firm; the parish priests from Jukkasjärvi, Vittangi and Karesuando; the leaders of the church councils; the chairman of the joint church council and the dean, Stefan Wikström. Rebecka Martinsson was the only woman present. The meeting had begun at eight o'clock. It was now quarter to ten. At ten o'clock coffee was to be served to finish off the meeting.

The priest's dining room served as a temporary conference room. The September sun was shining in through the hand-blown, uneven panes of the big barred windows. Wooden shelves full of books reached right up to the ceiling. There were no ornaments or flowers anywhere to be seen. Instead the windowsills were full of stones, some softly rounded and smooth, others rough and black with sparkling red garnet eyes. Strangely contorted branches lay on top of the stones. On the lawns and the gravel path outside lay drifts of rustling yellow leaves and fallen rowanberries.

Rebecka was sitting next to Bertil Stensson. She glanced at him. He was a youthful man in his sixties. Like a kindly uncle with a bad boy's haircut, pale silver. Sunburn and a warm smile.

A professional smile, she thought. It had been almost comical, watching him and Torsten standing and smiling at each other. You could easily have believed they were brothers, or old childhood friends. The priest had shaken Torsten by the hand and at the same time grabbed hold of Torsten's upper arm with his left hand. Torsten had seemed charmed. Smiled and run his hand through his hair.

She wondered if it was the priest who had brought home the stones and branches. It was usually women who did that sort of thing. Who went for walks by the sea and picked up smooth pebbles until their cardigans were dragging on the ground.

Torsten had made good use of his two hours. He'd quickly shrugged off his jacket and made sure his conversation was just personal enough. Entertaining without becoming flippant or slapdash. He'd served up the whole thing like a three-course meal. As an aperitif he'd poured a little flattery into them, things they already knew. That they had one of the wealthiest associations in the country. And one of the most beautiful. The starter consisted of small examples of areas where the church was in need of legal expertise, which was more or less every area, civil law, the law governing societies and associations, employment law, tax law . . . For the main course he had served hard facts, figures and calculations. Shown that it would be cheaper and more advantageous to sign an agreement with Meijer & Ditzinger, giving them access to the company's combined expertise in legal and economic matters. At the same time he had been quite open about the disadvantages, which were not significant, but even so . . . , and thus gave an impression of honesty and trustworthiness. They weren't dealing with a vacuum cleaner salesman here. Now he was busy spooning the dessert down their throats. He was giving a final example of how they had helped another community.

The church administration in this community had cost an enormous amount. A considerable number of churches and other buildings that had to be maintained, many lawns to be mown, graves dug, gravel paths raked, moss scraped off gravestones and goodness knows what, but all of that cost money. A lot of money. This community had employed a number of people on work placements, or whatever it was called, workers who were sponsored by the state through the department of employment. Anyway, this meant that the community didn't have high wage costs for these people, so it didn't really matter if the employees didn't exactly break into a sweat. But then they'd been taken on as temporary employees by the church, and the church was now responsible for paying the whole of their wages. There were a lot of them, and the majority weren't exactly working themselves into the ground, if he could put it like that. So they took on more people, but the work ethos had now become such that it no longer allowed people to come in and roll up their sleeves. Anyone who tried soon got frozen out. So it was difficult to get things done. Some of the employees even managed to hold down another full-time job alongside their full-time job with the church. And now the church was suddenly completely separate from the state, the community was an autonomous organization, and had to take responsibility for its own finances in a completely different way. The solution had been to help the community to put the church administration out to contract. Just as many others had done over the past fifteen years.

Torsten went through the exact figures showing how much money had been saved per year. The others exchanged glances.

Right on target, thought Rebecka.

"And," Torsten went on, "I still haven't included the saving the church makes by having responsibility for fewer employees. Besides more cash in the coffers, you have more time available for the real work of the church, meeting the spiritual needs of its members in different ways. Parish priests shouldn't have to be administrators, but they're often bogged down with that sort of work."

Bertil Stensson pushed a piece of paper sideways in front of Rebecka.

"You've certainly given us plenty to think about," it said.

Oh yes? thought Rebecka.

What was he up to? Did he want them to sit there scribbling notes to one another like two school kids keeping secrets from the teacher? She smiled and gave a slight nod.

Torsten finished off, answered a few questions.

Bertil Stensson stood up and announced that coffee would be served outside in the sun.

"Those of us who live up here have to seize the opportunity," he said. "We don't often get the chance to use our garden furniture."

He waved them out into the garden and as people made their way out he took Torsten and Rebecka into the living room. Torsten had to look at his Lars Levi Sunna painting. Rebecka Martinsson noticed that the priest gave Stefan Wikström a look that meant: wait outside with the others.

"I think this is just what the community needs," the priest said to Torsten. "Although I could really do with you now, not in twelve months' time when all this can actually become a reality."

Torsten considered the picture. It showed a gentle-eyed reindeer cow suckling her calf. Through the open door to the hall Rebecka could see a woman who had appeared from nowhere carrying out a tray of thermos pots and clinking coffee cups.

"We've had a very difficult time within the community," the priest went on, "I assume you've heard about the murder of Mildred Nilsson.

Torsten and Rebecka nodded.

"I need to fill her post," said the priest. "And it's no secret that she and Stefan didn't exactly get on. Stefan is against women priests. I don't share his opinion, but I have to respect it. And Mildred was our foremost local feminist, if I can put it that way. It was no easy job being in charge of them both. I know there's a well-qualified woman who's going to apply for the post when I advertise. I've nothing against her, quite the opposite. But for the sake of peace and quiet at work and at home, I want to fill the post with a man."

"Less well-qualified?" asked Torsten.

"Yes. Can I do that?"

Torsten rubbed his chin without taking his eyes off the picture.

"Of course," he said calmly. "But if the female applicant you've rejected decides to sue, you'll be liable for compensation."

"And I'd have to give her the job?"

"No, no. If the job's gone to the other person, you can't take it off him. I can find out how much compensation's been awarded in similar cases. I'll do it for free."

"He probably means you'll be doing it for free," the priest said to Rebecka with a laugh.

Rebecka smiled politely. The priest turned back to Torsten.

"I'd appreciate that," he said seriously. "Then there's another matter. Or two."

"Shoot," said Torsten.

"Mildred set up a foundation. We have a she-wolf in the forests around Kiruna, and Mildred felt very strongly about her. The foundation was to support the work of keeping her alive. Paying compensation to the Sami people, helicopter surveillance in conjunction with the Nature Conservancy Council . . ."

"Yes?"

"The foundation might not be quite so embedded in the community as she might have wished. Not that we're against having wolves, but we want to maintain an apolitical profile. Everybody, whether they hate wolves or love them, must be able to feel at home within the church."

Rebecka looked out through the window. The leader of the association of churches was peering in at them curiously. He was holding his saucer under his chin to catch the drips as he drank his coffee. The shirt he was wearing was appalling. Once upon a time it had presumably been beige, but it must have been in the wash with a blue sock.

Good job, he'd been able to find a tie to match it, thought Rebecka.

"We want to dissolve the foundation and use the resources for other projects which fit into the church better," said the priest.

Torsten promised to pass the question on to someone who was an expert in the law relating to societies and associations.

"And then there's quite a sensitive issue. Mildred Nilsson's husband is still living in the priest's house in Poikkijärvi. It feels terrible to turn him out of house and home, but . . . well, the house is needed for other things."

"Well, I'm sure that's no problem," said Torsten. "Rebecka, you're staying for a while, could you take a look at the lease and have a word with . . . what's the husband's name?"

"Erik. Erik Nilsson."

"If that's okay?" said Torsten to Rebecka. "Otherwise I can look at

THE BLOOD SPILT   65

it. The house is tied to the job, so if the worst comes to the worst we can get the police involved."

The priest grimaced.

"And if it gets that far," said Torsten calmly, "it's a good idea to have a bloody lawyer to blame."

"I'll sort it," said Rebecka.

"Erik's got Mildred's keys," the priest said to Rebecka. "The church keys. I want those back."

"Yes," she said.

"Including the key to her locker in the church office. It looks like this."

He took his keys out of his pocket and showed one of them to Rebecka.

"A locker," said Torsten.

"For money, notes from counseling sessions, and things you just don't want to lose," said the priest. "A priest isn't in the office much, and lots of other people are in and out all the time."

Torsten couldn't resist asking.

"The police haven't got it?"

"No," said the priest casually, "they haven't asked for it. Look, Bengt Grape's on his fourth helping. Come on, otherwise we're not going to get anything."

*   *   *

Rebecka drove Torsten to the airport. Indian summer sunshine over the dappled yellow birch trees.

Torsten looked at her from the side. He wondered if there'd been anything going on between her and Måns. At any rate, she was cross now. Shoulders up by her ears, mouth like a thin straight line.

"How long are you staying up here?" he asked.

"Don't know," she replied. "Over the weekend."

"Just so I know what to say to Måns, since I've mislaid his colleague."

"I shouldn't think he'll ask," she said.

Silence fell between them. In the end Rebecka couldn't keep quiet any longer.

"It's obvious the police don't even know that bloody locker exists," she exclaimed.

Torsten's voice became exaggeratedly patient.

"They must have missed it," he said. "But we're not here to do their job. We're here to do our job."

"She was murdered," said Rebecka quietly.

"Our job is to solve the client's problems, as long as it isn't illegal. It isn't illegal to get the church's keys back."

"No. And we'll help them work out how much sexual discrimination might cost, so they can build up their old boys' club."

Torsten looked out through the side window.

"And I've got to kick her husband out," Rebecka went on.

"I said you didn't have to."

Oh, pack it in, thought Rebecka. You didn't give me any choice. Otherwise you'd have got the police to chuck him out of the house.

She put her foot down.

The money comes first, she thought. That's the most important thing.

"Sometimes it just makes me want to throw up," she said tiredly.

"Goes with the job sometimes," said Torsten. "All you can do is wipe your shoes and carry on."

Inspector Anna-Maria Mella was driving to Lisa Stöckel's house. Lisa Stöckel was the chair of Magdalena, the women's group. Her house was in an isolated spot up on a ridge beyond Poikkijärvi chapel. Behind the house the ridge plunged down into huge gravel pits, and the river was on the other side of the ridge.

In the beginning the house had been a simple brown chalet built in the sixties. Later on it had been extended and adorned with ornate white window shutters and an excess of white ornamental carving on the porch. Nowadays it looked like a brown shoebox disguised as a gingerbread house. Next to the house was a tumble-down rectangular wooden building, painted Falun red, with a corrugated roof. One barred window, not double glazed. Woodshed, storeroom and former barn, guessed Anna-Maria. There must have been another house here at one time. And they pulled it down and built the chalet. Left the barn standing.

She drove very slowly into the yard. Three dogs were running to and fro in front of the car, barking. Some chickens flapped their wings and sought shelter under a currant bush. By the gatepost stood a cat in front of a shrew hole, rigid with concentration, ready to pounce. Only an irritated swishing of its tail gave away the fact that it had noticed the noisy Ford Escort.

Anna-Maria parked in front of the house. Through the side window she looked down into the jaws of the dogs who were leaping at the car door. True, their tails were wagging, but even so. One of them was unbelievably big. And it was black. She turned off the engine.

A woman came out of the house and stood on the porch. She was wearing an incredibly ugly Barbie-pink padded coat. She called to the dogs.

"Heel!"

The dogs immediately left the car and raced up onto the porch. The woman in the padded coat told them to lie down, and came over to the car. Anna-Maria got out and introduced herself.

Lisa Stöckel was in her fifties. She wore no makeup. Her face was sunburned after the summer. She had white lines around her eyes from squinting into the sun. Her hair was cut very short, a millimeter shorter and it would have stuck out from her head like a scrubbing brush.

Nice, thought Anna-Maria. Like a cowgirl. If you could imagine a cowgirl in that pink coat.

The coat really was hideous. It was covered in dog hair, and bits of the stuffing were sticking out from little holes and tears.

Girl? Anna-Maria did know women in their fifties who had girly lunches and would carry on being girls until the day they died, but Lisa Stöckel was no girl. There was something in her eyes that gave Anna-Maria the feeling that maybe she'd never been a girl, even when she was a child.

And then there was an almost imperceptible line that ran from the corner of her eye, under the eye and down toward the cheekbone. A dark shadow at the corner of the eyes.

Pain, thought Anna-Maria. In the body or in the soul.

They walked up to the house together. The dogs were lying on the porch, whimpering feverishly, desperate to be allowed to get up and greet the visitor.

"Stay," ordered Lisa Stöckel.

It was directed at the dogs, but Anna-Maria Mella obeyed as well.

"Are you frightened of dogs?"

"No, not as long as I know they're friendly," replied Anna-Maria, looking at the large black one.

The long pink tongue lolling out of its mouth like a tie. Paws like a lion.

"Okay, well, there's another one in the kitchen, but she's like a lamb. These are too, they're just a gang of village louts with no manners. Go on in."

She opened the door for Anna-Maria, who slid into the hall.

"Bloody hooligans," said Lisa Stöckel affectionately to the dogs. "Out!"

The dogs leapt up, their claws gouging long marks in the wood as they picked up speed; they took the steps down from the porch in one joyous bound and shot off across the yard.

Anna-Maria stood in the narrow hallway and looked around her. Half the floor was occupied by two dog beds. There was also a big stainless steel water bowl, Wellingtons, boots, tennis shoes and practical Gore-Tex shoes. There was hardly room for both her and Lisa Stöckel at the same time. The walls were covered in hooks and shelves, with several dog leads, work gloves, thick hats and gloves, overalls and all sorts of other things hanging from them. Anna-Maria wondered where she should hang her jacket; every hook was occupied, as was every coat hanger.

"Put your jacket over the back of the chair in the kitchen," said Lisa Stöckel. "Otherwise it'll get covered in hairs. Oh, no, don't take your shoes off whatever you do."

From the hallway one door led into the living room and one into the kitchen. In the living room stood several banana boxes full of books. There were piles of books on the floor. On one of the shorter walls stood the bookcase, empty and dusty, made of some kind of dark wood with a built-in display cabinet with colored glass.

"Are you moving?" said Anna-Maria.

"No, I'm just . . . You collect so much rubbish. And the books just gather dust."

The kitchen furniture was heavy, made of varnished yellow pine. A black Labrador retriever was asleep on a rustic kitchen sofa. She woke up when the two women came into the kitchen, thumping her tail against the sofa in greeting. Then she put her head down and went back to sleep.

Lisa introduced the dog as Majken.

"Tell me what she was like," said Anna-Maria when they'd sat down. "I know you worked together in this women's group, Magdalena."

"But I've already told him . . . a big guy with a moustache like this."

Lisa measured a couple of decimeters from her top lip with her hand. Anna-Maria smiled.

"Sven-Erik Stålnacke."

"Yes."

"Can you go over it again?"

"Where shall I start?"

"How did you get to know one another?"

Anna-Maria watched Lisa Stöckel's face. When people searched through their memories for a particular event they often dropped their guard. As long as it wasn't an event they were intending to lie about, of course. Sometimes they forgot the person sitting in front of them for a while. A wry, fleeting smile crossed Lisa Stöckel's face. Something softened for a moment. She'd liked the priest.

"Six years ago. She'd just moved into the priest's house. And in the autumn she was to be responsible for confirmation classes for the young people both here and in Jukkasjärvi. And she set about it like a gun dog. Contacted all the parents of the children who hadn't registered. Introduced herself and talked about why she thought confirmation classes were so important."

"Why were they important?" asked Anna-Maria, who hadn't thought they were the slightest use when she'd taken them a hundred years ago.

"Mildred thought the church should be a meeting place. She wasn't that bothered about whether people believed or not, that was between them and God. But if she could get them to church for a christening, confirmation, weddings and major festivals, so that people could meet one another and feel sufficiently at home in the church so they'd turn to it if life became too difficult, then . . . And when people said 'but he doesn't believe, it seems wrong if he's studying just to get presents,' she said it was good to get presents, no young people studied because they liked it, neither at school nor at church, but it was part of their general education to know why we celebrate Christmas, Easter, Whitsun and Ascension Day, and to be able to name the apostles."

"So you had a son or daughter who . . ."

"Oh, no. Well, yes, I have got a daughter, but she'd been confirmed several years ago. She works in the pub down in the village. No, it was my cousin's boy, Nalle. He's got special needs and Lars-Gunnar didn't want him confirmed. So she came to talk about him. Would you like a coffee?"

Anna-Maria said yes.

"She seems to have upset people," she said.

Lisa Stöckel shrugged her shoulders.

"That's just the way she was . . . always straight in. As if she only had forward gear."

"What do you mean?" asked Anna-Maria.

"I mean she never went round the houses about things. There was no room for diplomacy or fancy words. She thought something was wrong, and she just went for it."

Like when she got all the churchwardens against her, thought Lisa.

She blinked. But the picture in her head wasn't so easily gotten rid of. First of all it was two brimstone butterflies dancing around one another above the sweet scented arabis. Then the branches of the weeping birch swaying gently to and fro in the breeze from the calm summer river. And then Mildred's back. Her military march between the gravestones. Tramp, tramp, tramp over the gravel.

*   *   *

Lisa scuttles after Mildred along the path in Poikkijärvi churchyard. At the far end the team of churchwardens are having their coffee break. They have a lot of breaks, more or less all the time really. Work when the priest is watching. But nobody actually dares to make any demands of them. If you turn this lot against you, you'll end up holding a funeral in the middle of a pile of earth. Or trying to shout over the top of a lawn mower working two meters away. Preaching in a freezing cold church in the middle of winter. The parish priest is totally bloody useless, he does nothing. He doesn't need to, they know better than to mess with him.

"Don't start an argument about this," Lisa tries to divert her.

"I'm not going to start an argument."

And she really means it.

Mankan Kyrö catches sight of them first. He's the informal leader of the group. The boss of property services doesn't give a damn. Mankan decides. He's the one Mildred isn't going to start an argument with.

She dives straight in. The others listen with interest.

"The child's grave," she says, "have you dug it yet?"

"What do you mean?" says Mankan apathetically.

"I've just been talking to the parents. They said they'd chosen a spot with a view over the river, up there in the northern section, but that you'd advised them against it."

Mankan Kyrö doesn't answer. Instead he spits a huge lump of chewed snuff onto the grass and rummages in his back pocket for the snuff tin.

"You told them the roots of the weeping birch would grow through the coffin and go right through the baby's body," Mildred goes on.

"Well, wouldn't they?"

"That happens wherever you bury a coffin, and you know that perfectly well. You just didn't want to dig up there under the birch, because it's stony and there are so many roots. It was just too much like hard work. I just can't get my head round the fact that you valued your own comfort so highly that you thought it was okay to plant pictures like that in their heads."

She hasn't raised her voice the whole time. The gang around Mankan are staring at the ground. They're ashamed. And they hate the priest who's making them feel ashamed.

"So, what do you want me to do, then?" asks Mankan Kyrö. "We've already dug a grave—in a better spot if you ask me—but maybe we ought to force them to bury their child where you want."

"No way. It's too late now, you've terrified them. I just want you to know that if anything like this happens again . . ."

He's almost smiling now. Is she going to threaten him?

". . . then you'll be testing my love for you beyond the limit," she concludes, and walks away.

Lisa runs after her. Quickly so that she doesn't have to hear the comments behind her back. She can imagine. If the priest's husband gave her what she needed in bed, maybe she'd calm down.

*　*　*

"So who did she annoy?" asked Anna-Maria.

Lisa shrugged her shoulders and switched on the coffee machine.

"Where do I start? The headmaster of the school in Jukkasjärvi because she insisted he had to do something about bullying, the old biddies from social services because she got involved in their territory."

"What do you mean?"

"Well, there were always women with kids at her house, women who'd left their husbands . . ."

"She'd set up some sort of foundation for the wolf," said Anna-Maria. "There was a big debate about that."

"Mmm, I haven't got any cake or milk, you'll have to have it black."

Lisa Stöckel placed a chipped mug with some kind of advert on it in front of Anna-Maria.

"The parish priest and some of the other clergy couldn't stand her either."

"Why was that?"

"Well, because of us, the women in Magdalena, among other things. There are almost two hundred of us in the group. And there were plenty of people who liked her but weren't actually members, quite a lot of men, although no doubt people have told you the opposite. We used to study the Bible with her. Went to services where she was preaching. And did practical work as well."

"Like what?"

"Loads of things. Cooking, for example. We tried to think of something concrete we could do for single mothers. They thought it was hard, always being stuck on their own with the kids and having to spend all their time on practical things. Working, shopping, cleaning, cooking and then just the TV for company. So we have lunch together at the parish hall in town Monday to Wednesday, and out here at the priest's house Thursday and Friday. Sometimes you're on the duty roster, you pay twenty kronor for an adult and fifteen per child. It means for a few days in the week the mothers don't have to shop and cook. Sometimes they look after each other's kids so they can go off and do some exercise or just go into town in peace. Mildred was all for practical solutions."

Lisa laughed and went on:

"It was fatal, telling her something was wrong in the community or whatever. She struck like a pike, 'what can we do?' Before you knew what had hit you, you had a job. Magdalena was a really close group, what priest wouldn't want something like that around them?"

"So the other priests were jealous?"

Lisa shrugged her shoulders.

"You said Magdalena was a close group. Don't you exist any-more?"

Lisa looked down at the table.

"We do."

Anna-Maria waited for her to add something more, but Lisa Stöckel maintained a stubborn silence.

"Who was close to her?" asked Anna-Maria.

"Those of us who were on the committee of Magdalena, I sup-pose."

"Her husband?"

A movement of the iris in the eye, Anna-Maria spotted it. There was something there.

Lisa Stöckel, there's something you're not telling me, she thought.

"Of course," replied Lisa Stöckel.

"Did she feel threatened or afraid?"

"She must have had some sort of tumor or something that sup-pressed the part of her brain that feels fear . . . No, she wasn't afraid. And threatened, no more recently than at any other time, there was always somebody who felt the need to slash her tires or smash her car windows . . ."

Lisa Stöckel glared furiously at Anna-Maria.

"She stopped reporting things to the police a long time ago. It was just a load of trouble for nothing, you can never prove anything even if you know exactly who it is."

"But perhaps you could give me some names," said Anna-Maria.

*   *   *

Quarter of an hour later Anna-Maria Mella got into her Ford Escort and drove away.

Why get rid of all your books? she wondered.

Lisa Stöckel stood at the kitchen window watching Anna-Maria's car disappear down the hill in a cloud of oily smoke. Then she sat down on the kitchen sofa next to the sleeping Labrador. She stroked the dog's throat and chest just as a bitch licks her puppies to calm them. The dog woke up and thumped her tail affectionately a few times.

"What's the matter, Majken?" asked Lisa. "You don't even get up to say hello to people anymore."

Her throat constricted in a painful knot. Her eyelids prickled. There were tears in there. She wasn't going to shed them.

She must be in terrible pain, she thought.

She got up quickly.

Oh God, Mildred, she thought. Forgive me. Please forgive me. I'm . . . trying to do the right thing, but I'm afraid.

She had to get some air, suddenly felt ill. She made it out onto the porch and threw up a little pile of vomit.

The dogs were there at once. If she didn't want it, they could take care of it for her. She pushed them away with her foot.

That bloody policewoman. She'd got right inside her head and opened it up like a picture book. Mildred on every single page. She just couldn't look at those pictures anymore. Like that first time, six years ago. She remembered how she'd been standing by the rabbit hutches. It was feeding time. Rabbits, white, gray, black, spotted, got up on their hind legs and pushed their little noses through the chicken wire. She doled out pellets and shriveled bits of carrot and other root vegetables in little terra-cotta dishes. Felt a little bit of sorrow in her heart, because the rabbits would soon be in a stew down at the pub.

* * *

Then she's standing behind her, the priest who's just moved in. They haven't met before. Lisa hadn't heard her coming. Mildred Nilsson is a small woman, about the same age as her. Somewhere around fifty. She has a small, pale face. Her hair is long and dark brown. Lisa often hears people call her insignificant. They say "She's not pretty, but . . ." Lisa will never understand it.

Something happens inside her when she takes the slender hand that's being held out to her. She has to tell her own hand to let go. The priest is talking. Even her mouth is small. Narrow lips. Like a little red lingonberry. And while the lingonberry mouth talks and talks, the eyes sing a beautiful song. About something else altogether.

For the first time since—well, she can't remember when—Lisa is afraid the truth will show on her face. She could do with a mirror just to check. She, who has kept secrets all her life. Who knows the truth about being the prettiest girl in the village. She might have told people what it felt like to hear "look at the tits on that" all the time, how it made her stoop and gave her a bad back. But there are other things, a thousand secrets.

Daddy's cousin Bengt when she was thirteen. He's grabbed her by the hair and twisted it around his hand. It feels as if it's going to come out by the roots. "Keep your mouth shut," he says in her ear. He's forced her into the bathroom. Slams her head against the tiled wall so she'll understand he means it. With his other hand he unbuttons her jeans. The family is sitting downstairs in the living room.

She kept her mouth shut. Never said a word. Cut her hair off.

Or the last time she ever drank spirits, midsummer's eve 1965. She was well gone. They were three boys from town. Two of them still live in Kiruna, it wasn't long ago she bumped into one of them in the supermarket. But she's dropped the memory like a stone down a well, it's as if she dreamed it long ago.

And then there are the years with Tommy. That time he'd sat drinking with his cousins from Lannavaara. Late September. Mimmi can't have been more than three or four. The ice hadn't taken hold. And they'd given him an old fishing spear. Completely worthless, he'd never realized they were only playing a joke on him. Toward morning he'd rung her for a lift. She'd picked him up in the car, tried to get him to leave the spear there, but he'd managed to get it into the coupe somehow. Sat there with the window down and the spear sticking out. Laughing and stabbing out into the darkness.

When they got home he decided they had to go out fishing. It was two hours until daylight. She had to come with him, he said. To row and hold the torch. The girl's asleep, she said. Exactly, he said. She'd sleep for more than two hours. She tried to get him to put a life jacket on, the water was freezing cold. But he refused.

"You've turned into a real fucking Goody Two Shoes," he said. "I'm married to Goody fucking Two Shoes."

He thought that was very funny. Out on the water he kept repeating it to himself quietly. "Goody Two Shoes." "Steer her a bit nearer the point, Goody Two Shoes."

Then he fell in the water. Plop, and a second later he was clawing at the rail trying to find something to hang on to. Ice-cold water, dark night. He didn't scream or anything. Puffed and panted with exertion.

Oh, that split second. When she seriously wondered what she should do. Just one little push with the oar away from him. Just let the boat drift out of reach. With all that booze inside him. How long would it take? Five minutes maybe.

Then she pulled him up. It wasn't easy, she nearly fell in the water herself. They didn't find the spear. Maybe it sank. Maybe it floated away in the darkness. He was cross about it anyway. Furious with her too, although it was thanks to her he was alive. She could feel how much he wanted to hit her.

She never told anybody about that cold desire to watch him die. Drown like a kitten in a sack.

And now she's standing here with the new priest. She feels quite peculiar inside. The priest's eyes have climbed inside her.

Another secret to drop in the well. It falls down. Lies there sparkling like a jewel among all the rubbish.

It was almost three months since his wife had been found murdered. Erik Nilsson got out of his Skoda in front of the priest's
house. Still warm, although it was September. The sky bright blue,
not a cloud in sight. The light piercing the air like sharpened
knives.

He'd been to call in at work. It had felt good to see his colleagues. They were like another family. He'd go back soon. Give
him something else to think about.

He looked at the pots and containers lining the steps and the veranda. Wilted flowers drooped over the edges. He thought vaguely
that he must take the pots in. Before you knew it the grass would
be crisp with frost, and the cold would crack them.

He'd been shopping on the way home. Unlocked the door,
grabbed the carrier bags and pushed down the door handle with
his elbow.

"Mildred," he called out once he was inside.

He stopped dead. You could have heard a pin drop. The house
consisted of two hundred and eighty square meters of silence. The
whole world was keeping quiet. The house was drifting through a
silent dazzling universe like an empty spaceship. The only sound

was the earth, creaking around on its axis. Why on earth was he calling out to her?

When she was alive he'd always known whether she was at home or not. As soon as he got through the door. Nothing odd about that, he always used to say. A newborn baby could recognize the smell of its mother, even if she was in another room. You didn't lose that ability when you grew up. It just wasn't part of the conscious mind. So people talked about intuition or a sixth sense.

Sometimes it still felt like that when he got home. As if she was somewhere in the house. In the room next door all the time.

He dropped the bags on the floor. Walked into the silence.

Mildred, the voice in his head called out.

At the same moment the doorbell rang.

It was a woman. She was wearing a long fitted coat and high-heeled boots. She didn't fit in, couldn't have stood out more if she'd been dressed in just her underwear. She took off her right glove and held out her hand. Said her name was Rebecka Martinsson.

"Come in," he said, unconsciously running his hand over his beard and hair.

"Thank you, but there's no need, I just want to . . ."

"Come in," he said again, leading the way.

He told her to keep her boots on and asked her to sit down in the kitchen. It was clean and tidy. He'd done the cleaning and cooking when Mildred was alive, why stop now she was dead? He didn't touch her things, though. Her red sweater was still lying in a heap on the kitchen sofa. Her papers and her post were on the worktop.

"So," he said pleasantly.

He was good at that. Being pleasant to women. Over the years many had sat at this very kitchen table. Some had had a little one on their knee and another standing beside them clutching mummy's sweater in a small fist. Others hadn't been trying to get away from a man, but rather from themselves. Couldn't stand the loneliness in an apartment in Lombolo. The sort who stood out on the veranda smoking, cigarette after cigarette out in the cold.

"I'm here on behalf of your wife's employer," said Rebecka Martinsson.

Erik Nilsson had been on the point of sitting down, or perhaps asking if she'd like a cup of coffee. But he remained standing. When he didn't say anything, she went on:

"There are two things. First of all I would like her work keys. And then there's the matter of your moving out."

He looked out through the window. She kept talking, now she was the calm and pleasant one. She informed him that the house went with the job, that the church could help him find an apartment and a removal firm.

His breathing became heavy. His mouth a thin line. Every breath sounded like a snort down his nose.

He was gazing at her with contempt. She looked down at the table.

"Bloody hell," he said. "Bloody hell, it's enough to make you feel sick. Is it Stefan Wikström's wife who can't wait any longer? She never could stand the fact that Mildred had the biggest house."

"Look, I don't know anything about that. I . . ."

He slammed his hand down on the table.

"I've lost everything!"

He made a movement in the air with his fist, pulling himself together so as not to lose his self-control.

"Wait," he said.

He disappeared through the kitchen door. Rebecka could hear his footsteps going up the stairs and across the floor above. After a while he came back, flung the bunch of keys onto the table as if it had been a bag of dog shit.

"Was there anything else?" he asked.

"Your moving out," she said firmly.

And now she was looking him in the eye.

"How does it feel?" he asked. "How does it feel inside those fine clothes, when you've got a job like yours?"

She got up. Something changed in her face, it was a fleeting moment, but he'd seen it in this house many times. Silent anguish. He could see the answer in her eyes. Could hear it as clearly as if she'd spoken the words out loud. Like a whore.

She picked her gloves up from the table with stiff movements, slowly, as if she had to count them to make sure she had them all. One two. She picked up the big bunch of keys.

Erik Nilsson sighed heavily and rubbed his hand over his face.

"Forgive me," he said. "Mildred would have given me a kick up the backside. What day is it today?"

When she didn't reply he went on:

"A week, I'll be out of here in a week."

She nodded. He followed her to the door. Tried to think of something to say, it wasn't exactly the time to ask if she'd like a coffee.

"A week," he said to her departing back.

As if it could have made her feel happy.

Rebecka tottered away from the priest's house. Although that was just the way it felt. She wasn't actually tottering at all. Her legs and feet carried her away from the house with steady steps.

I'm nothing, she thought. There's nothing left inside me. No human being, no judgment, nothing. I do whatever they ask me to do. Of course. The people at the office are all I've got. I tell myself I can't cope with the idea of going back. But in fact I can't cope with the idea of ending up on the outside. I'll do anything, absolutely anything, to be allowed to belong.

She focused on the mailbox and didn't notice the red Ford Escort driving up the track until it slowed down and turned in between the gateposts.

The car stopped.

Rebecka felt as if she'd had an electric shock.

Inspector Anna-Maria Mella climbed out of the car. They'd met before, when Rebecka was defending Sanna Strandgård. And it had been Anna-Maria Mella and her colleague Sven-Erik Stålnacke who'd saved her life that night.

Anna-Maria had been pregnant then, shaped like a cube; now she was slim. But broad-shouldered. She looked strong although she was so small. Her hair in the same thick plait down her back as before. White, even teeth in her brown, sunburned horse face. A pony policewoman.

"Hi there!" exclaimed Anna-Maria.

Then she fell silent. Her whole body was a question mark.

"I . . ." said Rebecka, lost her way and tried again. "My firm has some business with the different communities within the Swedish church, we've had a sales meeting and . . . and there were one or two things they needed some help with regarding the priest's house and as we were up here anyway I've been to have a word with . . ."

She ended the sentence with a nod toward the house.

"But it's got nothing to do with . . ." asked Anna-Maria.

"No, when I came up here I didn't even know . . . no. What did you have?" asked Rebecka, trying to force a smile onto her face.

"A boy. I've just come back to work after my maternity leave, so I'm helping out with the investigation into Mildred Nilsson's murder."

Rebecka nodded. She looked up at the sky. It was completely empty. The bunch of keys weighed a ton in her pocket.

What am I? she thought. I'm not ill. I haven't got an illness. Just lazy. Lazy and crazy. I have no words of my own to speak. The silence is eating its way inward.

"Funny old world, isn't it?" said Anna-Maria. "First Viktor Strandgård and now Mildred Nilsson."

Rebecka nodded again. Anna-Maria smiled. She seemed completely unconcerned about the other woman's silence, but she was waiting patiently for Rebecka to say something.

"What do you think?" Rebecka managed to force out. "Is it somebody who'd been keeping a scrapbook about Viktor's murder, and decided to make a sequel of their own?"

"Maybe."

Anna-Maria gazed up into a pine tree. Heard a squirrel scampering up the trunk, but couldn't see it. It stayed on the other side, reached the top and rustled about among the branches.

Maybe it was some lunatic who was inspired by Viktor Strandgård's death. Or it might have been somebody who knew her. Who knew she'd conducted a service in the church, knew what time it finished and that she'd go down to where she kept the boat. She didn't defend herself. And why did somebody hang her up? It's like in the Middle Ages, when they used to impale people's heads on a spike. As a warning to others.

"How are you?" asked Anna-Maria.

Rebecka replied that she was fine. Just fine. Things had been difficult immediately afterward, of course, but she'd had help and support. Anna-Maria said that was good, really good.

Anna-Maria looked at Rebecka. She thought about that night when the police went to the cottage in Jiekajärvi and found her. She hadn't been able to go with them because her contractions had started. But she'd often dreamed about it afterward. In the dream she was riding a snowmobile through the darkness and the blizzard. Rebecka lay bleeding on the sledge. The snow spraying up into her face. All the time she was afraid of running into something. Then she got stuck. Standing there in the cold. The snowmobile roaring in vain. She usually woke up with a start. Lay there gazing at Gustav, sleeping and snuffling between her and Robert. On his back. Completely secure. Arms by his sides, pointing upward at a ninety degree angle, typical of new babies. Everything worked out fine, she usually thought. Everything worked out fine.

Everything didn't work out fine at all, she thought now.

"So are you off back to Stockholm now?" she asked.

"No, I've taken a bit of time off."

"Your grandmother had a house in Kurravaara, is that where you're staying?"

"No, I . . . no. Here in the village. The pub's got a couple of chalets."

"So you haven't been to Kurravaara?"

"No."

Anna-Maria looked searchingly at Rebecka.

"If you want some company we could go up there together," she said.

Rebecka thanked her, but said no. It was just that she hadn't had time yet, she explained. They said good-bye. Before they parted Anna-Maria said:

"You saved those children."

Rebecka nodded.

That's no consolation, she thought.

"What happened to them?" she asked. "I reported suspected abuse to social services."

"I don't think anything came of that investigation," said Anna-Maria. "Then the whole family moved away."

Rebecka thought about the girls. Sara and Lova. She cleared her throat and tried to think about something else.

"That sort of thing's so expensive for the community, you see," said Anna-Maria. "The investigations cost money. Having the children looked after costs a whole heap of money. Putting the case through the county court costs money. From the child's point of view it would be better if the whole apparatus was run by the state. But at the moment the best solution for the community is if the problem just goes away. Bloody hell, I've taken kids out of a fifty-two-square-meter war zone. Then you hear that the community's bought the family a tenancy in Örkelljunga."

She stopped. Noticed that she'd started babbling just because Rebecka Martinsson seemed to be so close to the edge.

As Rebecka walked on down toward the village bar, Anna-Maria gazed after her. She was seized by a sudden longing for her children. Robert was at home with Gustav. She wanted to press her nose against Gustav's soft skin, feel his strong little arms around her neck.

Then she took a deep breath and straightened her back. The sun on the yellow-white autumn grass. The squirrel, still busy up in the trees on the other side of the track. The smile poured back into her. It was never very far away. Time to talk to Erik Nilsson, the priest's husband. Then she'd go home to her family.

Rebecka Martinsson was walking down toward the bar. Behind her, the forest was talking. Come over here, it said. Come and walk deep inside. I am endless.

She could imagine that walk.

Slender pines of beaten copper. The wind high up in the crown of the trees sounds like rushing water. Firs that look charred and blackened, covered in beard lichen. The sound of her steps: the rustle of dry reindeer lichen and organ-pipe lichen, the crunch of the pinecones eaten by the woodpecker. Sometimes you walk on a soft carpet of needles along an animal track. All you hear then is the sound of thin twigs cracking beneath your feet.

You walk and walk. At first the thoughts in your head are like a tangled skein of wool. The branches scrape against your face or catch in your hair. One by one the threads are drawn from the skein. Get caught in the trees. Fly away with the wind. In the end your head is empty. And you are transported. Through the forest. Over steaming bogs, heavy with scent, where your feet sink between the still frozen tussocks and your body feels sticky. Up a hill. Fresh breeze. The dwarf birch creeping, glowing on the ground. You lie down. And then the snow begins to fall.

She suddenly remembered what it was like when she was a child. That longing to be transported into the endlessness of it all, like a Red Indian. The mountain buzzards soaring above her head. In her dreams she had a rucksack on her back and slept under the open sky. Her grandmother's dog Jussi was always there. Sometimes she traveled by canoe.

She remembered standing in the forest, pointing. Asking her father: "If I go that way, where will I end up?" And her father's reply. New poetry, depending on which direction the finger was pointing in, and where they were. "Tjålme." "Latteluokta." "Across the river Rauta." "Through Vistasvagge and over the Dragon's Back."

She had to stop. Almost thought she could see them. Hard to remember what her father's face had actually looked like. It's because
she has seen too many photographs of him. They've pushed out her
own memories. But she recognizes the shirt. Cotton, but soft as silk
from all the washing. White background, black and red lines making
a checked pattern. The knife in his belt. The leather dark and shiny.
The beautifully patterned bone handle. Herself, no more than
seven, she knows that for certain. Blue machine-knitted hat with a
pattern of white snowflakes. Sturdy boots. She has a knife in her belt
too, a small one. It's mostly for appearance's sake. Although she has
tried to use it. Wanted to carve something with it. Figures. Like
Astrid Lindgren's Emil in *Lönneberga*. But it's too feeble. If she's going
to use the knife she has to borrow Daddy's. It's better when she
wants to split wood or sharpen kebab sticks, sometimes for carving,
although it never quite turns out to be anything.

Rebecka looked down at her high-heeled boots from Lagerson's.

Sorry, she said to the forest. I'm not dressed appropriately these
days.

*   *   *

Micke Kiviniemi wiped over the bar counter with a cloth. It was just
after four on Tuesday afternoon. Their overnight guest, Rebecka
Martinsson, was sitting alone at one of the window tables gazing out
toward the river. She was the only female customer, had eaten elk
steak with mashed potato and Mimmi's wild mushrooms, drinking
from her glass of red wine from time to time, oblivious to the glances
of the village lads.

They were usually the first in. On a Saturday they came in as early
as three o'clock to have an early dinner, sink a few beers and kill the
empty hours until there was something good on TV. Malte Alajärvi
was chatting to Mimmi as usual. He enjoyed that. Later the evening
gang would turn up to have a few beers and watch the sport. It was
mostly single men who came to Micke's to eat. But a few couples

would turn up as well. And one or two from the women's group. And the staff from Jukkasjärvi tourist village often took the boat across the river and came in to eat.

"What the hell is this supposed to be?" Malte complained, pointing at the menu. "Gno . . ."

"Gnocchi," said Mimmi. "It's like little pieces of pasta. Gnocchi with tomato and mozzarella. And you can have a piece of grilled meat or chicken with it."

She positioned herself next to Malte and demonstratively took her notepad out of her apron pocket.

As if she needed it, thought Micke. She could take an order from a party of twelve and keep it in her head. Unbelievable.

He looked at Mimmi. If he had to choose between her and Rebecka Martinsson, Mimmi would win by a mile. Mimmi's mother Lisa had been a looker when she was young too, the old men in the village had plenty to say about her. And Lisa was still attractive. It was hard to hide, despite the fact that she always went around with no makeup, wore terrible clothes and cut her own hair. In the middle of the night with the sheep shears, as Mimmi said. But while Lisa shut off her beauty as much as she could, Mimmi showed hers off. Apron tight around her hips. The tendrils of stripy hair curling out from underneath the little handkerchief she'd knotted around her head. Low-cut, tight black sweaters. And when she leaned forward to wipe the table, anyone who wanted could get a very pleasant eyeful of her cleavage, her breasts swinging gently, held in place by a lacy bra. Always red, black or lilac. From behind you could get a glimpse of the tattoo of a lizard high up on her right buttock when her low-cut jeans slipped down as she bent forward.

He remembered when they'd first met. She'd been visiting her mother, and offered to work one evening. There were people wanting a meal, and as usual his brother hadn't turned up, although this whole bar thing had been his idea from the start, and so Micke was left on his own. She'd offered to throw together some bar food and do the serving. The word spread that same evening. The lads hadn't wasted any time ringing their mates on their cell phones. Everybody came in to have a look at her.

And so she stayed. For a while, she always said evasively when he tried to sort things out. When he tried to say it would be good for the business if he knew, so they could plan for the future, she sounded uncomfortable.

"Best not count on me, then."

Later, when they ended up in bed, he dared to ask her again. How long she'd be staying.

"Till something better turns up," she answered that time, and grinned.

And they weren't a couple, she'd made that very clear to him. He'd had quite a few girlfriends. Even lived with one of them for a while. So he knew what the words meant. You're a wonderful person, but . . . I'm not ready . . . If I were going to fall in love with anybody at the moment, it would be you . . . Can't tie myself down. They all meant one thing: I don't love you. You'll do for the moment.

She'd changed the whole place. Started by helping him get rid of his brother. Who neither worked nor did anything toward paying off the debts. Just came in and drank with his mates without paying. A bunch of losers who were quite happy to let his brother be king for the evening as long as he was getting the drinks in.

"It's a very simple choice," Mimmi had said to his brother. "Either we dissolve the whole thing, and you're left with a pile of debts. Or you pass it over to Micke."

And his brother signed. Red-rimmed eyes. The slightly stale body odor seeping through the T-shirt that hadn't been changed for days. And that new tone of anger in his voice. The alcoholic's temper.

"But the sign belongs to me," he'd informed them, shoving the contract away from him.

"I've got loads of ideas," he went on, tapping his head.

"Take it whenever you want," Micke had said.

Thought: that'll be the day.

He remembered how his brother had found the sign on the

Internet. An old bar sign from the USA. **"LAST STOP DINER,"** white neon letters on a red background. They'd been ridiculously pleased with it at the time. But why should Micke care about it now? He'd had other plans even then. **"Mimmi's"** was a good name for a bar. But she didn't want any of that. It ended up as **"Micke's Bar and Diner."**

"Why do you have to do such weird stuff?"

Malte looked down at the menu, his expression troubled.

"There's nothing weird about it," said Mimmi. "In fact it's just like dumplings, but smaller."

"Dumplings and tomatoes, how much weirder can it get? No, give me something out of the freezer. I'll have lasagne."

Mimmi disappeared into the kitchen.

"And forget the rabbit food," Malte shouted after her. "Did you hear me? No salad!"

Micke turned to Rebecka Martinsson.

"Will you be staying tonight as well?" he asked.

"Yes."

Where would I go? she thought. Where would I drive to? What would I do? At least there's nobody who knows me here.

"That priest," she said. "The one who died."

"Mildred Nilsson."

"What was she like?"

"Bloody good, I thought. She and Mimmi are the best things that have happened to this village. And this place too. When I started it was full of nothing but unmarried old men from eighteen to eighty-three. But when Mildred moved here the women started to come in. She sort of gave the village a new lease on life."

"Was it the priest who told them to come to the bar?"

Micke laughed.

"To eat! She was like that. Thought the women should get out a bit. Take a break from the kitchen. And then they brought their husbands with them and had a meal sometimes when they didn't feel like cooking. The atmosphere in here changed completely when the women started coming in. Before the old men used to just sit around moaning."

"No we didn't," interrupted Malte Alajärvi, who'd been eaves-dropping.

"You moaned then and you're still moaning now. Sitting here staring out across the river and complaining about Yngve Bergqvist and Jukkasjärvi . . ."

"Yes, but that Yngve . . ."

"And you whinge about the food and the government and the fact that there's never anything good on TV . . ."

"A load of bloody game shows!"

". . . and about everything else!"

"All I said about Yngve Bergqvist was that he's a bloody con artist who'll sell any damned thing as long as it says "Arctic" before it. It's Arctic sled dogs and Arctic safari and I swear the bloody Japanese will pay an extra two hundred to go to a genuine Arctic shit-house."

Micke turned to Rebecka.

"You see what I mean."

Then he became serious.

"Why are you asking? You're not a journalist, are you?"

"Oh no, I was just wondering. I mean, she lived here, and . . . No, that lawyer I was in here with yesterday evening, I work for him."

"Carry his bag and book his flights?"

"Something like that."

Rebecka Martinsson looked at the clock. She'd been afraid that a furious Anna-Maria Mella would turn up demanding the keys to the safe, but she'd wanted it to happen as well. But presumably the priest's husband hadn't mentioned it. Maybe he didn't know what the keys were for. It was a complete bloody mess. She looked out of the window. It was starting to get dark. She heard a car drive onto the gravel yard outside.

Her cell phone buzzed in her bag. She rooted it out and looked at the display. The law firm's number.

Måns, she thought, and hurried out onto the steps.

It was Maria Taube.

"How's it going?" she asked.

"I don't know," answered Rebecka.

"I was talking to Torsten. He said you'd hooked them anyway."

"Mmm . . ."

"And he said you'd stayed behind to take care of a few things."

Rebecka didn't reply.

"Have you been to the village where your grandmother's house is, what was it called again?"

"Kurravaara. No."

"Problem?"

"No, it's nothing."

"Why don't you go up there, then?"

"I just haven't got around to it," said Rebecka. "I've been a bit too busy helping our future clients sort out a load of crap."

"Don't snap at me, honey," said Maria gently. "Spill. What kind of crap?"

Rebecka told her. She suddenly felt so tired she wanted to sit down on the steps.

Maria sighed at the other end of the phone.

"Bloody Torsten," she said. "I'll . . ."

"No, you won't," said Rebecka. "The worst thing is the locker, though. It must have the priest's personal stuff in it. There could be letters and . . . anything. If anybody should have what's in there, it's her husband. And the police. There could be some sort of evidence, we don't know."

"I'm sure her boss will pass on anything that might be of interest to the police," Maria Taube ventured.

"Maybe," said Rebecka in subdued voice.

There was a silence between them for a moment. Rebecka kicked at the gravel with her shoe.

"But I thought you went up there to go into the lion's den," said Maria Taube. "That's why you went with Torsten, after all."

"Yeah yeah."

"For God's sake, Rebecka, don't give me the yeah-yeah! I'm your friend and I've got to say this. You just keep on backing off. If you daren't go into town and you daren't go up to Kurrkavaara . . ."

"Kurravaara."

". . . and you're just sitting there hiding in some village bar up the river, where are you going to end up?"

"I don't know."

Maria Taube didn't speak.

"It's not that easy," said Rebecka in the end.

"Do you think I think it is? I can come up and keep you company, if you want."

"No," Rebecka cut her off.

"Okay, I've said my piece. And I've made the offer."

"And I appreciate it, but . . ."

"You don't need to appreciate it. Now I've got to do some work if I'm going to get home before midnight. I'll call you. Måns asked how you were, by the way. I think he's worried. Rebecka, do you remember what it was like when you went to the swimming pool when you were at school? And you jumped from the top board straight away, so you wouldn't be scared of the other heights. Go up to the Crystal Church and go to one of their hallelujah services. Then you'll have got the worst over. Didn't you tell me last Christmas that Sanna and her family and Thomas Söderberg's family had moved away from Kiruna?"

"You won't tell him, will you?"

"Who?"

"Måns. That I . . . oh, I don't know."

"Of course not. I'll call, okay."

Erik Nilsson is sitting stock-still at the kitchen table in the priest's house. His dead wife is sitting opposite him. He daren't say anything for a long time. He hardly dares breathe. The least word or movement and reality cracks and splinters into a thousand pieces.

And if he blinks she's bound to be gone when he opens his eyes.

Mildred grins.

You're funny, you are, she says. You can believe that the universe is endless, that time is relative, that it can turn and go backwards.

The clock on the wall has stopped. The windows are mirrors. How many times has he invoked his dead wife these last three months? Wished that she would come gliding up to his bed in the darkness at night. Or that he might hear her voice as the wind whispers through the trees.

You can't stay here, Erik, she says.

He nods. It's just that there's so much. What shall he do with all the things, the books, the furniture? He doesn't know where to start. It's an insurmountable obstacle. As soon as he thinks about it, he's overwhelmed by such exhaustion that he has to go and lie down, even though it's the middle of the day.

Sod it, then, she says. Sod the lot of it. I don't care about all this stuff.

He knows it's true. All the furniture comes from her parents' home. She was the only daughter of a parish priest, and both her parents died while she was at university.

She refuses to feel sorry for him. She always has. It still makes him secretly angry with her. That was the bad Mildred. Not bad in the sense of nasty or malicious. But the Mildred who hurt him. Who wounded him. If you want to stay with me, then I'm pleased, she said when she was alive. But you're an adult, you choose your own life.

Was that right? he thinks as so many times before. Is it all right to be so uncompromising? I lived her life, all the way. True, I made my own choice. But shouldn't you meet halfway in love?

She looks down at the table. He can't start thinking about children again, because then she's bound to disappear like a shadow through the wall. He's got to pull himself together. He's always had to pull himself together. It's almost black in the kitchen.

She was the one who didn't want to. The first few years they did have sex. In the evenings. Or in the middle of the night, if he woke her up. Always with the light off. And still he could feel her stiff, ill-concealed reluctance if he wanted to do anything other than just stick it in. In the end it stopped of its own accord. He stopped making the approach, she didn't bother. Sometimes the wound opened and they'd quarrel. He might snivel that she didn't love him, that her job took everything. That he wanted children. And she, palms upward: What do you want from me? If you're unhappy, it's up to you to get up and go. His turn: Go where? Who to? The storms always passed. Everyday life stumbled on. And it was always, or almost always, good enough for him.

Her bony elbow on the table. The nail of her index finger tapping thoughtfully on the varnished surface. She looks deep in thought, with that stubborn expression she always gets when she's come up with some idea.

He's used to preparing food for her. Takes the plate covered with clingfilm out of the fridge when she gets home late, pops it in the microwave. Makes sure she eats. Or runs a bath. Tells her not to keep winding her hair round her finger, because she'll finish up bald. But now he doesn't know what to do. Or say. He wants to ask her what it's like. On the other side.

I don't know, she says. But it's drawing me toward it. It's powerful.

He might have bloody known it. She's here because she wants something. He's suddenly terrified that she'll disappear. Gone.

"Help me," he says to her. "Help me get out of here."

She can see that he won't manage it on his own. And she sees his rage. The secret hatred of the dependent, who can't cope on their own. But it doesn't matter anymore. She gets up. Places her hand on the back of his neck. Draws his face toward her breast.

Let's go, she says after a while.

It's quarter past seven when he closes the door of the house behind him for the very last time in his life. Everything he's taking with him fits into a supermarket carrier bag. One of the neighbors pulls the curtain aside, leans against the windowpane and watches him with curiosity as he chucks the bag into the backseat of the car.

Mildred gets into the passenger seat. When the car drives out through the gate he feels almost elated. Like the summer before they got married. When they drove around Ireland. And Mildred is definitely sitting there with a little smile on her face.

They stop on the track outside Micke's. He just wants to drop the key off with that Rebecka Martinsson.

To his surprise she's standing outside the bar. Her cell phone is in her hand, but she's not talking. Her arm is hanging straight down by her side. When she catches sight of him she almost looks as if she'd like to run away. He approaches her slowly, almost pleading. As if he were approaching a frightened dog.

"I thought I'd give you the key to the house," he says. "Then you can pass it on to the priest along with Mildred's work keys, and tell him I've moved out."

She doesn't say anything. Takes the key. Doesn't ask about his furniture or property. Stands there. Cell phone in one hand, the key in the other. He'd like to say something. Ask for forgiveness, perhaps. Take her in his arms and stroke her hair.

But Mildred has got out of the car and is standing by the side of the road calling to him.

Come away now! she shouts. There's nothing you can do for her. Somebody else will help her.

So he turns around and shambles back to the car.

As soon as he's sitting down the unhappiness Rebecka Martinsson has infected him with begins to ease. The road up to town is dark and exciting. Mildred is sitting beside him. He parks outside the Ferrum hotel.

"I've forgiven you," he says.

She looks down at her lap. Shakes her head slightly.

I didn't ask for forgiveness, she says.

It's two o'clock in the morning. Rebecka Martinsson is sleeping. Curiosity works its way in through the window like the tendrils of a climbing plant. Winds itself around her heart. Sends out roots and shoots, spreading through her body. Twining around her rib cage. Spinning a cocoon around her chest.

When she wakes up in the middle of the night it has grown into an irresistible compulsion. The sounds from the bar have died away in the autumn night. A branch is whipping and banging angrily on the metal roof of the chalet. The moon is almost full. The deathly pale light pours in through the window. Catches the bunch of keys, lying there on the pine table.

She gets up and dresses. Doesn't need to put the light on. The moonlight is enough. She looks at her watch. Thinks of Anna-Maria Mella. She likes the policewoman. She's a woman who's chosen to try to do the right thing.

She goes outside. There's a strong wind blowing. The rowans and the birch trees are whipping wildly to and fro. The trunks of the pine trees creak and groan.

She gets into the car and drives off.

She drives to the churchyard. It isn't far. Nor is it very big. She doesn't have to search for long before she finds the priest's grave. Lots of flowers. Roses. Heather. Mildred Nilsson. And an empty space for her husband.

She was born in the same year as Mum, thinks Rebecka. Mum would have been fifty-five in November.

Everything is silent. But Rebecka can't hear the silence. The wind is blowing so hard it's roaring in her ears.

She stands there for a while looking at the stone. Then she goes back to the car, parked on the other side of the wall. When she gets into the car, it's suddenly quiet.

What did you expect? she says to herself. Did you think the priest would be standing there, an apparition on her grave, pointing the way?

That would have made things easier, of course. But it's her own decision.

So the parish priest wants the key to Mildred Nilsson's locker. What's in there? Why hasn't anybody told the police about the locker? They want the key handed over discreetly. They're expecting Rebecka to do just that.

It doesn't matter, she thinks. I can do whatever I like.

Inspector Anna-Maria Mella woke up in the middle of the night. It was the coffee. Whenever she drank coffee late in the evening, she always woke up in the middle of the night and lay there tossing and turning for an hour before she could get back to sleep. Sometimes she'd get up. It was quite a nice time, really. The whole family was asleep, and she could listen to the radio with a cup of camomile tea in the kitchen, or fold laundry, or whatever, and lose herself in her thoughts.

She went down to the cellar and switched on the iron. Let the conversation with the husband of the murdered woman replay in her head.

ERIK NILSSON: We'll sit here in the kitchen so we can keep an eye on your car.

ANNA-MARIA: Oh yes?

ERIK NILSSON: Our friends usually park down by the bar or a little distance away. Otherwise there's the risk that you might get your tires slashed or the paint scratched or something.

ANNA-MARIA: I see.

ERIK NILSSON: Oh, it's not too bad. But a year ago there was a lot of
that sort of thing going on.

ANNA-MARIA: Did you report it to the police?

ERIK NILSSON: They can't do anything. Even if you know who it is,
there's never any proof. Nobody's ever seen anything. And people are scared. It might be their shed on fire next time.

ANNA-MARIA: Did somebody set fire to your shed?

ERIK NILSSON: Yes, it was a man in the village . . . At least we
think it was him. His wife left him and stayed here with us for
a while.

That was nice, thought Anna-Maria. Erik Nilsson had his chance to
have a go at her then, but he let it go. He could have let bitterness
creep into his voice, talked about how the police didn't do anything
and ended up blaming them for his wife's death.

She was ironing one of Robert's shirts, God, the cuffs were really
worn. The shirt steamed beneath the iron. There was a good smell
of freshly ironed cotton.

And he was well used to talking to women, that was obvious.
Sometimes she forgot herself and answered his questions, not to
gain his trust, but because he'd managed to gain hers. Like when he
asked about her children. He knew just what was typical at their
ages. Asked if Gustav had learned the word no yet.

ANNA-MARIA: It depends. If it's me saying no, he doesn't understand. But if it's him . . .

Erik Nilsson laughs, but all at once becomes serious.

ANNA-MARIA: Big house.

ERIK NILSSON: (sighs) It's never really been a home. It's half priest's
house and half hotel.

ANNA-MARIA: But now it's empty.

ERIK NILSSON: Yes, the women's group, Magdalena, thought there'd be too much talk. You know, the priest's widower consoling himself with assorted vulnerable women. They're probably right, I suppose.

ANNA-MARIA: I have to ask, how were things between you and your wife?

ERIK NILSSON: Must you?

ANNA-MARIA: —

ERIK NILSSON: Fine. I had an enormous amount of respect for Mildred.

ANNA-MARIA: —

ERIK NILSSON: She wasn't the sort of woman who's a dime a dozen. Not that sort of priest either. She was so incredibly . . . passionate about everything she did. She really felt she had a calling here in Kiruna and in the village.

ANNA-MARIA: Where did she come from originally?

ERIK NILSSON: She was born and bred in Uppsala. Daughter of a parish priest. We met when I was studying physics. She used to say she was fighting against moderation. "As soon as you feel too strongly about something, the church sets up a crisis group." She talked too much, too quickly and too loudly. And she was almost manic once she got an idea in her head. It could drive you mad. I wished a thousand times that she was a bit more moderate. But . . . [gestures with his hand] . . . when a person like that is snatched away . . . it isn't only my loss.

She'd looked around the house. There was nothing next to Mildred's side of the double bed. No books. No alarm clock. No Bible.

Suddenly Erik Nilsson was standing behind her.

"She had her own room," he said.

It was a little room under the eaves. There were no flowers in the window, just a lamp and some ceramic birds. The narrow bed was still unmade, just as she must have left it. A red fleecy dressing gown lay carelessly tossed across it. On the floor beside the bed, a tower of books. Anna-Maria had looked at the titles: *Beyond the Bible, Language for an Adult Belief*, a biblical reference book, some children's books and books for teenagers. Anna-Maria recognized *Winnie-the-Pooh, Anne of Green Gables*, and underneath the whole lot an untidy pile of torn out newspaper articles.

"There's nothing to see here," said Erik Nilsson tiredly. "There's nothing more for you to see."

*　　*　　*

It was odd, thought Anna-Maria, folding the children's clothes. It was as if he was hanging on to his dead wife. Her mail lay unopened in a big pile on the table. Her glass of water was still on the bedside table, and beside it her reading glasses. The rest of the house was so clean and tidy, he just couldn't bring himself to tidy her away. And it was a lovely home. Just like something out of one of those interior design magazines. And yet he'd said it wasn't a home, but "half priest's house, half hotel." And then he also said he "respected her." Strange.

Rebecka drove slowly into town. The gray white moonlight was absorbed by the asphalt and the rotting leaf canopy. The trees were pulled back and forth in the wind, seemed as if they were almost reaching out hungrily for the poor light, but getting nothing. They remained naked and black. Wrung out and tortured just before their winter sleep.

She drove past the parish hall. It was a low building made of white bricks and dark-stained wood. She turned up on to Gruvvägen and parked behind the old dry cleaner's.

She could still change her mind. No, actually, she couldn't.

What's the worst that can happen? she thought. I can get arrested and fined. Lose a job I've already lost.

Having got this far, it felt as if the worst she could do would be to go back to the chalet and back to bed. Get on the plane to Stockholm tomorrow morning and keep on hoping that she'd be sufficiently sorted out on the inside to go back to work again.

She thought about her mother. The memory rose to the surface, vivid and tangible. She could almost see her through the side window of the car. Nice hair. The pea green coat she'd made herself, with a wide belt around the waist and a fur collar. The one that made the neighbors roll their eyes to heaven when she swished past. Who exactly did she think she was? And the high-heeled boots that she hadn't even bought in Kiruna, but in Luleå.

It felt like a stab of love in her breast. She's seven years old, reaching out her hand for her mummy. Her coat is so beautiful. And her face too. Sometime when she was even younger she'd said, "You're like a Barbie doll, Mummy." And Mummy laughed and hugged her. Rebecka took the opportunity to breathe in all those wonderful aromas at close quarters. Mummy's hair smelled nice. The powder on her face too, but it smelled different. And the perfume in the hollow of her throat. Rebecka said the same thing on several occasions afterward too: "You look like a Barbie doll," just because Mummy had been so pleased. But she was never as pleased as that again. It was as if it had only worked the first time. "That's enough, now" her mother had said in the end.

Now Rebecka remembered. There was more. If you looked a little more closely. What the neighbors didn't see. That the shoes were cheap. The nails split and bitten right down. The hand that carried the cigarette to the lips shaking slightly, as it does when people are of a nervous disposition.

On the rare occasions when Rebecka thought about her, she always remembered her as being frozen. Wearing two thick sweaters and woolly socks at home by the kitchen table.

Or like now, shoulders slightly raised, there's no room for a thick sweater under the elegant coat. The hand that isn't holding the cigarette is hidden in the coat pocket. She peers into the car and finds Rebecka. Narrow, searching eyes. Corners of her mouth turned down. Who's crazy now?

I'm not crazy, thought Rebecka. I'm not like you.

She got out of the car and walked quickly toward the parish hall. Almost running away from the memory of the woman in the pea green coat.

Someone had kindly smashed the light above the back door of the hall. Rebecka tried the keys. There might be an alarm. Either the cheap version that only sounds inside the building, to frighten away thieves. Or a proper one that goes through to a security firm.

It's okay, she told herself. The national guard aren't likely to turn up; it'll be some tired security guy in a car who'll pull up outside the front door. Plenty of time to get away.

Suddenly one of the keys fitted. Rebecka turned it and slipped inside into the darkness. Silence. No alarm. No beeping noise to indicate that she had sixty seconds to punch in a code. The parish hall was in the basement, so the back door was upstairs and the main entrance was on the ground floor. She knew the office was upstairs. She didn't bother creeping about.

There's nobody here, she said to herself.

It felt as if her footsteps were echoing as she walked quickly across the stone floor to the office.

The room containing the lockers was inside. It was narrow and windowless; she had to put the light on.

Her pulse rate increased and she fumbled with the keys as she tried them in the locks of the unmarked gray lockers. If anybody came along now, she had no way of escape. She tried to listen out on to the stairs and the street. The keys were making more noise than church bells.

When she tried the third locker the key turned smoothly in the lock. It must be Mildred Nilsson's. Rebecka opened it and looked inside.

It was a small locker. There wasn't much, but it was almost full. A number of small boxes and fabric bags containing jewelry. A pearl necklace, some heavy gold rings with stones inset, earrings. Two wedding rings, worn smooth with age, left to her no doubt. A blue folder, containing a pile of papers. There were also several letters in the locker. The addresses on the envelopes were in different handwriting.

Now what do I do? thought Rebecka.

She wondered what the parish priest might know about the contents of the locker? Would he miss anything?

She took a deep breath, then went through the whole lot. Sat on the floor and sorted it all into piles around her. Her brain was working as it usually did now, quickly, taking in information, processing, sorting. Half an hour later Rebecka switched on the office's photocopier.

She took the letters as they were. There might be prints or traces on them. She put them in a plastic bag she found in a drawer.

She copied the papers from the blue folder. She put the copies along with the letters in the plastic bag. She put the folder back in the locker and locked it, turned off the light and left. It was half past three in the morning.

*   *   *

Anna-Maria Mella was woken by her daughter Jenny tugging at her arm.

"Mummy, there's somebody ringing the doorbell."

The children knew they weren't allowed to open the door at unusual times. As a police officer in a small town, you could get strange visitors at odd times. Tearful thugs looking for the only mother confessor they had, or colleagues with serious faces and the car engine running. And sometimes, very rarely, but it did happen, somebody who was angry or high on something, often both.

Anna-Maria got up, told Jenny to creep in beside Robert, and went down into the hall. She had her cell phone in the pocket of her dressing gown, the number to the main police switchboard already keyed in, checked through the spy hole first and then opened the door.

Rebecka Martinsson was standing outside.

Anna-Maria asked her in. Rebecka stood just inside the door. Didn't take her coat off. Didn't want a cup of tea or anything.

"You're investigating the murder of Mildred Nilsson," she said. "These are letters and copies of personal papers that belonged to her."

She handed over a plastic bag of papers and letters, and explained briefly how she'd got hold of the material.

"I'm sure you understand that it wouldn't look good for me if it came out that I'd passed this on to you. If you can come up with some other explanation, I'd be grateful. If you can't, well . . ."

She shrugged her shoulders.

". . . well, then I'll just have to roll with it," she said with a wry smile.

Anna-Maria peered into the bag.

"A locker in the priests' office?" she asked.

Rebecka nodded.

"Why didn't anybody tell the police that . . ."

She broke off and looked at Rebecka.

"Thank you!" she said. "I won't tell anybody how we got hold of them."

Rebecka made a move to go.

"You did the right thing," said Anna-Maria. "You do know that?"

It was difficult to know whether she was talking about what had happened two years ago in Jiekajärvi, or if she meant the photocopies and letters in the plastic bag.

Rebecka made a movement with her head. She might have been nodding. But she might have been shaking her head.

When she'd gone Anna-Maria stood there in the hall. She had an irresistible urge to scream out loud. What the hell, she wanted to yell. How the hell could they not hand this over to us?

Rebecka Martinsson is sitting on the bed in her chalet. She can see the contours of the back of the chair outlined against the gray rectangle of moonlight in the window.

Now, she thought. Now the panic ought to kick in. If anybody finds out about this, I'm toast. I'll be convicted of illegal entry and unauthorized interference, I'll never work again.

But the panic wouldn't come. No regrets either. Instead she felt quite light hearted.

I can always get a job as a ticket collector, she thought.

She lay down and looked up at the ceiling. Felt slightly elated in a crazy way.

A mouse was rustling about in the wall. Nibbling and scampering up and down. Rebecka knocked on the wall and it went quiet for a while. Then it started again.

Rebecka smiled. And fell asleep. With her clothes on and without having brushed her teeth.

She had a dream.

She is sitting up on Daddy's shoulders. It's blueberry time. Daddy's got the basket on his back. It's heavy, with the basket and Rebecka.

"Don't lean," he says when she stretches over to catch the beard lichen hanging from the trees.

Grandmother is walking behind them. Blue cardigan and gray head scarf. She has an economical way of moving in the forest. Doesn't lift her foot any higher than necessary. A kind of rapid trot with short steps. They have two dogs with them; Jussi, the gray dog, sticks with Grandmother. He's getting old, saving his strength. And Jacki, the youngster, some kind of pointer cross, rushes here and there, he can never get enough of the different smells, disappears from sight, sometimes you hear him barking several kilometers away.

Late in the afternoon she is lying by the fire and sleeping while the adults have gone a little further away to pick berries. She's using Daddy's Helly Hansen as a pillow. The afternoon sun warms her, but the shadows are long. The fire keeps the mosquitoes away. The dogs come and look at her from time to time. Nudge her face gently with their noses then scamper away before she has time to pat them or put her arms around their necks.

YELLOW LEGS

It's late winter. The sun climbs above the tops of the trees and warms the forest. Lumps of heavy snow slide down from the trees. A difficult time for hunting. During the day the deep white blanket is softened by the warmth. It's hard to run after prey. If the pack hunts at night by moonlight or at dawn, the icy surface slashes their pads to ribbons.

The alpha female begins to run. She is getting restless and irritable. Any of the pack who approach her can expect to be snapped at or told off. She positions herself in front of the subordinate males and urinates with her leg lifted so high that she almost has difficulty keeping her balance. The whole pack is affected by her moodiness. There is growling and howling. Scraps are constantly breaking out between the members of the pack. The young wolves roam around uneasily on the edge of the resting place. There is always one of the older wolves ready to put them in their place. At mealtimes the rank order is rigidly maintained.

The alpha female is Yellow Legs' half-sister. Two years ago she challenged the old alpha bitch at exactly this time of year. The lead bitch was about to start running, and was asserting her superiority over the other females. She turned to Yellow Legs' half-sister, stretched her gray-striped head forward, curled back her lips and bared her teeth with a threatening low growl. But instead of slinking backwards in fear, her tail pressed between her legs, Yellow Legs' half-sister took up the challenge. She looked the old bitch straight in the eyes and her hackles rose. The fight broke out in a split second and was over in a minute. The old alpha female lost. A deep bite in her side and a ragged ear were enough to make her retreat, whimpering. Yellow Legs' half-sister drove her away from the pack. And the pack had a new alpha female.

Yellow Legs never challenged the old leader. Nor does she stand up to her half-sister. And yet it seems as if her half-sister is particularly irritated by her. On one occasion she clamps Yellow Legs' muzzle firmly between her jaws and takes her on a half circuit through the pack. Yellow Legs slinks along humbly, her back bent, her eyes turned away. The young wolves get up and begin to walk around uneasily. Afterward Yellow Legs licks her half-sister's mouth submissively. She doesn't want to fight or assert herself.

It's hard to get the silver gray alpha male's attention. When the old female was there he used to follow her around for weeks before she finally decided to mate. He sniffed at her bottom and put the other males in their place so that she could see. Often, he would come back to her as she lay resting. He'd tap her with his front paw to ask "what about now?"

Now the alpha male is lying inert, apparently uninterested in Yellow Legs' half-sister. He's seven years old, and there's no one in the pack showing the least interest in taking his place. In a year or so he'll be older and weaker, and will have to assert himself more. But for the moment he can lie here and let the sun warm his fur while he licks his paws and snaps up a little bit of snow. Yellow Legs' half-sister is watching him. Squats down and urinates close to him in order to arouse his interest. Walks past him, very close. Keen and bloody around the base of her tail. In the end he obliges and covers her. The whole pack breathes a sigh of relief. The level of tension in the group drops immediately.

The two one-year-olds wake Yellow Legs and want to play. She has been lying under a pine tree a little distance away, half asleep. But now the youngsters hurl themselves upon her. One of them thumps his huge front paws down into the snow. His whole body bent playfully forward. The other comes hurtling over at full speed and jumps over her as she lies there. She leaps to her feet and sets off after them. Their barking and yapping echoes through the trees. A terrified squirrel shoots up a tree trunk like a red streak. Yellow Legs catches up with one of the youngsters and he does a double somersault in the snow. They wrestle for a while, then it's her turn to be chased. She flies like an arrow between the trees. Sometimes slows down so they can almost catch up with her, then shoots away again. She won't get caught until she wants to be.

THURSDAY SEPTEMBER 7

At half past six in the morning, Mimmi took her breakfast break. She'd been working in the bar since five. The aroma of coffee and newly baked bread mingled with the meaty smells of freshly made lasagne and stew. Fifty aluminum food containers stood cooling on the stainless steel worktop. She'd been working in the kitchen with the door propped open so that it wouldn't be so hot. And because they liked it, the old men. It was company for them, she supposed. Watching her fly about, working, filling up the coffee pot. And they could eat in peace, no critical eyes watching if they happened to chew with their mouths open or spill coffee down their shirts.

Before she sat down to eat her own breakfast, she dashed out into the dining room and gave the customers a little treat, going round with the coffee pot to offer a top-up. She pressed them to accept and offered round the bread basket. At that moment she belonged to all of them, she was their wife, their daughter, their mother. Her stripy hair was still damp from her morning shower, done up in a plait under the handkerchief she wore tied around her head. The looks she got said it all. She would never run around in the bar with loose, wet hair, dripping onto her tight sweater from H&M. Miss Wetter and Wetter T-shirt. She put the coffee pot down on the hot plate and announced:

"Just help yourselves, I'm going to sit down for quarter of an hour."

"Mimmi, come over here and have a chat," one of the men sang out in reply.

Some of them were on their way to work. They were the ones taking quick little gulps of coffee to get it down as rapidly as possible, although it was still too hot, bolting their sandwich in two bites. The others spent an hour or so here before they ambled home to loneliness. They tried to start conversations and flicked aimlessly through the previous day's newspaper, today's wouldn't be here for ages. In the village people didn't say they were unemployed or off sick or had taken early retirement. They said they were at home.

Their overnight guest Rebecka Martinsson was sitting alone at a table by the window, looking out over the river. Eating her muesli and drinking coffee, in no hurry.

Mimmi lived in a one-room apartment in town. She'd hung on to it although she practically lived with Micke in the house nearest the bar. When she'd decided to stick around for a while her mother had said something feeble about moving in with her. It had been so obvious that she'd felt obliged to offer, it would never have occurred to

Mimmi to say yes. She'd been running the bar with Micke for just about three years now, and it wasn't until last month that Lisa had given her a spare key to the house.

"You never know," she'd said, looking everywhere but at Mimmi. "If anything was to happen . . . I mean, the dogs are in there."

"Of course," Mimmi had replied, taking the key. The dogs.

Always those bloody dogs, she'd thought.

Lisa had seen that Mimmi was annoyed and sullen, but it wasn't her style to pretend she'd noticed something and to try and talk. No, it was time to leave. If it wasn't a meeting of the women's group, then it was the animals at home, maybe the rabbit hutches needed cleaning out or one of the dogs had to go to the vet.

Mimmi clambered up onto the oiled wooden worktop next to the refrigerator. If she drew up her legs she could squeeze in next to the fresh herbs growing in tin cans that had been washed out. It was a good place. You could see Jukkasjärvi on the other side of the river. A boat, sometimes. That window hadn't been there when the place was a workshop. Micke gave it to her as a gift. "I'd like a window just here," she'd said. And he'd sorted it.

It wasn't that she was angry with the dogs. Or jealous. Most of the time she called them her brothers. But when she was living in Stockholm, Lisa never once came to visit. Didn't even ring. "Of course she loves you," Micke always said. "She's your mother after all." He didn't understand anything.

There must be something genetically wrong with us, she thought. I mean, I'm incapable of loving as well.

If she met a guy who was a total shit, she could fall in love, of course—no, that was far too tame a word, the cheap supermarket version of the feeling she had; she became psychotic, dependent, an abuser. It had happened. There was one time in particular, when she lived in Stockholm. When you tore yourself free of a relationship like that, you left great chunks of flesh behind.

With Micke it was something quite different. She could have a child with him, if she'd actually believed she was capable of loving a child. But he was good, Micke was good.

Outside the window some of the hens were scratching about in the autumn grass. Just as she sank her teeth into her freshly baked bread, she heard the sound of a moped out on the track. It pulled into the yard and stopped.

Nalle, she thought.

He was always turning up at the bar in the mornings. If he woke up before his father and managed to sneak away without being heard. Otherwise the rule was that he was supposed to have breakfast at home.

After a little while he materialized outside the window where she was sitting and knocked on the glass. He was wearing a pair of bright yellow dungarees that had belonged to a telecom engineer once upon a time. The reflector strip down by his feet was almost completely worn away through frequent wearing and washing. On his head he had a blue cap of imitation beaver with big earflaps. His green fleecy jacket was much too short. Stopped at the waist.

He gave her one of his priceless crafty smiles. It split his powerful face, the big jaw shifting to the right, eyes narrowing, eyebrows shooting upward. It was impossible not to smile back, it didn't matter that she wasn't going to be able to have her sandwich in peace.

She opened the window. He shoved his hands into his jacket pockets and fished out three eggs. Looked at her as if he'd performed an amazing trick. He usually went into the henhouse and collected the eggs for her. She took them off him.

"Brilliant! Thanks! So, is it Hungry Harry who's come to visit us?"

A rumbling laugh emerged from his throat. Like a starter motor that isn't keen, in slow motion, hmmm-hmmm.

"Or maybe it's Dennis the Dishwasher?"

He answered with a delighted no, knew she was joking with him, but still shook his head vigorously to be on the safe side. He hadn't come here to wash up.

"Hungry?" she asked, and Nalle turned on his heel and vanished around the corner.

She jumped down from the worktop, closed the window, took a gulp of coffee and a big bite of her sandwich. By the time she got into the dining room, he was sitting opposite Rebecka Martinsson. He'd hung his jacket over the back of the chair next to him, but kept his cap on. It was a habit of his. Mimmi took off the cap and ruffled his thick, short hair.

"Wouldn't you rather sit over there instead? Then you can see if any cool cars go past."

Rebecka Martinsson smiled at Nalle.

"He's welcome to sit with me," she said.

Mimmi's hand reached out and touched Nalle again. Rubbed his back gently.

"Do you want pancakes or yogurt or a sandwich?"

She knew the answer, but it was good for him to talk. And to make his own decisions. She could see the word being shaped in his mouth for a few seconds before it came out. His lower jaw moved first in one direction, then the other. Then, decisively:

"Pancakes."

Mimmi disappeared into the kitchen. She took fifteen little pancakes out of the freezer and chucked them in the microwave.

Nalle's father Lars-Gunnar and her mother Lisa were cousins. Nalle's father was a retired policeman, and had been the leader of the local hunt for almost thirty years. That made him a powerful man. He was physically big too, just like Nalle. A policeman who commanded respect, in his day. And nice too, according to what people said. He still went to funerals when some old petty criminal died. On those occasions it was often only Lars-Gunnar and the priest who were there.

When Lars-Gunnar met Nalle's mother, he was already over fifty. Mimmi remembered when he brought Eva to see them for the first time.

I can't have been more than six, she thought.

Lars-Gunnar and Eva sat on the leather sofa in the living room. Lisa dashed in and out of the kitchen with cake and milk and more coffee and heaven knows what. That was the time when she was trying to fit in. Later on she got divorced and gave up baking and cooking altogether. Mimmi can almost imagine how Lisa eats her dinner in the cottage. Standing up, her bottom leaning against the worktop, shoveling down something out of a tin, maybe cold meat soup.

But that time. Lars-Gunnar on the sofa with his arm around Eva's shoulders, an unusually tender expression for a man in this village, and particularly for him. He was so proud. She was, maybe not pretty, but much younger than him, like Mimmi now, somewhere between twenty and thirty. Mimmi can't imagine where this social worker, a tourist on holiday, met Lars-Gunnar. But Eva gave up her job in . . . Norrköping, if Mimmi remembers rightly, got a job with the council and moved into the family home, where he still lived. After a year, Nalle was born. Although at the time he was called Björn. A suitable name for a big bear of a baby, but now everybody called him Nalle—"teddy bear."

It can't have been easy, thought Mimmi. Coming from a big town to live in a little village. Hauling the pram back and forth during her maternity leave, only the old dears to chat to. It's a wonder she didn't go crazy. Although that's exactly what she did, of course.

The microwave pinged and Mimmi cut two slices of ice cream and spooned strawberry jam over the pancakes. She poured a big glass of milk and spread butter on three thick slices of coarse bread. Took three hard-boiled eggs out of a pan on the gas stove, put the whole lot on a tray with an apple, and took it out to Nalle.

"And no more pancakes until you've eaten the rest," she said firmly.

When Nalle was three, he got inflammation of the brain. Eva rang the emergency helpline. She was told to wait awhile. And so things turned out the way they did.

And when he was five, Eva left. She left Nalle and Lars-Gunnar, and went back to Norrköping.

Or ran away, thought Mimmi.

There was a lot of talk in the village about how she'd abandoned her child. Some people just can't cope with taking responsibility, they said. And they asked how she could do it. How could she? Abandon her child.

Mimmi doesn't know. But she does know how it feels to be suffocated in the village. And she can imagine how Eva fell to pieces in the pink concrete house.

Lars-Gunnar stayed in the village with Nalle. Didn't like to talk about Eva.

"What could I do?" was all he said. "I mean, I can't force her."

When Nalle was seven, she came back. Or, to be more accurate, Lars-Gunnar fetched her from Norrköping. The next door neighbor told everyone how he'd carried her into the house in his arms. The cancer had almost eaten her away. Three months later, she was gone.

"What could I do?" said Lars-Gunnar again. "She was the mother of my son, after all."

Eva was buried in Poikkijärvi churchyard. Her mother and a sister came up for the funeral. They didn't stay long. Stuck around for the coffee and sandwiches afterward just as long as necessary. Carried Eva's shame for her. The other guests at the funeral didn't look them in the eye, stared at their backs.

"And Lars-Gunnar stood there consoling them," people said to each other. Couldn't they have looked after the woman when she was dying? Instead it was Lars-Gunnar who'd taken care of all that. And you could see it to look at him. He must have lost fifteen kilos. Looked gray and worn out.

Mimmi wondered what would have happened if Mildred had been there then. Maybe Eva would have fitted in with the women in Magdalena. Maybe she'd have got a divorce from Lars-Gunnar but stayed in the village, managed to look after Nalle. Maybe she could even have managed to stay married to him.

The first time Mimmi met Mildred, the priest was sitting on

Nalle's moped. He was going to be fifteen in three months. Nobody in the village said a word about the fact that an underage mentally handicapped boy was driving around on a moped. Good God, he was Lars-Gunnar's boy. Heaven knows they hadn't had an easy time. And as long as Nalle stuck to the road through the village . . .

"Ouch, my arse!" laughs Mildred inside Mimmi's head as she jumps off the moped.

Mimmi is sitting outside Micke's. She's taken one of the chairs outside and found a place sheltered from the spring breeze; she's smoking a cigarette and turning her face up toward the sun in the hope of getting a bit of color. Nalle looks pleased. He waves to Mimmi and Mildred, turns and rides off, the gravel spraying up around him. Two years earlier he'd been one of Mildred's confirmation candidates.

Mimmi and Mildred introduce themselves to each other. Mimmi is a bit surprised, she's not sure what she was expecting, but she's heard so much about this priest. That she's wonderful. That she's so wise. That's she's off her head.

And now she's standing here looking completely normal. Boring, in fact, if she's completely honest. Mimmi had expected some kind of electrical field around her, but all she sees is a middle-aged woman in unfashionable jeans and practical Ecco shoes.

"He's such a blessing!" says Mildred, nodding in the direction of the moped chugging along the village road.

Mimmi mumbles and sighs and says something about how things haven't been easy for Lars-Gunnar.

It's like a conditioned reflex. When the village sings its song about Lars-Gunnar and his feeble young wife and his handicapped boy, the chorus is always the same: "feel sorry for . . . what some people have to go through . . . things haven't been easy."

A deep crease appears between Mildred's eyebrows. She looks searchingly at Mimmi.

"Nalle is a gift," she says.

Mimmi doesn't reply. She doesn't buy any of that all-children-are-a-gift-and-there-is-a-purpose-in-everything-that-happens.

"I don't understand how people can keep talking about Nalle as if he were such a burden. Has it occurred to you what a good mood it puts you in, just being with him?"

It's true. Mimmi thinks about the previous morning. Nalle is too heavy. He's always hungry, and his father has his hands full making sure he doesn't eat all the time. An impossible task. The ladies in the village can't resist Nalle's pleas for food, and sometimes neither can Mimmi and Micke. Like yesterday. Suddenly Nalle was standing in the kitchen of the bar with one of the hens under his arm. Little Anni, a Cochin, not much of a layer, but nice and affectionate, doesn't mind being patted. But she doesn't want to be carted away from the flock. She's kicking with her little hen's legs and cackling uneasily under Nalle's huge arm.

"Anni!" says Nalle to Micke and Mimmi. "Sandwich."

He twists his head to the left and bends his neck so that he's looking at them sideways under his fringe. Looks crafty. It's impossible to decide whether he knows he's not fooling them for one second.

"Take the hen outside," says Mimmi, attempting to look stern.

Micke bursts out laughing.

"Does Anni want a sandwich? Well, she'd better have one then."

With a sandwich in one hand and the hen under the other arm, Nalle marches out into the yard. He puts Anni down and the sandwich disappears into his mouth at top speed.

"Hey!" Micke shouts from the veranda. "I thought that was for Anni?"

Nalle turns toward him with an expression of theatrical regret.

"Gone," he says haplessly.

Mildred is still talking:

"I mean, I know it's been difficult for Lars-Gunnar. But if Nalle hadn't had these problems, would he really have brought any greater happiness to his father? I wonder."

Mimmi looks at her. She's right.

She thinks about Lars-Gunnar and his brothers. She can't remember their father. Nalle's grandfather. But she's heard stories. Isak was a hard man. Kept the children in line with the strap. Sometimes worse. He had five sons and two daughters.

"Shit," said Lars-Gunnar once. "I was so scared of my own father that I wet myself sometimes. Long after I'd started school."

Mimmi remembers that comment very clearly. She was small then. Couldn't believe that great big Lars-Gunnar had ever been scared. Or little. Wet himself!

How they must have tried not to be like their father, those brothers. But yet he's there inside them. That contempt for weakness. A hardness passed down from father to son. Mimmi thinks about Nalle's cousins, some of them live in the village, they're in the hunting fraternity, they drink in the bar.

But Nalle is immune to all that. Lars-Gunnar's occasional outbursts of bitterness toward Nalle's mother, his own father, the world in general. His irritation over Nalle's shortcomings. The self-pity and hatred that only come out properly when the men are drinking, but are always there just beneath the surface. Nalle can hang his head, but for a few seconds at the most. He's a happy child in a grown man's body. Gentle and honest through and through. Bitterness and stupidity don't touch him.

If he hadn't been brain damaged. If he'd been normal. She can work out how the landscape between father and son would have looked then. Barren and poor. Tainted by that contempt for their own enclosed weakness.

Mildred. She doesn't know how right she is.

But Mimmi doesn't embark on any discussion. She shrugs her shoulders by way of a reply, says it was nice to meet you, but now she's got to get back to work.

* * *

Mimmi heard Lars-Gunnar's voice in the dining room.

"For God's sake, Nalle."

Not angry. But tired and resigned.

"I've told you, we have breakfast at home."

Mimmi came into the dining room. Nalle was sitting with his plate in front of him, hanging his head in shame. Licking the milk moustache off his upper lip. The pancakes were gone, so were the eggs and the bread, only the apple lay untouched.

"Forty kronor," said Mimmi to Lars-Gunnar, a fraction too cheerfully.

Old skinflint, she thought.

He had a freezer full of free meat from hunting. The women in the village helped him out for free with cleaning and washing; they turned up with home baked bread and invited him and Nalle to dinner.

When Mimmi started working at the bar, Nalle used to get his breakfast there free.

"You mustn't give him anything when he comes in," Lars-Gunnar explained. "He's just getting fat."

And Micke gave Nalle his breakfast, but because he didn't really have Lars-Gunnar's permission, he hadn't the guts to take payment for it.

Mimmi had.

"Nalle's had breakfast," she said to Lars-Gunnar the first time she had a morning shift. "Forty kronor."

Lars-Gunnar had looked at her in surprise. Looked around for Micke, who was at home fast asleep.

"You're not to give him anything when he comes begging," he began.

"If he's not allowed to eat, then you keep him away from here. If he comes in, he can eat. If he eats, you pay."

From then on, he paid up. Paid Micke too, if he was doing the morning shift.

Now he was even smiling at her, ordering coffee and pancakes for himself. He stood at the side of the table where Nalle and Rebecka were sitting. Couldn't decide where to sit. In the end he sat down at the table next to them.

"Come and sit here," he said. "Perhaps the lady wants to be left in peace."

The lady didn't answer, and Nalle stayed where he was. When Mimmi brought the coffee and pancakes, he asked:

"Can Nalle stay here today?"

"More," said Nalle, when he saw his father's mound of pancakes.

"The apple first," said Mimmi, immovable.

"No," she said then, turning to Lars-Gunnar. "I'm up to my eyes in it today. Magdalena are having their autumn dinner and planning meeting in here tonight."

A shiver of displeasure ran through him like a draft. As it did with most men when the women's group came up in conversation.

"Just for a little while?" he ventured.

"What about Mum?"

"I don't want to ask Lisa. She's got such a lot to do before the meeting tonight."

"One of the other women then? They all like Nalle."

She watched Lars-Gunnar consider the alternatives. Nothing in this world was free. There were women he could ask, no doubt about it. But that was just the problem. Having to ask a favor. Bother people. Owe someone a big thank you.

Rebecka Martinsson looked at Nalle. He was staring at his apple. Difficult to work out if he felt as if he were a nuisance, or if he just felt it was hard to be forced to eat the apple before he could have more pancakes.

"Nalle can stay with me if he'd like to," she said.

Lars-Gunnar and Mimmi looked at her in surprise. She was almost surprised at herself.

"I mean, I wasn't thinking of doing anything special today," she went on. "Maybe go for a bit of a trip . . . If he'd like to come along, then . . . I'll give you the number of my cell phone."

"She's staying in one of the cottages," Mimmi said to Lars-Gunnar. "Rebecka . . ."

". . . Martinsson."

Lars-Gunnar nodded a greeting to Rebecka.

"Lars-Gunnar, Nalle's father," he said. "If it's no trouble . . ."

Obviously it's trouble, but she'll brush that aside, thought Mimmi angrily.

"No trouble at all," Rebecka assured him.

I've jumped from the top board, she thought. Now I can do whatever I want.

In the conference room at the police station, Inspector Anna-Maria Mella was leaning back in her chair. She had called a morning meeting as a result of the letters and other papers found in Mildred Nilsson's locker.

Apart from herself, there were two men in the room: her colleagues Sven-Erik Stålnacke and Fred Olsson. Twenty or so letters lay on the table in front of them. Most were still in their envelopes, which had been slit open.

"Right then," she said.

She and Fred Olsson pulled on surgical gloves and began to read.

Sven-Erik was sitting with his clenched fists resting on the table, the great big squirrel's tail under his nose sticking straight out like a scrubbing brush. He looked as if he'd like to kill somebody. Eventually he pulled on the latex gloves as if they were boxing gloves.

They glanced through the letters. Most were from parishioners with problems. There were divorces and bereavements, infidelity, worries about the children.

Anna-Maria held up one letter.

"This is just impossible," she said. "Look, you just can't read it, it looks like a tangled telephone wire sprawling across the pages."

"Give it here," said Fred Olsson, stretching out his hand.

First of all he held the letter so close to his face that it was touching his nose. Then he moved it slowly away until in the end he was reading it with his arm stretched right out.

"It's a question of technique," he said as he alternated between screwing his eyes up and opening them very wide. "First of all you recognize the little words, 'and,' 'I,' 'so,' then you can move on from them. I'll look at it in a minute."

He put the letter down and went back to the one he'd been reading before. He enjoyed this kind of work. Searching databases, getting hits, linking registers, looking for people with no fixed abode. "The truth is out there," he always said as he logged on. He had a lot of good informers in his address book and a wide network of social contacts, people who knew about this and that.

"This one's not very happy," he said after a while, holding up a letter.

It was written on pale pink paper; there were galloping horses with flying manes up in the right-hand corner.

" 'Your time will soon be UP, Mildred,' " he read. " 'Soon the truth about you will be revealed to EVERYONE. You preach LIES and are living a LIE. MANY of us are tired of your LIES . . .' blah, blah, blah . . ."

"Put it in a plastic pocket," said Anna-Maria. "We'll send anything interesting to the lab. Shit!"

"Look!" she said. "Look at this!"

She unfolded a sheet of paper and held it up to her colleagues.

It was a drawing. The picture showed a woman with long hair, hanging from a noose. The person who had done the drawing was talented. Not a professional, but a skillful amateur, that much was obvious to Anna-Maria. Tongues of fire curled around the dangling body, and a black cross stood on top of a grave mound in the back-ground.

"What does it say down at the bottom?" asked Sven-Erik.

Anna-Maria read out loud:

" 'SOON MILDRED.' "

"That's . . ." began Fred Olsson.

"I'll send it to the lab in Linköping right away!" Anna-Maria went on. "If there are prints . . . We must ring them and tell them this has to have priority."

"You go," said Sven-Erik. "Fred and I will go through the rest."

Anna-Maria put the letter and the envelope in separate plastic pockets. Then she dashed out of the room.

Fred Olsson bent dutifully over the pile of letters again.

"This is nice," he said. "It says here she's an ugly man-hating hysteric who needs to be bloody careful because 'we've had enough of you, you fucking slag, be careful when you go out at night, look behind you, your grandkids won't recognize you.' She didn't have any children, did she? How could she have grandchildren, then?"

Sven-Erik was still staring at the door Anna-Maria had disappeared through. All summer. These letters had been lying in the locker all summer, while he and his colleagues fumbled around in the dark.

"All I want to know," he said without looking at Fred Olsson, "is how the hell those priests could not tell me Mildred Nilsson had a private locker in the parish office!"

Fred Olsson didn't reply.

"I've got a good mind to give them a good shaking and ask what the hell they're playing at," he went on. "Ask them what they think we're doing here!"

"But Anna-Maria's promised Rebecka Martinsson . . ."

"But I haven't promised anything," barked Sven-Erik, slamming the flat of his hand down onto the table so hard it jumped.

He got up and made a hopeless gesture with his hand.

"Don't worry," he said. "I'm not going to run away and do anything stupid. I just need to, I don't know, sort myself out for a bit."

With these words he left the room. The door slammed behind him.

Fred Olsson went back to the letters. It was all for the best, really. He liked working alone.

Bertil Stensson and Stefan Wikström were standing in the little room inside the parish office looking into Mildred Nilsson's locker. Rebecka Martinsson had handed in the key to the house in Poikkijärvi and the key to the locker.

"Just calm down," said Bertil Stensson. "Think about . . ."

He ended the sentence with a nod in the direction of the office where the clerks were sitting.

Stefan Wikström glanced at his boss. The parish priest's mouth contracted into a thoughtful expression. Smoothed itself out, contracted again. Like a little hamster mouth. The short, stocky body in a beautifully ironed pink shirt from the Shirt Factory. A bold color, it was the priest's daughter who kitted him out. Went well with the tanned face and the silvery, boyish haircut.

"Where are the letters?" said Stefan Wikström.

"Maybe she burned them," said the priest.

Stefan Wikström's voice went up an octave.

"She told me she'd kept them. What if somebody in Magdalena's got them? What am I going to say to my wife?"

"Maybe nothing," said Bertil Stensson calmly. "I need to get in touch with her husband. To give him her jewelry."

They stood in silence.

Stefan Wikström gazed at the locker without speaking. He had thought this would be a moment of liberation. That he would hold the letters in his hand and be free of Mildred for good. But now. Her grip on the back of his neck was as tight as ever.

What is it you want of me, Lord? he thought. It is written that you do not test us beyond our capability, but now you have driven me to the limit of what I can cope with.

He felt trapped. Trapped by Mildred, by his job, by his wife, by his vocation, just giving and giving without ever getting anything back. And after Mildred's death he had felt trapped by his boss Bertil Stensson.

Before, Stefan had enjoyed the father-son relationship that had grown between them. But now he recognized the price that would have to be paid. He was under Bertil's thumb. He could see what Bertil said about him behind his back from the way the women in the office looked at him. They put their heads on one side, and there was just a hint of pity in their eyes. He could almost hear Bertil: "Things aren't easy for Stefan. He's more sensitive than you'd think." More sensitive as in weak. The fact that the parish priest had taken some of his services hadn't gone unnoticed. Everyone had been informed, apparently by chance. He felt diminished and exploited.

I could disappear, he thought. God takes care of the sparrow.

Mildred. Back in June she was gone. All of a sudden. But now she was back. Magdalena, the women's group, had got back on its feet. They were vociferously demanding more women priests in the parish. And it was as if Bertil had already forgotten what she was really like. When he spoke about her nowadays, there was warmth in his voice. She had a big heart, he sighed. She had a greater talent as a pastor than I myself, he maintained generously. That implied that she had a greater talent as a pastor than Stefan, since Bertil was a better pastor than Stefan.

At least I'm not a liar, thought Stefan angrily. She was an aggressive troublemaker who drew damaged women to her and gave them fire instead of balm. Death couldn't change that fact.

It was a disturbing thought, that Mildred had set damaged people on fire. Many might say she'd set him on fire too.

But I'm not damaged, he thought. That wasn't why.

He stared into the locker. Thought about autumn 1997.

*   *   *

Bertil Stensson has called Stefan Wikström and Mildred Nilsson to a meeting. Mikael Berg, the rural dean, is with him in his capacity as the person responsible for personnel issues. Mikael Berg sits bolt upright on his chair. He's in his fifties. The trousers he's wearing are ten to fifteen years old. And at that time Mikael was ten to fifteen kilos heavier. His thin hair is plastered to his skull. From time to time he takes a deep breath. His hand shoots up, doesn't know where to go, smooths his hair down, drops back to his knee.

Stefan is sitting opposite him. Thinking he'll remain calm. During the whole conversation ahead of him, he'll remain calm. The others can raise their voices, but he's not like that.

They're waiting for Mildred. She's coming straight from a service in a school and has let them know that she'll probably be a few minutes late.

Bertil Stensson is looking out of the window. A deep furrow between his eyebrows.

Mildred arrives. Walks in through the door at the same time as she knocks. Red cheeks. Her hair slightly frizzy from the damp autumn air outside.

She chucks her jacket onto a chair, pours herself a coffee from the flask.

Bertil Stensson explains why they're there. The community is being split in two, he says. A Mildred-section and, he doesn't say a Stefan-section, and the rest.

"I'm delighted with the sense of involvement you spread around you," he says to Mildred. "But this is an insupportable situation for me. It's beginning to resemble a war between the feminist priest and the priest who hates women."

Stefan nearly leaps out of his seat.

"I most certainly don't hate women," he says, upset.

"No, but that's the way it looks," says Bertil Stensson, pushing Monday's newspaper across the table.

Nobody needs to look at it. Everybody has read the article. "Woman Priest Answers Her Critics," says the headline. The article quotes Mildred's sermon from the previous week. She said that the stole was in fact a Roman female garment. That it's been worn since the fourth century, when liturgical costume was first worn. "What priests are wearing today is actually women's clothes, according to Mildred Nilsson," says the article. "I can still accept male priests, after all it says in the Bible: there is neither female nor male, neither Jew nor Greek."

Stefan Wikström has also had the opportunity to express his views in the article. "Stefan Wikström maintains that he doesn't see the sermon as a personal attack. He loves women, he just doesn't want to see them in the pulpit."

Stefan's heart is heavy. He feels he's been tricked. True, that is what he said, but it's come out completely wrong in that context. The journalist asked him:

"You love your brothers. What about women? Do you hate women?"

And he'd naïvely answered absolutely not. He loved women.

"But you don't want to see them in the pulpit."

No, he'd replied. Broadly speaking that was true. But there was no value judgment in that, he'd added. In his eyes the work of the deaconess was every bit as important as that of the priest.

The parish priest is saying that he doesn't want to hear any more comments like this from Mildred.

"And what about Stefan's comments?" she says calmly. "He and his family don't come to church when I'm preaching. We can't hold a joint confirmation, because he refuses to work with me."

"I can't go against what it says in the Bible," says Stefan.

Mildred makes an impatient movement with her head. Bertil clothes himself in patience. They've heard this before, Stefan realizes, but what can he do, it's still true.

"Jesus chose twelve men as his disciples," Stefan persists. "The chief priest was always a man. How far can we move away from the word of the Bible in our attempt to fit in with the values prevalent in modern society before it stops being Christianity at all?"

"All the disciples and the chief priests were Jews as well," replies Mildred. "How do you get round that? And read the epistle to the Hebrews, Jesus is our chief priest today."

Bertil holds up his hands in a gesture that means he doesn't want to get involved in a discussion they've had several times before.

"I respect you both," he says. "And I've agreed not to place a woman in your district, Stefan. I want to stress once again that you're placing both me and the church in an extremely difficult position. You're shifting the focus to a conflict. And I want to ask you both not to get involved in polemics, above all not from the pulpit."

He changes the expression on his face. From stern to forgiving. He almost winks at Mildred, as if they share a secret understanding.

"I'm sure we can make an effort to concentrate on our common goals. I don't want to have to hear words like male power and the power balance between the sexes being bandied about in church. You have to believe Stefan, Mildred. It isn't a value judgment if he doesn't come to church when you're preaching."

Mildred's expression doesn't alter at all. She stares Stefan straight in the eye.

"It's what the Bible says," he maintains, staring right back at her. "I can't find a way around that."

"Men hit women," she says, takes a deep breath and carries on. "Men belittle women, dominate them, persecute them, kill them.

Or they cut off their genitals, kill them when they're newborn babies, force them to hide behind a veil, lock them up, rape them, prevent them from educating themselves, pay them lower wages and give them less opportunity to take power. Deny them the right to become priests. I can't find a way around that."

There is complete silence for about three seconds.

"Now, Mildred," ventures Bertil.

"She's sick in the head," yells Stefan. "Are you calling me . . . Are you comparing me with men who abuse women? This isn't a discussion, it's slander, and I don't know . . ."

"What?" she says.

And now they're both on their feet, somewhere in the background they can hear Bertil Stensson and Mikael Berg: calm down, sit down.

"What part of that was slander?"

"There's no room to maneuver," says Stefan, turning to Bertil. "There's no common ground. I don't have to put up with . . . it's impossible for us to work together, you can see that for yourself."

"You never could work with me," he hears Mildred saying behind his back as he storms out of the room.

*   *   *

Bertil Stensson stood in silence in front of the locker. He knew his young colleague was waiting for him to say something reassuring. But what could he say?

Of course she hadn't burned the letters, or thrown them away. If only he'd known about them. He felt very annoyed with Stefan because he hadn't said anything about them.

"Is there anything else I should know?" he asked.

Stefan Wikström looked at his hands. The vow of confidentiality could be a heavy cross to bear.

"No," he said.

To his amazement, Bertil Stensson discovered that he missed her. He had been distressed and shocked when she was murdered. But he hadn't thought he'd miss her. He was probably being unfair. But what had seemed good about Stefan before, his helpfulness and his . . . oh, it was a ridiculous word, his admiration for his boss. Now Mildred was gone, it all seemed somehow coquettish and irritating. They had balanced each other out, his little ones. That's how he'd often thought of them. Although Stefan was over forty and Mildred over fifty. Perhaps because they were both the children of parish priests.

She'd certainly known how to annoy a person. Sometimes in the smallest ways.

The Epiphany dinner, for example. Looking back now, he felt that it was petty of him to have got so annoyed. But then he hadn't known that it would be Mildred's last.

*　　*　　*

Stefan and Bertil are staring at Mildred's advance down the table in front of them as if they are under a spell. The church is holding its Epiphany dinner, a tradition that's been established for a few years now. Stefan and Bertil are sitting next to one another opposite Mildred. The staff are clearing away the main course and Mildred is mobilizing her troops.

She started by recruiting soldiers for her little army. Grabbed the salt cellar in one hand and the pepper mill in the other. Brought them together, then took them for a bit of a march around while she followed the conversation, apparently lost in thought; it was probably about how busy things had been over Christmas, but now at least it was over, and maybe about the latest winter cold that was doing the rounds, that sort of thing. She was pushing down the edges of the candle too. Even at that stage Bertil could see how Stefan was almost having to hold on to the edge of the table to stop himself snatching the candle off her and shouting stop fiddling with everything!

Her wineglass still stood by her side like the queen on a chessboard, waiting for her turn.

When Mildred starts talking about the wolf that was in the papers over Christmas, she distractedly pushes the salt and pepper over to Bertil and Stefan's side of the table. The wineglass is on the move as well. Mildred says the wolf has made its way across the Russian and Finnish borders, and the glass makes great sweeps across the table, as far as her arm can reach, crossing all possible borders.

She keeps talking, her cheeks rosy from the wine, constantly moving the objects on the table. Stefan and Bertil feel crowded and strangely disturbed by her advance across the tablecloth.

Keep to your own side, they want to shout.

She tells them she's been thinking. She's been thinking they ought to set up a foundation within the church to protect the wolf. The church owns the land, after all, it's part of the church's responsibility, she thinks.

Bertil has been somewhat affected by the one woman game of chess on the tablecloth, and comes back at her.

"In my opinion the church should devote itself to its main task, working within the community, and not to forestry. Purely as a matter of principle, I mean. We shouldn't even own any forest. We should leave the administration of capital to others."

Mildred doesn't agree.

"Our task is to take care of the earth," she says. "Land is exactly what we should own, not shares. And if the church owns land, it can be looked after in the right way. This wolf has made its way into Swedish territory, onto land owned by the church. If it doesn't get special protection, it won't live for long, you know that. Some hunter or reindeer farmer will shoot it."

"So this foundation . . ."

"Would prevent that, yes. With money and cooperation with the Nature Conservancy Council, we can tag the wolf and keep an eye on it."

"And by doing so you would push people away," objects Bertil. "There must be room for everybody within the church, hunters, the

Sami people, people who like wolves—everybody. But the church can't take sides like that."

"What about our duty of care, then?" says Mildred. "We are supposed to care for the earth, and that has to include species threatened with extinction, surely? As for not adopting a political stance, if the church had had that attitude down the ages, wouldn't we still have slavery?"

They have to laugh at her in the end. She always has to exaggerate and go too far.

*   *   *

Bertil Stensson closed the locker door, turned the key and dropped it in his pocket. In February Mildred had set up her foundation. Neither he nor Stefan Wikström had objected.

The whole idea of the foundation had irritated him. And now as he looks back and tries to be honest with himself, it irritates him to realize that he didn't stand up to her because of cowardice. He was afraid of being seen as a wolf-hater and God knows what else. But he did get Mildred to agree to a less provocative name than the Northern Wolf Protection Foundation. It became Jukkasjärvi Community Wildlife Protection Foundation instead. And he and Stefan were signatories along with Mildred.

And later in the spring, when Stefan's wife took the youngest child and went to stay with her mother in Katrineholm and didn't come back for a long time, Bertil hadn't really thought anything of it.

Now, of course, it bothered him.

But Stefan should have said something, he thought in his defense.

Rebecka parked the car outside her grandmother's house in Kurravaara. Nalle jumped out and scampered around the outside of the house, curious.

Like a happy dog, thought Rebecka as she watched him disappear around the corner.

The next second her conscience pricked. You shouldn't compare him to a dog.

September sun on the gray building. The wind blowing gently through the tall autumn grass, faded and lacking in nutrients. Low water, a motorboat far away. From another direction, the sound of someone chopping wood. A soft breeze against her face, like a gentle hand.

She looked at the house again. The windows were in a terrible state. They needed taking out, scraping down, new putty, fresh paint. The same dark green color as before, nothing else. She thought about the mineral wool packed in the entrance to the cellar to stop the cold air that would come pouring up otherwise, forming rime frost on the walls that would turn to patches of gray damp. It needed pulling out. The place needed sealing properly, insulation, install the right kind of ventilation. Make a decent cellar for storage. Somebody ought to save the hollow-eyed house before it was too late.

"Come on, let's go in," she shouted to Nalle who had run down to Larsson's red-timbered storehouse and was tugging at the door.

Nalle lumbered over the potato patch. The bottom of his shoes was soon thick with mud.

"You," he said, pointing at Rebecka when he had reached the veranda.

"Rebecka," answered Rebecka. "My name's Rebecka."

He nodded in reply. He'd ask her again soon. He'd already asked her several times, but still hadn't said her name.

They went up the steps into her grandmother's kitchen. A bit damp and chilly. Felt colder than outside. Nalle went first. In the kitchen he opened every wardrobe and closet, every cupboard and drawer, completely without embarrassment.

Good, thought Rebecka. He can open them and all the ghosts can fly away.

She smiled at his big lumbering figure, at the crafty, crooked smile he directed at her from time to time. It felt good to have him there.

A knight can look like that too, she thought.

A sense of security came over her—everything was just the same. It put its arm around her. Pulled her down onto the sofa beside Nalle, who'd found a banana box full of comics. He sorted out the ones he liked. They had to be in color, and he chose mostly Donald Duck. He put Agent 69, The Phantom, and Buster back in the box. She looked around. The blue painted chairs around the old gate-legged table, shiny with use. The refrigerator humming away. The tiles above the black Näfveqvarn stove, decorated with pictures of different spices. Next to the woodstove stood the electrical one, with knobs of brown and orange plastic. Grandmother's hand everywhere. The rack above the stove was crammed with dried flowers, pans and stainless steel ladles. Uncle Affe's wife Inga-Lill still hung bunches of flowers there to dry. Cat's foot, tansy, cotton grass, buttercups and yarrow. There were also some bought pink everlasting flowers, they'd never have been there in Grandmother's day. Grandmother's woven rag rugs on the floor, even on the sofa to protect it. Embroidered cloths on every surface, even covering the treadle sewing machine in the corner. The embroidered tray holder, where the tray Grandfather had made out of matchsticks the last time he was ill still hung.

She'd woven or crocheted the cushion covers.

Could I live here? wondered Rebecka.

She looked down on to the meadow. Nobody was cutting or burning it nowadays, that was obvious. Big tussocks, the grass growing up through a rotting layer of the previous year's grass. Thousands of holes made by field mice and voles, no doubt. From up here she had a better view of the roof of the barn. The question was whether it could still be saved. All at once she felt downhearted. A house dies when it's abandoned. Slowly but surely. It crumbles away, it stops breathing. It cracks, subsides, goes moldy.

Where do you start? thought Rebecka. The windows alone are more than a full-time job. I can't put a new roof on. It won't be safe to walk on the veranda before long.

Then the house shook. The door slammed downstairs. The little chime of bells just inside the door with the text "Jopa virkki puu visainen kielin kantelon kajasi tuota soittoa suloista" shook and emitted a few delicate notes.

Sivving's voice rang through the house. Made its way up the stairs and pushed through the door.

"Hello!"

A few seconds later he appeared in the doorway. Grandmother's neighbor. A big man. His hair white and soft as pussy willow on his head. A yellowish white military vest underneath a blue imitation beaver jacket. A big grin when he caught sight of Rebecka. She got up.

"Rebecka," was all he said.

In two paces he was beside her. Put his arms around her.

They didn't usually hug each other, hardly even when she was a little girl. But she stopped herself from stiffening. Closed her eyes for the two seconds the embrace lasted. Drifted out on a sea of tranquillity. If you didn't count handshakes, nobody had touched her since . . . since Erik Rydén welcomed her to the firm's party on Lidö. And before that, six months ago when they took blood tests at the clinic.

Then the hug was over. But Sivving Fjällborg held on to her, his right hand around her left upper arm.

"How are you?" he asked.

"Fine," she smiled back.

His face grew more serious. He held her for a second longer before he let go. Then the smile was back.

"And you've got a friend with you."

"I have, this is Nalle."

Nalle was absorbed in a Donald Duck comic. Difficult to know whether he could actually read, or whether he was just looking at the pictures.

"Well, I think you should both come with me and have some coffee, because I've got something really special to show you at home. What do you think, Nalle? Juice and a cake? Or do you drink coffee?"

* * *

Nalle and Rebecka followed close behind Sivving like two calves.

Sivving, thought Rebecka, and smiled. It'll be all right. I can do one window at a time.

Sivving's house was on the other side of the road. Rebecka explained that she'd come up to Kiruna because of work, and stayed on for a short holiday. Sivving didn't ask any awkward questions. Why she wasn't staying in Kurravaara, for example. Rebecka noticed his left arm was hanging limply by his side, and that his left foot was dragging slightly, not a lot, but still. She didn't ask either.

Sivving lived down in the boiler room in the cellar. It meant there was less cleaning to do, and it was cosier. He only used the rest of the house when his children and grandchildren came to visit. But it was a very pleasant boiler room. The china and household equipment he needed from day to day were on a string shelf, stained brown. There was a bed and a little Formica table, a chair, a chest of drawers and an electric hob.

In her basket next to the bed lay Sivving's pointer bitch, Bella. And beside her lay four puppies. Bella got up quickly, wagging her tail, and came to say hello to Rebecka and Nalle. She hadn't time to allow herself to be patted, just gave them a quick sniff, then butted her master a couple of times and gave him a lick.

"Good girl," said Sivving. "So, Nalle, what do you think? Aren't they nice?"

Nalle seemed as if he hardly heard what was said. He was staring at the puppies the whole time, with an ecstatic expression on his face.

"Oh," he said, "oh," and squatted down beside the basket, reaching out for a sleeping puppy.

"I don't know . . ." began Rebecka.

"No, leave him," said Sivving. "Bella is a much calmer mother than I'd have thought she would be."

Bella lay down beside the three puppies that were still in the basket. She kept an eye on Nalle all the time as he lifted the fourth and settled himself, leaning back against the wall with the puppy on his lap. The puppy woke up and attacked Nalle's hand and sleeve with all its might.

"They're funny," laughed Sivving. "It's as if they've got an on-off switch. One minute they're charging about like lunatics, the next, bang, fast asleep."

They drank their coffee in silence. It didn't matter. It was enough just watching Nalle lying on his back on the floor with the puppies tumbling over his legs, tugging at his clothes and clambering up onto his stomach. Bella took the opportunity to beg for a bun at the table. She was dribbling as she sat down beside Rebecka.

"You've learned some fine manners," laughed Rebecka.

"Basket," said Sivving to Bella, waving his hand.

"You know, I think there's something the matter with her hearing in the ear on your side," said Rebecka, laughing even more.

"I've only got myself to blame," said Sivving. "But you know how it is, when you're sitting here all on your own, it's easy to give in and share. And then . . ."

Rebecka nodded.

"Anyway," said Sivving cheerfully. "Since you've got this big strong lad with you, you can give me a hand to lift the jetty. I was thinking of trying to pull it up with the tractor, but I'm afraid it won't hold."

* * *

The jetty was sodden and heavy. The river low and sluggish. Nalle and Sivving stood in the water, one on each side, struggling away. The summer's last flies took the opportunity to bite the back of their necks. The sun and the effort meant that their clothes ended up in a pile up on the bank. Nalle was wearing Sivving's spare boots. Rebecka had fetched some other clothes from her grandmother's house. One boot was split, so her right foot had soon got wet. Now she was standing on the bank pulling, her sock squelching inside the boot. She could feel rivulets of sweat pouring down her back. And her scalp. Wet and salty.

"This certainly lets you know you're alive," she groaned to Sivving.

"Your body, anyway," replied Sivving.

He looked at her with pleasure. Knew there was a kind of release in hard physical work when the soul was tormented. He'd certainly get her working if she came back.

Afterward they had meat soup and crispbread in Sivving's boiler room. Sivving had conjured up three stools, they just fitted around the table. Rebecka had found some dry socks.

"Glad to see you're enjoying that," said Sivving to Nalle, who was shoveling down the soup along with big pieces of crispbread spread with a thick layer of butter and cheese. "You can come and help me again."

Nalle nodded, his mouth full of food. Bella was lying in her basket, the snuffling puppies beneath her stomach. Her ears moved occasionally. She was checking up on people even though her eyes were closed.

"And you, Rebecka," said Sivving, "you're always welcome."

She nodded and looked out through the cellar window.

Time passes more slowly here, she thought. Although you do notice that it's passing. A new jetty. New to me, it's already been around for many years. The cat disappearing in the grass isn't the Larssons' Mirri. She's dead and gone, long ago. I don't know the names of the dogs I hear barking far away. I used to know. Recognized Pikki's hoarse, bad-tempered bark, always looking for a fight. She could keep going forever. Sivving. Soon he'll need help with clearing the snow and shopping for food. Maybe I could cope with staying here?

Anna-Maria Mella drove her red Ford Escort into Magnus Lindmark's yard. According to Lisa Stöckel and Erik Nilsson, this was the man who'd made no secret of the fact that he'd hated Mildred. Who'd slashed her tires and set fire to her shed.

He was washing his Volvo, and he turned off the water and put down the hose as she drove in. Around forty. A bit on the short side, but he looked strong. Rolled up his shirtsleeves when she got out of the car. Probably wanted to show off his muscles.

"You're driving a steam engine," he joked.

The next moment he realized she was from the police. She could see how his face changed. A mixture of contempt and cunning. Anna-Maria felt she should have had Sven-Erik with her.

"I don't think I want to answer any questions," said Magnus Lindmark before she'd even managed to open her mouth.

Anna-Maria introduced herself. Took out her ID as well, although she wasn't in the habit of waving it about unnecessarily.

Now what do I do? she thought. There's no chance of forcing him.

"You don't even know what it's about," she ventured.

"Now let me guess," he said, screwing his face up into an exaggerated expression of thoughtfulness and rubbing his chin with his index finger. "A slag of a priest who got what she deserved, maybe? And now I'm supposed to feel something or other, well no way, I don't feel like talking about it."

My my, thought Anna-Maria, he's really enjoying this.

"Okay," she said with an unconcerned smile. "In that case I'll get back in my steam engine and chug away."

She turned around and walked to the car.

He'll call out, she just had time to think.

"If you catch the guy who did it," he yelled, "give me a ring so I can come in and shake him by the hand."

She walked the last few steps to her car. Turned toward him, her hand on the handle. Said nothing.

"She was a fucking slag who got what she deserved. Haven't you got your notebook? Write that down."

Anna-Maria pulled a notebook and pen out of her pocket. Wrote down "fucking slag."

"She seems to have got on quite a few people's nerves," she said, as if she were talking to herself.

He came over to her, positioned himself threateningly close.

"Too fucking right," he said.

"Why were you annoyed with her?"

"Annoyed," he spat. "Annoyed, I get annoyed with the fucking dog when she stands there barking at a squirrel. I'm not the hypocritical type, I've got no problem admitting I hated her. And I wasn't the only one."

Keep talking, thought Anna-Maria, nodding sympathetically.

"Why did you hate her?"

"Because she broke up my marriage, that's why! Because my son starting pissing in his bed when he was eleven years old! We had problems, Anki and me, but once she'd spoken to Mildred there was no more talk of sorting things out. I said 'do you want to go to family counseling, I'll do that if you want,' but no, that fucking priest messed with her head until she left me. And took the kids with her. You didn't think the church approved of that sort of thing, did you?"

"No. But you . . ."

"Anki and I used to quarrel, sure. But maybe you and your old man have words now and again?"

"Often. But you got so angry that you . . ."

Anna-Maria broke off and leafed through her notebook.

". . . set fire to her shed, punctured her tires, smashed the glass in her greenhouse."

Magnus Lindmark smiled broadly at her and said sweetly:

"But that wasn't me."

"So what were you doing the night before midsummer's eve?"

"I've already said, I stayed over with a friend."

Anna-Maria read from her notebook.

"Fredrik Korpi. Do you often stay over with your little friends?"

"When you're too fucking pissed to drive home . . ."

"You said you weren't the only one who hated her? Who else?"

He made a sweeping gesture with his arm.

"Just about anybody."

"Well liked, I heard."

"By a load of hysterical old women."

"And a number of men."

"Who are nothing but hysterical old women. Ask any, excuse the expression, real man and they'll tell you. She was after the hunting fraternity as well. Wanted to cancel their permit and fuck knows what else. But if you think Torbjörn killed her, then you've got that fucking wrong as well."

"Torbjörn?"

"Torbjörn Ylitalo, the church's forest warden and the chairman of the hunting club. They had a terrible quarrel back in the spring. I reckon he'd have liked to stick his shotgun in her mouth. And then she started that fucking wolf foundation. And that's a class thing, you know. It's easy for a load of fuckers from Stockholm to love wolves. But the day a wolf comes down to their golf courses and their terrace bars and gobbles up their poodles for breakfast, they'll be out there hunting!"

"But Mildred Nilsson wasn't from Stockholm, was she?"

"No, but somewhere down there. Torbjörn Ylitalo's cousin had his old dog killed by a wolf when he went down to Värmland to visit his in-laws at Christmas ninety-nine. He sat there in Micke's crying when he was telling us about finding the dog. Or the remains of the dog, I should say. There was only the skeleton left, and a few bloody scraps of fur."

He looked at her. She kept her face expressionless—did he think she was going to faint because he was talking about skeletons and scraps of fur?

When she didn't say anything he turned his head aside, his gaze sweeping away across the pine trees to the ragged clouds scudding across the chilly blue autumn sky.

"I had to get a lawyer before I was allowed to meet my own kids, for fuck's sake. I hope she suffered. She did, didn't she?"

*   *   *

When Rebecka and Nalle got back to Micke's bar, it was already five o'clock in the afternoon. Lisa Stöckel was walking down toward the bar from the road, and Nalle ran to meet her.

"Dog!" he shouted, pointing at Lisa's dog Majken. "Little!"

"We've been looking at puppies," explained Rebecka.

"Becka!" he yelled, pointing at Rebecka.

"Wow, you're popular," Lisa smiled at Rebecka.

"The puppies swung it," Rebecka replied modestly.

"He loves anything to do with dogs," said Lisa. "You like dogs, don't you, Nalle? I heard you looked after Nalle today, thanks for that. I can pay if you've had any expenses for food and so on."

She took a wallet out of her pocket.

"No, no," said Rebecka, waving her hand, and Lisa dropped the wallet on the ground.

All her cards fell out onto the gravel, her library ticket, supermarket loyalty card, her Visa card and her driving license.

And the photograph of Mildred.

Lisa bent down quickly to gather everything up, but Nalle had already picked up the photograph of Mildred. It had been taken during a coach trip the Magdalena group had gone on, to a retreat in Uppsala. Mildred was smiling at the camera, surprised and reproachful. Lisa had been holding the camera. They'd stopped to stretch their legs.

"Illred," said Nalle to the photograph, and laid it against his cheek.

He smiled at Lisa as she stood there, her hand impatiently outstretched. She had to exercise an iron control not to snatch it off him. It was a bloody good job nobody else was there.

"They were friends, those two," she said, nodding toward Nalle, who still had the photograph pressed against his cheek.

"She seems to have been a very special priest," said Rebecka seriously.

"Very," said Lisa. "Very."

Rebecka bent down and patted the dog.

"He's such a blessing," said Lisa. "You forget all your troubles when you're with him."

"Isn't it a bitch?" asked Rebecka, peering under the dog's stomach.

"I was talking about Nalle," said Lisa. "This is Majken."

She stroked the dog absentmindedly.

"I've got a lot of dogs."

"I like dogs," said Rebecka, stroking Majken's ears.

Not so keen on people, though? thought Lisa. I know. I was like that myself for a long time. Probably still am.

But Mildred had got Lisa to do whatever she wanted. Right from the start. Like when she got Lisa to give talks about budgeting. Lisa had tried to refuse. But Mildred had been . . . stubborn was a ridiculous word. You couldn't contain Mildred in that word.

*   *   *

"Don't you care?" asks Mildred. "Don't you care about people?"

Lisa is sitting on the floor with Bruno lying alongside her. She's clipping his claws.

Majken is standing beside them like a nurse, supervising. The other dogs are lying in the hallway hoping it will never be their turn. If they keep really still and quiet, maybe Lisa will forget about them.

And Mildred is sitting on the sofa in the kitchen and explaining. As if the problem was that Lisa didn't understand. Magdalena, the women's group, wants to help women who've gone adrift in purely financial terms. Long term unemployed, those on benefit because they're signed off sick for a long time, with the authorities after them and the kitchen drawers stuffed full of papers from debt collecting agencies and God knows who else. And Mildred just happens to know that Lisa works as a debt counselor and budgeting advisor for the council. Mildred wants Lisa to run a course for these women. So they can get their private finances sorted out.

Lisa wants to say no. Say that she doesn't actually care about people. That she cares about her dogs, cats, goats, sheep, lambs. The female elk that turned up the winter before last, thin as a rake, so she fed her and looked after her.

"They won't turn up," Lisa replies.

She clips Bruno's last claw. He gets a pat and disappears to join the rest of the gang in the hall. Lisa gets up.

"They'll say 'yeah, yeah, brilliant' when you invite them," she goes on. "But they won't turn up."

"We'll see," says Mildred, narrowing her eyes. Then her little lingonberry mouth widens into a smile. A row of tiny teeth, like a child's.

Lisa goes weak at the knees, looks away, says "okay, I'll do it" just to get rid of the priest before she collapses completely.

Three weeks later Lisa is standing in front of a group of women, talking. Drawing on a whiteboard. Circles and pieces of pie, red, green and blue. Glances at Mildred, hardly dares look at her. Looks at the rest of her audience instead. They've got dressed up, God help us. Cheap blouses. Bobbly cardigans. Gold colored costume jewelry. Most of them are listening obediently. Others are staring at Lisa, almost with hatred in their eyes, as if the way their lives have turned out might be her fault.

Gradually she's drawn into other projects with the women's group. She just gets carried along. She even attends the Bible study group for a while. But in the end it just doesn't work anymore. She can't look at Mildred, because it feels as if the others can read her face like an open book. She can't avoid looking at her the whole time, that's just as obvious. She doesn't know where to turn. Doesn't hear what they're talking about. Drops her pen and makes a fuss. In the end she stops going.

She keeps away from the women's group. Her restlessness is like an incurable illness. She wakes up in the middle of the night. Thinks about the priest all the time. She starts running. Mile after mile. Along the roads at first. Then the ground dries out and she can run in the forest. She goes to Norway and buys another dog, a Springer spaniel. It keeps her busy. She renews the putty in all the windows and doesn't borrow the rotovator from her neighbor for the potato patch as she usually does, but turns it over by hand instead during the light May evenings. Sometimes she thinks she can hear the telephone ringing in the house, but she doesn't answer it.

"Can I have the picture, Nalle?" said Lisa, trying to make her voice sound neutral.

Nalle was holding on to the picture with both hands. His smile went from one ear to the other.

"Illred," he said. "Swinging."

Lisa stared at him, took the picture off him.

"Yes, that's right," she said in the end.

She spoke to Rebecka, a little too quickly, but Rebecka didn't appear to notice anything:

"Nalle was confirmed by Mildred. And her confirmation classes were quite . . . unconventional. She understood that he was a child, so there was plenty of playing on the swings and boat trips and eating pizza. Isn't that right, Nalle, you and Mildred, you used to have pizza. Quattro Stagione, wasn't it?"

"He had three helpings of meat soup today," said Rebecka.

Nalle left them and set off toward the henhouse. Rebecka shouted a good-bye after him, but he didn't seem to hear.

Lisa didn't seem to hear either when Rebecka said good-bye and went off to her chalet. Answered distractedly, staring after Nalle.

* * *

Lisa padded after Nalle like a fox stalking its prey. The henhouse was at the back of the bar.

She thought about what he'd said when he saw the picture of Mildred.

"Illred. Swinging." But Nalle didn't go on the swings. She'd like to see the swing he could fit into. So they can't have gone to the playground together to go on the swings.

Nalle opened the henhouse door. He usually collected the eggs for Mimmi.

"Nalle," said Lisa, trying to attract his attention. "Nalle, did you see Mildred swinging?"

He pointed above his head with his hand.

"Swinging," he replied.

She followed him inside. He stuck his hand under the hens and collected the eggs they were sitting on. Laughed when they pecked angrily at his hand.

"Was she high up? Was it Mildred?"

"Illred," said Nalle.

He stuffed the eggs in his pockets and went out.

My God, thought Lisa. What am I doing? He just repeats whatever I say.

"Did you see the space rocket?" she asked, making a flying movement with her hand. "Whoosh!"

"Whoosh!" smiled Nalle, taking an egg out of his pocket with a sweeping movement.

Out on the road Lars-Gunnar's car stopped, and the horn sounded.

"Your daddy," said Lisa.

She raised a hand and waved to Lars-Gunnar. She could feel how stiff and awkward it was. Her body betrayed her. It was completely impossible for her to meet his eyes or even exchange a word.

She stayed behind the bar as Nalle hurried off toward the car.

Don't think about it, she said to herself. Mildred's dead. Nothing can change that.

*   *   *

Anki Lindmark lived in an apartment on the second floor at Kyrkogatan 21D. She opened the door when Anna-Maria rang the bell, and peered over the security chain. She was in her thirties, maybe a bit younger. She'd bleached her hair herself, and the roots were showing. She was wearing a long sweater and a denim skirt. As Anna-Maria looked at her through the narrow opening, it struck her that the woman was quite tall, at least half a head taller than her ex-husband. Anna-Maria introduced herself.

"Are you Magnus Lindmark's ex?" she asked.

"What's he done?" asked Anki Lindmark.

Suddenly the eyes behind the security chain widened.

"Is it to do with the boys?"

"No," said Anna-Maria. "I just want to ask a few questions. It won't take long."

Anki Lindmark let her in, put the chain back on and locked the door.

They went into the kitchen. It was clean and tidy. Porridge oats, O'Boy drinking chocolate powder and sugar in Tupperware containers on the worktop. A little cloth covering the microwave. On the windowsill stood wooden tulips in a vase, a glass bird, and a little miniature cart made of wood. Children's drawings were fastened to the refrigerator and freezer with magnets. Proper curtains with tiebacks, a pelmet and frilled edges.

At the kitchen table sat a woman in her sixties. She had carrot-colored hair and was staring angrily at Anna-Maria. Shook a menthol cigarette out of its packet and lit up.

"My mother," explained Anki Lindmark when they'd sat down.

"Where are the children?" asked Anna-Maria.

"At my sister's. It's their cousin's birthday today."

"Your ex-husband, Magnus Lindmark . . ." Anna-Maria began.

When Anki Lindmark's mother heard her former son-in-law's name she blew out a cloud of smoke like a snort.

". . . he's said himself that he hated Mildred Nilsson," Anna-Maria went on.

Anki Lindmark nodded.

"He caused damage to her property," said Anna-Maria.

The next second she could have bitten off her tongue. "Caused damage to her property," what kind of official jargon was that? It was the smoking carrot-woman's narrow eyes that were making her be so formal.

Sven-Erik, come and help me, she thought.

He knew how to talk to women.

Anki Lindmark shrugged her shoulders.

"Anything we discuss is just between you and me," said Anna-Maria in an attempt to push the continental shelves together. "Are you afraid of him?"

"Tell her why you live here," said her mother.

"Well," said Anki Lindmark. "In the beginning, after I left him, I lived in Mum's cottage in Poikkijärvi . . ."

"It's been sold now," said her mother. "We can't go out there anymore. Carry on."

". . . but Magnus kept giving me articles out of the evening paper about fires and so on, and in the end I didn't dare live there anymore."

"And the police can't do a thing," said the mother with a mirthless smile.

"He's not bad to the boys, you mustn't think that. But sometimes when he drinks . . . well, he sometimes comes up and shouts and yells at me . . . whore and all sorts . . . kicking the door. So it's best to live here where we've got neighbors and no windows at ground level. But before I got this apartment and found the courage to live on my own with the boys, I stayed with Mildred. But she got her windows smashed and he . . . and slashed tires . . . and then her shed caught fire."

"And that was Magnus?"

Anki Lindmark looked down at the table. Her mother leaned over to Anna-Maria.

"The only people who don't believe it was him are the bloody police," she said.

Anna-Maria refrained from explaining the difference between believing something and being able to prove it. She nodded thoughtfully instead.

"I just hope he'll find somebody new," said Anki Lindmark. "Preferably have children with her. But things have been better lately, since Lars-Gunnar talked to him."

"Lars-Gunnar Vinsa," said her mother. "He's a policeman, or he was—he's retired now. And he's the leader of the hunting club. He talked to Magnus. And if there's one thing Magnus doesn't want, it's to lose his place with the hunt."

Lars-Gunnar Vinsa, Anna-Maria knew who he was. But he'd only worked for a year after she started in Kiruna, and they'd never worked together. So she couldn't say she knew him. He had a mentally handicapped son, she remembered. She remembered how she'd found that out too. Lars-Gunnar and a colleague had arrested a heroin user who was playing up down at the Cupola club. Lars-Gunnar had asked if she had any needles in her pockets before he searched her. No bloody chance, they were at home in her apartment. So Lars-Gunnar had stuck his hands in her pockets to go through them and had jabbed himself with a needle. The girl had come into the station with her upper lip like a burst football and blood pouring from her nose. His colleagues had talked Lars-Gunnar out of owning up, that's what Anna-Maria had heard. That was in 1990. It took six months to get a definite result from an HIV test. After that there was a lot of talk about Lars-Gunnar and his six-year-old son. The boy's mother had abandoned the child and Lars-Gunnar was all he had.

"So Lars-Gunnar spoke to Magnus after the fire?" asked Anna-Maria.

"No, it was after the cat."

Anna-Maria waited in silence.

"I used to have a cat," said Anki, clearing her throat as if she had something stuck in it. "Puss. When I left Magnus I shouted for her, but she'd been gone for a while. I thought I'd come back later to collect her. I was so nervous. I didn't want to meet Magnus. He kept ringing me. And my mother. In the middle of the night, sometimes. Anyway, he rang me at work and said he'd hung a carrier bag with some things of mine in it on the door of the apartment."

She stopped speaking.

Her mother blew a cloud of smoke at Anna-Maria. It drifted apart in thin veils.

"Puss was in the bag," she said, when her daughter didn't speak. "And her kittens. Five of them. They'd all had their heads chopped off. It was just blood and fur."

"What did you do?"

"What could she do?" her mother went on. "You lot can't do anything. Even Lars-Gunnar said the same. If you report something to the police, it has to be a crime. If they'd suffered, it could have been cruelty to animals. But as he'd chopped their heads off, they wouldn't have suffered at all. It could have been criminal damage if they'd had any financial value, if they'd been pedigree cats or an expensive hunting dog or something. But they were just farm cats."

"Yes," said Anki Lindmark. "But I don't think he'd kill . . ."

"Okay, what about later then?" said her mother. "After you'd moved here? Don't you remember what happened with Peter?"

Her mother stubbed out her cigarette, got out a new one and lit it.

"Peter lives in Poikkijärvi. He's divorced too, but such a nice, kind guy. Anyway, he and Anki started seeing each other now and again . . ."

"Just as friends," Anki interjected.

"One morning when Peter was on his way to work, Magnus pulled out straight in front of him. Magnus stopped the car and jumped out. Peter couldn't drive around, because Magnus had parked sort of diagonally across the narrow gravel track. And Magnus jumps out and goes to the trunk and gets out a baseball bat. Walks over to Peter's car. And Peter's sitting there thinking he's going to die and thinking about his own kids, thinking maybe he's dead meat. Then Magnus just lets out a loud guffaw, gets back in his own car and screeches away with the gravel spraying up around his tires. So that was the end of the dating, wasn't it, Anki?"

"I don't want to quarrel with him. He's very good to the boys."

"But you hardly dare go to the supermarket. There's hardly any difference from before, when you were married to him. I'm so bloody tired of the whole thing. The police! They can do sod all."

"Why was he so angry with Mildred?" asked Anna-Maria.

"He said she'd kind of influenced me to leave him."

"And had she?"

"No, she hadn't," said Anki. "I'm an adult. I make my own decisions. And I've told Magnus that."

"And what did he say?"

" 'Did Mildred tell you to say that?' "

"Do you know what he was doing the night before midsummer's eve?"

Anki Lindmark shook her head.

"Has he ever hit you?"

"He's never hit the boys."

Time to go.

"Just one last thing," said Anna-Maria. "When you were staying with Mildred. What impression did you get of her husband? How were things between them?"

Anki Lindmark and her mother exchanged glances.

The talk of the village, thought Anna-Maria.

"She came and went like the cat," said Anki. "But he seemed happy with things as they were . . . I mean, they never fell out or anything."

*   *   *

The evening was closing in. The hens went into the henhouse and nestled close together on their perches. The wind eased and lay down on the grass. Details were obliterated. Grass, trees and buildings floated away into the dark blue sky. Sounds crept closer, became clearer.

Lisa Stöckel listened to the sound of the gravel beneath her feet as she walked down the track to the bar. Her dog Majken trailed behind her. In an hour the women's group would be holding its autumn meeting and dinner at Micke's.

She'd stay sober and take it easy. Put up with all that talk about how everything must carry on without Mildred. How Mildred felt just as close now as when she was alive. All she could do was bite the insides of her lips, hang on to the chair and not stand up and shout: We're finished! Nothing can carry on without Mildred! She isn't close! She's a rotting lump down in the ground! Earth to earth! And you, you can all go back to being home-birds, making the coffee, discussing your fibromyalgia, gossiping like old women. You can read your magazines and serve your men.

She walked in and the sight of her daughter interrupted her train of thought.

Mimmi. Wiping the tables and windowsills with a cloth. Her tri-colored hair in two big bunches above her ears. Pink lacy bra peeping over the neckline of her tight black jumper. Cheeks rosy with warmth, presumably she'd been in the kitchen getting the food ready.

"What are we having?" asked Lisa.

"I've gone for a bit of a Mediterranean theme. Little olive bread rolls with dips to start," answered Mimmi without slowing down her actions with the cloth. It was swishing across the shiny bar counter. She followed it with the hand towel she always carried folded over the waistband of her apron.

"There's tzatziki, tapenade and hummus," she went on. "Then bean soup with pistou, it made sense to do vegetarian for everybody, because half of you are grass eaters . . ."

She looked up and grinned at Lisa, who was just taking off her cap.

"But Mum," she exclaimed, "what on earth do you look like? Are you letting the dogs chew your hair off when it gets too long?"

Lisa ran her hand over her cropped hair to try and flatten it. Mimmi looked at her watch.

"I'll fix it," she said. "Pull up a chair and sit down."

She disappeared through the swing door into the kitchen.

"Mascarpone ice cream with cloudberries for dessert," she shouted from the kitchen. "It's absolutely . . ."

She finished the sentence with an appreciative wolf whistle.

Lisa pulled up a chair, took off her jacket and sat down. Majken immediately lay down at her feet; just this short walk had worn her out, or she was in pain, probably the latter.

Lisa sat as still as in church as Mimmi's fingers worked through her hair and the scissors evened it all out to the width of a finger.

"What's going to happen now, without Mildred?" asked Mimmi. "Your hair grows in three circles in a row just here."

"I suppose we'll just carry on as normal."

"With what?"

"Meals for mothers and children, the clean panties and the wolf."

The clean panties project had begun as an appeal. When it came to the practical help social services offered women who were on drugs, it turned out to be very much focused on men. There were disposable razors and underpants in the clothing pack, but no women's panties or tampons. Women had to make do with sanitary towels like nappies, and men's underpants. Magdalena had offered to work with social services, buying panties and tampons as well as things like deodorant and moisturizer. They had also provided a contact list. The name of the contact person was given to a landlord who could be persuaded to let a room to the woman who was using. If there were problems, the landlord could ring the contact person.

"What are you going to do about the wolf?"

"We're hoping for some kind of monitoring in association with the Nature Conservancy Council. When the snow comes and they can start tracking on scooters, she's going to be at serious risk if we can't get something sorted out. But we've got some money in the foundation, so we'll see."

"You realize you're stuck with it now, don't you?" said Mimmi.

"What do you mean?"

"You're the one who'll have to be the driving force in Magdalena."

Lisa blew away a few prickly hairs that had settled under her eye.

"Never," she said.

Mimmi laughed.

"What makes you think you've got a choice? I think it's quite funny, I mean you've never actually been one for joining clubs and things, I bet you never thought this would happen. My God, when I heard you'd been elected chairwoman . . . Micke had to give me first aid."

"I can imagine," said Lisa dryly.

No, she thought. I never imagined this would happen. There were a lot of things I'd never have imagined I'd do.

Mimmi's fingers moved through her hair. The sound of the scissors' blades against each other.

That evening in early summer . . . thought Lisa.

She remembered sitting in the kitchen, sewing new covers for the dogs' beds. The sound of the scissors' blades against each other. Snip, snip, clip, clip. The television was on in the living room. Two of the dogs were lying on the sofa in there, you could almost imagine they were drowsily watching the news. Lisa was listening with half an ear as she cut the material. Then the sewing machine rattling across the fabric in straight lines, the pedal right down to the floor.

Karelin was lying in the basket in the hallway, snoring. Nothing looks more ridiculous than a sleeping, snoring dog. He was lying on his back, back legs in the air and splayed out to the sides. One ear had flopped over his eye like a pirate's eye patch. Majken was lying on the bed in the bedroom, her paw over her nose. From time to time she made little noises in her throat and her legs twitched. The new Springer spaniel lay happily beside her.

All at once Karelin wakes up with a start. He leaps up and begins to bark like mad. The dogs in the living room jump off the sofa and join in. Majken and the spaniel puppy come racing in and almost knock Lisa over; she has got up too.

As if she might not have understood, Karelin comes into the kitchen and tells Lisa at the top of his voice that there's somebody outside, they've got a visitor, somebody's coming.

It's Mildred Nilsson, the priest. She's standing out there on the veranda. The evening sun behind her turns the edges of her hair into a golden crown.

The dogs are all over her. They're ecstatic about the visit. Barking, racketing about, whining, Bruno even sings a note or two. Their tails thud against the door frame and the balustrade.

Mildred bends down to say hello to them. That's good. She and Lisa can't look at each other for too long. As soon as Lisa saw her out there, it felt as if they'd both waded out into a fast-flowing river. Now they've got a bit of time to get used to it. They glance at each other, then look away. The dogs lick Mildred's face. Her mascara ends up just below her eyebrows, her clothes are covered in hairs.

The current is strong. It's a question of standing firm. Lisa holds on to the door handle. She sends the dogs to their baskets. Normally she yells and shouts, that's how she normally speaks to them and it doesn't bother them at all. This time the command is almost a whisper.

"Go to your baskets," she says, waving feebly in the direction of the house.

The dogs look at her in bewilderment, isn't she going to yell at them? But they lope off anyway.

Mildred doesn't waste any time. Lisa can see she's angry. Lisa is a head taller than her, Mildred has to stretch her neck slightly.

"Where have you been?" says Mildred furiously.

Lisa raises her eyebrows.

"Here," she replies.

Her eyes fasten on the marks of summer on Mildred. She's got freckles. And the light down on her face, on her upper lip and around her jawbone, has turned blonde.

"You know what I mean," says Mildred. "Why aren't you coming to the Bible study group?"

"I . . ." begins Lisa, scrabbling around in her head for a sensible excuse.

Then she gets angry. Why should she need to explain? Isn't she an adult? Fifty-two years old, surely at that age it's okay to do what you want?

"I've had other things to do," she says. Her tone is more abrupt than she would like.

"What other things?"

"You know perfectly well!"

They stand there like two reindeer, vying to be leader of the herd. Their rib cages heaving up and down.

"You know perfectly well why I haven't been coming," says Lisa in the end.

They've waded out up to their armpits now. The priest loses her footing in the current. Takes a step toward Lisa, amazed and angry all at the same time. And something else in her eyes too. Her mouth opens. Takes a deep breath just as you do before you disappear under the water.

The current carries Lisa along with it. She loses her grip on the door handle. Moves toward Mildred. Her hand ends up round the back of Mildred's neck. Her hair feels like a child's beneath Lisa's fingers. She draws Mildred toward her.

Mildred in her arms. Her skin is so soft. They stagger into the hallway entwined around each other, the door is left open, banging against the balustrade. Two of the dogs sneak out.

The only sensible thought in Lisa's head: They'll stay in the yard.

They stumble over shoes and dog baskets in the hallway. Lisa is walking backwards. Her arms still around Mildred, one around her waist, one around the back of her neck. Mildred very close, pushing her into the house, her hands beneath Lisa's sweater, fingers on Lisa's nipples.

They stumble through the kitchen, land on the bed in the bedroom. Majken is lying there smelling of damp dog, she couldn't resist a dip in the river earlier in the evening.

Mildred on her back. Off with their clothes. Lisa's lips on Mildred's face. Two fingers deep inside her.

Majken raises her head and looks at them. Settles down with a sigh, nose between her paws. She's seen members of the congregation coupling before. There's nothing strange about it.

*　　*　　*

Afterward they make coffee and thaw out some buns. Eat as if they were starving, one after the other. Mildred gives the dogs tidbits and laughs, until Lisa tells her off, they'll be sick, but she's laughing all the time she's trying to be stern.

They sit there in the kitchen in the middle of the light summer night. Each with a sheet around them, sitting on opposite sides of the table. The dogs have picked up on the party atmosphere and are playing about.

Now and again their hands creep across the table to meet.

Mildred's index finger asks the back of Lisa's hand: "Are you still here?" The back of Lisa's hand answers: "Yes!" Lisa's index finger and middle finger ask the inside of Mildred's wrist: "Guilt? Regret?" Mildred's wrist replies: "No!"

And Lisa laughs.

"I'd better come back to the Bible study group, then," she says.

Mildred bursts out laughing. A piece of half-chewed cinnamon bun falls out of her mouth and onto the table.

"I don't know, the things you have to be prepared to do to get people to the Bible study group."

*   *   *

Mimmi stood in front of Lisa and examined her work. The scissors in her hand like a drawn sword.

"There," she said. "Now I don't have to be ashamed of you."

She ruffled Lisa's hair with a quick gesture. Then she pulled the kitchen towel out of the waistband of her apron and vigorously brushed the hairs off Lisa's neck and shoulders.

Lisa ran her hand over the stubble.

"Don't you want to look in the mirror?" asked Mimmi.

"No, I'm sure it's fine."

The autumn meeting of Magdalena, the women's group. Micke Kiviniemi had set up a little drinks table outdoors, just outside the door by the steps that led into the bar. It was dark now, almost black outside. And unusually warm for the time of year. He'd created a little pathway from the road across the graveled yard up to the steps, edged it with tea lights in glass jars. Several handmade candlesticks stood on the steps and on the drinks table.

He got his reward. Heard their ohs and ahs from as far away as the road. Here they came. Tripping along, walking, tiptoeing across the gravel. Thirty or so women. The youngest just under thirty, the oldest just turned seventy-five.

"This is lovely," they said to him. "It feels just like being abroad."

He smiled back. But didn't reply. Sought sanctuary behind the drinks table. Felt like somebody in a hide, watching the wildlife. They wouldn't take any notice of him. They'd just behave naturally, as if he weren't there. He felt excited, as if he were a boy lying on the fallen leaves among the trees, spying on them.

The yard outside the bar, like a big room in the darkness, full of sounds. Their feet on the gravel, giggling, chattering, cackling, nattering. The sounds traveled. Soared recklessly upward toward the

black star-spangled sky. Rushed shamelessly across the river, reaching the houses on the other side. Were absorbed by the forest, the
black fir trees, the thirsty moss. Ran along the road and reminded
the village: we exist.

They smelled good and had dressed up for the occasion. Although
it was obvious they weren't well off. Their dresses were out of fash-
ion. Long cotton cardigans buttoned over flowery bell-shaped skirts.
Home permed hair. Shoes from the OBS store.

They got through the business of the meeting in about half an
hour. The duty rosters were quickly filled with the names of volun-
teers, more hands in the air than were needed.

Then they had dinner. Most of them weren't used to drinking,
and quickly got tipsy, to their slightly dismayed delight. Mimmi gig-
gled at them as she moved between the tables. Micke stayed in the
kitchen.

"Heavens," exclaimed one of the women as Mimmi carried in the
dessert, "I haven't had this much fun since . . ."

She broke off and waved her skinny arm around, searching for the
answer.

It stuck out from the sleeve of her dress like a matchstick.

". . . since Mildred's funeral," somebody shouted.

There was silence for less than a second. Then they all burst out
into hysterical laughter, telling each other it was true, Mildred's funeral had been . . . well, to die for, and they shouted and laughed as
much as the feeble joke was worth.

The funeral. They'd stood there in their black clothes as the coffin was lowered. The bright early summer sun had stabbed at their
eyes. The bumblebees banging about among the funeral flowers.
The birch leaves young and shiny, as if they'd been waxed. The tops
of the trees like green churches, chock full of male birds keen to
mate, and the females answering them. Nature's way of saying: I
don't care, I never stop, earth to earth.

The whole of that incredibly beautiful early summer's day as the
background to that terrible hole in the ground, the polished coffin.

The images in their heads of how she looked. Her skull like a broken plant pot inside the skin.

Majvor Kangas, one of the women in the group, had invited them
back to her house afterward.

"Come with me!" she'd said. "My old man's gone to the cottage, I
don't want to be on my own."

So they'd gone along. Sat there subdued in the lounge on the
black, squashy leather sofa. Hadn't had much to say, not even about
the weather.

But Majvor was feeling rebellious.

"Right, you lot!" she'd said. "Give me a hand!"

She'd fetched a tall stool with two steps from the kitchen, clambered up and opened the little cupboard above the hall stand. She'd
passed down a dozen or so bottles: whisky, Cognac, liqueurs,
Calvados. Some of the others took them off her.

"These are good," one of them had said, reading the labels.
"Twelve-year-old single malt."

"Our daughter-in-law always brings them for us when she goes
abroad," explained Majvor. "But Tord never opens them, it's just his
home brewed hooch and grog if he offers somebody a drink. And
I'm not much of a one for this sort of stuff, but . . ."

She'd allowed a meaningful pause to finish the sentence. Was
helped down from the stool like a queen from her throne. A woman
on each side of her, holding her hands.

"What's Tord going to say?"

"What can he say?" Majvor had said. "He didn't even open any of
them when it was his sixtieth birthday last year."

"Let him drink his own fox poison!"

And so they'd got a bit tipsy. Sung hymns. Expressed their devo-
tion to each other. Given speeches.

"Here's to Mildred," Majvor had shouted. "She was the most in-
domitable woman I've ever met!"

"She was mad!"

"Now we'll have to be mad on our own!"

They'd laughed. Cried a bit. But mostly laughed.

That was the funeral.

Lisa Stöckel looked at them. They were eating mascarpone ice cream and praising Mimmi as she swept past.

They'll be all right, she thought. They'll manage.

It made her happy. Or maybe not happy, but relieved.

And at the same time: loneliness had her on its hook, a barb through her heart, reeling her in.

*   *   *

After Magdalena's autumn meeting Lisa strolled home through the darkness. It was just after midnight. She passed the churchyard and wandered up onto the ridge that ran upstream alongside the river. She went past Lars-Gunnar's house, could just make it out in the moonlight. The windows were dark.

She thought about Lars-Gunnar.

The village chief, she thought. The strong man of the village. The man who got the firm with the contract to clear the snow and plow the road down to Poikkijärvi first, before he plowed down to Jukkasjärvi. The one who helped Micke when there was a problem with the bar license.

Not that Lars-Gunnar himself drank in the bar much. These days he hardly ever drank. It had been different in the past. In the old days the men used to drink all the time. Friday, Saturday and at least one day in the middle of the week as well. And at that time they really drank. Then it was a beer or two most days. That's the way it was. But there comes a time when you had to ease up, otherwise the only way was downhill.

No, Lars-Gunnar didn't bother much with spirits. The last time Lisa had seen him really drunk was six years ago. The year before Mildred moved to the village.

He actually came to her house that time. She could still see him sitting there in her kitchen. The chair disappears beneath his bulk.

His elbow is resting on his knee, his forehead on his palm. Breathing heavily. It's just after eleven o'clock at night.

It's not just that he's been drinking. The bottle is on the table in front of him. He had it in his hand when he arrived. Like a flag: I've been drinking, and I'm going to bloody well carry on drinking for a good while yet.

She'd already gone to bed when he knocked on the door. Not that she heard him knock, the dogs told her he was there as soon as he set foot on her veranda.

Of course it shows a kind of trust, coming to her when he's like this. Weakened by alcohol and his feelings. She just doesn't know what to do with it. She isn't used to it. People confiding in her. She's not the kind of person who invites that kind of behavior.

But she and Lars-Gunnar are related, after all. And she can keep her mouth shut, he knows that.

She stands there in her dressing gown, listening to his song. The song about his unhappy life. His unhappy and disappointing love. And Nalle.

"Sorry," Lars-Gunnar mumbles into his fist. "I shouldn't have come here."

"It's okay," she says hesitantly. "You keep talking while I . . ."

She can't think what to do, but she's got to do something to stop herself running straight out of the house.

". . . while I get the food ready for tomorrow."

And so he keeps talking while she chops meat and vegetables for soup. In the middle of the night. Celeriac and carrots and leeks and swede and potatoes and everything but the kitchen sink. But Lars-Gunnar doesn't seem to think there's anything strange about it. He's too taken up with his own affairs.

"I had to get away from the house," he confesses. "Before I left . . . I'm not sober, I admit that. Before I left I was sitting by the side of Nalle's bed holding a shotgun to his head."

Lisa doesn't say anything. Slices a carrot as if she hadn't heard.

"I thought about how things are going to be," he sighs. "Who's going to look after him when I'm gone? He's got nobody."

*   *   *

And that's true, thought Lisa.

She'd arrived at her gingerbread house up on the ridge. The moon cast a silvery sheen over the extravagant carving on the veranda and window frames.

She went up the steps. The dogs were barking and charging about like mad things inside, recognizing her footsteps. When she opened the door they hurtled out for their evening pee on the grass.

She went into the living room. All that was left in there was the empty, gaping bookcase and the sofa.

Nalle's got nobody, she thought.

YELLOW LEGS

Spring is coming. The odd patch of snow beneath the blue gray pines and the tall firs. A warm breeze from the south. The sun filtering through the branches. Small animals rustling about all over the place in last year's grass. Hundreds of scents floating about in the air, like in a stew. Pine resin and the smell of new birch leaves. Warm earth. Open water. Sweet hare. Bitter fox.

The alpha female has dug a new lair this year. It's an old fox's den on a south-facing slope, two hundred meters above a mountain lake. The ground is sandy and easy to dig out, but the alpha female has worked hard, widening the entrance so that she can get in, clearing out all the old rubbish left by the foxes, and digging out a chamber to live in three meters beneath the slope. Yellow Legs and one of the other females have been allowed to help sometimes, but she's done most of the work herself. Now she spends her days close to the lair. Lies in front of the entrance in the spring sunshine, dozing. The other wolves bring food. When the alpha male approaches her with something to eat, she gets up and comes to meet him. Licks and whimpers affectionately before gulping down his gifts.

* * *

One morning the alpha female goes into the lair and doesn't come out again that day. Late in the evening she squeezes out the cubs. Licks them clean. Eats up the membranes, umbilical cords and the placenta. Nudges them into the right place beneath her stomach. No stillborn cub to carry out. The fox and the crow will have to manage without that meal.

The rest of the pack live their lives outside the lair. Catching mostly small prey, staying close by. Sometimes they can hear a faint squeaking when one of the cubs has wriggled in the wrong direction. Or been pushed out by one of its siblings. Only the alpha male has permission to crawl in and regurgitate food for the alpha female.

After three weeks and a day, she carries them out of the lair for the first time. Five of them. The other wolves are beside themselves with joy. Greet them carefully. Sniffing and nudging. Licking the little ones' rotund tummies, and under their tails. After just a short while the alpha female carries them back into the lair. The cubs are completely worn out by all the new impressions. The two one-year-olds hurtle joyfully through the forest, chasing one another.

It's the beginning of a wonderful time for the pack. They all want to help with the little ones. They play tirelessly. And the rest are infected by their playfulness. Even the alpha female joins in a tug-of-war over an old branch. The cubs are growing, they're always hungry. Their muzzles grow longer and their ears more pointed. It happens quickly. The one-year-olds take turns to lie on guard outside the lair when the others go off hunting. When the adults return, the youngsters come forward, tails wagging. Begging and whimpering and licking the corners of the older wolves' mouths. In reply the adult wolves bring up red mounds of the meat they've swallowed. If there's anything left over, the babysitters can have it.

Yellow Legs doesn't go off on her own. During this period she stays with the pack and the new cubs. She lies on her back playing the helpless prey beneath two of them. They hurl themselves at her, one sinks his needle-sharp teeth into her lips and the other attacks her tail like a mad thing. She pushes the one who was dangling from her lip aside and places her enormous paw on top of it. It's all the cub can do to free itself. Wriggling and struggling. Finally it escapes. Gallops around her on its fluffy paws, comes back and throws itself at her head, growling recklessly. Bites her ear aggressively. Then all of a sudden they fall into a deep, peaceful sleep. One lying between her front legs, the other with its head on its sibling's stomach. Yellow Legs takes the opportunity to have a little doze as well. She snaps half-heartedly at a wasp that comes too close, misses, the sleepy hum of insects above the flowers. The morning sun rises above the tops of the pine trees. The birds swoop through the air, hunting for food to regurgitate into the gaping mouths of their babies.

Playing with cubs makes you tired. Happiness flows through her like spring water.

Friday September 8

Inspector Sven-Erik Stålnacke woke up at half past four in the morning.

Bloody cat, was his first thought.

It was usually his cat Manne who woke him up around this time. The cat would leap up from the floor, landing with a surprisingly heavy thud on Sven-Erik's stomach. If Sven-Erik just grunted and turned on his side, Manne would stalk up and down the side of Sven-Erik's body like a mountain climber on top of a high ridge. Sometimes the cat would let out a terrible wail, which meant that he either wanted food, or to be let out. Usually both. Straightaway.

Sometimes Sven-Erik tried refusing to get up, muttered "it's the middle of the night you stupid bloody cat," and wrapped himself in the bedclothes. Then the promenade up and down his body was carried out with the claws extended further and further each time. In the end Manne would scratch Sven-Erik's head.

Pushing the cat onto the floor or shutting him out of the bedroom didn't really help. Then Manne started on the soft furnishings and curtains with all his might.

"That cat's too bloody crafty," Sven-Erik always said. "He knows I'll put him outside when he does that. And that's exactly what he wanted all along."

He was a man who commanded respect. Strong upper arms, broad hands. Something in his face and bearing bore witness to years of dealing with most things, human misery, fired-up troublemakers. And he found pleasure in being ruled by a cat.

But this morning it wasn't Manne who'd woken him. He woke up anyway. Out of habit. Maybe because he was missing that stripy young man who constantly terrorized him with his demands and whims.

He sat up heavily on the edge of the bed. He wouldn't be able to get back to sleep. This was the fourth night the bloody cat had been missing. He'd gone missing before for one night, occasionally two. That was nothing to worry about. But four.

He went downstairs and opened the outside door. The night was like gray wool, on the way toward the day. He gave a long whistle, went into the kitchen, fetched a tin of cat food and stood on the steps banging the tin with a spoon. No cat. In the end he had to give up, he was getting cold in just his underpants.

That's the way it is, he thought. That's the price of freedom. The risk of getting run over or taken by the fox. Sooner or later.

He spooned coffee into the percolator.

Still, it's better that way, he thought. Better than Manne getting weak and ill, and having to be taken to the vet. That would have been bloody awful.

The percolator got going with a gurgle, and Sven-Erik went up to the bedroom to get dressed.

Maybe Manne had made himself at home somewhere else. That had happened before. He'd come home after two or three days and hadn't been the least bit hungry. Obviously well fed and well rested. It was probably some old dear who'd felt sorry for him and taken him in. Some pensioner who had nothing else to do but cook him salmon and give him the cream off the top of the milk.

Sven-Erik was suddenly filled with an unreasoning anger against this unknown individual who took in and adopted a cat that didn't belong to the person in question. Didn't this person realize that there was somebody worrying and wondering where the cat had gone? You could tell Manne wasn't homeless, with his shiny coat and affectionate ways. He'd get him a collar. Should have done it a long time ago. It was just that he was afraid he'd get caught up somewhere. That's what had stopped him, the thought of Manne caught in some undergrowth starving to death, or hanging in a tree.

He ate a good breakfast. The first few years after Hjördis had left him, breakfast had usually consisted of a cup of coffee, drunk standing up. But he'd mended his ways since then. He shoveled down spoonfuls of low fat yogurt and muesli without really tasting it. The percolator had fallen silent, and the aroma of freshly brewed coffee filled the kitchen.

He'd taken over Manne from his daughter when she moved to Luleå. He should never have done it. He realized that now. It was nothing but bloody trouble, that's all it was, bloody trouble.

*   *   *

Anna-Maria Mella was sitting at the kitchen table with her morning coffee. It was seven o'clock. Jenny, Petter and Marcus were still asleep. Gustav was awake. He was bouncing around in the bedroom upstairs, clambering all over Robert.

In front of her on the table lay a copy of the horrific drawing of the hanged Mildred. Rebecka Martinsson had made copies of a number of papers as well, but Anna-Maria didn't understand a bloody word. She hated numbers and maths and that sort of thing.

"Morning!"

Her son Marcus ambled into the kitchen. Dressed! He opened the door of the refrigerator. Marcus was sixteen.

"So," said Anna-Maria, looking at the clock. "Is there a fire upstairs, or something?"

He grinned. Picked up milk and cereal and sat down opposite Anna-Maria.

"I've got an exam," he said, spooning down milk and cornflakes. "You can't just jump out of bed and dash in at the last minute. You have to prime your body."

"Who are you?" said Anna-Maria. "And what have you done with my son?"

It's Hanna, she thought. God bless her.

Hanna was Marcus' girlfriend. Her keen attitude toward schoolwork was catching.

"Cool," said Marcus, sliding the drawing of Mildred toward him. "What's this?"

"Nothing," answered Anna-Maria, taking the drawing off him and turning it upside down.

"No, seriously. Let me have a look!"

He took the picture back.

"What does this mean?" he said, pointing at the grave mound visible behind the dangling body.

"Well, maybe that she's going to die and be buried."

"Yes, but what does it mean? Can't you see it?"

Anna-Maria looked at the picture.

"No."

"It's a symbol," said Marcus.

"It's a grave mound with a cross on top."

"Look! The outlines are twice as thick as in the rest of the picture. And the cross carries on down into the ground and ends in a hook."

Anna-Maria looked. He was right.

She got up and shuffled the papers together. Resisted the urge to give her son a kiss, ruffled his hair instead.

"Good luck in the exam," she said.

In the car she rang Sven-Erik.

"Yes," he said when he'd fetched his copy of the picture. "It's a cross that goes through a semicircle and ends in a hook."

"We need to find out what it means. Who'll know the answer to something like that?"

"What did they say at the lab?"

"They'll probably get the picture today. If there are clear prints they'll get them off this afternoon, otherwise it takes longer."

"There must be some professor of religion who knows about the symbol," said Sven-Erik thoughtfully.

"You're a clever boy!" said Anna-Maria. "Fred Olsson can sort somebody out, then we can fax it to them. Go and get dressed and I'll pick you up."

"Oh yes?"

"You can come to Poikkijärvi with me. I want to talk to Rebecka Martinsson, if she's still there."

*   *   *

Anna-Maria pointed her light red Ford Escort in the direction of Poikkijärvi. Sven-Erik sat beside her, pushing his foot down to the floor in a reflex action. Why did she always have to drive like a boy racer?

"Rebecka Martinsson gave me copies too," she said. "I don't understand any of it. I mean, it's something financial, but . . ."

"Shouldn't we ask the economic crimes team to have a look at it?"

"They're always so busy. You ask a question, and you get the answer a month later. It's just as well to ask her. I mean, she's already seen it. And she knows why she gave it to us."

"Is this really a good idea?"

"Have you got a better idea?"

"But will she really want to get dragged into all this?"

Anna-Maria shook her plait impatiently.

"She was the one who gave me the copies and the letters! And she's not going to get dragged into anything. How long can it take? Ten minutes of her holiday."

Anna-Maria braked sharply and turned left on to Jukkasjärvivägen, accelerated up to ninety, braked again and turned right down toward Poikkijärvi. Sven-Erik clung to the door handle, thinking that maybe he should have taken a travel sickness pill; from there his thoughts turned spontaneously to the cat, who hated travelling by car.

"Manne's disappeared," he said, gazing out at the pine trees, sparkling in the sunshine as they swept by.

"Oh no," said Anna-Maria. "How long's he been gone?"

"Four days. He's never been away this long."

"He'll come back," she said. "It's still warm out, it's natural for him to want to be outside."

"No," said Sven-Erik firmly. "He's been run over. I'll never see that cat again."

He longed for her to contradict him. To protest and reassure. He would stick to his conviction that the cat was gone for good. So he could express a little of his anxiety and sorrow. So she could give him a little hope and consolation. But she changed the subject.

"We won't drive all the way up," she said. "I don't think she wants to attract attention."

"What's she actually doing here?" asked Sven-Erik.

"No idea."

Anna-Maria was on the point of saying she didn't think Rebecka was all that well, but she didn't. Sven-Erik was bound to insist they cancel the visit. He was always softer than she was when it came to that sort of thing. Maybe it was because she had children living at home. Most of her protective instincts and consideration for others were used up at home.

Rebecka Martinsson opened the door of her chalet. When she saw Anna-Maria and Sven-Erik, two deep grooves appeared between her eyebrows.

Anna-Maria was standing in front, something eager in her eyes, a setter who'd picked up a scent. Sven-Erik behind, Rebecka hadn't seen him since she'd been in the hospital almost two years ago. The thick hair growing around his ears had turned from dark gray to silver. The moustache still like a dead rodent beneath his nose. He looked more embarrassed, seemed to realize they weren't welcome.

Even if you did save my life, thought Rebecka.

Fleeting thoughts flowed through her mind. Like silk scarves through a magician's hand. Sven-Erik by the side of her hospital bed: "We went into his apartment and realized we had to find you. The girls are okay."

I remember best what happened before and after, thought Rebecka. Before and after. I ought to ask Sven-Erik really. What it looked like when they arrived at the cottage. He can tell me about the blood and the bodies.

You want him to tell you you did the right thing, said a voice inside her. That it was self-defense. That you had no choice. Just ask, he's bound to say what you want to hear.

They sat down in the little cottage. Sven-Erik and Anna-Maria on Rebecka's bed. Rebecka on the only chair. On the little radiator hung a T-shirt, a pair of tights and a pair of panties over the "ei saa peittää" sticker.

Rebecka glanced anxiously at the wet clothes. But what could she do? Bundle up the wet panties and chuck them under the bed? Or out through the window, maybe?

"Well?" she said tersely, couldn't manage politeness.

"It's about the photocopies you gave me," Anna-Maria explained. "There are some things I don't understand."

Rebecka clasped her knees.

But why? she thought. Why do we have to remember? Wallow in it all, go over things over and over again? What do we gain from that? Who can guarantee that it will help? That we won't just drown in the darkness?

"The thing is . . ." she said.

She spoke very quietly. Sven-Erik looked at her slender fingers around her knees.

". . . I'm going to have to ask you to leave," she went on. "I gave you the photocopies and the letters. I got them by committing a crime. If that comes out, it'll cost me my job. Besides which, people round here don't know who I am. I mean, they know my name. But they don't know I was involved in what happened out in Jiekajärvi."

"Please," begged Anna-Maria, staying where she was as if her bottom was welded to the bed, although Sven-Erik had made a move to get up. "A woman's been murdered. If anybody asks what we were doing here, tell them we were looking for a missing dog."

Rebecka looked at her.

"Good plan," she said slowly. "Two plainclothes detectives looking for a missing dog. Time for the police authorities to look at how their resources are used."

"It might be my dog," said Anna-Maria, slightly abashed.

Nobody spoke for a little while. Sven-Erik felt as if he were about to die of embarrassment, perched on the edge of the bed.

"Let's have a look, then," said Rebecka in the end, reaching out for the folder.

"It's this," said Anna-Maria, taking a sheet of paper out of the folder and pointing.

"It's an extract from somebody's accounts," said Rebecka. "This entry's been marked with a highlighter pen."

Rebecka pointed at a figure in a column headed 1930.

"Nineteen thirty is a current account, a check account. It's been credited with one hundred and seventy-nine thousand kronor from account seventy-six ten. It's down as additional staff costs. But here in the margin somebody's written in pencil 'Training?' "

Rebecka pushed a strand of hair behind her ear.

"What about this, then?" asked Anna-Maria. " 'Ver,' what does that mean?"

"Verified, authenticated. Could be an invoice or something else to show what the costs consisted of. It seems to me as if she was wondering about this particular cost, that's why I took it."

"What company is it, then?" Anna-Maria wondered.

Rebecka shrugged her shoulders. Then she pointed at the top right-hand corner of the page.

"The number of the organization begins with eighty-one. That means it must be a foundation."

Sven-Erik shook his head.

"Jukkasjärvi church nature conservancy foundation," said Anna-Maria after a second or two. "A foundation she set up."

"She was wondering about that particular expenditure for training," said Rebecka.

Silence fell once again. Sven-Erik swatted at a fly that kept wanting to land on him.

"She seems to have got on quite a lot of people's nerves," said Rebecka.

Anna-Maria smiled mirthlessly.

"I was talking to one of them yesterday," she said. "He hated Mildred Nilsson because his ex-wife stayed at her house with the children after she'd left him."

She told Rebecka about the decapitated kittens.

"And we can't do a thing," she concluded. "Those farm cats don't have any financial value, so it isn't criminal damage. Presumably they didn't have time to suffer, so it isn't cruelty to animals. You just feel so powerless. As if you might be more useful selling fruit and vegetables in the supermarket. I don't know, do you feel like that as well?"

Rebecka smiled wryly.

"It's very rare I have anything to do with criminal cases," she said evasively. "And when I do, it's financial crime. But yes, this business of being on the side of the suspect . . . Sometimes I do feel a sort of revulsion toward myself. When you're representing somebody who really has no conscience whatsoever. You keep repeating 'everybody is entitled to a defense' like a kind of mantra against the . . ."

She didn't actually say self-contempt, but allowed a shrug of her shoulders to finish the sentence.

Anna-Maria had noticed that Rebecka Martinsson often shrugged her shoulders. Shaking off unwelcome thoughts, perhaps, a way of interrupting a difficult train of thought. Or maybe she was like Marcus. His constant shrugs were a way of marking the distance between him and the rest of the world.

"You've never thought about changing sides, then?" asked Sven-Erik. "They're always looking for public prosecutors, people don't stay up here."

Rebecka's smile was rather strained.

"Of course," said Sven-Erik, obviously feeling like a complete idiot, "you must earn three times as much as a prosecutor."

"It's not that," said Rebecka. "I'm not actually working at the moment, so the future is . . ."

She shrugged her shoulders again.

"But you told me you were up here with your job," said Anna-Maria.

"Yes, I'm working a bit now and again. And when one of the partners was coming up here, I wanted to come along."

She's off sick, Anna-Maria realized.

Sven-Erik gave her a lightning glance, he'd understood as well.

Rebecka stood up, indicating that the conversation was at an end.
They said good-bye.

When Sven-Erik and Anna-Maria had gone just a few paces, they
heard Rebecka Martinsson's voice behind them.

"Threatening behavior," she said.

They turned around. Rebecka was standing on the cottage's little
veranda, her hand resting on one of the posts that supported the
roof, leaning against it slightly.

She looks so young, thought Anna-Maria. Two years ago she was
one of those real career girls. She'd seemed so super-slim and super-
expensive, her long dark hair beautifully cut, not just chopped off
like Anna-Maria's. Now Rebecka's hair was longer. And just
chopped off. She was wearing jeans and a T-shirt. No makeup. Her
hip bones stuck out where they met the waistband of her jeans, and
her tired but stubbornly upright posture as she leaned against the
post made Anna-Maria think about the kind of grown-up children
she sometimes met through her job. Coping with impossible circumstances, taking care of their alcoholic or mentally ill parents,
looking after their brothers and sisters, keeping the facade up as far
as possible, lying to the police and social services.

"The man with the kittens," Rebecka went on. "It's threatening
behavior. It appears that his action was intended to frighten his ex-
wife. According to the law, a threat doesn't actually have to be
spelled out. And she was frightened, I presume. It might be harassment of a female. Depending on what else he's done, there could be
grounds for an injunction to stop him going anywhere near her."

*   *   *

As Sven-Erik and Anna-Maria were walking along the road on
the way back to the car, they met a lion yellow Merc. In it sat

Lars-Gunnar and Nalle Vinsa. Lars-Gunnar gave them a long look. Sven-Erik raised his hand in a wave, after all it wasn't that many years since Lars-Gunnar had retired.

"Of course," said Sven-Erik, gazing after the car as it disappeared in the direction of Micke's bar. "He lives down here in the village, I wonder how things are going with that lad of his."

*   *   *

Bertil Stensson was holding a lunchtime service in Kiruna church. Once every two weeks the townspeople could receive the Eucharist during their lunch break. About twenty people were gathered in the small chapel.

Stefan Wikström was sitting in the seat nearest the aisle on the fifth row, wishing he hadn't turned up.

A memory popped into his head. His father, also a parish priest, at home on the kitchen sofa. Stefan beside him, maybe ten years old. The boy babbling on, he's holding something, something he wants to show his father, he can't remember what it was now. His father with the newspaper held up in front of his face like the veil in the temple. And suddenly the boy begins to cry. Then his mother's pleading voice behind him: you could at least listen to him for a while, he's been waiting for you all day. Out of the corner of his eye Stefan can see she's wearing her apron. It must be dinnertime. His father lowers the paper, annoyed at the interruption to his reading, the only restful time of the day before dinner, feeling injured at the accusation in her voice.

Stefan's father had been dead for many years. His poor mother too. But that was exactly how the priest was making him feel now. Like that annoying child in need of attention.

Stefan had tried to avoid going to the lunchtime service. A voice inside him had said quite clearly: "Don't go!" But still he went. He'd persuaded himself it was for Bertil Stensson's sake, not because he was in need of the Eucharist.

He'd thought things would get easier when Mildred was gone,

but on the contrary, everything was more difficult. Much more difficult.

It's like the prodigal son, he thought.

He'd been the dutiful, conscientious son, the one who stayed at home. He'd done so much for Bertil over the years: taken boring funerals, boring services in hospitals and old people's homes, relieved the parish priest of paperwork—Bertil was useless when it came to administration—unlocked the church for the youngsters on a Friday night.

Bertil Stensson was vain. He'd taken over all the work involving the ice hotel in Jukkasjärvi. Any weddings or christenings in the ice hotel were his. He also bagged any event that had even the slightest chance of ending up in the local press, like the crisis group set up after the road accident when seven young people on a ski trip lost their lives, or specially arranged services for the Sami district court. In between all this, he was very fond of his free time. And it was Stefan who made all this possible, who covered up for him and took over.

Mildred Nilsson had been like the prodigal son. Or more accurately: like the prodigal son must have been while he was still living at home. Before restlessness took him away to foreign lands. Troublesome and difficult, he must have got on his father's nerves, just like Mildred.

Everybody believed Stefan had been the one who really couldn't stand Mildred. But they were wrong, it was just that Bertil had been more adept at hiding his dislike.

Things had been different then, when she was alive. Everything the woman touched was surrounded by trouble and arguments. And Bertil had been pleased to have Stefan, grateful for the son who stayed at home. Stefan could see in his mind's eye how Bertil would come into his room at the parish hall. He had a particular way with him, a code that meant: you are my chosen one. He would appear in the doorway, owl-like with his thick, silvery hair and his stocky body, his reading glasses either perched crookedly on top of his head or on the end of his nose. Stefan would look up from his papers. Bertil would glance almost imperceptibly over his shoulder, sidle in and close the door behind him. Then he would sink down into Stefan's armchair with a sigh of relief. And a smile.

Something clicked inside Stefan every time. More often than not Bertil didn't want anything in particular, he might want to talk about a few minor matters, but he gave the impression that he wanted a bit of peace for a little while. Everybody ran to Bertil, Bertil sneaked off to Stefan.

But after Mildred's death, things had changed. She was no longer there, like a rough seam chafing in the priest's shoe. Now it was Stefan's dutiful conscientiousness that seemed to chafe. Nowadays Bertil often said: "I'm sure we don't need to be quite so formal," and "I'm sure God will allow us to be practical," words he'd adopted from Mildred.

And when Bertil talked about Mildred it was in such glowing terms that Stefan felt physically sick from all the lies.

And Bertil had stopped visiting Stefan in his office. Stefan sat there, incapable of getting anything done, agonizing, waiting.

Sometimes the priest walked past the open door. But now the code had changed, the signals were different: rapid footsteps, a glance through the wide-open door, a nod, a quick smile. In-a-hurry-how's-things, that meant. And before Stefan had even managed to return the smile, the priest had disappeared.

Before he'd always known where the priest was, nowadays he had no idea. The office staff asked about Bertil and looked strangely at Stefan when he forced a smile and shook his head.

It was impossible to conquer Mildred now she was dead. In that foreign land she had become her father's favorite child.

The service was almost over. They sang a concluding hymn and departed in the peace of God.

Stefan should have left now. Gone straight out and just gone home. But he couldn't help it, his feet made a beeline for Bertil.

Bertil was chatting to a member of the congregation, gave Stefan a sideways glance, didn't let him into the conversation, Stefan could wait.

Everything was wrong nowadays. If Bertil had just acknowledged him, Stefan could have thanked him briefly for the service and left. Now it seemed as if he had something in particular on his mind. He was forced to come up with something.

At long last the parishioner left. Stefan felt obliged to explain his presence.

"I felt I needed to take communion," he said to Bertil.

Bertil nodded. The churchwarden carried out the wine and the wafer, gave the priest a look. Stefan trailed after Bertil and the churchwarden to the sacristy, joined in the prayer over the bread and wine without being asked.

"Have you heard anything from that firm?" he asked when the prayer was over. "About the wolf foundation and so on?"

Bertil removed his chasuble, alb and stole.

"I don't know," he said. "Perhaps we won't dissolve it after all. I haven't decided yet."

The churchwarden was taking all the time in the world to pour the wine into the piscina and place the wafers in the ciborium. Stefan ground his teeth.

"I thought we were agreed that the church couldn't have a foundation like that," he said quietly.

Besides which it's the church council's decision, not just yours, he thought.

"Well, yes, but for the time being it exists anyway," said the priest, and Stefan could clearly hear the impatience beneath the mild voice. "Whether I think we should pay for protection for the wolf or spend the money on training is something we can take up later in the autumn."

"And the hunting lease?"

Bertil was smiling broadly now.

"Now now, that's not something for you and I to stand here arguing about. That's a decision for the church council when the time comes."

He patted Stefan on the shoulder and left.

"Say hello to Kristin!" he said, without turning round.

Stefan had a lump in his throat. He looked down at his hands, the long, stiff fingers. Real piano fingers, his mother used to say when she was alive. Toward the end, when she was sitting in her apartment in the care home and mixing him up with his father more often than not, all this talk about his fingers used to upset him. She would hold on to his hands and order the nurses to look at his hands: just look at these hands, completely unmarked by physical work. Piano fingers, desk hands.

Say hello to Kristin.

If he dared to start looking at things as they really were, marrying her had been the biggest mistake of his life.

Stefan could actually feel himself hardening inside. Hardening toward Bertil, toward his wife.

I've carried them long enough, he thought. It has to end.

His mother must have realized about Kristin. What he'd fallen for was her resemblance to his mother. The slightly doll-like appearance, the graceful manner, the good taste.

But his mother had definitely realized. "So personal," his mother had said about Kristin's home the first time she visited her son's girl-friend, "very pleasant." That was when he was studying in Uppsala. Pleasant and personal, two good words to use when you couldn't say beautiful or tasteful without lying. And he remembered his mother's amused smile when Kristin showed off her arrangement of dried everlasting flowers and roses.

No, Kristin was a child who had a mediocre talent for imitating and copying. She'd never become the kind of priest's wife his mother had been. And what a shock he'd had the first time he went to messy Mildred's house. All her colleagues and their families had been invited to Mildred's for a Christmas drink. It had been an interesting collection of people: the priests and their families, Mildred herself, her husband with his beard and apron, pretending to be under the thumb, and the three women who had temporarily sought refuge in the priest's house at Poikkijärvi. One of the women had two children who must have had every kind of behavioral difficulty in the book.

But Mildred's home had been like a Carl Larsson painting. The same light touch, warm and welcoming without being over the top, the same tasteful simplicity as in Stefan's childhood home. Stefan couldn't see how it fitted in with Mildred's personality. Is this her home? he'd thought. He'd been expecting bohemian chaos, with piles of newspaper cuttings on storage shelves and oriental cushions and rugs.

He remembered Kristin afterward: "Why don't we live in the priest's house in Poikkijärvi?" she'd wondered. "It's bigger, it would be better for us, we've got children after all."

No doubt his mother had seen that the fragile side of Kristin that attracted Stefan wasn't just fragile, but broken. Something cracked and sharp that Stefan would hurt himself on sooner or later.

He was suddenly seized by an upsurge of bitterness toward his mother.

Why didn't she say anything? he thought. She should have warned me.

And Mildred. Mildred who'd used poor Kristin.

He remembered that day at the beginning of May when she came in waving that letter.

He tried to push Mildred out of his mind. But she was just as insistent now as she had been then. Pushing. Just like then.

*   *   *

"Right," says Mildred, bursting into Stefan's office.

It's May 5. In less than two months she'll be dead. But now she's more than alive. Her cheeks and her nose are as red as freshly waxed apples. She kicks the door shut behind her.

"No, sit down!" she says to Bertil, who's trying to escape from the armchair. "I want to talk to both of you."

Talk to, what kind of introduction is that. That alone tells you everything about what she could be like.

"I've been thinking about this business with the wolf," she begins.

Bertil's leg crosses over the other leg. His arms fold themselves across his chest. Stefan leans back in his chair. Away from her. They feel criticized and told off before she's even managed to say what's on her mind.

"The church leases its land to Poikkijärvi hunting club for a thousand kronor a year," she goes on. "The lease runs for seven years, and is automatically renewed if it isn't cancelled. This has been the case since 1957. The parish priest at the time lived in the priest's house in Poikkijärvi. And he liked to hunt."

"But what has that got to do with . . ." Bertil begins.

"Let me finish! True, anybody can join the club, but it's the board and the elite hunting team who actually make use of the leased land. And since the number in the elite team is set in the statutes at twenty, no new members are allowed in. In practice it's only when somebody dies that the board elects a new member. And every single person on the board is a member of the team. So it's the same bunch of old men there as well. In the last thirteen years, not one new member has joined."

She breaks off and looks Stefan straight in the eye.

"Except for you, of course. When Elis Wiss left the team voluntarily, you were elected—that must have been six years ago?"

Stefan doesn't reply, it's the way she says "voluntarily." On the inside he's white with rage. Mildred goes on:

"According to the statutes, only the hunting team is allowed to hunt with shotguns, so therefore the team has commandeered all elk hunting. As far as other hunting is concerned, suitable members can buy a one day license, but the kill must be divided up between active members of the club, and surprise surprise, it's the board members who make the decision as to how that division takes place. But this is what I'm thinking. Both the mining company, LKAB, and Yngve Bergqvist are interested in the lease, LKAB for its employees and

Yngve for tourists. That would mean we could increase the fee significantly. And I'm talking about big money here; it would allow us to look at a sensible approach to forestry. I mean, seriously, what does Torbjörn Ylitalo actually do? Runs errands for the team! We're even providing that bunch of old farts with a free employee."

Torbjörn Ylitalo is the forestry officer in the church. He's one of the twenty members of the elite team, and the chairman of the hunting club. Stefan is conscious of the fact that much of Torbjörn's working day is spent planning hunts with Lars-Gunnar who is the team leader, maintaining the church's hunting lodges and watchtowers and clearing tracks.

"So," Mildred concludes. "We'll have money to manage the forest properly, but above all money to protect the wolf. The church can donate the lease to the foundation. The Nature Conservancy Foundation has tagged her, but we need more money to monitor her."

"I can't see why you're taking this up with me and Stefan," Bertil breaks in, his voice very calm; "Surely any changes to the lease are a matter for the church council?"

"You know what," says Mildred, "I think this is a matter for the whole church community."

The room falls silent. Bertil nods once. Stefan becomes aware of an ache in his left shoulder, pain working its way up the back of his neck.

They understand precisely what she means. They can see exactly how this discussion will look if it's carried out within the whole community and, of course, in the press. The bunch of old men hunting for free on church land, and on top of that claiming the animals they haven't even killed themselves.

Stefan is a member of the hunting team, he won't escape.

But the parish priest has his own reasons for keeping well in with the hunting team. They keep his freezer well filled. Bertil can always show off, offering his guests elk steak and game birds. And there's no doubt the team members have done other things to compensate the priest for his silent approval of their empire. Bertil's log cabin, for example. The team built it and they maintain it.

Stefan thinks about his place on the team. No, he feels it. As if it were a warm, smooth pebble in his pocket. That's what it is, his secret mascot. He can still remember when he got the place. Bertil's arm around his shoulders as he was introduced to Torbjörn Ylitalo. "Stefan hunts," the priest had said, "he'd be really pleased if he got a place on the team." And Torbjörn, the feudal lord in the church's forest kingdom, nodded, not allowing even a hint of displeasure to cross his face. Two months later Elis Wiss had given up his place on the team. After forty-three years. Stefan was elected as one of the twenty.

"It isn't fair," says Mildred.

The priest gets up from Stefan's armchair.

"I'm prepared to discuss this when you're somewhat calmer," he says to Mildred.

And he leaves. Leaves Stefan with her.

"How's that supposed to work?" Mildred says to Stefan. "As soon as I start thinking about this I'm anything but calm."

Then she gives him a big smile.

Stefan looks at her in surprise. What's she grinning at? Doesn't she understand that she's just made her position completely and totally impossible? That she's just delivered an unequivocal declaration of war? It's as if inside this extremely intelligent woman (and he has to admit that she is), there lives a retarded babbling idiot. What's he supposed to do now? He can't rush out of the room, it's his room. He stays in his seat, irresolute.

Then suddenly she looks at him with a serious expression, opens her handbag and takes out three envelopes, which she holds out to him. It's his wife's handwriting.

He stands up and takes the letters. He has stomach cramps.

Kristin. Kristin! He knows what kind of letters they are without reading them. He slumps back onto his chair.

"The tone of two of them is quite unpleasant," says Mildred.

Yes, he can imagine. It isn't the first time. This is what Kristin usually does. With slight variations, it's always the same. He's been through this twice already. They move to somewhere new. Kristin runs the children's choir and Sunday school, a sweet little songbird singing the praises of the new place to the skies. But when the first flush of love, that's the only thing he can call it, has passed, her discontent begins to show. Real and imagined injustices which she collects like bookmarks in an album. A period of headaches, visits to the doctor and accusations hurled at Stefan, who doesn't take her concerns seriously. Then something goes seriously wrong between her and some employee or member of the church community. And soon she's off on a crusade all over the district. In the last place it turned into a real circus in the end, with the union dragged in and an employee in the parish offices who wanted their nervous breakdown classified as a work-related injury. And Kristin, who just felt that she'd been unjustly accused. And finally the unavoidable move. The first time it was with one child, the second time with three. The eldest boy is at high school now, it's a critical time.

"I've got two more in the same vein," says Mildred.

When she's gone, Stefan sits there with the letters in his right hand.

She's snared him like a ptarmigan, he thinks, and he doesn't even know whether he means Mildred or his wife.

Rebecka Martinsson's boss Måns Wenngren was sitting on his office chair, creaking. He hadn't noticed it before, but it made a really irritating grating noise when you raised or lowered it. He thought about Rebecka Martinsson. Then he stopped thinking about her.

He actually had loads to do. Calls to make, e-mails to answer. Customers and clients to entertain. His junior associates had begun placing papers and yellow Post-it notes on his chair so that he'd see them. But it was only an hour until lunch, so he might as well put everything off for a bit longer.

He always said he was a restless soul. He could almost hear his ex-wife Madelene saying: "Well, it sounds better than moody, unfaithful and running away from yourself." But restless was true as well. A sense of unease had already got its claws into him in the cradle. His mother used to tell people how he'd screamed all night for the first year. "He calmed down a bit when he learned to walk. For a while."

His brother, three years older than Måns, never tired of telling the story of how they'd sold Christmas trees one year. One of the family's tenants had offered Måns and his brother a part-time job selling the trees. They were only kids, Måns had only just started school. But he could already count and add up, his brother said. Especially when it came to money.

And so they'd sold trees. Two little lads, seven and ten. "And Måns earned loads more money than the rest of us," his brother would say. "We just couldn't understand it, he was only getting four kronor per tree in commission, the same as everybody else. But while the rest of us were just standing around shivering and waiting for five o'clock to come, Måns was running about chatting to everybody as they looked at the trees. And if somebody thought a tree was too tall, he offered to chop the top off then and there. Nobody could resist, a nipper with a saw nearly as tall as he was. And this is the best bit: he took the top part that he'd sawed off, chopped off the branches and bound them together into big bundles, then sold them for five kronor apiece! And those five kronor went straight into his own pocket. The tenant—what the hell was his name, was it Mårtensson—was absolutely livid. But what could he do?"

His brother would pause at this point in the story and raise his eyebrows in a gesture that said all there was to say about the tenant's powerlessness in the face of the landowner's crafty son. "A business-man," he would conclude, "always a businessman."

Even when he was middle-aged, Måns was still defending himself against the label. "The law isn't the same thing as business," he said.

"Of course it bloody is," his brother used to reply. "Of course it is."

His brother had spent his early adult life abroad doing God knows what, and in the end he'd come back to Sweden, done a degree in social sciences, and was now in charge of the benefits office in Kalmar.

Anyway, Måns had gradually stopped defending himself. And why did you always have to apologize for success?

"That's right," he'd reply nowadays, "business and money in the bank." And then he'd tell him about the latest car he'd bought, or some smart deal on the stock market, or just about his new cell phone.

Måns could read all about his brother's hatred in his sister-in-law's eyes.

Måns just didn't get it. His brother had kept his marriage together. The children came to visit.

No, he thought, getting up from the creaky chair, I'm going to do it now.

*   *   *

Maria Taube chirruped a "bye then" into the telephone and hung up. Bloody clients, ringing up and churning out questions that were so vague and general it was impossible to answer them. It took half an hour just to try and work out what they wanted.

There was a knock on her door, and before she had time to answer Måns appeared.

Didn't you learn anything at Lundsberg? she thought crossly. Like waiting for "come in," for example?

As if he'd read the thought behind her smile, he said:

"Have you got a minute?"

When did anybody last say no to that question? thought Maria, waving at the chair and switching off her incoming calls.

He closed the door behind him. A bad sign. She tried desperately to think of something she'd overlooked or forgotten, some client who had a reason to be dissatisfied. She couldn't come up with anything. That was the worst thing about this job. She could cope with the stress and the hierarchy and the overtime, but there was that black abyss that sometimes opened up right beneath your feet. Like the mistake Rebecka had made. So damned easy, to lose a few million.

Måns sat down and looked around, his fingers beating a tattoo on his thigh.

"Nice view," he said with a grin.

Outside the window loomed the grubby brown facade of the building next door. Maria laughed politely, but didn't speak.

Come on, out with it, she thought.

"How's . . ."

Måns finished off the question with a vague gesture in the direction of the piles of paper on her desk.

"Fine," she replied, and stopped herself from launching into details of something she was working on.

He doesn't want to know, she told herself.

"So . . . have you heard anything from Rebecka?"

Maria Taube's shoulders dropped a centimeter.

"Yes."

"I heard from Torsten that she was staying up there for a bit."

"Yes."

"What's she doing?"

Maria hesitated.

"I don't really know."

"Don't be so bloody difficult, Taube. I know it was your idea for her to go up there. And to be perfectly honest, I don't think it was such a brilliant idea. And now I want to know how she's doing."

He paused.

"She does work here after all," he said in the end.

"You ask her then," said Maria.

"It's not that easy. The last time I tried she made a hell of a scene, if you remember."

Maria thought about Rebecka, rowing away from the firm's party. She was crazy.

"I can't talk to you about Rebecka, you know that. She'd be bloody livid."

"And what about me?" asked Måns.

Maria Taube smiled sweetly.

"You're always bloody livid anyway," she said.

Måns grinned, perked up by the insult.

"I remember when you started working for me," he said. "Nice and sweet. Did as you were told."

"I know," she said. "What this place does to people . . ."

Rebecka Martinsson and Nalle turned up outside Sivving Fjällborg's door like two casual laborers. He greeted them as if he'd been expecting them and invited them down to the boiler room. Bella was lying in a wooden box on a bed of rag rugs, sleeping with the puppies in a heap under her stomach. She just opened one eye and thumped her tail in greeting when the visitors came in.

At around one o'clock she'd called at Nalle's house and rung the doorbell. Nalle's father Lars-Gunnar had opened the door. A big man, filling the doorway. She'd stood out on the porch feeling like a five-year-old asking her friend's parents if her friend can come out to play.

Sivving put the coffee on and got out thick mugs with a pattern of big flowers in yellow, orange and brown. He put some bread in a basket and took margarine and sausage out of the refrigerator.

It was cool down in the cellar. The smell of dog and fresh coffee blended with faint traces of earth and concrete. The autumn sun shone down through the narrow window below the ceiling.

Sivving looked at Rebecka. She must have found some clothes stored at her grandmother's. He recognized the black anorak with the white snowflakes on it. He wondered if she knew it had belonged to her mother. Probably not.

And it was unlikely that anybody would have told her how much she looked like her mother. The same long, dark brown hair and distinctive eyebrows. Square-shaped eyes, the iris an indefinable light sandy color with a dark ring.

The puppies woke up. Big paws and ears, tumbling playfully, tails like little propellers against the side of the box. Rebecka and Nalle sat down on the floor and shared their sandwiches with them as Sivving cleared away.

"Nothing else smells quite this good," said Rebecka, inhaling deeply with her nose pressed against a puppy's ear.

"That particular one isn't spoken for yet," said Sivving. "Want to stake your claim?"

The puppy was chewing on Rebecka's hand with needle sharp teeth. His coat was chocolate brown, the hair so soft and short it felt like silky skin. His back paws had been dipped in white.

She put him back in the box and stood up.

"I can't. I'll wait outside."

She'd been on the point of saying she worked too hard to have a dog.

*   *   *

Rebecka and Sivving were lifting potatoes. Sivving went in front pulling off the tops with his good hand. Rebecka followed with the hoe.

"Just dig and hoe," said Sivving, "that's great. Otherwise I was going to ask Lena, she's coming up at the weekend with the boys."

Lena was his daughter.

"I'm happy to do it," said Rebecka.

She pushed the hoe back and forth; it was easy to work in the sandy soil. Then she picked up the almond potatoes that had come away from the tops and remained in the ground.

Nalle was running around on the lawn with an old bird's wing on a string, playing with the puppies. From time to time Rebecka and Sivving straightened their backs and looked across at them. You had to smile. Nalle with his hand holding the string high up in the air, yelling and shouting, his knees pumping up and down as he ran. The puppies chasing after him, full of the excitement of the chase. Bella was lying on her side on the grass, enjoying the warmth of the autumn sunshine. Lifted her head from time to time to snap at an annoying horsefly or to check on the little ones.

I'm just not normal, thought Rebecka. I can't cope with being around my work colleagues who are the same age as me, but with an old man and somebody who's retarded I feel as if I can be myself.

"I remember when I was little," she said. "When the adults had lifted the potatoes, you always lit a fire out on the field in the evening. And we were allowed to bake the potatoes that were left behind."

"Charred black on the outside, reasonably well cooked just inside the skin, and raw on the inside. Oh, I remember. And what you looked like when you came in later. Covered in soot and soil from top to toe."

Rebecka smiled at the memory. They had learned to respect fire, the children weren't really allowed to be responsible for a fire on their own, but the evening after potato picking was an exception. Then the fire belonged to them. There was Rebecka, her cousins, and Sivving's Mats and Lena. They used to sit there in the darkness of the autumn evening, gazing into the flames. Poking at it with sticks. Feeling just like Red Indians in a boys' adventure story.

They wouldn't go in to Grandmother until ten or eleven o'clock—it was practically the middle of the night. Happy and filthy. The adults had taken a sauna much earlier, and were sitting around drinking and chatting. Grandmother and Uncle Affe's wife Inga-Lill and Sivving's wife Maj-Lis drinking tea, Sivving and Uncle Affe with a Tuborg. She remembered the picture of the old men on the label. "Hvergang."

She and the other children had had the sense to stay in the hall-way rather than trailing half the potato field into the kitchen.

"My, here come the Hottentots," Sivving would laugh. "I can't tell how many there are, because the hall is as dark as a mine shaft and their skin is as black as coal. Come on, let's see you laugh so we can count the rows of teeth!"

They used to laugh. Take towels from Grandmother. Run down to the sauna by the river and get themselves clean in the fading heat.

Torbjörn Ylitalo, the chairman of Poikkijärvi hunting club, was out in his yard sawing wood when Anna-Maria Mella arrived. She stopped the car and got out. His back was toward her. His red ear protectors meant that he hadn't heard her. She took the opportunity to have a little look around in peace.

Well-looked-after geraniums in the window behind checked curtains. Presumably married, then. Tidy flower beds. Not a single fallen leaf on the lawn. The fence beautifully painted Falun red, with white tips.

Anna-Maria thought about her own fence, covered in patches of algae, and the paint flaking off the southern gable in great lumps.

We must paint it next summer, she thought.

But wasn't that just what she'd thought last autumn?

Torbjörn Ylitalo's chainsaw bit through the wood with a piercing shriek. When he threw the last piece to one side and bent down to pick up a fresh meter-long piece, Anna-Maria shouted to attract his attention.

He turned around, took off his ear protectors and switched off the saw. Torbjörn Ylitalo was in his sixties. A bit rough, but somehow well groomed. The remaining hair on his head was just like his beard, gray and well cut. When he had taken off his goggles, he opened his shiny blue work jacket and took out a pair of flexible, rimless Sven-Göran Eriksson glasses which he fixed firmly on his big lumpy nose. Sunburned and weather-beaten above the white neck. His earlobes were two big flaps of skin, but Anna-Maria noticed that the razor had been over them as well.

Not like Sven-Erik, she thought.

Sometimes there were clumps of hair like witches' brooms growing out of his ears.

*   *   *

They sat down in the kitchen. Anna-Maria accepted the offer of a cup of coffee when Torbjörn Ylitalo said he was having one himself anyway.

He measured coffee into the machine and rummaged ineffectually in the freezer, seemed relieved when Anna-Maria said she didn't want anything to eat.

"Are you on holiday before the elk hunting season starts?" asked Anna-Maria.

"No, but I've got very flexible working hours, you know."

"Mmm, you're the forestry officer for the church."

"That's right."

"Chairman of the hunting club, and a member of the hunting team."

He nodded.

They chatted for a while about hunting and gathering berries.

Anna-Maria took a notepad and pen out of the inside pocket of her jacket, which she'd kept on. She placed them on the table in front of her.

"As I said outside, this is about Mildred Nilsson. You and she didn't get on, according to what I've heard."

Torbjörn Ylitalo looked at her. He wasn't smiling, he hadn't smiled once so far. He took a sip of his coffee without hurrying, placed the cup on the saucer and asked:

"Who told you that?"

"Was it true?"

"What can I say, I don't like to speak ill of the dead, but she sowed a lot of discord and bitterness in this village."

"In what way?"

"I'll be honest with you: she hated men. I really believe she wanted the women in the village to leave their men. And there isn't much you can do in that situation."

"Are you married?"

"Tick the yes box!"

"Did she try to get your wife to leave you?"

"No, not her. But there were others."

"So exactly what did you and Mildred fall out about?"

"Well, it was this bloody stupid idea of having a quota system in the hunting team. Top-up?"

Anna-Maria shook her head.

"You know, every other member a woman. She thought that should be a condition if the lease was to be renewed."

"And you thought that was a bad idea."

A little more energy crept into his almost leisurely way of speaking.

"Well, there wasn't really anybody who thought it was a good idea, apart from her. And I certainly don't hate women, but I do think people should compete for places on the board of a company, or for parliament, or for that matter for our little hunting team, on equal terms. It really would be inequality if you got a place just because you were a woman. And how would you gain any respect? And besides— what's wrong with letting the men do the hunting? Sometimes I think hunting is our last outpost. Leave us to do at least that in peace. I didn't bloody well insist on joining her women's Bible group."

"So you fell out about that, you and Mildred?"

"Well, I wouldn't say we fell out—she knew what I thought."

"Magnus Lindmark said you'd have liked to put your shotgun in her mouth."

Anna-Maria wondered for a moment whether she should have told him that. Then again, it would serve the bastard who chopped the heads off the kittens bloody well right.

Torbjörn Ylitalo didn't seem bothered. He even smiled slightly for the first time. A tired, almost imperceptible smile.

"That's probably more to do with Magnus' own feelings," he said. "But Magnus didn't kill her. And neither did I."

Anna-Maria didn't answer.

"If I'd killed her, I would have shot her and buried her deep in some bog," he said.

"Did you know she wanted to cancel the lease?"

"Yes, but nobody on the church council was on her side, so it didn't mean a thing."

Torbjörn Ylitalo stood up.

"Well, if there's nothing else, I really need to get on with the wood."

Anna-Maria got up. She watched him place their cups on the draining board.

Then he took the coffee pot and placed it in the refrigerator, the coffee still warm.

She didn't comment. And they parted amicably out in the yard.

*   *   *

Anna-Maria drove away from Torbjörn Ylitalo. She wanted to go and see Erik Nilsson again. Ask if he knew who'd sent the drawing to his wife.

She parked the car outside the gates to the priest's house. The mailbox was overflowing with newspapers and letters, the lid jammed open. Soon it would be raining into the box. Bills, junk mail and newspapers would turn into one great big papier-mâché lump. Anna-Maria had seen overflowing mailboxes like this before. The neighbors ring, the mailbox looks like that, the police go in, and there's death in the house. One way or another.

She took a deep breath. She'd try the door first of all. If the priest's husband was lying in there, it might well be unlocked. If it was locked she'd look in through the windows on the ground floor.

She went up onto the porch. It was decorated with pretty white carved wood, white wicker chairs and big blue glazed pots, the contents of which had dried to a solid cement containing the brown, withered remains of summer flowers.

Just as she touched the door handle, it was pressed downward and the door opened from the inside. Anna-Maria didn't scream. Her expression probably didn't even change. But inside she jumped. Her stomach tied itself in knots.

A woman came out onto the porch, almost collided with Anna-Maria, and gave a little scream of fear.

She was around forty, wide-open dark brown eyes with long, thick eyelashes. Not much taller than Anna-Maria, so quite short. But she was slimmer, more fine-boned. The hand that flew up to her breast had long, slender fingers, the wrist was small.

"Oh," she smiled.

Anna-Maria Mella introduced herself.

"I'm looking for Erik Nilsson."

"Ah," said the woman. "He's . . . he isn't here."

Her voice faded away.

"He's moved away," she said. "I mean, the house belongs to the church. Nobody actually forced him to go, but . . . I'm sorry, my name's Kristin Wikström."

She extended the delicate hand toward Anna-Maria. Then she seemed embarrassed, as if she felt the need to explain her presence.

"My husband, Stefan Wikström, is going to move in here now Mildred's . . . Well, not just him. Me and the children too, of course."

She gave a short laugh.

"Erik Nilsson hasn't moved his furniture or his belongings and we don't know where he is and . . . well, I came here to see how much there was to do."

"So you don't know where Erik Nilsson's staying?"

Kristin Wikström shook her head.

"What about your husband?" asked Anna-Maria.

"He doesn't know either."

"No, but I'm wondering: where's he at the moment?"

Small furrows appeared above Kristin Wikström's upper lip.

"What do you want with him?"

"Just a few questions."

Kristin Wikström shook her head slowly, her expression troubled.

"I'd really prefer it if he were left in peace," she said. "He's had a very difficult summer. No holiday. The police around all the time. Journalists, they even ring at night, you know, and we daren't unplug the phone because my mother's old and ill, what if she were trying to ring us? And we're all afraid that it was some lunatic who . . . You daren't let the children out on their own. I'm worried about Stefan all the time."

But she didn't mention the grief over a lost colleague, Anna-Maria noted coldly.

"Is he at home?" she asked mercilessly.

Kristin Wikström sighed. Looked at Anna-Maria as if she were a child who'd disappointed her. Disappointed her a great deal.

"I don't actually know," she said. "I'm not the kind of woman who has to keep tabs on my husband all the time."

"Then I'll try the priest's house in Jukkasjärvi first, and if he's not there I'll go into town," said Anna-Maria, resisting the urge to roll her eyes to heaven.

*   *   *

Kristin Wikström remains standing on the porch of the priest's house in Poikkijärvi. She watches the departing red Ford Escort. She didn't like that woman detective. She doesn't like anyone. No, that isn't true, of course. She loves Stefan. And the children. She loves her family.

In her head she has a film projector. She doesn't think it's very common. Sometimes it just shows rubbish. But now she is going to close her eyes and watch a film she likes very much. The autumn sun warms her face. It's still late summer, it's hard to believe this is Kiruna, when it's as warm as this. It fits in very well. Because the film is from last spring.

The spring sun is shining in through the window and warming her face. The colors are muted. The picture is in soft focus, so it looks as if she has a halo around her hair. She is sitting on a chair in the kitchen. Stefan is sitting on the chair next to her. He is leaning forward, his head on her lap. Her hands are caressing his hair. She says: ssh. He is weeping. "Mildred," he says. "I can't cope much longer." All he wants is peace and quiet. Peace at work. Peace at home. But with Mildred spreading her poison through the congregation . . . She strokes his soft hair. It's a sacred moment. Stefan is so strong. He never seeks consolation from her. She enjoys being needed by him. Something makes her look up. In the doorway stands their eldest son Benjamin. What a mess he looks, with his long hair and his tight black ripped jeans. He stares at his parents. Doesn't say a word. But his eyes look completely crazy. She indicates with her eyebrows that he should disappear. She knows Stefan won't want the children to see him like this.

The film ends. Kristin grabs hold of the banister. This will be her and Stefan's house. If Mildred's husband thinks he can just leave all the furniture behind, and that nobody will dare to move it out, then he's wrong. As she walks toward the car, she allows the film in her head to run once more. This time she edits out her son Benjamin.

A nna-Maria drove into the yard of the priest's house at Jukkasjärvi. She rang the bell, but nobody answered.

When she turned, a boy was walking toward the house. He was about the same age as Marcus, maybe fifteen. His hair was long and dyed deep black. Beneath his eyes was a black, sooty line of kohl. He was wearing a scruffy black leather jacket and tight black trousers with huge holes in the knees.

"Hi!" shouted Anna-Maria. "Do you live here? I'm looking for Stefan Wikström, do you know if . . ."

She didn't get any further. The boy stared at her. Then he turned on his heel and ran. Ran off along the road. For a moment Anna-Maria considered running after him, but then she came to her senses. What for?

She got in the car and drove toward the town. Kept an eye open for the boy dressed in black as she was driving through the village, but there was no sign of him.

Could he have been one of the priest's children? Or was it somebody who'd maybe been thinking of breaking in? Who was surprised because there was somebody there?

Something else was tapping her on the head as well.

Stefan Wikström's wife. She was called Kristin Wikström.

Kristin. She recognized that name.

Then she remembered. Pulled over to the side of the road and stopped the car. Reached out for the pile of letters to Mildred that Fred Olsson had sorted out and thought might be of interest.

Two of them were signed "Kristin."

Anna-Maria glanced through them. One was dated in March, and was neatly handwritten:

> Leave us in peace. We want peace and quiet. My husband needs a peaceful working life. Do you want me to beg on my knees? I'm on my knees. And I'm begging: Leave us in peace.

The second was dated just a month later. It was obviously written by the same person, but the handwriting was all over the place, the downward strokes of the letter g were long, and some words had been scribbled out:

> Perhaps you think we don't KNOW. But everybody knows it wasn't just chance that you went for the job in Kiruna just one year after my husband had taken up his post here in town. But I can ASSURE you, we KNOW. You are working with groups and organizations whose SOLE aim is to work against him. You are poisoning wells with your HATRED. You shall drink that HATRED yourself!

Now what do I do? thought Anna-Maria. Go back and get her up against a wall?

She rang Sven-Erik Stålnacke on her cell phone.

"Let's talk to her husband instead," he suggested. "I was on the way to the parish offices in any case to pick up the books of that wolf foundation."

*   *   *

Stefan Wikström sighed heavily, sitting behind his desk. Sven-Erik Stålnacke had settled himself in the armchair. Anna-Maria was leaning against the door with her arms folded.

Sometimes she was just so . . . unprofessional, thought Sven-Erik, looking at Anna-Maria.

He really should have dealt with this little runt himself, that would have been better. Anna-Maria didn't like him, and couldn't hide the fact. Of course, Sven-Erik had read about the quarrel between Mildred and this priest, but they were here to work.

"Yes, I know about the letters," said the priest.

His left elbow was resting on the desk, his forehead supported by his thumb and fingertips.

"My wife . . . she . . . sometimes she's not well. I don't mean she's mentally ill, but she's a bit unstable at times. She's not really like this."

Neither Sven-Erik Stålnacke nor Anna-Maria Mella spoke.

"Sometimes she sees ghosts in broad daylight. But she wouldn't . . . you can't think she . . . ?"

He lifted his head and banged the desk with the palm of his hand.

"If that's what you think, it's completely ridiculous. My God, Mildred had a hundred enemies."

"Including you?" asked Anna-Maria.

"Certainly not! Am I a suspect as well? Mildred and I disagreed on some professional matters, that's true, but to think that either I or poor Kristin would have anything to do with her murder . . ."

"That isn't what we said," interjected Sven-Erik.

He frowned in a way that made Anna-Maria keep quiet and listen.

"What did Mildred say about these letters?" asked Sven-Erik.

"She told me she'd received them."

"Why do you think she kept them?"

"I don't know, I mean, I even keep all the Christmas cards I get."

"Did anybody else know about them?"

"No, and I'd be grateful if we could keep it that way."

"So Mildred didn't tell anybody else."

"No, not as far as I know."

"Did that make you feel grateful?"

Stefan Wikström blinked.

"What?"

He almost burst out laughing. Grateful. Was he supposed to have felt grateful to Mildred? The idea was just bizarre. But what could he say? He couldn't tell them anything. Mildred still had him trapped in a cage. And she'd made his wife into the padlock. And expected gratitude.

In the middle of May he'd gone crawling to Mildred and asked her for the letters. He joined her as she walked along Skolgatan on the way down to the hospital. She was going to visit somebody. It was the worst time of the year. Not at home in Lund, of course. But in Kiruna it was. The streets were full of gravel and all kinds of crap that appeared as the snow melted. Nothing green. Just dirt, rubbish and great drifts of gravel.

Stefan had spoken to his wife on the telephone. She was staying with her mother in Katrineholm with the youngest children. Her voice sounded more cheerful. Stefan looks at Mildred. She seems cheerful too. Turns her face up to the sun and sometimes takes deep, pleasurable breaths. It must be a blessing to have no sense of beauty. That must mean your mood isn't affected by dirt and gravel.

It's very odd, he thinks, not without some bitterness, that Kristin feels happier and draws strength from being away from him for a while. That isn't really what he thinks marriage should be about, you should gain strength from each other and support each other. He accepted long ago that she wasn't the support he'd hoped for. But now it's beginning to feel as if she doesn't think he's enough for her either. "Oh, just a bit longer," she answers evasively when he wonders how long she's going to be away.

Mildred doesn't want to give him the letters.

"You could smash my life to bits at any moment," he says to her with a twisted smile.

She looks at him steadily.

"Then you must get used to trusting me," she says.

He looks at her sideways. As they walk along side by side, it's obvious how small she is. Her front teeth really are unnaturally narrow. She looks exactly like a shrew.

"I'm thinking of raising the question of the hunting lease for Poikkijärvi hunting club with the church council. The lease expires at Christmas. If we lease the rights to somebody who can pay . . ."

He can't believe his ears.

"So that's the way things are," he says, surprised at how calm he sounds. "You're threatening me! If I vote for the lease to stay with the club, you'll tell everybody about Kristin. That stinks, Mildred. You're really showing your true colors now."

He can feel his mouth, living a life of its own. It contorts into a grimace, close to tears.

If Kristin can just get some rest, she'll get back on track. But if this business with the letters comes out . . . he knows she won't be able to cope. He can already hear her accusing people of talking about her behind her back. She'll have even more enemies. Soon she'll be waging war on several fronts simultaneously. And then they'll go under.

"No," says Mildred. "I'm not threatening you. I'll keep quiet whatever happens. I just wish you could . . ."

"Feel grateful?"

". . . accommodate me in this one matter."

"Go against my conscience?"

And now she flares up. Shows her real self.

"Oh, come on! It's hardly that, is it? A question of conscience?"

*　*　*

Sven-Erik Stålnacke repeats his question.

"Did you feel grateful about the letters? Bearing in mind that you weren't exactly the best of friends, it was generous of her not to tell anybody about the letters."

"Yes," Stefan ground out after a while.

"Hmm," said Sven-Erik. Anna-Maria's back moved away from the door.

"One more thing," said Sven-Erik. "The wolf foundation's books. Are they kept here?"

Stefan Wikström's irises moved uneasily across the whites of his eyes like goldfish in a bowl.

"What?"

"The books for the wolf foundation. Are they here?"

"Yes."

"We'd like to have a look at them."

"Don't you need some sort of warrant from the prosecutor to do that?"

Anna-Maria and Sven-Erik glanced at each other. Sven-Erik stood up.

"Excuse me," he said. "I just need to go to the bathroom. Where . . . ?"

"To the left, out through the office door, then immediately left again."

Sven-Erik disappeared.

Anna-Maria took out the drawing of the hanged Mildred.

"Somebody sent this to Mildred Nilsson. Have you seen it before?"

Stefan Wikström took it from her. His hand was steady.

"No," he said.

He handed the drawing back to her.

"You haven't received anything similar?"

"No."

"And you've no idea who might have sent it? She never mentioned it?"

"Mildred and I didn't confide in each other."

"Maybe you could make me a list of people you think she might have talked to. I mean people who worked in the church or here in the parish hall."

Anna-Maria watched him as he was writing. She hoped Sven-Erik would do what he had to do out there as quickly as possible.

"Have you got children?" she asked.

"Yes. Three boys."

"What age is the oldest?"

"Fifteen."

"What does he look like? Is he like you?"

Stefan Wikström's voice suddenly acquired a slight drawl.

"Impossible to tell. You can't tell what he looks like underneath all the hair dye and makeup. He's . . . going through a phase."

He looked up and smiled. Anna-Maria realized the fatherly smile, the deliberate pause and the word "phase" were something he used as a matter of routine when he talked about his son.

Stefan Wikström's smile suddenly disappeared.

"Why are you asking about Benjamin?" he asked.

Anna-Maria took the list out of his hand.

"Thank you for your help," she said, and left.

Sven-Erik Stålnacke went straight from Stefan Wikström's room into the parish office. There were three women in there. One of them was watering the plants on the windowsills, the other two were sitting at their computers. Sven-Erik went over to one of them and introduced himself. She was about the same age as him, around sixty, shiny nose and a pleasant expression.

"We'd like to have a look at the books for the wolf foundation," he said.

"Okay."

She went over to one of the bookshelves and came back with a folder that had next to nothing in it. Sven-Erik looked at her quizzically. Accounts ought to consist of great heaps of paper, invoices, columns and calculations.

"Is that all there is?" he asked incredulously.

"Yes," she said. "There aren't that many transactions, it's mostly credits."

"I'll just borrow this for a while."

She smiled.

"Keep it, it's only printouts and photocopies. I'll get some new ones off the computer."

"Er," said Sven-Erik, lowering his voice. "I'd like to ask you about something, could we just . . ."

He nodded in the direction of the empty stairwell.

The woman followed him out.

"There's an invoice to do with training costs," said Sven-Erik. "Quite a large sum . . ."

"Yes," said the woman. "I know the one you mean."

She thought for a little while, as if she were gathering herself.

"It wasn't right," she said. "Mildred was very angry. Stefan and his family went on holiday to the USA at the end of May on the foundation's money."

"How come?"

"He and Mildred and Bertil were all independent signatories for the foundation, so there was no problem. He probably thought nobody would notice, or he might have done it to annoy her, how should I know."

"What happened?"

The woman looked at him.

"Nothing," she said. "I suppose they drew a line under it. And Mildred said he'd visited Yellowstone where there's a wolf project going on, so as far as I know there wasn't any trouble about it."

Sven-Erik thanked her and she went back to her computer. He wondered whether he should go back to Stefan's office and ask about the trip. But there was no hurry; they could talk to him about it the following day. He instinctively felt he needed to think it over for a while. And in the meantime there was no point in frightening people.

*　*　*

"His face didn't change at all," Anna-Maria said to Sven-Erik in the car. "When I showed Stefan Wikström the drawing, his expression didn't alter. Either he has no feelings, or he was too busy hiding what he felt. You know how it is, you're so hell-bent on appearing calm that you forget you still ought to pretend to react in some way."

Sven-Erik mumbled something.

"He should at least have been slightly interested," said Anna-Maria. "Had a look at it. That's how I'd have reacted. Got upset, if it was somebody I cared about. Or slightly disturbed if I didn't know her, or actually disliked her. I'd have looked at it for a while."

He didn't actually answer my last question, she thought later. When I asked if he had any idea who might have sent it? He just said he and Mildred didn't confide in each other.

*   *   *

Stefan Wikström went out into the office. He felt slightly queasy. He ought to go home and have dinner.

The girls in the office looked at him curiously.

"They were just asking routine questions about Mildred," he said.

They nodded, but he could see they were still wondering. What an expression. Routine questions.

"Did they talk to you?" he asked.

The woman who'd spoken to Sven-Erik answered.

"Yes, the tall man wanted the wolf foundation's accounts."

Stefan went rigid.

"But you didn't give them to him? They've no right to ..."

"Of course I did! There's nothing secret in them, is there?"

She looked at him sharply. He could feel the others' eyes on him as well. He turned on his heel and went quickly back into his room.

The parish priest could say what he liked. Stefan needed to speak to him now. He rang Bertil on his cell phone.

Bertil was in his car. His voice broke up from time to time.

Stefan told him the police had been there. And that they'd taken the foundation's accounts away with them.

Bertil didn't seem particularly bothered. Stefan said that as they were both on the board of the foundation, nothing that was actually illegal had taken place, but even so.

"If this gets out you know how it'll sound. They'll have us down as embezzlers."

"I'm sure it'll be fine," said the parish priest calmly. "Look, I've got to park, talk to you later."

From his calm tone, Stefan understood that Bertil wouldn't stand by him if the trip to the USA came out. He would never admit that they'd both talked it over and agreed. "There's plenty of money just lying there in the foundation's account," Bertil himself had said. And they'd discussed some kind of developmental trip. They were on the board of a nature conservancy foundation, but knew nothing about wolves. And so it had been decided that Stefan would take a trip to Yellowstone. And somehow Kristin and the younger boys had ended up going too, that's how he'd got them back from Katrineholm.

It was understood that neither of them was going to tell Mildred that the money came from the foundation. But of course somebody in the office had to go running to her with the story.

She'd confronted him when he got back from the trip. He'd calmly explained the necessity of having someone on the board with some degree of knowledge. He was the most appropriate person, as a hunter and somebody who knew the ways of the forest. He could gain a respect and understanding that Mildred would never achieve if she tried for a thousand years.

He'd been expecting an outburst of rage. Some small hidden part of him was almost looking forward to it. Anticipating with pleasure the red evidence of her loss of control against the deep blue background of his own assured calm.

Instead she had leaned against his desk. Heavily, in a way that made him think for a moment that she might have some secret illness, something to do with her kidneys or her heart. She'd turned her face toward him. White beneath the early spring suntan. The eyes two black circles. An absurd cuddly toy with button eyes that's come alive and begun to speak, and is suddenly very frightening.

"When I speak to the church council about the hunting permit at the end of the year, you're to lie low, do you understand?" she said. "Otherwise we'll let the police sort out whether this was right or wrong."

He'd tried to say that she was making herself look ridiculous.

"Your choice," she said. "I've no intention of pandering to you forever."

He'd gazed at her in amazement. When had she pandered to him? She was like a bundle of nettles.

Stefan thought about the parish priest. He thought about his wife. He thought about Mildred. He thought about the looks the office staff had given him. Suddenly it felt as if he'd lost control of his breathing. He was panting like a dog in a car. He must try to calm down.

I can get out of this, he thought. What's the matter with me?

Even when he was a boy he'd gravitated toward companions who oppressed and exploited him. He had to run errands and give them his sweets. Later on he had to slash tires and throw stones to prove the priest's son wasn't a coward. And now he's an adult seeking out people and situations where he ends up being treated like dirt.

He reached for the telephone. Just one call.

Lisa Stöckel is sitting on the steps of her gingerbread house. The drugged-up pastry-chef's tour de force, as Mimmi calls it. She'll be going down to the bar soon. She eats there every day now. Mimmi doesn't seem to think it's strange. In her kitchen Lisa now has only a bowl, a spoon and a tin opener for the dog food. The dogs are wandering about outside by the fence. Sniffing and pissing on the currant bushes. She almost thinks they look slightly quizzical when she doesn't shout at them.

Piss wherever you want, she thinks with a half-smile.

The hardness of the human heart is a remarkable thing. It's like the soles of your feet in summer. You can walk on pinecones and on gravel. But if the heel cracks, it goes deep.

Hardness has always been her strength. Now it's her weakness. She tries to find the words to say to Mimmi, but it's hopeless. Everything that needs saying should have been said long ago, and now it's too late.

And what would she have said then? The truth? Hardly. She remembers when Mimmi was sixteen. She and Tommy had already been divorced for many years. He drank his way through the weekends. It was lucky he was such a good tiler. As long as he had a job, he stuck to beer from Monday to Thursday. Mimmi was worried. Obviously. Thought Lisa ought to talk to him. Asked: "Don't you care about Daddy?" Lisa had answered yes. It was a lie. And she was the one who'd decided there was to be no more lying. But Mimmi was Mimmi. Lisa didn't give a shit about Tommy. Another time, Mimmi had asked: "Why did you actually marry Daddy?" Lisa had realized she didn't have a clue. It was a staggering discovery. She hadn't managed to remember what she'd thought or felt during the time when they started going out, went to bed together, got engaged, when he put his ring on her finger. And then Mimmi came along. She'd been such a wonderful child. And at the same time the bond that would always link Lisa with Tommy. She'd worried about her maternal instinct. How is a mother supposed to feel about her child? She didn't know. "I could die for her," she'd sometimes thought as she stood watching Mimmi sleep. But it meant nothing. It was like promising people trips abroad if you won millions on the lottery. Easier to die for your child in theory than to sit and read to them for quarter of an hour. The sleeping child made her feel sick with longing and pangs of conscience. But when Mimmi was awake, with her small hands grabbing at Lisa's face and up her sleeves searching for skin and closeness, it made Lisa's flesh crawl.

Getting out of the marriage had felt like an impossible task. And when she finally did it, she was surprised at how easy it was. All she had to do was pack and move out. The tears and the screaming were like oil on water.

Things are never complicated with the dogs. They don't care about her awkwardness. They are totally honest and relentlessly cheerful.

Like Nalle. Lisa has to smile when she thinks of him. She can see it in his new friend Rebecka Martinsson. When Lisa saw her for the first time last Tuesday evening, she was wearing that calf-length coat and the shiny scarf, definitely real silk. A stuck-up top-notch secretary, or whatever she was. And there was something about her, a microsecond's hesitation perhaps. As if she always had to think before she spoke, made a gesture or even smiled. Nalle doesn't bother about things like that. He goes marching into people's hearts without taking his shoes off. One day with Nalle, and Rebecka Martinsson was walking around in an anorak from the seventies, her hair tied back with a rubber band, the sort that pulls out half your hair when you take it off.

And he doesn't know how to lie. Every other Thursday Mimmi serves afternoon tea at the bar. It's become one of those events that the ladies from town travel out to Poikkijärvi for. Freshly baked scones with jam, a wide variety of cakes. The previous Thursday Mimmi had shouted angrily: "Who's taken a bite out of my cakes?" Nalle, who'd been sitting there having a snack of a sandwich and a glass of milk, had immediately shot his hand up in the air and confessed: "Me!"

Blessed Nalle, thinks Lisa.

The very words Mildred used a thousand times.

Mildred. When Lisa's hardness cracked, Mildred poured in. Lisa was totally contaminated.

It's only three months since they lay on the kitchen sofa. They often ended up there, because the dogs had taken over the beds, and Mildred used to beg "don't push them off, can't you see how cozy they are?"

Mildred is always really busy at the beginning of June. End of term services in schools, confirmations, playgroups breaking up for the summer, church youth groups finishing off and lots of weddings. Lisa is lying on her left side, leaning on her elbow. She is holding a cigarette in her right hand. Mildred is asleep, or she might be awake, or more likely somewhere in between the two. Her back is covered in hairs, a soft down all along the length of her spine. It's like a special gift, the fact that Lisa who is so fond of dogs has a lover whose back is like a puppy's tummy. Or perhaps a wolf's stomach.

"What is it with you and that wolf?" asks Lisa.

Mildred has had a real wolf spring. She got ninety seconds on the evening news program, talking about wolves. There was a concert, with the proceeds going to the wolf foundation. She's even preached a sermon about the she-wolf.

Mildred turns onto her back. She takes the cigarette from Lisa. Lisa doodles on Mildred's stomach with her finger.

"Well," she says, and it's obvious she's making a real effort to answer the question. "There's something about wolves and women. We're alike. I look at that she-wolf and she reminds me of what we were created for. Wolves are incredibly patient. Just imagine, they can live in polar regions where it's minus fifty degrees, and in the desert where it's plus fifty. They're territorial, their boundaries are set in stone. And they roam for miles, completely free. They help each other within the pack, they're loyal, they love their cubs more than anything. They're like us."

"You haven't got any cubs," says Lisa, regretting it almost immediately, but Mildred isn't offended.

"I've got you lot," she laughs.

"They're brave enough to stay in one place when it's necessary," Mildred continues her sermon, "they're brave enough to move on when they have to, they're not afraid to fight and attack if need be. And they're . . . alive. And happy."

She tries to blow smoke rings while she thinks about it.

"It's to do with my faith," she says. "The whole of the Bible is full of men with a major task to do, a task that comes before everything, wife, children and . . . well, everything. There's Abraham and Jesus and . . . my father followed in their footsteps in his work as a priest, you know. My mother was responsible for where we lived, visits to the dentist, Christmas cards. But for me Jesus is the one who allows women to start thinking, to move on if they have to, to be like a she-wolf. And when I'm starting to feel bitter and weepy, he says to me: Come on, be happy instead."

Lisa carries on doodling on Mildred's stomach, her index finger traces a path across her breasts and her hip bones.

"You know they hate her, don't you?" she says.

"Who?" asks Mildred.

"The men in the village," says Lisa. "The ones on the hunting team. Torbjörn Ylitalo. At the beginning of the eighties he was convicted of hunting crimes. He shot a wolf down in Dalarna. That's where his wife comes from."

Mildred sits bolt upright.

"You're joking!"

"I'm not joking. He should really have lost his gun license. But Lars-Gunnar is a policeman, and you know how it is. And it's the police authorities who decide these things, and he used his contacts, and . . . Where are you going?"

Mildred has shot up off the kitchen sofa. The dogs come rushing in. They think they're going out. She doesn't take any notice of them. Pulls on her clothes.

"Where are you going?" asks Lisa again.

"Those bloody old men," says Mildred furiously. "How could you? How could you have known about this all along and not said anything?"

Lisa sits up. She's always known. After all, she was married to Tommy and Tommy was a friend of Torbjörn Ylitalo. She looks at Mildred, who fails to fasten her wristwatch and pushes it into her pocket instead.

"They hunt for free," snaps Mildred. "The church gives them everything, they won't let a single bloody person in, least of all women. But the women, they work and sort things out and have to wait for their reward in heaven. I'm so bloody tired of it. It really does send out a message about how the church regards men and women, but enough is damned well enough!"

"My God, you can swear!"

Mildred turns to Lisa.

"You ought to try it," she says.

Magnus Lindmark was standing by his kitchen window in the dusk. He hadn't switched on the lights. Every contour, every object both inside and outside had become blurred, begun to dis- solve, disappearing into the darkness.

However, he could still see Lars-Gunnar Vinsa, the leader of the hunting team, and Torbjörn Ylitalo, the chairman of the hunting club, walking up the road toward Magnus' house. He hid behind the curtain. What the hell did they want? And why weren't they driving? Had they parked a little way off and walked the last part? Why? He had a really bad feeling about this.

Whatever they wanted, he was bloody well going to tell them he didn't have time. Unlike those two, he did actually have a job. Well, okay, Torbjörn Ylitalo was a forester, but he didn't do any bloody work, nobody could pretend he did.

Magnus Lindmark didn't often get visitors nowadays, not since Anki and the boys left. He used to think it was a pain in the ass, all her relatives and the boys' friends coming round. And it wasn't his style to pretend and smile sweetly. So in the end her sisters and friends used to clear off when he got home. That had suited him

down to the ground. He couldn't do with people sitting around rab-
biting for hours. Hadn't they got anything else to do?

They were on the porch now, knocking on the door. Magnus' car
was in the yard, so he couldn't pretend he wasn't home.

Torbjörn Ylitalo and Lars-Gunnar Vinsa came in without waiting for Magnus to open the door. They were standing in the kitchen.

Torbjörn Ylitalo switched the light on.

Lars-Gunnar looked around. Suddenly Magnus realized what his
kitchen looked like.

"It's a bit . . . I've had a lot . . ." he said.

The sink was overflowing with dirty dishes and old milk cartons.
Two bags crammed full of empty stinking cans by the door. Clothes
he'd just dropped on the floor on his way into the shower, he should
have chucked them in the laundry room. The table covered in junk
mail, letters, old newspapers and a bowl of yogurt, the yogurt dried
up and cracked. On the worktop next to the microwave lay a boat
engine in bits; he was going to fix it sometime.

Magnus asked, but neither of them wanted coffee. Nor a beer.
Magnus himself opened a Pilsner, his fifth of the evening.

Torbjörn got straight down to business.

"What have you been saying to the police?" he asked.

"What the fuck do you mean?"

Torbjörn Ylitalo's eyes narrowed. Lars-Gunnar's stance became
somehow heavier.

"Let's not be stupid, Magnus," said Torbjörn. "You told them I
wanted to shoot the priest."

"Crap! That cow of a detective's full of crap, she . . ."

He didn't get any further. Lars-Gunnar had taken a step forward
and hit him with a blow that was like having your ears boxed by a
grizzly.

"Don't you stand there lying to us!"

Magnus blinked and raised his hand to his burning cheek.

"What the fuck," he whimpered.

"I've stuck up for you," said Lars-Gunnar. "You're a bloody loser,

I've always thought so. But for your father's sake we've let you into the team. And we've let you stay, despite your bloody antics."

A hint of defiance flared in Magnus.

"Oh, so you're a better person than me, are you? You're superior in some way, are you?"

Now it was Torbjörn's turn to give him a thump in the chest. Magnus staggered backwards, cannoning into the worktop with the back of his thighs.

"Right, now you just listen!"

"I've put up with you," Lars-Gunnar went on. "Going out shooting at road signs with your new gun, you and your pals. That bloody fight in the hunting lodge a couple of years ago. You can't hold your drink. But you carry on boozing and do such stupid bloody things."

"What the fuck, the fight, that wasn't me, that was Jimmy's cousin, he . . ."

A new thump in the chest from Torbjörn. Magnus dropped the can of beer. It lay there, the beer trickling out onto the floor.

Lars-Gunnar wiped the sweat from his brow. It was running past his eyebrows and down his cheeks.

"And those bloody kittens . . ."

"Yes, for fuck's sake," Torbjörn chipped in.

Magnus managed a foolish, drunken giggle.

"What the fuck, a few cats . . ."

Lars-Gunnar punched him in the face. Clenched fist. Right on the nose. It felt as if his face had split open. Warm blood poured down over his mouth.

"Come on then!" roared Lars-Gunnar. "Here, come on, here!"

He pointed at his own chin.

"Come on! Here! Now you've got the chance to fight a real man. You cowardly little bastard, tormenting women. You're a fucking disgrace. Come on!"

He beckoned Magnus toward him with both hands. Stuck his chin out to entice him.

Magnus was holding his right hand under his bleeding nose, the blood was running up his shirtsleeve. He waved Lars-Gunnar away with his left hand.

Suddenly Lars-Gunnar leaned heavily on the kitchen table.

"I'm going outside," he said to Torbjörn Ylitalo. "Before I do something I might regret."

Before he went out through the door, he turned around.

"You can report me if you want," he said. "I don't care. That's just what I'd expect from you."

"But you're not going to do that," said Torbjörn Ylitalo when Lars-Gunnar had gone. "And you're going to keep your mouth shut about anything to do with me and the hunting team. Have you got that?"

Magnus nodded.

"If I hear you've been opening your big mouth again, I personally will make sure you regret it. Understand?"

Magnus nodded again. He was tilting his face upward in an effort to stop the blood pouring out of his nose. It ran back into his throat instead, tasted like iron.

"The hunting permit will be renewed at the end of the year," Torbjörn went on. "If there's a lot of talk or trouble . . . well, who knows. Nothing's certain in this world. You've got your place in the team, but only if you behave yourself."

There was silence for a little while.

"Right then, make sure you put some ice on that," said Torbjörn eventually.

Then he left as well.

Lars-Gunnar Vinsa was sitting out on the steps, his head in his hands.

"Let's get out of here," said Torbjörn.

"Fuck," said Lars-Gunnar. "But my father used to hit my mother, you know. So it just makes me furious . . . I should have killed him, my father, I mean. When I'd finished my police training and moved back here, I tried to get her to divorce him. But back then, in the six-ties, you had to talk to the priest first. And the bastard persuaded her to stay with the old man."

Torbjörn Ylitalo gazed out across the overgrown meadow bor-dering on to Magnus' property.

"Come on," he said.

Lars-Gunnar got up with some difficulty.

He was thinking about that priest. His bald, shiny pate. His neck, like a pile of sausages. Fuck. His mother, sitting there with her best coat on. Her bag on her knee. Lars-Gunnar sitting beside her to keep her company. The priest, a little smile on his face. As if it were some bloody joke. "Old lady," the priest had said to her. His mother had just turned fifty. She would live for more than thirty years. "Will you not be reconciled with your husband instead?" Afterward she'd been very quiet. "That's it, it's all sorted," Lars-Gunnar had said. "You've spoken to the priest, now you can get a divorce." But his mother had shaken her head. "It's easier now you youngsters have left home," she'd replied. "How would he manage without me?"

*   *   *

Magnus Lindmark watched the two men disappear down the road. He opened the freezer and rummaged about. Took out a plastic bag of frozen mince, lay down on the living room sofa with a fresh can of beer, placed the frozen mince on his nose and switched on the TV. There was some documentary about dwarves, poor bastards.

Rebecka Martinsson is buying a packed meal from Mimmi. She is on her way down to Kurravaara. She might stay there tonight. When Nalle was there, it felt fine. Now she's going to try it on her own. She's going to have a sauna and swim in the river. She knows how it will feel. Cold water, sharp stones beneath her feet. The sharp intake of breath when you jump in, quick strokes as you swim out. And that inexplicable feeling of being at one with yourself at different ages. She's bathed there, swum there as a six-year-old, a ten-year-old, a teenager, right up until she moved away from the town. The same big stones, the same shoreline. The same chilly autumn evening air, pouring like a river of air over the river of water. It's like a Russian doll with all the little dolls safely inside, so that you can screw the top part and the bottom part back together, knowing that even the tiniest is safe and sound inside.

Then she'll eat alone in the kitchen and watch television. She can have the radio on while she washes up. Maybe Sivving will come over when he sees the light.

"So you were off on an adventure with Nalle today?"

It's Micke who's asking, the bar owner. He's got kind eyes. They don't really go with his muscular, tattooed arms, his beard and his earring.

"Yes," she replies.

"Cool. He and Mildred were often out and about together."

"Yes," she says.

I've done something for her, she thinks.

Mimmi has arrived with Rebecka's food.

"Tomorrow evening," says Micke, "do you fancy working here for a few hours? It's Saturday, everybody's back from their holidays, the schools have gone back, it'll be packed in here. Fifty kronor an hour, eight till one, plus tips."

Rebecka looks at him in amazement.

"Sure," she says, trying not to look too pleased. "Why not?"

She drives away. Feels full of mischief.

YELLOW LEGS

November. The gray light of dawn comes slowly. It has snowed during the night, and feather light flakes are still floating down in the silent forest. From somewhere comes the croaking of a raven.

The wolf pack is sleeping in a little hollow, completely covered in snow. Not even their ears are sticking up. All the cubs but one have survived the summer. There are eleven members of the pack now.

Yellow Legs stands up and shakes off the snow. Sniffs the air. The snow has settled like a blanket over all the old scent trails. Swept the air and the ground clean. She sharpens her senses. The keen eye. The alert ear. And there. She hears the sound of an elk rising from its overnight resting place, shaking off the snow. It's a kilometer away. Hunger makes its presence known like an aching void in her stomach. She wakes the others and gives the signal. There are many of them now, they can hunt such large prey.

The elk is a dangerous quarry. It has strong hind legs and sharp hooves. It could easily break her jaw with one kick, like a branch. But Yellow Legs is a skillful hunter. And she is daring.

The pack trots calmly in the direction of the elk. Soon they will pick up the scent. The cubs, now seven months old, are told with irritated silent yelps and nudges to stay behind the rest of the pack. They have already begun to catch small animals, but on this hunt they are allowed to come along only as observers. They know something big is happening, and are quivering with suppressed excitement. The older wolves are saving their strength. It is only their noses, raised in the air from time to time, that reveal the fact that this is not just a normal relocation, but the beginning of a demanding hunt. It is more likely that it will fail than succeed, but there is a determination in the way Yellow Legs moves. She's hungry. And these days she works hard for the pack, all the time. Daren't leave to go off on her own as she used to do. She senses that she is on the way to being driven out. One fine day, she may not be allowed to return. Her half-sister, the alpha female, keeps her on a tight rein. Yellow Legs always approaches the alpha pair with her hind legs bent and her back low in order to show them her submissiveness. Her backside drags along the ground. She crawls and licks the corners of their mouths. She is the most skillful hunter in the pack, but that no longer helps. They can manage without her, and somehow they all know that her days are numbered.

Physically, it is Yellow Legs who is superior. She is fast and long-legged. The biggest female in the pack. But she doesn't have the mind of a leader. Likes to take little trips on her own, away from the pack. Doesn't like trouble, prefers to turn aside a quarrel or a fight by fawning and starting a game instead. Her half-sister, on the other hand, gets up after a rest and stretches, looking around at the same time with a rock hard question in her eyes: "Well? Anyone thinking of taking me on today?" She is uncompromising and unafraid. You fit in with her or you leave, soon her cubs will learn that lesson. She wouldn't hesitate to kill them if there were a fight. With her as one of the leading pair, rival packs have to be wary of encroaching on their territory. Her restlessness gets the whole pack on its feet in the hunt for prey, or moving on to extend their territory.

The elk has got the scent of the pack. It's a young bull. They hear the crack of breaking branches as they gather speed through the forest. Yellow Legs moves up to a gallop. The fresh snow isn't deep, there is a considerable risk that the elk will get away from them. Yellow Legs breaks away from the rest and runs in a semicircle to overtake it.

After two kilometers the pack catches up with the elk. Yellow Legs has made it stop, launching small attacks but keeping well away from its antlers and hooves. The others gather around the massive animal. The bull tramps around in a circle, ready to defend itself against the first one who dares to attack. It's one of the males. He sinks his teeth into the elk's haunch. The elk pulls itself free. There's a deep wound, muscles and sinews torn away. But the wolf doesn't move away quickly enough; the elk kicks him over and he rolls backwards. When he gets up on his feet he's limping slightly. Two ribs are broken. The other wolves retreat a few paces and the elk breaks away. Bleeding from its haunch, it disappears into the brush.

It has too much strength left. Best to let it run for a while, bleeding, let it tire itself out. The wolves set off in pursuit of their prey. The pack is spaced out this time, trotting along. There's no hurry. They'll soon catch him again. The wolf that was kicked limps along after them. For the immediate future he'll be totally dependent on the others' success in hunting in order to survive. If the prey is too small, there won't be anything but bones left for him when he's permitted to eat. If they have to travel too far to hunt, he won't be strong enough to go with them. When the snow gets deep, it will be painful to get along.

After five kilometers the pack attacks again. This time it's Yellow Legs who moves in first. She closes on the elk at a gallop. The distance between the pack and the elk diminishes rapidly. The others are so close behind her that she can feel their heads with her hind legs. There is only the big elk, nothing else. His blood in her nose.

She's caught up. She seizes the elk's haunch. This is the most dangerous moment, she doesn't let go, and the next second a wolf is cling-
ing to its other haunch. Another instantly takes over from Yellow
Legs when she lets go. She dashes ahead and fastens her jaws around
the elk's throat. The elk falls to its knees in the snow. Yellow Legs
tugs at its throat. The huge animal tries to summon its strength to
get to its feet. Stretches its head up to the sky. The alpha male sinks
its teeth into the elk's muzzle and drags its head down to the ground.
Yellow Legs gets a fresh grip on the throat and rips it open.

Life runs quickly out of the elk. The snow is stained red. The cubs
are given a signal. Help yourselves. They come racing along and hurl
themselves at the dying animal. They are allowed to share in the tri-
umph of the hunt, shaking its legs and muzzle. The older wolves slit
the bull open with their powerful jaws. Steam rises from the body in
the chilly morning air.

In the trees up above, black birds gather.

SATURDAY SEPTEMBER 9

Anna-Maria Mella looked out through the kitchen window. The
woman next door was wiping the windowsills outside her house.
Again! She did it once a week. Anna-Maria had never been in their
house, but she could imagine it—formidably tidy, not a speck of dust
in sight, and nicely decorated.

The neighbors worked hard on their house and garden. Constantly crawling around uprooting dandelions. Carefully clearing
away the snow and building perfect banks at the side of the path.
Cleaning windows. Changing curtains. Sometimes Anna-Maria was
filled with a completely unreasonable irritation. Sometimes with
sympathy. And at the moment with a kind of envy. To have the entire
house clean and tidy at some point, that would really be something.

"She's wiping down the windowsills again," she said to Robert.

Robert grunted from somewhere around the bottom of the sports pages and his coffee cup. Gustav was sitting in front of the cupboard where the pots and pans were kept, taking everything out.

Anna-Maria was overcome by a slow wave of revulsion. They were supposed to be making a start on the Saturday housework. But she was the one who had to take the initiative. Roll up her sleeves and get the others started. Marcus had stayed the night at Hanna's. Dodging out of his duties! She should be pleased, of course. That he had a girlfriend and mates. The worst nightmare was for your children to be different, to be outsiders. But his room!

"Can you tell Marcus today that he needs to clean his room?" she said to Robert. "I can't keep going on at him."

"Hello!" she said after a while. "Am I talking to myself?"

Robert looked up from the paper.

"Well, you could answer me! So I know whether you've actually heard or not!"

"Fine, I'll tell him," said Robert. "What's the matter?"

Anna-Maria pulled herself together.

"Sorry," she said. "It's just . . . Marcus' bloody room. It frightens me. I really think it's dangerous to go in there. I've been in junkies' squats that have looked like something out of *Ideal Homes* compared with that."

Robert nodded seriously.

"Talking hairy apple cores . . ." he said.

"They frighten me!"

". . . dancing in a drug-induced trance brought on by the fumes of a fermenting banana skin. We'll have to buy some hamster cages for our new friends."

Best strike while the iron's . . .

"If you do the kitchen I'll make a start upstairs," suggested Anna-Maria.

It was best that way. Upstairs was total chaos. Their bedroom floor was covered in dirty washing and half-full plastic bags and cases from their driving holiday that still hadn't been unpacked. The windowsills were speckled with dead flies and leaves. The toilet was disgusting. And the children's room . . .

Anna-Maria sighed. All that sorting and putting away wasn't Robert's strong point. It would take him forever. It would be better if he could clean the oven, get the dishwasher going and vacuum downstairs.

It was so damned depressing, she thought. They'd said a thousand times that they'd do the cleaning on a Thursday evening instead. Then everything would be clean and tidy for Friday afternoon, when the weekend started. They could have a really nice meal on Friday, the weekend would be longer, Saturday could be spent doing something more enjoyable and everybody would be together and ecstatically happy in their nice clean house.

But it always turned out like this. On Thursday everybody was completely shattered, cleaning didn't even come into the equation. On Friday they shut their eyes to the mess, rented a film that always sent her to sleep, then Saturday had to be spent cleaning, half the weekend ruined. Sometimes they didn't get around to it until Sunday, and then the housework usually started with her having a complete fit.

And then there were all the things that never got done. The piles of washing waiting to be done, she never caught up, it was impossible. All those disgusting wardrobes. The last time she'd stuck her head into Marcus' wardrobe, helping him look for something or other, she'd lifted up the pile of sweaters and other stuff and some little insect had crawled out and disappeared into the lower layers of clothes. She didn't even want to think about it. When had she last taken off the bath panel? All those bloody kitchen drawers full of crap. How did everybody else find the time? And the energy?

Her work phone played its little tune out in the hallway. A zero-eight number she didn't recognize was showing on the display.

It was a man who introduced himself as Christer Elsner, a professor of the history of religion. It was to do with the symbol the police authorities in Kiruna had asked about.

"Yes?" said Anna-Maria.

"Unfortunately I haven't been able to find this particular symbol. It's similar to the alchemists' sign for a test or an examination of something, but the hook that carries on down through the semicircle is different. The semicircle often represents something incomplete, or sometimes it represents humanity."

"So it doesn't exist?" asked Anna-Maria, disappointed.

"Oh, well, now we're getting into difficult territory straightaway," said the professor. "What exists? What doesn't exist? Does Donald Duck exist?"

"No," said Anna-Maria. "He only exists as a fantasy figure."

"In your mind?"

"Yes, and in others' minds, but not in reality."

"Hmm. What about love, then?"

Anna-Maria laughed in surprise. It felt as if something pleasant was spreading through her body. She was exhilarated by thinking a new thought for once.

"Now it's getting tricky," she said.

"I haven't been able to find the symbol, but I've been looking at historical sources. Symbols do originate somewhere. It might be new. There are many symbols within certain musical genres. Similarly certain types of literature, fantasy and the like."

"Who'd know about that sort of thing?"

"People who write about music. When it comes to books, there's a very well-stocked bookstore for science fiction and fantasy here in Stockholm. In Gamla Stan, the Old Town."

They ended the conversation. Anna-Maria thought it was a shame. She would have liked to carry on talking. Although what would she have said to him? It would be nice to be able to turn herself into his dog. Then he could take the dog out into the forest for walks. And talk about his latest ideas and thoughts, lots of people did that with their dogs. And Anna-Maria, temporarily transformed into his dog, could listen. Without feeling pressured to come up with any intelligent answers.

She went into the kitchen. Robert hadn't stirred.

"I've got to go to work," she said. "I'll be back in an hour."

She wondered briefly whether she ought to ask him to make a start on the cleaning. But she left it. He wouldn't do it anyway. And if she'd asked him, she'd have been furious and disappointed when she came back and found him sitting here at the kitchen table in exactly the same spot as she'd left him.

She kissed him good-bye. It was better not to fall out.

* * *

Ten minutes later Anna-Maria was at work. In her mailbox was a fax from the lab. They'd found plenty of fingerprints on the sketch— Mildred Nilsson's fingerprints. They'd keep trying. It would take a few days.

She rang directory inquiries and asked for the number of a science fiction bookstore somewhere in Gamla Stan. The man on the other end of the line found it straightaway and put her through.

She explained what she wanted to the woman at the other end, described the symbol.

"Sorry," said the bookseller. "I can't think of anything at the moment. But fax the picture over and I'll ask some of my customers."

Anna-Maria promised to do that, thanked her for her help and hung up.

Just as she put the phone down it rang again. She picked up the receiver. It was Sven-Erik Stålnacke.

"You need to come," he said. "It's that priest Stefan Wikström."

"Yes?"

"He's disappeared."

Kristin Wikström was standing in the kitchen of the priest's house in Jukkasjärvi weeping inconsolably.

"Here!" she screamed at Sven-Erik Stålnacke. "Stefan's passport! How can you even ask that? I'm telling you, he hasn't gone away. Would he leave his family? He's the best . . . I'm telling you, something's happened to him."

She threw the passport on the floor.

"I do understand," said Sven-Erik, "but we still have to go through this in order. Couldn't you sit down?"

It was as if she couldn't hear him. She moved around the kitchen in despair, bumping into furniture and hurting herself. Two boys aged five and ten were sitting on the sofa, playing with Lego on a green base; they didn't seem particularly bothered by their mother's hysteria or the fact that Sven-Erik and Anna-Maria were in the kitchen.

Kids, thought Anna-Maria. They can accommodate anything.

All at once the problems between her and Robert seemed totally insignificant.

So what if I do more housework than him? she thought.

"What's going to happen?" yelled Kristin. "However will I manage?"

"So he didn't come home last night," said Sven-Erik. "Are you sure about that?"

"He hasn't slept in our bed," she whimpered. "I always change the sheets on a Friday, and his side hasn't been disturbed."

"Maybe he got home late and slept on the sofa?" ventured Sven-Erik.

"We're married! Why wouldn't he sleep with me?"

Sven-Erik Stålnacke had gone down to the priest's house in Jukkasjärvi to ask Stefan Wikström about the trip abroad the family had taken at the foundation's expense. He'd been met by Stefan's wife, her eyes huge. "I was just about to call the police," she'd said.

First of all he'd borrowed the key to the church and run down there. There was no dead priest hanging from the organ loft. Sven-Erik had almost had to sit down on a pew, he was so relieved. He'd phoned in to the station and got people out checking the rest of the churches in town. Then he'd phoned Anna-Maria.

"We need the numbers of your husband's bank accounts—have you got those?"

"What's the matter with you? Aren't you listening? You need to get out there and look for him. Something's happened, I tell you! He'd never . . . He might be lying . . ."

She fell silent and stared at her sons. Then she stormed outside. Sven-Erik went after her. Anna-Maria took the opportunity to have a look around.

She quickly opened the kitchen drawers. No wallet. No jacket in the hallway with a wallet in the pocket. She went upstairs. It was just as Kristin Wikström had said. Nobody had slept on one side of the double bed.

From the bedroom you could see the mooring where Mildred Nilsson had kept her skiff. The place where she'd been murdered.

And it was still light, thought Anna-Maria. The night before midsummer's eve.

No watch on his bedside table.

He seemed to have had his watch and his wallet with him.

She went back downstairs. One of the rooms appeared to be Stefan's study. She tugged at the desk drawers, they were locked. After searching for a while she found the key behind some books on the bookshelf. She opened the drawers. There wasn't much. A few letters that she glanced through. None of them seemed to have anything to do with him and Mildred. None of them was from a lover, if he had one. She peered out through the window. Sven-Erik and Kristin were still out there talking. Good.

Normally they would have waited a few days. People usually disappeared because they wanted to.

A serial killer, thought Anna-Maria. If he's found dead, that's what we're dealing with. Then we'll know.

Outside Kristin Wikström had sunk down on a garden seat. Sven-Erik was coaxing information out of her about all kinds of things. Who they could ring to take care of the children. The names of Stefan Wikström's close friends and relatives, maybe one of them knew more than his wife. If they had a summer cottage anywhere. If the family only owned one car, the one parked in the yard?

"No," sniveled Kristin. "His car's gone."

Tommy Rantakyrö rang to report that they'd checked all the churches and chapels. No dead priest.

A big cat came strolling confidently along the path toward the house. He hardly even glanced at the stranger in his garden. He didn't change course, nor did he slink into the tall grass. He might possibly have lowered his belly and his tail slightly. He was dark gray. His fur was long and soft, it looked almost fluffy. Sven-Erik thought he looked unreliable. Flat head, yellow eyes. If a big bastard like that had attacked Manne, Manne wouldn't have had a chance.

Sven-Erik could see Manne in his mind's eye, lying hidden as cats do, in a ditch maybe, or under a house. Knocked about, weak. In the end he'd be easy prey for a fox or a hunting dog. All they'd have to do was snap his spine. Snip snap.

Anna-Maria's hand brushed against his shoulder. They went off to one side. Kristin Wikström was staring straight ahead. Right hand clenched in front of her face, chewing at the index finger.

"What do you think?" asked Anna-Maria.

"We'll start searching for him," said Sven-Erik, looking at Kristin Wikström. "I've got a really bad feeling about this one. Nationally to start with. Customs too. We'll check flights and his accounts and his cell phone. And we need to have a chat with his colleagues and friends and relatives."

Anna-Maria nodded.

"Overtime."

"Yes, but what the hell can the prosecutor say? When the press get wind of this . . ."

Sven-Erik spread his hands in a helpless gesture.

"We need to ask her about the letters as well," said Anna-Maria. "The ones she wrote Mildred."

"But not now," said Sven-Erik decisively. "When somebody's come and taken the boys away."

* * *

Micke Kiviniemi looked out over the room from his strategic position behind the bar. King of all he surveyed. His noisy, messy kingdom, smelling of fried food, cigarette smoke, beer and aftershave with undertones of sweat. He was pouring beers one after the other, with the odd glass of red or white wine or a whisky in between. Mimmi was scampering between the tables like a performing mouse, bickering happily with the customers as she wiped down tables and took orders. He could hear her saying "chicken casserole or lasagne, take it or leave it."

The TV was on in the corner and behind the bar the stereo was doing its best. Rebecka Martinsson was sweating away in the kitchen. Food in and out of the microwave. Collecting baskets of dirty glasses from behind the bar and bringing out clean ones. It was like a really nice film. All the bad stuff seemed a long way off. The tax office. The bank. Monday mornings when he woke up feeling so bloody tired, deep in his bones, lying there listening to the rats in the garbage.

If only Mimmi could have been a little bit jealous because he'd given Rebecka Martinsson a job, everything would have been perfect. But she'd just said that was great. He'd stopped himself from saying that Rebecka Martinsson was something new for the old men to look at. Mimmi wouldn't have said anything, but he had the feeling she had a little box hidden away somewhere. And in that little box she was collecting all the times he'd made a mistake or overstepped the mark, and when the box was full she'd pack her bags and go. Without any warning. It was only girls who cared who gave a warning.

But right now his kingdom was as full of life as an anthill in the spring.

*   *   *

I can do this job, thought Rebecka Martinsson as she sluiced down the plates before putting the tray into the dishwasher.

You didn't need to think or concentrate. Just carry, work hard, get a move on. Keep up the tempo all the time. She was unaware of how her whole face was smiling as she carted a basket of clean glasses out to Micke.

"Okay?" he asked, and smiled back.

She felt her telephone buzzing in her apron pocket and got it out. No chance that it would be Maria Taube. She worked all the time, that was true, but not on a Saturday night. She'd be out and about, people buying her drinks.

Måns' number on the display. Her heart turned over.

"Rebecka," she yelled into the phone, pressing her hand against her other ear so she could hear.

"Måns," he yelled back.

"Hang on," she shouted. "Just a minute, it's so noisy in here."

She rushed out through the bar, waving the phone at Micke and holding up the fingers of her other hand; she mouthed "five minutes," moving her lips clearly. Micke nodded in agreement and she slipped outside. The cool night air made the hairs on her arms stand on end.

She could hear a lot of noise at the other end of the phone too. Måns was in a bar. Then things quieted down.

"Okay, I can talk now," she said.

"Me too. Where are you?" asked Måns.

"Outside Micke's Bar & Restaurant in Poikkijärvi, that's a village not far from Kiruna. What about you?"

"Outside Spyan, that's a little village bar on the edge of Stureplan in Stockholm."

She laughed. He sounded happy. Not so damned dismissive. He was probably drunk. She didn't care. They hadn't spoken to each other since the evening when she'd rowed away from Lidö.

"Are you out partying?" he asked.

"No, actually I'm working illegally."

Now he'll get mad, thought Rebecka. Then again, maybe not, it was a gamble.

And Måns laughed out loud.

"I see, and what is it you're doing?"

"I've got a brilliant job washing up," she said with exaggerated enthusiasm. "I'm earning fifty kronor an hour, that'll be two hundred and fifty for the night. And they've promised I can keep the tips as well, but I don't know about that, there aren't that many people coming into the kitchen to give a tip to the washer-up, so I reckon I've been taken for a bit of a ride there."

She could hear Måns laughing at the other end. A kind of snort that ended up in an almost pleading hoot. She knew he did that when he was wiping his eyes.

"Bloody hell, Martinsson," he sniveled.

Mimmi stuck her head round the door and gave Rebecka a look that meant "crisis."

"Look, I've got to go," said Rebecka. "Otherwise they'll dock my pay."

"Then you'll end up owing them money. When are you coming back?"

"I don't know."

"I'll probably end up having to come and fetch you," said Måns. "You're just not reliable."

You do that, thought Rebecka.

*   *   *

At half-past eleven Lars-Gunnar Vinsa came in. Nalle wasn't with him. He stood in the middle of the bar looking around. It was like grass in the wind. Everybody was affected by his presence. A few hands raised in the air in greeting, a few nods, a few conversations broken off or slowed, only to resume. A few heads turned. His arrival had been registered. He leaned over the counter and said to Micke:

"That Rebecka Martinsson, has she cleared off or what?"

"No," said Micke. "Actually, she's working here tonight."

Something in Lars-Gunnar's expression made him go on:

"It's just a one-off, it's really busy tonight and Mimmi's already got her hands full."

Lars-Gunnar reached over the counter with his bearlike arm and hauled Micke toward the kitchen.

"Come with me, I want to talk to her and I want you to be there."

Mimmi and Micke managed to exchange a glance before Micke and Lars-Gunnar disappeared through the swing door into the kitchen.

What's going on? asked Mimmi's eyes.

How should I know, replied Micke.

Grass in the wind again.

Rebecka Martinsson was standing in the kitchen rinsing dishes.

"So, Rebecka Martinsson," said Lars-Gunnar. "Come out the back with Micke and me, we need to talk."

They went out through the back door. The moon like a fish scale above the black river. The dull sounds from the bar. The wind soughing in the tops of the pine trees.

"I want you to tell Micke here who you are," said Lars-Gunnar Vinsa calmly.

"What do you want to know?" said Rebecka. "My name is Rebecka Martinsson."

"Maybe you should tell him what you're doing here?"

Rebecka looked at Lars-Gunnar. If there was one thing she'd learned in her job, it was that you should never start babbling and chattering.

"You seem to have something on your mind," she said. "You carry on."

"This is where you come from, well, not here, but Kurravaara. You're a lawyer, and you're the one that killed those three pastors in Jiekajärvi two years ago."

Two pastors and one sick boy, she thought.

But she didn't correct him. Stood there in silence.

"I thought you were a secretary," said Micke.

"You must understand we're wondering, those of us who live in the village," said Lars-Gunnar. "Why a lawyer's got herself a job in the kitchen, working under false colors. What you're earning tonight is probably what you'd normally pay for lunch in the city. We're wondering why you've wormed your way in here . . . poking about. I mean, I don't really care. People can do what they want as far as I'm concerned, but I thought Micke had a right to know. And besides . . ."

His eyes slid away from her and he looked out across the river. Let out a deep sigh. A weight settled on his shoulders.

". . . there's the fact that you were using Nalle. He's only a little boy inside his head. But you had the stomach to worm your way in here with his help."

Mimmi appeared in the doorway. Micke gave her a look that made her come outside to join them, closing the door behind her. She didn't speak.

"I thought I recognized the name," Lars-Gunnar went on. "I used to be in the police, so I'm well aware of what happened in Jiekajärvi. But then the penny dropped. You murdered those people. Vesa Larsson, anyway. It may well be that the prosecutor didn't think there was a case to answer, but I can tell you as far as the police are concerned, that doesn't mean a thing. Not a bloody thing. Ninety percent of cases where you know someone's guilty finish up not even going to court. And you must be feeling really pleased with yourself. Getting away with murder, that's clever. And I don't know what you're doing here. I don't know if that business with Viktor Strandgård gave you the taste for more, and you're here playing the private eye off your own bat, or if you're maybe working for some newspaper. I don't give a shit which it is. But in any case, the charade stops right here."

Rebecka looked at them.

I ought to make a speech, of course, she thought. Speak out in my defense.

And say what? That this had given her something else to think about, other than putting stones in her jacket pockets and sewing them up. That she couldn't cope with being a lawyer anymore. That she belonged to this river. That she'd saved the lives of Sanna Strandgård's daughters.

She untied her apron and handed it to Micke. Turned away without a word. She didn't go back through the bar. Instead she went straight past the henhouse and over the road to her chalet.

Don't run! she told herself. She could feel their eyes on her back.

Nobody followed her demanding an explanation. She pushed her belongings into her suitcase and overnight bag, threw them on the backseat of her rented car and drove away.

She didn't cry.

What does it matter? she thought. It's completely and utterly insignificant. Everything is insignificant. Nothing matters at all.

YELLOW LEGS

Bitter cold February. The days are growing longer, but the cold is hard, like God's fist. Still implacable. The sun is nothing more than an image in the sky, the air is like solid glass. Under a thick white blanket the mice and voles find their way about. The cloven-footed animals gnaw through the icy bark on the trees. They are growing thinner, waiting for the spring.

But minus forty degrees or the snowstorms that cover the whole landscape in a slow white wave of destruction don't bother the wolf pack. Quite the contrary. This is the best time. The best weather. They have picnics with outdoor activities in the blizzards. There is sufficient food. Their territory is extensive, their hunters skillful. No heat to torment them. No bloodsucking insects.

As for Yellow Legs, her days are numbered. The glint of the alpha female's sharp teeth tell her it's time. Soon. Soon. Now. Yellow Legs has tried everything. Crawled on her knees, begging to be allowed to stay. This February morning, the time has come. She is not permitted to approach the family. The alpha female lunges at her, jaws snapping at the air.

The hours pass. Yellow Legs does not leave straightaway. Stays a short distance away from the pack. Hoping for a sign that she will be allowed to return. But the alpha female is implacable. Gets up and drives her away.

One of the males, Yellow Legs' brother, turns away from her. In her mind she wants to bury her nose in his fur, sleep with her head resting on his shoulder.

The young wolves look at Yellow Legs with their tails down. Her yellow legs want to run, to chase them through the trees, tumbling over and over in a play fight, then up on her feet being chased by them in her turn.

And the cubs, soon they'll be a year old, cocky, foolhardy, still like puppies. They understand enough about what's happening now to keep calm and stay out of it. Whimpering uncertainly. She wants to drop an injured hare at their feet and watch them set off after it, ecstatic at the chance to hunt, leaping over one another in their eagerness.

She tries one last time. Takes a tentative step forward. This time the alpha female chases her right to the edge of the forest. In under the gray branches of the old fir trees, stripped of their needles. She stands there watching the pack and the alpha female, calmly making her way back to the others.

Now she must sleep alone. Until now she has rested among the sleepy sounds of the pack, yelping and hunting in their dreams, grunting and sighing, farting. From now on her ears will remain alert while she herself drifts into an uneasy sleep.

From now on unfamiliar scents will fill her nose, eroding the memory of her sisters and brothers, half-siblings and cousins, cubs and elders.

She sets off at a slow trot. Travelling in one direction. Yearning to be going the other way. She has lived here. She will survive there.

Sunday September 10

It is Sunday evening. Rebecka Martinsson is sitting on the floor in her grandmother's house in Kurravaara. She's lit a fire in the stove. A blanket over her shoulders, her arms around her knees. From time to time she takes a log out of the wooden box from the Swedish Sugar Company. She is gazing into the fire. Her muscles are tired. During the day she has carried rugs, blankets, quilts, mattresses and cushions outside. She's beaten them and left them hanging out there. She has scrubbed the floor with yellow soap and cleaned the windows. Washed all the china and wiped out the kitchen cupboards. She's left the ground floor at that. She's had the windows wide open all day to air the place, get rid of all the old, stale air. Now she's lit a fire in both the kitchen stove and the other room to drive out the last of the damp. She has kept the Sabbath day holy. Her mind has rested. Now it is resting in the fire. In the age-old way.

*   *   *

Inspector Sven-Erik Stålnacke is sitting in his living room. The television is on, but with no sound. Just in case there might be a cat miaowing outside. It doesn't matter, he's seen this film before. It's Tom Hanks, falling in love with a mermaid.

The whole house feels empty without the cat. He's walked along the side of the road, looking in the ditch and calling quietly. Now he feels very tired. Not from walking, but from listening so hard all the time. From keeping going. Although he knows there's no point.

And no sign of life from the priest who's vanished. Both evening papers had got hold of it on Saturday. Center page spread on the disappearance. A comment from the national police profiling team, but nothing from the female psychiatrist who did actually help them with a profile. One of the evening papers had found some old case from the seventies, where some lunatic in Florida had murdered two revivalist preachers. The murderer had been killed himself by a fellow prisoner while he was cleaning the toilets, but during his time in jail he'd boasted that he'd committed other murders he hadn't gone down for. Big picture of Stefan Wikström. The words "priest," "father of four," "despairing wife" appeared in the text under the picture. Not a word about possible embezzlement, thank the Lord. Sven-Erik also noticed that it didn't say anything about Stefan Wikström being opposed to women priests.

There were, of course, no resources for the protection of priests and pastors in general. His colleagues had felt their hearts sink when one of the papers wrote: **"Police Admit: We Cannot Protect Them!"** The *Express* offered advice to those who felt under threat: Make sure you're always with somebody, change your normal routines, take a different route home from work, lock the door, don't park next to a delivery van.

It was a madman, of course. The sort who would just carry on until his luck ran out. Sven-Erik thinks about Manne. In a way, his disappearance was worse than if he'd died. You couldn't grieve. You were just tormented by not knowing. Your head like a cesspit, full of horrible speculation about what might have happened.

But good God, Manne was just a cat. If it had been his daughter. That idea is too big. Impossible to grasp.

*   *   *

Bertil Stensson is sitting on the sofa in his living room. A glass of Cognac stands on the windowsill behind him. His right arm is resting along the back of the sofa, behind his wife's neck. With his left hand he is caressing her breast. She doesn't take her eyes off the TV, it's some old film with Tom Hanks, but the corners of her mouth turn up approvingly. He caresses one breast and one scar. He remembers how upset she was four years ago, when they took it off. "A woman still wants to be desired even though she's turned sixty," she said. But he's come to love the scar more than the breast that was there before. As a reminder that life is short. Before your pots can feel the thorns, he shall take them away as with a whirlwind, both living, and in his wrath. That scar puts everything into perspective. Helps him to maintain a balance between work and leisure, duty and love. Sometimes he's thought he'd like to preach a sermon about the scar. But of course that isn't really an option. Besides, it would feel as if he were overstepping the mark in some inexplicable way. It would lose its power in his life if he put it into words. It is the scar that preaches to Bertil. He has no right to take over that sermon and pass it on to others.

It was Mildred he spoke to, four years ago. Not Stefan. Not the bishop, although they've been friends for many years. He remembers that he wept. That Mildred was a good listener. That he felt he could rely on her.

She drove him mad. But as he sits here now, his wife's scar beneath his left forefinger, he can't really remember what it was that used to provoke him so. Even if she was a bluestocking who didn't really appreciate what did and didn't fall within the remit of the church.

She disqualified him from his role as her boss. That bothered him. Never asked for permission. Never asked for advice. Found it very difficult to keep in line.

He almost gives a start at his own choice of words, keep in line. He really isn't that kind of boss. He prides himself on giving his employees freedom and responsibilities of their own. But he's still their boss.

Sometimes he'd had to point that out to Mildred. Like that business with the funeral. It was a man who'd left the church. But he'd been attending Mildred's services the year before he got ill. Then he died. And he'd made it known that he wanted Mildred to officiate. And she'd conducted a civil funeral. Of course, he could have turned a blind eye to that little infringement of the rules, but he'd reported her to the cathedral chapter, and she'd had to go and see the bishop. At the time he'd thought it was the right thing to do. What was the point of having rules and regulations if they weren't followed?

She came back to work and behaved exactly as she always had. Didn't even mention the interview with the bishop. Didn't seem upset, didn't sulk, didn't seem to feel she'd been treated unfairly. This gave Bertil a sneaking feeling that the bishop might have been on her side. That he might have said he had to speak to her and rap her knuckles because Bertil had insisted, something along those lines. That they'd been in silent agreement that Bertil was easily offended, insecure in his position and perhaps even slightly jealous. Because he hadn't been asked to officiate at the funeral.

It isn't often people really take a close look at themselves. But now he's sitting before the scar, as if he were in the confessional.

It was true. He had been a bit jealous. A bit irritated by that simple love she drew from so many people.

"I miss her," Bertil says to his wife.

He misses her, and he will grieve for her for a long time to come.

His wife doesn't ask who he means. She abandons the film and turns the sound down.

"I didn't support her as I should have done when she worked here," he goes on.

"That's not true," says his wife. "You gave her the freedom to work in her own way. Managed to keep both her and Stefan in the church, that was quite an achievement."

The two troublesome priests.

Bertil shakes his head.

"Support her now, then," says his wife. "She's left so much behind. She used to be able to take care of it all herself, but maybe now she needs your support more than ever."

"How?" he laughs. "Most of the women in Magdalena regard me as their greatest enemy."

His wife smiles at him.

"Then you must help and support without receiving either thanks or love in return. You can have a little love from me instead."

"Maybe we should go to bed," suggests the priest.

*   *   *

The wolf, he thinks as he sits down to pee. That's what Mildred would have wanted. Use the money in the foundation to pay for her to be protected this winter.

As soon as the idea occurs to him, it's as if the whole bathroom is almost electrified. His wife is already in bed, calling out to him.

"Won't be a minute," he answers. Almost afraid to shout out loud. Her presence is so tangible. But fleeting.

What do you want? he asks, and Mildred comes closer.

It's just typical of her. Just when he's sitting on the toilet with his trousers down.

I'm in the church all day, he says. You could have come to find me there.

And at that very moment he knows. The money in the foundation won't be enough. But if the hunting permit is renegotiated.

Either the hunting club can start paying the proper rate. Or they find a new lessee. And that money can go to the foundation.

He can feel her smiling. She knows what she's asking of him. Every one of the men will be against him. There'll be trouble, letters to the paper.

But she knows he can do it. He can get the church council on his side.

I'll do it, he tells her. Not because I think it's the right thing to do. But for your sake.

* * *

Lisa Stöckel is out in the yard, tending a bonfire. The dogs are shut in, sleeping in their beds.

Bloody gangsters, she thinks lovingly.

She's got four now. For most of her life she's had five.

There's Bruno, a short-haired pure brown pointer. Everybody calls him the German. It's his air of self-control and his slightly military stiffness that have earned him the nickname. When Lisa gets out her rucksack and the dogs realize they're off on a long trip, bedlam breaks out in the hallway. They scurry round and round like a carousel. Barking, prancing, yelping, whining, giving little yaps of happiness. Almost knocking her over, trampling all over the packing. Looking at her with eyes that say: We can come with you, can't we? You won't go without us?

All except the German. He sits there like a statue in the middle of the floor, apparently unmoved. But if you lean forward and look at him carefully, you can see a trembling beneath his skin. An almost imperceptible quiver of suppressed excitement. And if it all gets too much for him in the end, if he has to let his feelings out before he breaks in two, he might just stamp with his front paws as he sits there, twice. Then you know he's really excited.

Then there's Majken, of course. Her old Labrador bitch. But she's slowing down nowadays. Gray muzzle, tired. Majken's looked after them all. She really loves puppies. The newcomers to the pack have been allowed to sleep on her stomach, she's been their new mummy. And if she didn't have a puppy to look after, she had a phantom pregnancy instead. Until only two years ago Lisa would come home and find the sheets on her bed raked up and completely reorganized. Majken would be lying there among the pillows and covers, with her little pretend puppies: a tennis ball, a shoe, or one time when Majken had been really lucky, a soft toy she'd found somewhere in the forest.

And then Karelin, her big black Schaefer/Newfoundland cross. He'd come to Lisa as a three-year-old. The vet in Kiruna had phoned and asked if she wanted him. He was going to be put down, but the owner had said he'd rather see him re-homed. He just didn't fit in in town. "I can well believe it," the vet had said to Lisa, "you should have seen him dragging his master along after him on the lead."

And finally Sicky-Morris, her Norwegian Springer spaniel. Show champion and award winning hunting stock. Talent completely wasted out here with the rest of the rogues. And Lisa doesn't even hunt. He loves to sit by her side and have his chest stroked, plonks his paw in her lap to remind her he exists. A nice, gentle man. Silky coat and curly hair on his ears like a girl, suffers badly from car sickness.

But now all four of them are lying inside. Lisa is throwing everything possible onto the fire. Mattresses and old dog blankets, books and some furniture. Papers. More papers. Letters. Old photographs. It makes a real blaze. Lisa gazes into the flames.

It became such hard work in the end, loving Mildred. Creeping about, keeping quiet, waiting. They quarreled. It was like a bad sitcom.

*   *   *

They're arguing in Lisa's kitchen. Mildred closes the windows.

That's the most important thing, thinks Lisa. That nobody hears.

Lisa lets it all out. All the words are the same. She's sick of them before they've been uttered. That Mildred doesn't love her. That she's tired of being something to pass the time. Tired of the hypocrisy.

Lisa is standing in the middle of the floor. She wants to throw things around. Her despair makes her shrill and wordy. She's never been like this before.

And Mildred is kind of cringing. Sitting on the sofa with Sicky-Morris pressed against her. Sicky-Morris is cringing too. Mildred is patting the dog as if she were consoling a child.

"What about the church, then?" she asks. "And Magdalena? If we were to live together openly, that would be the end of it. It would be the final proof that I'm nothing but a bitter man-hater. I can't test people's tolerance beyond their capability."

"So you prefer to sacrifice me?"

"No, why does it have to be like that? I'm happy. I love you, I can say it a thousand times, but you seem to want some kind of proof."

"It's not a question of proof, it's a question of being able to breathe. Real love wants to be seen. But that's the problem. You don't want that, you don't love me. Magdalena's just your bloody excuse for keeping your distance. Erik might fall for that, but not me. Get yourself another lover, I'm sure there's plenty who wouldn't say no."

Mildred begins to cry. Her mouth tries to hold back. She buries her face in the dog's fur. Wipes her tears with the back of her hand.

This is where Lisa wanted her. Maybe what she really wanted to do was hit her. She longs for her tears and her pain. But she isn't satisfied. Her own pain is still hungry.

"You can stop crying," she says harshly. "It means nothing to me."

"I'll stop," Mildred promises like a child, her voice cracking, her hand still wiping away the tears.

And Lisa who has always accused herself of her inability to love delivers her verdict:

"You just feel sorry for yourself, that's all. I think there's something wrong with you. There's something missing inside you. You say you love me, but who can open up another person and look inside and see what that means? I could leave everything, put up with anything. I want to marry you. But you . . . you're incapable of feeling love. You're incapable of feeling pain."

Then Mildred looks up from the dog. A candle in a brass holder is burning on the kitchen table. She puts her hand over the flame, it burns right into her palm.

"I don't know how to prove I love you," she says. "But I'll show you I'm capable of feeling pain."

Her mouth narrows to a thin line of agony. Tears pour from her eyes. A horrible smell fills the kitchen.

In the end, it feels like an eternity, Lisa takes hold of Mildred's wrist and pulls her hand away from the candle. The wound on her palm is burned and fleshy. Lisa looks at it in horror.

"You'll have to go to hospital," she says.

But Mildred shakes her head.

"Don't leave me," she begs.

Now Lisa is crying too. She leads Mildred out to the car, fastens the seat belt around her as if she were a child who couldn't do it herself, fetches a pack of frozen spinach.

It's weeks before they quarrel again. Mildred turns the inside of her bandaged hand toward Lisa from time to time. By chance, as it were, pushing her hair behind her ear or something like that. It's a secret love sign.

*   *   *

It's dark now. Lisa stops thinking about Mildred and goes to the henhouse. The chickens are asleep on their perches. Pressed close together. She takes them one by one. Lifts the chicken down from the perch. Carries it out to the fence. Keeps it pressed close against her body so it feels safe, clucking quietly. There's a stump of wood over there that she uses when she's chopping wood.

Grabs the legs quickly, swings it against the stump, a blow that stuns it. Then the axe, held with one hand right next to the axe head, one single chop, just hard enough, in exactly the right place. She keeps hold of the legs till it stops flapping, closes her eyes so she doesn't get feathers or anything else in them. Altogether there are ten hens and a cockerel. She doesn't bury them. The dogs would just dig them up straightaway. She chucks them in the garbage can instead.

*   *   *

Lars-Gunnar Vinsa is driving home to the village in the darkness. Nalle is asleep in the passenger seat beside him. They've been out in the forest all day picking lingon berries. Lots of thoughts. Coming into his head now. Old memories.

All of a sudden he can see Eva, Nalle's mother, standing in front of him. He's just got home from work. He's been on the evening shift and it's dark outside, but she hasn't put the lights on. She's standing quite still in the darkness right next to the wall in the hallway when he walks in.

It's such peculiar behavior that he's forced to ask her:

"What's the matter?"

And she replies:

"I'm dying here, Lars-Gunnar. I'm sorry, but I'm dying here."

What should he have done? As if he weren't tired to death as well. At work he was dealing with all kinds of misery day in and day out. Then he came home to take care of Nalle. He still can't work out what she did all day. The beds were never made. She hardly ever cooked dinner. He went to bed. Asked her to come up with him, but she didn't want to. The following morning, she was gone. Took nothing more than her handbag. She didn't even think he was worth a letter. He had to clean her out of the house. Packed her bits and pieces in boxes and put them in the attic.

After six months she phoned. Wanted to speak to Nalle. He explained that it just wasn't on. She'd only have upset the boy. He told her how Nalle had looked for her, asked about her and cried at first. But things were better now. He told her how the boy was getting on, sent her his drawings. He could see people in the village thought he was being too soft. Too indulgent. But he didn't wish her any harm. What would that achieve?

The old biddies from social services kept on about Nalle going to a residential center.

"He can stay there from time to time," they said. "It'll give you some respite."

He'd gone to have a look at their bloody residential center. Just walking through the door made you depressed. Everything was depressing. The ugliness of it all, every single object screamed "institution," "storeroom for loonies, the retarded and the crippled." The ornaments that had been made by the inmates—plaster casts, tiles covered in beads, vile pictures in cheap frames. And the way the staff chattered on. Their striped cotton overalls. He remembers looking at one of them. She can't have been more than one meter fifty. He thought:

Are you going to intervene if there's a fight?

Nalle was big, that was true, but he couldn't defend himself.

"Never," Lars-Gunnar said to social services.

They tried to insist.

"You need respite," they said. "You've got to think about yourself."

"No," he'd said. "Why? Why have I got to think about myself? I'm thinking about the boy. The boy's mother was thinking about herself, tell me what good came of that."

*   *   *

They're home now. Lars-Gunnar slows down as he approaches the entrance to his property. He checks out the yard. You can see quite well in the moonlight. In the trunk of the car is his elk rifle. It's loaded. If there's a police car in the yard he'll just keep on going. If they notice him, he'll still have a minute. Before they manage to start the car and pull out onto the road. Well, thirty seconds anyway. And that's enough.

But there's nothing in the yard. Highlighted against the moon he sees an owl on a low reconnaissance flight along the riverbank. He parks the car and lowers the back of his seat as far as it will go. He doesn't want to wake Nalle. The boy will wake up anyway in an hour

or so. Then they can go in and go to bed. Lars-Gunnar is just going
to close his eyes for a little while.

YELLOW LEGS

Yellow Legs trots out of her own territory. She can't stay there. Over
the border into another pack's territory. She can't stay there either.
It's extremely dangerous. A clearly marked area. Fresh scent mark-
ings are like a barbed wire fence between the tree trunks. A wall of
scents runs through the long grass sticking up through the snow;
they've sprayed here, scratched with their back feet. But she has to
get through, she has to go north.

The first day goes well. She's running on an empty stomach. Urinates low, pressing herself to the ground so the smell won't spread,
maybe she'll make it. She's got the wind behind her, that's good.

The next morning they pick up her scent. Two kilometers behind
her, five wolves are sniffing at her trail. They set off after her. They
take turns to lead, and soon make visual contact.

Yellow Legs senses their presence. She has crossed a river, and
when she turns she can see them on the other side, less than a kilometer downstream.

Now she's running for her life. An intruder will be killed immediately. Her tongue is hanging outside her mouth. Her long legs carry
her through the snow, but there is no well-trodden track to follow.

Her legs find the tracks of a scooter, going in the right direction.
The others follow it, but not so quickly.

When they are just three hundred meters behind her, they suddenly stop. They've chased her out of their territory, and a little bit
further.

She's escaped.

One more kilometer, then she'll lie down. Eat some snow.

The hunger is gnawing at her stomach like a vole.

*   *   *

She continues her journey northward. Then, where the White Sea separates the Kola peninsula from Karelia, she turns northwest.

The early spring keeps her company. It's hard to run.

Forest. A hundred years old and older. Conifers halfway to the sky. Naked, spindly, bare of needles almost all the way to the top. And right up there, their green, swaying, creaking arms build a roof. The sun can hardly penetrate, can't manage to melt the snow yet. There are just patches of light and the drip of melting snow from high in the trees. Dripping, trickling, dribbling. Everything can smell spring and summer. Now it's possible to do more than merely survive. The beat of heavy wings from the birds in the forest, the fox out of its den more and more often, the shrew and the mouse scampering along the icy crust of the snow in the mornings. And then the sudden silence as the whole forest stops, sniffs and listens to the she-wolf passing by. Only the black woodpecker continues his constant hammering on the tree trunks. The dripping doesn't stop either. The spring is not afraid of the wolf.

*   *   *

Bog country. Here the early spring is a torrent of water beneath a mushy, sodden covering of snow that turns to gray slush under the slightest pressure. Every step sinks deep. The she-wolf begins to travel by night. The icy crust on the snow will bear her weight. She settles in a hollow or under a pine tree during the day. On her guard even when she's asleep.

*   *   *

Hunting is different without the pack. She catches hares and other small wild animals. Not much for a wolf on a long journey.

Her relationship to other animals is different too. Foxes and ravens are quite happy to be with a pack of wolves. The fox eats the pack's leftovers. The raven prepares the wolf's table. He shouts from the trees: There's prey over here! It's a rutting deer! Busy rubbing his antlers against a tree! Come and get him! A bored raven can sometimes plump down in front of a sleeping wolf, peck its head and take a few hops backwards, looking slightly ridiculous and clumsy. The wolf snaps at it. The bird takes off at the very last second. They can entertain each other like this for quite some time, the black and the gray.

But a lone wolf is no playmate. She doesn't turn down any prey, doesn't want to play with birds, isn't willing to share.

One morning she surprises a vixen outside her earth. Several holes have been dug in a slope. One of the holes is hidden beneath a tree root. Only her tracks and a little bit of soil on the snow outside gives away its location. The vixen emerges from the hole. The wolf has picked up the acrid scent and taken a slight diversion from her route. She moves down the slope into the wind, sees the fox poke her head out, the spindly body. The wolf stops, freezes on the spot, the fox has to come out a little bit further, but as soon as it turns its head in this direction it will see her.

She pounces. As if she were a cat. A fight through the bushes and the branches of a fallen young spruce. Bites the fox right across her back. Snaps the spine. Eats her greedily, holding the body down with one paw as she rips the flesh, gulping down what little there is.

Two ravens immediately appear, working together to try to secure a share. One risks its life, coming dangerously close to make her chase it so that its companion can quickly steal a morsel. She snaps at them as they dive-bomb her head, but her paw doesn't leave the body of the fox. She gobbles every scrap, then trots around all the other holes, sniffing. If the fox had cubs and they're not too far down, she can dig them out, but there's nothing there.

She returns to her original route. The legs of the lone wolf move restlessly onward.

MONDAY SEPTEMBER 11

"It's just as if he's been swallowed up by the ground."

Anna-Maria Mella looked at her colleagues. It was the morning meeting in the prosecutor's office. They had just established that they had no trace whatsoever of Stefan Wikström, the missing priest.

You could have heard a pin drop for the next six seconds. Inspector Fred Olsson, Prosecutor Alf Björnfot, Sven-Erik Stålnacke and Inspector Tommy Rantakyrö looked distressed. That was the worst thing imaginable, that he actually had been swallowed up by the ground. Buried somewhere.

Sven-Erik looked particularly upset. He'd been the last to arrive at the prosecutor's morning service. It wasn't like him. There was a small plaster on his chin. It was stained brown with blood. The sign that a man is having a bad morning. The stubble on his throat below his Adam's apple had escaped the razor in his haste, and was protruding from his skin like coarse gray tree trunks. Below one corner of his mouth were the remains of dried-up shaving foam, like white adhesive.

"Okay, so far it's still just a missing person," said the prosecutor. "He was a servant of the church, after all. And then he found out we were onto him about that trip he went on with his family with the wolf foundation's money. That could well be enough to make him run. The fear of his reputation being ruined. He might pop up somewhere like a jack-in-the-box."

There was silence around the table. Alf Björnfot looked at the people sitting there. Difficult to motivate this shower. They seemed to be just waiting for the priest's body to turn up. With clues and proof to give the investigation a new lease on life.

"What do you know about the period just before he disappeared?" he asked.

"He rang his wife from his cell phone at five to seven on Friday evening," said Fred Olsson. "Then he was busy with the youngsters in the church, opened up their club, held an evening service at half nine. He left there just after ten, and nobody's seen him since."

"The car?" asked the prosecutor.

"Parked behind the parish hall."

It was such a short distance, thought Anna-Maria. It was perhaps a hundred meters from the youngsters' club to the back of the parish hall.

She remembered a woman who'd disappeared some years before. A mother of two who'd gone out one evening to feed the dogs in their run. And then she was gone. The genuine despair of her husband, his assurances and everybody else's that she would never leave her children of her own free will had led the police to prioritize her disappearance. They'd found her buried in the forest behind the house. Her husband had killed her.

But Anna-Maria had thought exactly the same then. Such a short distance. Such a short distance.

"What did you find out from checking phone calls, e-mails and his bank account?" asked the prosecutor.

"Nothing in particular," said Tommy Rantakyrö. "The call to his wife was the last one. Otherwise there were a few work-related calls with various members of the church and the parish priest, a call to the leader of the hunting team about the elk hunt, his wife's sister . . . I've got a list of the calls here, and I've made a little note of what the calls were about."

"Good," said Alf Björnfot encouragingly.

"What did the sister and the parish priest have to say?" wondered Anna-Maria.

"He called the sister to tell her he was worried about his wife. Worried she was going to be ill again."

"She wrote those letters to Mildred Nilsson," said Fred Olsson. "Things seem to have been pretty bad between the Wikströms and Mildred Nilsson."

"So what did Stefan Wikström talk to the parish priest about?" asked Anna-Maria.

"Well, he got a bit worked up when I asked him," said Tommy Rantakyrö. "But he told me Stefan was worried because we'd borrowed the accounts for the wolf foundation."

An almost imperceptible frown appeared on the prosecutor's brow, but he didn't say anything about improper conduct and seizing items without permission. Instead he said:

"Which could indicate that he disappeared of his own free will. That he's staying away because he's afraid of the shame. Believe me, the most common reaction to this sort of thing is to bury your head in the sand. You say to yourself 'can't they see they're just making things worse for themselves,' but often they've gone beyond sensible logic."

"Why didn't he take the car?" asked Anna-Maria. "Did he just walk off into the wilderness? There weren't any trains at that time. Nor any flights."

"Taxi?" asked the prosecutor.

"No pickups," answered Fred Olsson.

Anna-Maria looked at Fred appreciatively.

You stubborn little terrier, she thought.

"Right, then," said the prosecutor. "Tommy, I'd like you to . . ."

". . . start knocking on doors in the area around the parish hall asking if anybody's seen anything," said Tommy with resignation in his voice.

"Exactly," said the prosecutor, "and . . ."

". . . and talk to the kids from the church youth club again."

"Good! Fred Olsson can go with you. Sven-Erik," said the prosecutor. "Maybe you could ring the profiling group and see what they've got to say?"

Sven-Erik nodded.

"How did you get on with the drawing?" the prosecutor asked.

"The lab is still working on it," said Anna-Maria. "They haven't come up with anything yet."

"Good! We'll meet again first thing tomorrow morning, unless anything major happens in the meantime," said the prosecutor, folding his glasses with a snap and pushing them into his breast pocket.

That brought the meeting to an end.

*　*　*

Before Sven-Erik went to his office he called by to speak to Sonja on the exchange.

"Listen," he said. "If anybody rings and says they've found a gray tabby cat, let me know."

"Is it Manne?"

Sven-Erik nodded.

"It's a week now. He's never been away that long."

"We'll keep our eyes open," promised Sonja. "He'll be back, you'll see. It's still warm. He's probably out courting somewhere."

"He's been neutered," said Sven-Erik gloomily.

"Okay," she said. "I'll tell the girls."

*　*　*

The woman from the national police profiling team answered her direct line straightaway. She sounded cheerful when Sven-Erik introduced himself. Far too young to be working with this kind of crap.

"I suppose you've read the papers?" said Sven-Erik.

"Yes, have you found him?"

"No, he's still missing. What do you think, then?"

"What do you mean?"

Sven-Erik tried to marshal his thoughts.

"Well," he began. "If we assume the papers have got it right."

"That Stefan Wikström has been murdered and we're dealing with a serial killer," she supplied.

"Exactly. But in that case, this is peculiar, isn't it?"

She didn't speak. Waited for Sven-Erik to carry his thought through to its conclusion.

"What I mean," he said, "is that it's peculiar that he's disappeared. If the murderer hung Mildred up from the organ, why doesn't he do the same thing with Stefan Wikström?"

"Maybe he needs to scrub him clean. You found a dog hair on Mildred Nilsson, didn't you? Or maybe he wants to hang on to him for a while."

She broke off and seemed to be thinking.

"I'm sorry," she said at last. "When the body turns up—if it turns up, he might have gone of his own accord—we can talk again. See if there's a pattern."

"Okay," said Sven-Erik. "He could have gone of his own accord. He hadn't been completely honest in his dealings with a foundation that belonged to the church. Then he found out that we were on the trail of his grubby little story."

"His grubby little story?"

"Yes, it was a matter of about a hundred thousand kronor. And it's doubtful there would have been enough to make a case. It was a study trip that was actually more of a private holiday."

"So you don't think that was any reason for him to run?"

"Not really."

"So what if it was just the fact that the police were getting closer that frightened him?"

"What do you mean?"

She laughed.

"Nothing!" she said, stressing the word.

Then she suddenly sounded formal.

"I wish you luck. Let me know if anything happens."

As soon as they'd hung up, Sven-Erik realized what she'd meant. If Stefan had murdered Mildred . . .

His brain immediately started to protest.

If we just assume that's what happened, Sven-Erik persisted. Then he would have been scared enough to run if the police were getting closer. Whatever we wanted. Even if we just wanted to ask him the time.

Anna-Maria's phone rang. It was the woman from the science fiction bookstore.

"I've found something out about that symbol," she said, coming straight to the point.

"Yes?"

"One of my customers was familiar with it. It's on the cover of a book called *The Gate*. It's by Michelle Moan, that's a pseudonym. There isn't a Swedish version available. I haven't got a copy, but I can order one for you. Shall I do that?"

"Yes please! What's it about?"

"Death. It's a book of death. Really expensive—fifty-two pounds. And then there'll be the postage on top of that. I actually rang the publisher in England."

"And?"

"I asked if they'd had any orders from Sweden. A few—and one in Kiruna."

Anna-Maria held her breath. Long live amateur detectives.

"Did you get a name?"

"Yes, Benjamin Wikström. I got an address too."

"Don't need it," said Anna-Maria. "Thanks. I'll be in touch."

*   *   *

Sven-Erik was standing by Sonja on the exchange. He hadn't been able to stop himself going out to ask.

"What did the girls say? Had any of them heard anything about the cat?"

She shook her head.

Tommy Rantakyrö suddenly materialized behind Sven-Erik.

"Has your cat gone missing?" he asked.

Sven-Erik grunted in reply.

"He'll have moved in with somebody else," said Tommy breezily. "You know what cats are like, they don't get attached to anybody, it's just our own . . . projectifi . . . that you read your own feelings into the situation. They can't feel affection, it's been scientifically proven."

"You're talking crap," growled Sven-Erik.

"No, it's absolutely true," said Tommy, not reading the warning in Sonja's eyes. "When they start rubbing up against your legs and winding themselves round you, they're only doing that to mark you with their scent, because you're a sort of restaurant and resting place that belongs to them. They're not pack animals."

"No, maybe not," said Sven-Erik. "But he still comes up and sleeps in my bed like a baby."

"Because it's warm. You don't mean any more to the cat than an electric blanket."

"But you're a dog person," Sonja cut him off short. "You can't go making all these statements about cats."

To Sven-Erik she said:

"I'm a cat person too."

At that precise moment the glass door flew open. Anna-Maria came hurtling in. She grabbed hold of Sven-Erik and dragged him away from reception.

"We're going to the priest's house at Jukkasjärvi," was all she said.

*   *   *

Kristin Wikström opened the door wearing her dressing gown and slippers. Her makeup was smudged beneath her eyes. Her blonde hair was tucked behind her ears and lay flat and uncombed at the back of her head.

"We're looking for Benjamin," said Anna-Maria. "We'd like a word with him. Is he at home?"

"What do you want?"

"To talk to him. Is he at home?"

Kristin Wikström's voice went up a notch.

"What do you want him for? What do you want to talk to him about?"

"His father's disappeared," said Sven-Erik patiently. "We need to ask him one or two questions."

"He's not home."

"Do you know where he is?" asked Anna-Maria.

"No, and you should be looking for Stefan. That's what you two should be doing right now."

"Can we have a look at his room?" asked Anna-Maria.

His mother blinked tiredly.

"No, you can't."

"In that case we're very sorry to have disturbed you," said Sven-Erik pleasantly, dragging Anna-Maria to the car.

They drove out of the yard.

"Fuck!" Anna-Maria burst out once they were through the gateposts. "How could I be so stupid as to come out here without a search warrant?"

"Pull up a bit further on and let me out," said Sven-Erik. "You drive like hell and get the warrant sorted out and then come back. I want to keep an eye on her."

Anna-Maria stopped the car, Sven-Erik slid out.

"Get a move on," he said.

*   *   *

Sven-Erik trotted back to the priest's house. He positioned himself behind one of the gateposts where he was hidden by a rowan bush. He could see both the outside door and the chimney.

If there's any smoke, I'm going in, he thought.

After quarter of an hour Kristin Wikström came out. She'd changed from her dressing gown into jeans and a sweater. She was holding a garbage bag in her hand, tied at the top. She was heading for the garbage can. Just as she lifted the lid, she turned her head and caught sight of Sven-Erik.

Only one thing to do. Sven-Erik hurried over to her and held out his hand.

"Okay," he said. "I'll take that."

She passed him the bag without a word. He noticed that she'd dragged a brush through her hair and put a little bit of color on her lips. Then the tears began to flow. No gestures, hardly even a change of expression, just the tears. She might just as well have been peeling onions.

Sven-Erik undid the bag. It contained cuttings about Mildred Nilsson.

"Now now," he said, pulling her toward him. "There now. Tell me where he is."

"In school, of course."

She let him put his arms around her, let herself be held. Wept silently into his shoulder.

"But what is it you're thinking?" asked Sven-Erik as he and Anna-Maria were parking the car outside the Högalid school. "Do you think he murdered Mildred Nilsson and his father?"

"I don't think anything at all. But he's got a book with the same symbol that was on that threatening drawing sent to Mildred. Presumably he drew it. And he had a load of cuttings about her murder."

The headteacher of the school was a charming woman in her fifties. She was slightly plump, and was wearing a knee-length skirt with a dark blue jacket that didn't match. She had a bright scarf around her neck, like a piece of jewelry. The very sight of her cheered Sven-Erik up. He liked women who seemed to crackle with energy.

Anna-Maria explained that she would like Benjamin Wikström to be sent for without any fuss. The head took out a timetable. Then she rang the teacher taking Benjamin's class and had a brief conversation.

While they were waiting, she asked what it was all about.

"We think he might have been threatening Mildred Nilsson, the priest who was murdered last summer. So we just need to ask him a few questions."

The teacher shook her head. "I'm sorry," she said, "but I find that very difficult to believe. Benjamin and his friends—they look appalling. Black hair, white faces. Their eyes sooty with makeup. And sometimes when you look at their tops! Last term one of Benjamin's friends was wearing a top with a picture of a skeleton eating newborn babies."

She laughed and pretended to shudder. Became serious when Anna-Maria failed to smile.

"But they're really nice kids," she went on. "Benjamin had a few problems last year, but I'd happily let him babysit my children. If I had small children, that is."

"What do you mean, he had problems?" asked Sven-Erik.

"His schoolwork wasn't going very well. And he became so very . . . They want to be different, mark themselves out by the way they dress and so on. Sometimes I think they actually wear their sense of being outsiders. Make it their own choice. But he didn't feel good. He had lots of little sores on his arm, and he was always sitting there picking the scabs off. He ended up with a patch of sores that just wouldn't heal. Then sometime after Christmas things straightened themselves out. He got a girlfriend and started a band."

She smiled.

"That band. My God, they did a gig here at the school last spring. Somehow they'd got hold of a pig's head, and they stood there on the stage hacking at it with axes. They were ecstatic."

"Is he good at drawing?" asked Sven-Erik.

"Yes," said the headteacher. "Yes, he is actually."

There was a knock at the door and Benjamin Wikström walked in.

Anna-Maria and Sven-Erik introduced themselves.

"We'd like to ask you a few questions," said Sven-Erik.

"I'm not talking to you," said Benjamin Wikström.

Anna-Maria Mella sighed.

"In that case I shall have to arrest you on suspicion of making illegal threats. You'll have to come down to the station."

Eyes fixed on the ground. The lank hair hanging in front of the face.

"Whatever."

"Okay," said Anna-Maria to Sven-Erik. "Shall we talk to him, then?"

Benjamin Wikström was sitting in interview room one. He hadn't uttered a single word since they picked him up. Sven-Erik and Anna-Maria had got themselves a coffee. And a Coca-Cola for Benjamin Wikström.

Chief Prosecutor Alf Björnfot came cantering along the corridor toward them.

"Who've you picked up?" he panted.

They told him.

"Fifteen," said the prosecutor. "His guardian has to be present, is his mother here?"

Sven-Erik and Anna-Maria exchanged glances.

"Get her here," said the prosecutor. "Give the kid something to eat if he wants it. And ring social services. They need to send a representative as well. Call me later."

He disappeared.

"I don't want to do all that!" groaned Anna-Maria.

"I'll go and get her," said Sven-Erik.

* * *

After an hour they were sitting in the interview room. Sven-Erik Stålnacke and Anna-Maria Mella were sitting on one side of the table. On the other side sat Benjamin Wikström, with a representative from social services on his left. On his right was Kristin Wikström, her eyes red-rimmed.

"Did you send this drawing to Mildred Nilsson?" asked Sven-Erik. "We'll have prints from it very shortly. So if you did do it, we might as well talk about it."

Benjamin Wikström maintained a stubborn silence.

"My God," said Kristin. "What's going on, Benjamin? How could you do something like this? It's just sick!"

Benjamin's cheeks stiffened. He looked down at the table. Arms pressed tightly against his body.

"Maybe we should take a little break," said the woman from social services, putting her arm around Kristin.

Sven-Erik nodded and switched off the tape recorder. Kristin Wikström, the social services woman and Sven-Erik left the room.

"Why don't you want to talk to us?" asked Anna-Maria.

"Because you don't understand anything," said Benjamin Wikström. "You don't understand anything at all."

"That's what my son always says to me. He's the same age as you. Did you know Mildred?"

"It's not her on the drawing. Don't you get it? It's a self-portrait."

Anna-Maria looked at the drawing. She'd assumed it was Mildred. But Benjamin had long dark hair too.

"You were friends!" exclaimed Anna-Maria. "That's why you had those cuttings."

"She understood," he said. "She understood."

Behind the veil of hair, slow tears dripped onto the surface of the desk.

*   *   *

Mildred and Benjamin are sitting in her room at the parish hall. She's invited him for meadowsweet tea with honey. She's been given the tea by one of the women in Magdalena who picked the leaves and dried them herself. They're laughing because it tastes bloody awful.

One of Benjamin's friends was confirmed by Mildred. And through his friend he and Mildred got to know one another.

The Gate is lying on Mildred's desk. She's finished reading it.

"So what did you think?"

It's a thick book. Really thick. Lots of writing, in English. Lots of colored pictures too.

It's about "the gate" to the unbuilt house, to the world you create.

It's encouraging you to create the world you want to live in for all eternity, through various rites and in your head. It's about the way you get there. Suicide. Collectively or alone. The English publisher has been sued by a group of parents. Four young people took their lives together in the spring of 1998.

"I like the idea that you create your own heaven," she says.

Then she listens. Passes him tissues when he weeps. He does that when he's talking to Mildred. It's the feeling that she cares that starts him off.

"He hates me," he says. "And it doesn't make any difference. If I cut my hair and went around in a shirt and smart trousers and worked hard at school and became chairman of the school council, he still wouldn't be satisfied. I know that."

There's a knock on the door. Mildred frowns in annoyance. When the red light's showing . . .

The door opens and Stefan Wikström walks in. It's actually his day off.

"So this is where you are," he says to Benjamin. "Get your jacket and go and sit in the car. Now."

To Mildred he says:

"And you can stay out of my family's business. He's wasting his time at school. The way he dresses is enough to make you throw up. He does everything he can to embarrass the family. With every encouragement from you, I can see that. Giving him tea when he's truanting from school. Did you hear what I said? Jacket, car."

He taps his watch.

"You've got Swedish now, I'll give you a lift."

Benjamin stays where he is.

"Your mother's sitting at home crying. Your form tutor rang and wondered where you were. You're making your mother ill. Is that what you want?"

"Benjamin wanted to talk," says Mildred. "Sometimes . . ."

"You should talk to your family!" says Stefan.

"Yeah, right!" shouts Benjamin. "But you just refuse to answer.

Like yesterday, when I asked if I could go along with Kevin's family up to the Riksgränsen ski center. 'Get your hair cut and dress like a normal person, then I'll talk to you like a normal person.' "

Benjamin stands up and picks up his jacket.

"I'll cycle to school. You don't need to give me a lift."

He rushes out.

"This is your fault," says Stefan, pointing at Mildred as she sits there, still holding her teacup.

"I feel sorry for you, Stefan," she replies. "The landscape around you must be very desolate."

*　　*　　*

"We're letting him go," said Anna-Maria to the prosecutor and her colleagues. She went out to the rest area and asked the woman from social services to take mother and son home.

Then she went into her office.

She felt tired and dispirited.

Sven-Erik called in to see if she wanted to go out for lunch.

"But it's three o'clock," she said.

"Have you eaten?"

"No."

"Get your jacket. I'll drive."

She grinned.

"Why?"

Tommy Rantakyrö materialized behind Sven-Erik.

"You need to come," he said.

Sven-Erik looked at him grimly.

"I'm not even speaking to you," he said.

"Because of that business about the cat? I was only kidding. But you need to hear this."

*　　*　　*

They followed Tommy to interview room two. A woman and a man were sitting there. They were both dressed for the forest. The man was quite tall; he was holding a khaki cap from the army surplus store in his fist, and he was wiping the sweat from his brow. The woman was unnaturally skinny. Had those deep furrows above her lips and in her face that you get from smoking for many years. Bandana on her head, berry stains on her jeans. Both of them stank of smoke and mosquito repellent.

"Please could I have a glass of water," said the man as the three detectives entered the room.

"Just leave it!" said the woman, in a tone that indicated that nothing the man could say or do would be right.

"Could you just tell us again what you told me?" asked Tommy Rantakyrö.

"Oh, you tell them!" the woman snapped at her husband.

She was clearly stressed; her eyes flickered from one detective to the other.

"Well, we were north of Lower Vuolusjärvi picking berries," said the man. "My brother-in-law's got a cabin out there. Amazing cloudberries when the time's right, but at the moment it's lingon . . ."

He glanced up at Tommy Rantakyrö who was gesturing to indicate that the man really ought to get to the point.

"Anyway, we heard a noise during the night," said the man.

"It was a scream," his wife stated firmly.

"Yes, yes. Anyway, then we heard a shot."

"And then another shot," supplied his wife.

"Oh, you tell them, then!" snapped the husband.

"I said, didn't I, I said you're going to have to talk to the police! I said that."

The woman pursed her lips.

"That's about it, really," concluded the husband.

Sven-Erik gazed at them in amazement.

"When was this?" he asked.

"Friday night," said the man.

"And it's Monday now," said Sven-Erik slowly. "Why have you only just come in?"

"I told you, didn't I . . ." the woman began.

"Just shut up, will you," the man cut her off.

"I said we ought to come in straightaway," the woman said to Sven-Erik. "And when I saw the headlines about that priest . . . do you think it's him?"

"Did you see anything?" said Sven-Erik.

"No, we'd gone to bed," said the man. "We just heard what I told you. Well, we heard a car as well. But that was much later. There's a road that runs from Laxforsen out there."

"Didn't you realize this might be something serious?" asked Sven-Erik quietly.

"How should I know," said the man sullenly. "It's the elk hunting season, so it's hardly surprising if people are shooting in the forest."

Sven-Erik's voice was unnaturally patient.

"It was the middle of the night. During the hunting season no shooting is permitted from one hour before sunset. And who screamed? The elk, was it?"

"I did say . . ." the woman began.

"Look, noises can sound very strange in the forest," said the man, looking uncooperative. "It might have been a fox. Or a rutting stag, barking. Have you ever heard that? Anyway, we've told you all about it now. So perhaps we can go home."

Sven-Erik was staring at the man as if he'd taken leave of his senses.

"Go home!" he yelled. "Go home? You're staying right here! We'll get a map and take a look at the area. You're going to tell me where the shot came from. We'll work out if it was a bullet or shot. You're going to think about what sort of scream it was, whether you could make out any words. And we're going to talk about the car you heard as well. Where it came from, how far away it was, the whole lot. I want exact times of when this all happened. And we're going to go over this very carefully. Several times. Got it?"

The wife looked appealingly at Sven-Erik.

"I told him we ought to go straight to the police, but once he's got started on the berry picking . . ."

"Yes, and now look what's happened," said her husband. "I've got three thousand kronors' worth of lingonberries in the car. Whatever happens I'll have to phone the lad to come and collect them. I'm not having the bloody berries ruined."

Sven-Erik's chest was heaving up and down.

"But the car was a diesel, anyway," said the man.

"Are you taking the piss?" asked Sven-Erik.

"No, it's not bloody difficult to recognize a diesel, is it. The cabin's some distance from the road, but even so. But like I said, that was much later. Might not have had anything to do with the shot."

At quarter past four in the afternoon Anna-Maria and Sven-Erik were flying north by helicopter. The river Torne meandered below them like a silver ribbon. A few isolated clouds were casting their shadows on the mountainsides, but otherwise the sun was shining down on the golden yellow terrain.

"You can see why they'd want to stay out here picking berries instead of coming in and ruining their trip," said Anna-Maria.

Sven-Erik had to agree, and laughed.

"What is it with people?"

They looked down at the map.

"If the cabin's here at the northern end of the lake, and the shot came from the south . . ." said Anna-Maria, pointing.

"He thought it sounded really close."

"That's right, and further down you've got some cottages right on the shoreline. And they heard a car. It can't be more than one, at the most two kilometers, starting from the cabin."

They'd circled an area on the map. The following day the police would start searching the area, along with the local military.

The helicopter began to drop. Followed the long oval shape of the lake, Lower Vuolusjärvi, northward. They located the cabin where the berry pickers had been staying.

"Go lower and we'll check it out as best we can," Anna-Maria yelled to the pilot.

Sven-Erik had the telescope. Anna-Maria thought it was easier without. Birch trees, lots of marshy ground. The forest road, following the edge of the lake almost to its northern point. The odd reindeer gazing stupidly at them, and a female elk with a calf, galloping off into the undergrowth.

But still, thought Anna-Maria as she squinted, trying to see something other than mountain birches and brushwood. You can't bury somebody without leaving some kind of trace. Roots, shit like that.

"Wait," she suddenly shouted. "Look over there."

She pulled at Sven-Erik's arm.

"See?" she said. "There's a boat just there, down by the reindeer pen. We'll check it out."

*   *   *

The lake was over six kilometers long. A track led down to the lake from the road through the forest. There were planks over the last section. The white plastic skiff had been pulled ashore. Turned neatly upside down so it wouldn't get filled with water.

They turned it over together.

"Nice and clean," said Sven-Erik.

"Very nice and clean indeed," said Anna-Maria.

She bent down and examined the bottom of the boat carefully. Looked up at Sven-Erik and nodded. He bent down too.

"That's definitely blood," he said.

They looked out across the lake. It was smooth and calm. A ripple on the surface. Somewhere a black-throated diver was calling.

Down there, thought Anna-Maria. He's in the lake.

"We'll go back," said Sven-Erik. "No point trampling around and annoying the scene of crime team. We'll get Krister Eriksson and Tintin here. If they find anything, we'll send for a diver. We won't use the track, there could be traces or something."

Anna-Maria Mella checked the time.

"We can do it before it gets dark," she said.

*   *   *

It was half past four in the afternoon by the time they gathered at the lake again, Anna-Maria Mella, Sven-Erik Stålnacke, Tommy Rantakyrö and Fred Olsson. They were waiting for Krister Eriksson and Tintin.

"If he's anywhere round here, Tintin will find him," said Fred Olsson.

"Although she's not as good as Zack," said Tommy.

Tintin was a black Alsatian bitch. She belonged to Inspector Krister Olsson. When he'd moved up to Kiruna five years ago, he'd brought Zack with him. A male Alsatian with a thick coat, black and tan. Broad head. Not exactly a show dog. A one man dog. It was only Krister who mattered to him. If anyone else tried to say hello or pat him, he turned his head away indifferently.

"It's an honor to be allowed to work with him," Krister himself had said about the dog.

The mountain rescue team had also sung his praises, loud and long. Zack was the best avalanche dog they'd ever seen. He'd been good at searching as well. The only time Krister Eriksson was to be seen in the staff room at the station was when Zack was treating everyone to cakes. Or to put it more accurately, when some grateful relative or somebody who's life he'd saved was buying the cakes. Otherwise Krister Eriksson spent his coffee breaks walking the dog or training.

He just wasn't the sociable type. Maybe it was because of the way he looked. According to what Anna-Maria had heard, his injuries had been caused by a house fire when he was a teenager. She'd never dared to ask, he just wasn't the type. His face was like bright pink parchment. His ears were two holes that just went straight into his head. He had no hair at all, no eyebrows, no eyelashes, nothing.

There wasn't much left of his nose either. Two oblong holes right through his skull. Anna-Maria knew his colleagues called him Michael Jackson.

When Zack was alive, people had joked about the dog and his master. Said they sat together in the evenings, sharing a beer and watching the sport. That it was Zack who picked most of the winners.

Since Krister had got Tintin, she'd heard nothing. Presumably the jokes were still going on, but as Tintin was a bitch they were probably too coarse to repeat when Anna-Maria was around. "She'll be fine," Krister always said about Tintin. "She's a bit too overenthusiastic at the moment. Too young in the head, but it'll sort itself out."

Krister Eriksson arrived at the scene ten minutes after the others. Tintin was sitting in the front seat, fastened in with her own seat belt. He let her out.

"Has the boat arrived?" he asked.

The others nodded. A helicopter had dropped it at the northern end of the lake. It was orange, made for the shallows, equipped with spotlights and an echo sounder.

Krister Eriksson put on Tintin's life jacket. She knew exactly what that meant. A job. An exciting job. She sniffed eagerly round his legs. Her mouth was open and expectant. Her nostrils were twitching in all directions.

They walked down to the boat. Krister Eriksson positioned Tintin on the small platform and pushed off. His colleagues stayed where they were, watching them glide away. They heard Krister start up the engine. They were searching in a headwind. At first Tintin was moving her feet up and down in excitement, whimpering and dancing. At last she settled. Sat in the prow, seemed to be thinking of something else.

Forty minutes passed. Tommy Rantakyrö scratched his head.

Tintin was lying down. The boat moved to and fro across the lake. Working north to south. The detectives moved along the shoreline.

"Bloody mosquitoes," said Tommy Rantakyrö.

"Men with dogs. That's your sort of thing, isn't it?" Sven-Erik said to Anna-Maria.

"Pack it in," growled Anna-Maria warningly. "It wasn't even his dog, anyway."

"What's this?" wondered Fred Olsson.

"Nothing!" said Anna-Maria.

"But if you've started . . ." said Tommy Rantakyrö.

"It was Sven-Erik who started," said Anna-Maria. "Go on then, tell them. You carry on and humiliate me."

"Well, it was when you were living in Stockholm, wasn't it?" began Sven-Erik.

"When I was at the police training college."

"Anna-Maria moved in with this guy. And it hadn't been going on for very long."

"We'd been living together for two months, and we hadn't been going out for that much longer."

"And one day when she got home, correct me if I'm wrong, there was a leather thong on the bedroom floor."

"And it was just like the ones you see in porn movies. It even had a hole at the front. It wasn't too difficult to work out what was meant to be sticking out of that."

She paused and looked at Fred Olsson and Tommy Rantakyrö. She'd never seen them looking so happy and expectant in her life.

"And," she said, "there was a sanitary towel on the floor as well."

"Get away!" said Tommy Rantakyrö attentively.

"I was really shocked," Anna-Maria went on. "I mean, what do we really know about another person? So when Max got home and called out in the hallway, I was just sitting there in the bedroom. He just said 'How's things?' And I pointed at the leather underwear and said 'We need to talk. About that.'

"And he didn't even react. 'Oh,' he said, 'it must have fallen off the wardrobe.' And he put the thong and the sanitary towel back on top of the wardrobe. He was completely blasé about the whole thing."

Then she grinned.

"It was a pair of dog's underpants. His mother had a boxer bitch that he used to look after sometimes. And when they went out she used to wear the underpants with the towel in, and the hole was for her tail. It was that simple."

The laughter of the three men echoed across the lake.

They went on giggling for a long time afterward.

"Bloody hell," said Tommy Rantakyrö, wiping his eyes.

Then Tintin got to her feet in the boat.

"Look," said Sven-Erik Stålnacke.

"As if any of us would even consider not looking at this particular moment," said Tommy Rantakyrö, stretching his neck.

Tintin had positioned herself. Her body was completely rigid. Her nose was pointing in toward the lake like the needle of a compass. Krister Eriksson slowed the boat so that it was barely moving, and steered in the direction indicated by Tintin's nose. The dog began to whimper and bark, walking round and round on the platform and scratching. Her barking became more and more agitated until the front part of her body was hanging down over the water. When Krister Eriksson picked up the lead-weighted buoy to mark the spot, Tintin couldn't control herself. She jumped into the water and swam around the buoy, barking and sneezing from the water.

Krister Eriksson called her, grabbed the handle on the life jacket and pulled her out. For a while it looked as if he might end up in the water himself. In the boat Tintin carried on whining and whimpering with pleasure. They could hear Krister Eriksson's voice above the noise of the engine and the dog's yelping.

"Well done, girl. Good girl."

When Tintin leapt ashore she was as wet as a sponge. She shook herself vigorously, making sure everybody had a good shower.

Krister Eriksson praised her and stroked her head. She was only still for a second. Then she shot off into the forest, shouting out loud how bloody wonderful she was. They could hear her bark coming from different directions.

"Was she supposed to jump in?" asked Tommy Rantakyrö.

Krister Eriksson shook his head.

"She just got so excited," he said. "But when she's successful and finds something she's looking for, it has to be an entirely positive experience for her, so you can't tell her off for jumping in, but . . ."

He gazed in the direction of the barking with a mixture of immeasurable pride and thoughtfulness.

"She's bloody amazing," said Tommy, impressed.

The others agreed. The last time they'd met Tintin they were looking for a seventy-six-year-old woman with senile dementia who'd gone missing; Tintin found her in the forest up beyond Kaalasjärvi. It had been a huge area to search, and Krister Eriksson had driven a jeep very slowly along old logging tracks. He'd fixed a bath mat on the bonnet for Tintin so she wouldn't slip. She'd sat there like a sphinx, her nose in the air. An impressive performance.

You didn't often get to have such long conversations with Krister Eriksson. Tintin came back from her victory lap, and even she was affected by the sudden feeling of group solidarity. She even went so far as to scamper among the detectives and have a quick sniff at Sven-Erik's trousers.

Then the moment had passed.

"Right, well, that's us done, then," said Krister almost crossly, called the dog and took off her life jacket.

It was getting dark.

"All we can do now is ring the technicians and the divers," said Sven-Erik. "They can get up here as soon as it's light tomorrow morning."

He felt both happy and sad. The worst had happened. Another priest had been murdered, they could be more or less certain of that now. But on the other hand, there was a body down there. There were traces of blood in the skiff, and there were bound to be some on the track as well. They knew it had been a diesel car. They had something to work with again.

He looked at his colleagues. He could see the same electricity in them all.

"They can get themselves up here tonight," said Anna-Maria. "They can at least make an attempt in the dark. I want him out of there now."

Måns Wenngren was sitting in the Grodan club looking at his cell phone. All day he'd been telling himself not to call Rebecka Martinsson, but now he couldn't actually remember why not.

He'd call her and just ask casually how her job on the side was going.

He was thinking the kind of thoughts he'd had when he was fifteen. What her face would look like at the exact moment he pushed inside her.

Embarrassing old fool! he said to himself as he keyed in the number.

She answered after three rings. Sounded tired. He asked casually about the job on the side, just as he'd planned.

"It didn't work out very well," she said.

Then the whole story came pouring out, how she'd been accused of snooping by Nalle's father.

"It was really nice, not being 'the woman who killed three men,' " she said. "I wasn't keeping it a secret, but there was no reason to tell anybody either. The worst thing is I left without paying the bill."

"You can probably pay it by account transfer or something," said Måns.

Rebecka laughed.

"I don't think so."

"Do you want me to sort it out for you?"

"No."

No, of course not, he thought. Can do it herself.

"Then you'll just have to go back there and pay it," he said.

"Yes."

"You haven't done anything wrong, you don't need to go crawling."

"No."

"Even if you have done something wrong, you shouldn't crawl," Måns went on.

Silence at the other end of the phone.

"This is turning into hard work, Martinsson," said Måns.

"Sorry," she said.

"Forget about it now," said Måns. "I'll ring you first thing to-morrow and give you a bit of a pep talk. Going to pay a bill in some godforsaken little place, you can do that. Remember the time you had to deal with Axling Import all by yourself?"

"Mmm."

"I'll call you tomorrow."

He won't call, she thought when they'd rung off. Why should he?

*   *   *

The divers found Stefan Wikström's body in the lake at five past ten that evening. They managed to get him up with a stretcher made from a net, but he was heavy. An iron chain had been wound around his body. His skin was completely white and porous, as if it had been steeped in the water and faded. There were half centimeter wide entry holes in his forehead and chest.

YELLOW LEGS

It's the beginning of May. The leaves that have been lying beneath the snow have been compacted to form a brown shell over the ground. Here and there something green is tentatively emerging. Warm breezes from the south. Birds flying overhead.

The she-wolf is still on the move. Sometimes she is overwhelmed by her great loneliness. Then she stretches her throat up to the sky and lets everything out.

Fifty kilometers south of Sodankylä there is a village with an open garbage tip. She roots around there for a while, finds some discarded food and digs out fat, terrified rats. Fills her stomach well.

A little way outside the village there is a Karelian elkhound on a chain. When the she-wolf emerges from the edge of the forest, he doesn't start barking like a thing possessed. Nor does he feel afraid and try to get away. He stands there in silence, waiting for her.

True, the smell of human beings frightens her, but she has been alone for a long time now, and this unafraid dog will do her very well. For three days she returns to him as darkness falls. Dares to come right up to him. Sniffs, allows herself to be sniffed. They court one another. Then she returns to the edge of the forest. Stops and looks at him. Waits for him to follow her.

And the dog pulls at his chain. During the day, he stops eating.

When the she-wolf returns on the fourth evening, he is no longer there. She stands at the edge of the forest for a little while. Then she trots off into the forest once again. And continues her journey.

*   *   *

The snow has completely gone. The ground is steaming, quivering with longing for life. Everywhere things are crawling, chirruping, crackling and playing. Leaves burst open on the aching trees. Summer is coming from below like a green, unstoppable wave.

She moves twenty kilometers northward along the river Torne. Crosses the bridge made by humans in Muonio.

Shortly afterward a man kneels before her for the second time in her life. She is lying in the birch woods with her tongue hanging out of her mouth. Her legs don't exist. The trees above her a vague blur.

The man on his knees is a researcher in wolf behavior from the Nature Conservancy Council.

"You're so beautiful," he says, stroking her flanks, her long yellow legs.

"Yes, she's very pretty," the vet agrees.

She gives her a vitamin injection, checks her teeth, flexes her limbs carefully.

"Three, maybe four years old," she guesses. "Excellent condition, no scabies, nothing."

"A real princess," says the researcher, screwing the radio transmitter together around her neck, "a special piece of jewelry for a royal lady."

The helicopter's engine is still going. The ground is so soft the pilot daren't turn it off, because the helicopter might sink down and be unable to lift off.

The vet gives the she-wolf another injection and then it's time to leave her.

The researcher stands up. Still touching her. The thick, healthy coat. Wool next to the skin. Coarse, long hairs on the outer layer. The heavy paws.

When they have lifted off they can see her getting to her feet. A little bit wobbly.

"Tough lady," the vet comments.

The researcher sends a thought to the powers that be. A prayer for protection.

TUESDAY SEPTEMBER 12

It's all in the morning papers. And they're talking about it on the news on the radio. The missing priest has been found in a lake with chains around his body. Shot twice. Once in the chest. Once in the head. An execution, according to a police source, describing the fact that the body was found as more luck than skill.

Lisa is sitting at the kitchen table. She's folded up the newspaper and turned off the radio. She's trying to sit completely still. As soon as she moves, it's as if there's a wave inside her, a wave that surges through her body, getting her up on her feet, making her walk round and round in her empty house. Into the living room with the gaping bookshelves and the empty windowsills. Into the kitchen. The dishes have been washed. The cupboards wiped out. All the drawers full of rubbish have been emptied. No papers or unpaid bills lying around. Into the bedroom. Last night she slept without any bed linen, just pulled her quilted coat over her, fell asleep, much to her surprise. The cover is folded up at the foot of the bed, the pillows placed on top of it. Her clothes are gone.

By sitting completely still she can curb her longing. Her longing to scream and cry. Or her longing for pain. To place her hand on the burning hotplate. It will soon be time to go. She's had a shower and put on clean underwear. Her bra is chafing under her arms; it doesn't usually do that.

It's not so easy to fool the dogs. They come up to her, wagging their tails. The sound of their claws on the floor, clickety-clickety-click. They don't take any notice of her stiff body, rejecting them. They push their noses against her stomach and between her legs, wriggle their heads under her hands and demand to be patted. She pats them. It takes an enormous effort. To shut everything off to the extent that she can manage to stroke them, feel their soft fur, the warmth of the living blood flowing beneath it.

"In your baskets," she says in a voice which is not her own.

And they go to their baskets. Then they come straight back and start walking around her again.

When it's half past seven, she gets up. Rinses out her coffee mug and places it on the draining board. It looks strangely abandoned.

Out in the yard the dogs start playing up. Normally they just jump straight into the car, knowing it means a long day in the forest. But now they're messing about. Karelin scampers off and pees on the currant bushes. The German sits down and stares at her as she stands there ordering them into the car through the open tailgate. Majken is the first to give in. Scuttles across the yard, crouching, tail pressed down between her legs. Karelin and the German jump in after her.

Sicky-Morris is never very keen on travelling by car. But now he's worse than ever. Lisa has to chase after him, shouting and swearing until he stops. She has to drag him to the car.

"Get in, for Christ's sake!" she shouts, slapping him on the backside.

And then he jumps in. He understands. They all do. Looking at her through the window. She sits down on the bumper, worn out already. The last thing she's doing is fighting with them, that wasn't the way she wanted it to be.

* * *

She drives to the churchyard. Leaves the dogs in the car. Walks down to Mildred's grave. As usual there are lots of flowers, small cards, even photographs that have warped and thickened with the dampness.

They're keeping it nice for her, all the women.

She should have had something with her to place on the grave, of course. But what could she have brought?

She tries to think of something to say. A thought to think. She stares at Mildred's name on the wet, gray stone. Mildred, Mildred, Mildred. Drives the name into her body like a knife.

My Mildred, she thinks. I held you in my arms.

* * *

Erik Nilsson is watching Lisa from a distance. She stands there passive and rigid, as if she's looking right through the stone. The other women always get down on their knees and poke about in the earth, busying themselves and tidying, talking to other visitors.

He's on his way to the grave, but he stops for a moment. He usually comes here on weekday mornings. To have his time there in peace. He's got nothing against the Magdalena crowd, but they've taken over Mildred's grave. There's no room for him among the grieving. They clutter the place with flowers and candles. Place little pebbles on top of the headstone. His contributions are lost among all the bits and pieces. No doubt it's okay for the others, this sense of collective grieving. It's a consolation to them that so many miss her. But for him. It's a childish thought, he knows. He wants people to point at him and say: "He was her husband, you have to feel sorry for him most of all."

Mildred passes behind him.

Shall I go down there? he asks.

But she doesn't reply. She's staring at Lisa.

He walks over to Lisa. Clears his throat in plenty of time so as not to startle her, she seems so absorbed in her thoughts.

"Hi," he says tentatively.

They haven't met since the funeral.

She nods and tries to force a smile.

He's just about to say "so you've got a breakfast meeting here as well," or something equally meaningless to oil the wheels between them. But he changes his mind. Instead he says seriously:

"We only had her on loan. If we could only bloody realize that while they're still with us. I was often angry with her because of what she didn't give me. Now I wish I'd . . . I don't know . . . accepted what she did give with pleasure, instead of being tormented by what I didn't get from her."

He looks at her. She looks back without any expression on her face.

"I'm just talking," he says defensively.

She shakes her head.

"No, no," she manages to get out. "It's just . . . I can't . . ."

"She was always so busy, working all the time. Now that she's dead it feels as if we've finally got time for one another. It's as if she's retired."

He looks at Mildred. She's crouching down, reading the cards on the grave. Sometimes she gives a big smile. She picks up the pebbles on the top of the headstone and holds them in her hand. One after the other.

He stops speaking. Waits for Lisa to ask him how he's getting on, perhaps. How he's coping.

"I've got to go," she says. "The dogs are in the car."

Erik Nilsson watches her as she leaves. When he bends down to change the flowers in the vase buried in the ground, Mildred has gone.

L isa gets into the car.

"Lie down," she says to the dogs in the back.

I should have lain down myself, she thinks. Instead of wandering round the house waiting for Mildred. Then. The night before midsummer's eve.

It's the night before midsummer's eve. Mildred is already dead. Lisa doesn't know that. She wanders round and round. Drinking coffee, although she shouldn't do that when it's this late.

Lisa knows Mildred was conducting midnight mass in Jukkasjärvi. All the time she's been expecting Mildred to come to her afterward, but now it's getting very late. Maybe somebody stayed behind to chat. Or maybe Mildred's gone home to bed. Home to Erik. Lisa's stomach ties itself in knots.

Love is like a plant, or an animal. It lives and develops. Is born, gets bigger, grows old, dies. Produces strange new shoots. Not so long ago, her love for Mildred was a burning, vibrating joy. Her fingers always thinking about Mildred's skin. Her tongue thinking of her nipples. Now it's just as big as before, just as strong. But in the darkness it's become pale and needy. It absorbs everything that is in Lisa. Her love for Mildred makes her exhausted and unhappy.

She is just so incredibly tired of thinking about Mildred all the time. There's no room for anything else in her head. Mildred and Mildred. Where she is, what she's doing, what she said, what she meant by this or that. She can yearn for her all day long, only to quarrel with her when she finally arrives. The wound on Mildred's hand healed long ago. It's as if it had never been there.

Lisa looks at the time. It's well after midnight. She puts Majken on the lead and walks down to the main road. Thinks she'll go down to the jetty to see if Mildred's boat is there.

On the way she passes Lars-Gunnar and Nalle's house.

She notices that the car isn't there.

Afterward. Every single day afterward, she thinks about that. All the time. That Lars-Gunnar's car wasn't there. That Lars-Gunnar is all Nalle's got. That nothing can bring Mildred back to life.

Måns Wenngren rings and wakes Rebecka Martinsson. Her voice is warm, a little bit hoarse because it's early.

"Up you get!" he orders. "Get yourself a coffee and something to eat. Have a shower and get yourself ready. I'll ring again in twenty minutes. You need to be ready by then."

He's done this before. When he was married to Madelene and still putting up with her periodic agoraphobia and panic attacks and God knows what else, he used to talk her through visits to the dentist, meals with relatives, buying shoes at the NK department store. Every cloud . . . at least he knows the technique by now.

He rings after twenty minutes. Rebecka answers like an obedient Girl Guide. Now she's to get in the car, drive into town and take out enough money to pay the rent on her cabin in Poikkijärvi.

The next time he calls, he tells her to drive down to Poikkijärvi, park outside the bar and ring him.

"Right," says Måns when she calls him. "It'll take a minute and a half, then the whole thing will be behind you. Go in and pay. You don't need to say a word if you don't want to. Just hold out the money. When you've done that, get back in the car and call me again. Okay?"

"Okay," says Rebecka, like a child.

She sits in the car and looks at the bar. It looks white and slightly scruffy in the bright autumn sunshine. She wonders who's there. Micke or Mimmi?

Lars-Gunnar opens his eyes. It's Stefan Wikström who wakes him through the dream. His pathetic cries, whining and whimpering as he falls to his knees by the lake. When he knows.

He's been asleep in the armchair in the living room. His gun is on his knee. He gets up with difficulty, his back and shoulders stiff. He goes up to Nalle's room. Nalle is still fast asleep.

He should never have married Eva, of course. But he was just a stupid man from Norrland. Easy prey for somebody like her.

He's always been big. He was fat even as a child. At that time children were skinny little sprats chasing after footballs. They were thin and quick and threw snowballs at fat boys lumbering home as fast as their legs would carry them. Home to Dad. Who hit them with his belt if he felt like it.

I've never raised a hand to Nalle, he thinks. I never would.

But Lars-Gunnar the fat boy grew up and did very well in school despite the hassles. He trained to be a policeman and moved back home. And now he was a different man. It's not easy to return to the village of your childhood without falling back into the role you had before. But Lars-Gunnar had changed during his year at the police training college. And you don't mess with a policeman. He had new friends too. In town. Colleagues. He got a place on the hunting team. And because he wasn't afraid of hard work and was good at planning and organizing, he soon became the leader of the hunt. The idea had been to make it a rotating post, but it never happened. Lars-Gunnar thinks it probably suited the rest of them to have somebody planning and organizing things. In a little corner of his mind he's also aware that nobody would have dared to question his right to continue as leader. That's good. No harm in a bit of respect. And he's earned that respect. Not exploited it as some would have done.

No, his problem has been that he's too nice. Always thinks well of his fellow men. Like Eva.

It's hard not to blame himself. But he'd turned fifty when he met her. Lived alone all those years, because things never worked out with women. He was still kind of slow with them, conscious that his body was far too big. And then there was Eva. Who leaned her head against his chest. Her head almost disappeared in his hand when he held her close. "My little one," he used to say.

But when it didn't suit her any longer, she'd cleared off. Left him and the boy.

He can hardly remember the months that dragged by after she left. It was like a darkness. He'd thought people were looking at him in the village. Wondered what they were saying about him behind his back.

Nalle turns over laboriously in his sleep. The bed creaks beneath him.

I must . . . thinks Lars-Gunnar, and loses the thread of his thought.

It's difficult to concentrate. But everyday life. That has to carry on. That's the whole point. His and Nalle's everyday life. The life Lars-Gunnar has created for them both.

I must get some shopping, he thinks. Milk and bread and margarine. Everything's running out.

He goes downstairs and rings Mimmi.

"I'm going into town," he says. "Nalle's asleep and I don't want to wake him up. If he comes over to you, give him some breakfast, will you?"

* * *

"Is he there?"

Anna-Maria Mella had phoned the medical examiner's office in Luleå. Anna Granlund, the autopsy technician, answered, but Anna-Maria wanted to speak to Lars Pohjanen, the senior police surgeon. Anna Granlund kept an eye on him like a mother looking after her sick child. She kept the autopsy room in perfect order. Opened up the bodies for him, lifted out the organs, put them back when he'd finished, stitched them up and wrote the major part of his reports as well.

"He can't retire," she'd said to Anna-Maria on one occasion. "It's like a marriage in the end, you know; I've got used to him, I don't want anybody else."

And Lars Pohjanen kept plodding on. Seemed as if he were breathing through a pipe, sucking out the fluid. Just talking made him breathless. A year or so earlier he'd had an operation for lung cancer.

Anna-Maria could see him in her mind's eye. He was probably asleep on the scruffy seventies sofa in the staff room. The ashtray beside his well-worn clogs. His green scrubs spread over him like a blanket.

"Yes, he's here," Anna Granlund replied. "Just a minute."

Pohjanen's voice on the other end of the phone, scratchy and rattling.

"Tell me," said Anna-Maria, "you know how bloody useless I am at reading."

"There isn't much. Hrrrm. Shot in the chest from the front. Then in the head, at very close range. There's an explosive effect in the exit wound from the head."

A long intake of breath, the sucking noise.

". . . waterlogged skin, but not swollen . . . although you know when he disappeared . . ."

"Friday night."

"I'd assume he's been there since then. Minor damage to those parts of the skin not covered by clothing, the hands and face. The fish have been nibbling. Not much more. Have you found the bullets?"

"They're still looking. Any signs of a struggle? No other injuries?"

"No."

"And otherwise?"

Pohjanen's voice became snappy.

"Nothing, I told you. You'll have to ask somebody . . . to read the report out loud for you."

"I meant how were things with you."

"Oh, I see," he said, his tone instantly more amiable. "Everything's crap, of course."

*   *   *

Sven-Erik Stålnacke was talking to the police psychiatrist. He was sitting in the parking lot in his car. He liked her voice. Right from the start he'd taken to its warmth. And he liked the fact that she spoke slowly. Most women in Kiruna talked too bloody fast. And loudly. It was like a hail of bullets, you didn't stand a chance. He could hear Anna-Maria's voice in his head: "What do you mean, you don't stand a chance, we're the ones that don't stand a chance. No chance of getting a sensible answer within a reasonable amount of time. You ask: How was it, then? And then there's silence, and more bloody silence, and after an interminable consideration the answer comes: Good. Then it's hell trying to squeeze out anything more— from Robert, anyway. So we have to kind of talk for two. Don't stand a chance? Do me a favor."

Now he was listening to the psychiatrist's voice and he could hear her sense of humor. Although the conversation was serious. If he'd just been a few years younger . . .

"No," she said. "I don't believe it's a copycat murder. Mildred Nilsson was put on display. Stefan Wikström's body wasn't even meant to be found. And no use of violence to relieve tension either. This is a completely different modus operandi. It could be another person altogether. So the answer to your question is no. It's highly unlikely that Stefan Wikström was murdered by a serial killer suffering from a psychological disorder, and that the murder was committed in a highly emotional state and inspired by Viktor Strandgård. Either it was somebody else, or Mildred Nilsson and Stefan Wikström were killed for a more, how shall I put it, down to earth reason."

"Yes?"

"I mean, Mildred's murder seems very . . . emotional. But Stefan's murder is more like . . ."

". . . an execution."

"Exactly! It feels a bit like a crime of passion. I'm just speculating now, I want you to bear that in mind, I'm just trying to communicate the emotional picture I'm getting . . . okay?"

"Fine."

"Like a crime of passion, then. Husband kills his wife in a rage. Then kills the lover in a more cold-blooded way."

"But they weren't a couple," said Sven-Erik.

Then he thought, as far as we know.

"I don't mean they're a married couple. I just mean . . ."

She fell silent.

". . . I don't know what I mean," she said. "There could be a link. It could definitely be the same perpetrator. Psychopath. Certainly. Maybe. But not necessarily, not at all. And not to the extent that your grasp on reality has completely lost its basis in reality."

It was time to hang up. Sven-Erik did so with a pang of loss. And Manne was still missing.

Rebecka Martinsson walks into Micke's. Three people are having breakfast in the bar. Elderly men who look at her appreciatively. A real live beautiful woman. Always welcome. Micke's mopping the floor.

"Hi," he says to Rebecka, putting the mop and bucket aside. "Come with me."

Rebecka follows him into the kitchen.

"I'm really sorry," he says. "Everything turned out wrong on Saturday. But when Lars-Gunnar told us, I just didn't know what to think. Were you the one that killed those pastors in Jiekajärvi?"

"Yes. Although it was actually two pastors and a . . ."

"I know. A madman, wasn't it? It was in all the papers. Although they never said what your name was. They never put Thomas Söderberg's name or Vesa Larsson's either, but everybody around here knew who it was. It must have been terrible."

She nods. It must have been.

"On Saturday, I thought maybe what Lars-Gunnar said was true. That you'd come here to snoop. I did ask you if you were a journalist and you said no, but then I thought well, no, maybe she isn't a journalist, but she works for a newspaper all the same. But you don't, do you?"

"No, I . . . I ended up here by mistake, because Torsten Karlsson and I were looking for somewhere to eat."

"The guy who was with you the first time?"

"Yes. And it isn't something I usually tell people. Everything that happened . . . then. Anyway, I ended up staying here, because I wanted some peace, and because I didn't dare go out to Kurravaara. My grandmother's house is out there and . . . but in the end I went there with Nalle after all. He's my hero."

The last remark is accompanied by a smile.

"I came to pay for the cabin," she says, holding out the money.

Micke takes it and gives her change.

"I've included your wages as well. What does your other boss think about you working in a bar on the side?"

Rebecka laughs.

"Oh, now you've got a hold over me!"

"You ought to say good-bye to Nalle, you'll be passing his house on your way. If you take a right up toward the chapel . . ."

"I know, but it's probably a really bad idea, his father . . ."

"Lars-Gunnar's in town and Nalle's on his own at home."

No chance, thinks Rebecka. There are limits.

"Say good-bye for me," she says.

Back in the car she rings Måns.

"I've done it," she says.

Måns Wenngren answers her the way he used to answer his wife. He doesn't even need to think about it.

"That's my girl!"

Then he quickly adds:

"Well done, Martinsson. I've got to go to a meeting now. Talk to you soon."

Rebecka sits there with her cell phone in her hand.

Måns Wenngren, she thinks. He's like the mountains. It's raining and it's horrible. Howling wind. You're tired and your shoes are soaked through and you don't really know who you are. The map doesn't seem to match the reality. And then all of a sudden the clouds part. Your clothes dry out in the wind. You sit on the side of the mountain looking down over a sun-drenched valley. Suddenly it's all worth it.

She tries to call Maria Taube, but gets no reply. Sends a text: "Everything fine. Call me."

She drives away down the main road. Tunes the car radio to some kind of background music.

By the turning off toward the chapel, she meets Nalle. A shiver of guilt and sorrow runs down her spine. She raises her hand and waves to him. In the rearview mirror she can see him waving back at her. Waving like mad. Then he starts to run after the car. He's not very fast, but he won't give up. Suddenly she sees him fall. It looks bad. He tumbles down into the ditch.

Rebecka stops the car by the side of the road. Looks in the rearview mirror. He doesn't get up. She moves fast now. Jumps out of the car and runs back.

"Nalle!" she shouts. "Nalle!"

What if he's hit his head on a stone?

He's lying there in the ditch, smiling up at her. Like a beetle on its back.

"Becka!" he says when she appears.

Of course I have to say good-bye, she thinks. What kind of person am I?

He gets to his feet. She brushes him down.

"Bye then, Nalle," she says. "It was really good fun . . ."

"Come with," he says, tugging at her arm like a child. "Come with!"

He turns on his heel and lumbers away up the road. He's going home.

"No, really, I . . ." she begins.

But Nalle keeps on going. Doesn't turn around. Is confident that she's following him.

Rebecka looks at the car. It's parked tidily by the side of the road. Clearly visible to other drivers. She could go with him for a little while. She sets off after him.

"Wait for me, then!" she calls.

Lisa stops the car outside the vet's. The dogs know exactly where they are. This is not a nice place. They all get up and look out through the car window. Jaws hanging open. Tongues lolling. The German begins to shed dandruff. He always does that when he's nervous. White scales work their way up through his fur and cover his brown coat like snow. Their tails are plastered to their stomachs.

Lisa goes in. The dogs are left in the car.

Aren't we coming with you? their eyes ask her. Are we going to get away without any injections, examinations, frightening smells and those humiliating white plastic funnels round our heads?

Annette, the vet, comes to meet her. They sort out the payment, Annette deals with it herself. There's only the two of them there. No other staff. Nobody in the waiting room. Lisa is moved by her consideration.

The only thing Annette asks is:

"Are you taking them with you?"

Lisa shakes her head. She hasn't actually thought that far

ahead. She's only just managed to think this far. And now she's here. They'll become garbage. She pushes aside the idea of how unworthy that is. That she owes them more than that.

"How shall we do this?" asks Lisa. "Shall I bring them in one at a time, or what?"

Annette looks at her.

"That'll be too hard for you, I think. Let's bring them all in, then I can give them something to calm them down first."

Lisa staggers out.

"Stay!" she warns them as she opens the tailgate.

She puts on their leads. Doesn't want to risk any of them running away.

Into reception, the dogs around her legs. Through the waiting room, past the office and the treatment room.

Annette opens the door to the operating room.

The panting. The sound of their claws clicking and scrabbling across the floor. They get entangled in each other's leads. Lisa pulls at them and tries to untangle them as she walks toward that room, just get them in there.

They've made it at last. They're in that ugly room with its ugly red plastic floor and blotchy brown walls. Lisa catches her thigh on the black operating table. All the claws that have scratched the floor have enabled the dirt to work its way down into the plastic matting so that it's impossible to scrub it clean. It's turned into a dark red pathway from the door and around the table. On one of the wall cupboards there's a ghastly poster of a little girl surrounded by a sea of flowers. She's holding a floppy-eared puppy on her lap. The clock on the wall has a text running across the face from the ten to the two: "The time has come."

The door glides shut behind Annette.

Lisa unclips their leads.

"We'll start with Bruno," says Lisa. "He's so stubborn, he'll still be the last to lie down. You know what he's like."

Annette nods. While Lisa strokes Bruno's ears and chest, Annette gives him a sedative injection into the muscle of his foreleg.

"Who's my best boy?" asks Lisa.

Then he looks at her. Straight in the eye, although that isn't what dogs do. Then he glances quickly away. Bruno is a dog who maintains the correct etiquette. Looking the leader of the pack in the eye is not allowed, no way.

"You're a patient boy, aren't you," says Annette, giving him a pat when she's finished.

Soon Lisa is sitting on the floor beneath the window. The radiator is burning into her back. Sicky-Morris, Bruno, Karelin and Majken are lying on the floor around her, half asleep. Majken's head resting on one thigh. Sicky-Morris on the other. Annette pushes Bruno and Karelin closer to Lisa, so that she has them all with her.

There are no words. Only a terrible ache in her throat. Their warm bodies beneath her hands.

To think you've managed to love me, she thinks.

Someone who carries such a hopeless weight inside her. But a dog's love is simple. You run about in the forest. You're happy. You lie basking in each other's warmth. Relax and feel good.

The electric razor buzzes, then Annette inserts a canula into their forelegs.

It happens quickly. All too quickly. Only the last thing is left to do. Where are her farewell thoughts? The ache in her throat swells into an unbearable pain. It hurts so much, everywhere. Lisa is shaking as if she has a fever.

"I'll do it, then," says Annette.

And she gives them the injection that puts them to sleep.

It takes half a minute. They are lying there as they were before. Their heads on her lap. Bruno's back pressed against the bottom of her back. Majken's tongue is lolling out of her mouth in a way that it doesn't do when she's asleep.

Lisa thinks she'll get up. But she can't.

The tears are just beneath the skin of her face. Her face is trying to resist. It's like a tug-of-war. The muscles are fighting against it. Wanting to pull her mouth and eyebrows back into their normal expression, but the tears squeeze their way out. Finally she cracks into a grotesque, sobbing grimace. Tears and snot pour out. To think it can be so unbearably painful. The tears have been waiting behind her eyes, and it's been like pressing down the lid of a pan. Now they've boiled over and are running down her face. Down onto Sicky-Morris.

A cross between a groan and a whimper emerges from her throat. It sounds so ugly. A kind of oohoo, oohoo. She can hear it herself, this dried up condemned old woman moaning. She gets up on all fours. Hugs the dogs. Her movements are violent and reckless. She crawls among them, pushing her arms under their limp bodies. Strokes their eyelids, their noses, their ears, their stomachs. Pushes her face against their heads.

The tears are like a storm. They snatch and tear at her body. She snivels and tries to swallow. But it's hard to swallow when she's on all fours with her head down. In the end the snot trickles out of her mouth. She wipes it away with her hand.

At the same time, she can hear a voice. Another Lisa who is standing there watching her. Who says: What kind of a person are you? What about Mimmi?

And she stops crying. Just as she's thinking it'll never stop.

It's remarkable. The whole summer has been a list of things to do. One by one she's ticked them off. Tears weren't on the list. They put themselves there. She didn't want them. She's afraid of them. Afraid of drowning in them.

And when they came. At first they were horrible, an unbearable torment, darkness. But then. Then the tears became a refuge. A place to rest. A waiting room before the next thing on the list. Then a part of her suddenly wanted to stay there among the tears. Put off the other thing which is going to happen. And then the tears leave her. Say: that's it, then. And just stop.

She gets up. There's a hand basin, she grabs the edge and pulls herself to her feet. Annette has obviously left the room.

Her eyes are swollen, they feel like half tennis balls. She presses her icy fingertips against her eyelids. Turns on the tap and splashes her face. There are some rough paper towels beside the basin. She dries her face and blows her nose, avoids looking in the mirror. The paper rasps against her nose.

She looks down at the dogs. She's so exhausted, worn out with her tears, that she isn't capable of feeling so strongly any longer. The overwhelming grief is just like a memory. She crouches down and gives each dog a much more thoughtful caress.

Then she leaves the room. Annette is busy at the computer in the office. All Lisa needs to do is mutter a good-bye.

Out into the September sunshine. That stabs and torments her. Sharply defined shadows. The sun is in her eyes, except when a few clouds drift by. She gets in the car and flips down the sun visor. Starts the car and drives through town before driving out onto the road to Norway.

She thinks about precisely nothing during the journey. Except for how the road curves its way forward. How the pictures change. Bright blue sky. White, ragged clouds shredding themselves as they scud along high above the mountains. Sharply defined, rugged ravines. The length of Torneträsk, like a shining blue stone with yellow gold spun around it.

When she has passed Katterjåkk it appears. A huge truck. Lisa keeps driving fast. She undoes her seat belt.

Rebecka Martinsson followed Nalle down into the cellar. A stone staircase painted green made its way down beneath the house. He opened a door. Inside was a room that was used as a larder, and for carpentry and general storage. Lots of things everywhere. It was damp. The white paint was covered with black spots in places. Here and there the plaster had come away. There were basic storage shelves covered in jam jars, boxes of nails and screws and all kinds of bits and pieces, tins of paint, tins of varnish that had evaporated, brushes that had gone hard, sandpaper, buckets, electrical tools, piles of flex. Tools hung on the walls where there was space.

Nalle shushed her. Placed his forefinger on his lips. He took her hand and led her to a chair; she sat down. He knelt down on the cellar floor and tapped on it with his fingernail.

Rebecka sat in silence, waiting.

He took an almost empty packet of biscuits out of his breast pocket. Rustled the packet as he unfolded it, took out a biscuit and broke it into pieces.

And then a little mouse came scampering across the floor. It ran over to Nalle following an S-shaped route, stopped by his knees, reared up on its hind legs. It was brownish gray, no more than four or five centimeters long. Nalle held out half a biscuit. The mouse tried to take it from him, but as Nalle didn't let go, it stayed and ate. The only sound was small nibbling noises.

Nalle turned to Rebecka.

"Mouse," he said loudly. "Little."

Rebecka thought it would be frightened away when he spoke so loudly, but it stayed where it was and kept right on nibbling. She nodded at him and gave him a big smile. It was a strange sight. Great big Nalle and the tiny mouse. She wondered how it had come about. How he'd managed to get it to overcome its fear. Could he have been patient enough to sit quietly down here, waiting for it? Maybe.

You're a very special boy, she thought.

Nalle reached out his forefinger and tried to pat the mouse on the back, but then fear overcame hunger. It shot away like a gray streak and disappeared among all the rubbish standing by the wall.

Rebecka watched it.

Time to go. Couldn't leave the car parked like that indefinitely.

Nalle was saying something.

She looked at him.

"Mouse," he said. "Little!"

A feeling of sorrow came over her. She was standing here in an old cellar with a mentally handicapped boy. She felt closer to him than she'd been to another human being for a long, long time.

Why can't I? she thought. Can't like people. Don't trust them. But you can trust Nalle. He can't pretend to be what he's not.

"Bye then, Nalle," she said.

"Bye then," he said, without the least trace of sorrow in his voice.

She went up the green stone staircase. She didn't hear the car pull up outside. Didn't hear the footsteps on the porch. Just as she opened the door into the hallway, the outside door was opened. Lars-Gunnar's enormous bulk filled the doorway. Like a mountain blocking her path. Something shriveled up inside her. And she looked into his eyes. He looked at her.

"What the hell," was all he said.

The scene of crime team found a rifle bullet at nine thirty in the morning. They dug it out of the ground by the shore of the lake. Caliber 30-06.

By quarter past ten the police had matched the firearms register with the motor vehicle database. All those who owned a diesel car and were registered as owning a gun.

Anna-Maria Mella leaned back in her office chair. It really was a luxury item. You could recline the back so you were almost lying down, just like in a bed. Like a dentist's chair, but without the dentist.

Four hundred and seventy-three people matched. She glanced through the names.

Then she caught sight of one name she recognized. Lars-Gunnar Vinsa.

He owned a diesel Merc. She checked in the firearms register. He was registered for three weapons. Two rifles and one shotgun. One of the rifles was a Tikka. Caliber 30-06.

What they really ought to do was take in all the guns of the right caliber for testing. But maybe they ought to talk to him first. Although that wasn't likely to be particularly pleasant when it was a former colleague.

She checked the time. Half ten. She could drive out there with Sven-Erik after lunch.

Lars-Gunnar Vinsa looks at Rebecka Martinsson. Halfway to town he'd remembered that he'd forgotten his wallet, and turned back.

What kind of bloody conspiracy was this? He'd told Mimmi he was going out. Had she phoned that lawyer? He can hardly believe it. But that's what must have happened. And she's come dashing down here to snoop around.

The cell phone in the woman's hand rings. She doesn't answer it. He stares doggedly at her ringing phone. They stand there motionless. The phone goes on ringing and ringing.

* * *

Rebecka thinks she ought to answer. It's probably Maria Taube. But she can't. And when she doesn't answer, it's suddenly written in his eyes. And she knows. And he knows that she knows.

The paralysis passes. The phone ends up on the floor. Did he knock it out of her hand? Did she throw it down?

He's standing in her way. She can't get out. A feeling of absolute terror seizes her.

She turns and runs up the staircase to the top floor. It's narrow and steep. The wallpaper dirty with age. A flowery pattern. The varnish on the stairs is like thick glass. She scrabbles rapidly on all fours, like a crab. Mustn't slip now.

She can hear Lars-Gunnar. Heavy behind her.

It's like running into a trap. Where will she go?

The bathroom door in front of her. She dashes inside.

Somehow she manages to shut the door and makes her fingers turn the lock.

The handle is pressed down from the outside.

There's a window, but there's nothing left inside her that can manage to try and escape. The only thing that exists is fear. She can't stand up. Sinks down on the toilet seat. Then she begins to shake. Her body is jerking and shuddering. Her elbows are pressed against her stomach. Her hands are in front of her face, they're shaking so violently that she involuntarily hits herself on the mouth, the nose, the chin. Her fingers are bent like claws.

A heavy thud, a crash against the outside of the door. She screws her eyes tight shut. Tears pour out. She wants to press her hands against her ears, but they won't obey, they just keep shaking and shaking.

"Mummy!" she sobs as the door flies open with a bang. It hits her knees. It hurts. Someone is lifting her up by her clothes. She refuses to open her eyes.

*   *   *

He lifts her by the collar. She's whimpering.

"Mummy, Mummy!"

He can hear himself whimpering. Äiti, äiti! It's more than sixty years ago, and his father is throwing his mother around the kitchen like a glove. She's locked Lars-Gunnar and his brother and sisters in the bedroom. He's the eldest. The little girls are sitting on the sofa, ashen-faced and silent. He and his brother are hammering on the door. His mother sobbing and pleading. Things falling on the floor. His father wanting the key. He'll get it soon. Soon it will be Lars-

Gunnar's and his brother's turn, while the girls watch. His mother will be locked in the bedroom. The strap will come into play. For something. He can't remember what. There were always so many reasons.

He slams her head against the hand basin. She shuts up. The child's tears and his mother's "Älä lyö! Älä lyö!" also fall silent in his head. He lets go of her. She falls down onto the floor.

When he turns her over she looks at him with big, silent eyes. Blood is pouring from her forehead. It's just like that time he hit a reindeer on the way to Gällivare. The same big eyes. And the shaking.

He grabs hold of her feet. Drags her out into the hallway.

Nalle is standing on the stairs. He catches sight of Rebecka.

"What?" he shouts.

A loud, anxious cry. He sounds like a long-tailed skua.

"What?"

"It's nothing, Nalle!" shouts Lars-Gunnar. "Out you go."

But Nalle is terrified. Not listening. Takes a few more steps up the stairs. Looks at Rebecka lying there. Shouts again, "What?"

"Didn't you hear what I said?" roars Lars-Gunnar. "Outside!"

He lets go of Rebecka's feet and waves his hands at Nalle. In the end he goes down the stairs and pushes him out into the yard. He locks the door.

Nalle stands outside. He can hear him out there. "What? What?" Fear and confusion in his voice. Can see him in his mind's eye, walking round and round on the porch, completely at a loss.

He feels an overwhelming rage toward the woman upstairs. It's her fault. She should have left them in peace.

He takes the stairs in three bounds. It's like Mildred Nilsson. She should have left them in peace. Him and Nalle and this village.

* * *

Lars-Gunnar is standing out in the yard, pegging out washing. It's late May. No leaves yet, but one or two things are starting to appear in the flower beds. It's a sunny, windy day. Nalle will be thirteen in the autumn. It's six years since Eva died.

Nalle is running around in the yard. He's good at amusing himself. It's just that you can never be alone. Lars-Gunnar misses that. Being left in peace sometimes.

The spring breeze tugs and pulls at the washing. Soon the sheets and underclothes will be hanging between the birch trees like a row of dancing flags.

Behind Lars-Gunnar stands the new priest Mildred Nilsson. How she can talk. It seems as if she'll never stop. Lars-Gunnar hesitates as he reaches for the underpants that are a bit tatty. They don't come up very white either, although they are clean.

But then he thinks, what the hell. Why should he be embarrassed in front of her?

She wants Nalle to be confirmed in the church.

"Listen," he says. "A couple of years ago some of those hallelujah types turned up here wanting to pray for him to be healed. I threw them out on their ear. I'm not that keen on the church."

"I'd never do that!" she says firmly. "I mean, of course I'll pray for him, but I promise to do it quietly at home, in my own room. But I'd never want him to be any different. You really have been blessed with a fine boy. He couldn't be any better."

* * *

Rebecka draws up her knees. Pushes them down. Draws them up. Pushes them down. Shuts herself in the bathroom again. Can't manage to get up. Crawls as far away as she can, into a corner. He's coming back up the stairs.

* * *

It was so bloody simple for Mildred to say that Nalle was a blessing, Lars-Gunnar thinks. She didn't have to look after him day and night. And she wasn't the one with a broken marriage behind her because of the child they'd had. She didn't need to worry. About the future. How Nalle would manage. About Nalle's puberty and sexuality. Standing there with the soiled sheets, wondering what the hell to do. No girl would want him. A mass of strange fears in his head, that he could become dangerous.

After the priest's visit the village women came running. Let the boy be confirmed, they said. And they offered to organize everything. Said Nalle would be bound to enjoy it, and if he didn't, they could just stop. Even Lars-Gunnar's cousin Lisa came to say her bit. Said she could sort out a suit, so he wouldn't be standing there in something that was too small.

Then Lars-Gunnar lost his temper. As if it was about the suit or the present.

"It's not about the money!" he roared. "I've always paid for him, haven't I? If I'd wanted to save money I'd have shoved him in an institution long ago! All right then, he can be confirmed!"

And he'd paid for a suit and a watch. If you had to pick two things Nalle had no use whatsoever for, it would be a suit and a watch. But Lars-Gunnar didn't say a word about it. Nobody was going to say he was mean behind his back.

Afterward it was as if something had changed. As if Mildred's friendship with the boy took something away from Lars-Gunnar. People forgot about the price he'd had to pay. Not that he had any big ideas about himself. But he hadn't had an easy life. His father's brutality toward the family. Eva's betrayal. The burden of being the single parent of a disturbed child. He could have made other choices. Simpler choices. But he educated himself and returned to the village. Became someone.

He hit rock bottom when Eva left. He stayed at home with Nalle, feeling as if nobody wanted him. The shame of being surplus to requirements.

And yet he still looked after Eva when she was dying. He kept Nalle at home. Looked after him. If you listened to Mildred Nilsson, he was bloody lucky to have such a fine boy. "Of course," Lars-Gunnar had said to one of the women, "but it's a heavy responsibility as well. A lot to worry about." And he'd got his answer: parents always worry about their children. He wouldn't have to be separated from Nalle, as other parents were when their children grew up and left home. They talked a load of crap. People who hadn't a clue what it was really like. But after that he kept quiet. How could anybody understand.

It was the same with Eva. Since Mildred had arrived, whenever Eva came up in the conversation, people said: "Poor soul." About her! Sometimes he wanted to ask what they meant by that. If they thought he was such a bastard to live with that she'd even left her own son?

He got the feeling they were talking about him behind his back.

Even then he regretted agreeing to Nalle's confirmation. But it was already too late. He couldn't forbid him to spend time with Mildred in the church, because that would just look like sour grapes. Nalle was enjoying himself. He hadn't the wit to see through Mildred.

So Lars-Gunnar let it carry on. Nalle had a life away from him. But who washed his clothes, who carried the responsibility and the worry?

And Mildred Nilsson. Lars-Gunnar now thinks he was her target all the time. Nalle was just a means to an end.

She moved into the priest's house and organized her female Mafia. Made them feel important. And they let themselves be led along like cackling geese.

It's obvious she had a grudge against him from the start. She envied him. He had a certain standing in the village, after all. Leader of the hunting team. He'd been a policeman. He listened to people too. Put others' needs before his own. And that gave him a certain level of respect and authority. She couldn't stand that. It was as if she set herself the task of taking everything away from him.

It turned into a kind of war between them, but only they could see it. She tried to discredit him. He defended himself as best he could. But he'd never had any aptitude for that kind of game.

*   *   *

The woman has crawled back into the bathroom. She's curled up on the floor between the toilet and the hand basin, holding her arms up over her face to protect herself. He grabs her feet and drags her down the stairs. Her head thumps rhythmically on every step. Thud, thud, thud. And Nalle's cry from outside: "What? What?" It's hard to close his ears to that. There has to be an end to it. There has to be an end to it now, at long last.

*   *   *

He remembers the trip to Majorca. It was one of Mildred's bright ideas. All of a sudden the young people in the church were going to a camp abroad. And Mildred wanted Nalle to go too. Lars-Gunnar had said no, definitely not. And Mildred had said the church would send an extra member of staff along, just for Nalle. The church would pay. "And just think," she said, "how much kids of this age normally cost. Slalom gear, trips, computer games, expensive stuff, expensive clothes . . ." And Lars-Gunnar had understood. "It's not about money," he'd said. But he'd realized that in the eyes of the villagers, that's exactly what it would look like. That he begrudged Nalle having things. That Nalle had to do without. That when Nalle finally had the opportunity to do something that would be fun . . . So Lars-Gunnar had to give in. All he could do was get out his wallet. And everybody said to him how nice it was that Mildred was so good to Nalle. Lucky for the boy that she'd moved here.

But Mildred wanted to see him go under, he knows that. When her windows got smashed, or when that idiot Magnus Lindmark tried to set fire to her shed, she didn't report it to the police. And so there was talk. Just as she'd intended. The police can't do anything. When you really need them, all they can do is just stand there. It really got to Lars-Gunnar. He was the one who had to put up with the embarrassment.

And then she turned her attention to his place on the hunting team.

It might be the church's mark on the paper. But the forest belongs to him. He's the one who knows it. It's true that the cost of the lease has been low. But really, in all fairness, the hunters ought to get paid for shooting. Elk cause enormous damage to the forest, chewing the bark of the trees.

The autumn elk hunt. Planning with the other guys. Walking through the forest in the early morning. Before sunrise. The dogs are excited, pulling on their leads. Sniffing at the gray darkness deep in the forest. Somewhere in there is their quarry. The hunt itself, during the day. Autumn air, the sound of dogs barking far away. The sense of togetherness when you're dealing with the kill. Struggling with the body in the slaughterhouse. Chatting around the fire in the cabin in the evening.

She wrote a letter. Didn't dare bring it up face-to-face. Wrote that she knew Torbjörn had been convicted of breaking the law on hunting. That he hadn't lost his firearms license. That it was Lars-Gunnar who'd sorted it all out. That he and Torbjörn couldn't be permitted to hunt on church land. "It isn't only inappropriate, but also objectionable in view of the fact that the church is intending to offer protection to the she-wolf," she wrote.

He can feel the pressure squeezing his chest as he thinks about it. She would plunge him into isolation, that's what she wanted. Make him into a fucking loser. Like Malte Alajärvi. No job, no hunting.

He'd talked to Torbjörn Ylitalo. "What the fuck can we do?" Torbjörn had said. "I'll be glad if I can just hang on to my job." Lars-Gunnar had felt as if he were sinking into a swamp. He could see himself in a few years. Growing old, stuck at home with Nalle. They could sit there like two idiots, gawping at game shows on TV.

It wasn't right. All that business about the license! It was nearly twenty years ago, after all! It was just an excuse to do him some damage.

"Why?" he'd said to Torbjörn. "What does she want to do to me?" And Torbjörn had shrugged his shoulders.

A week went by without him speaking to a single soul. A foretaste of what life would be like. In the evenings he drank, just so that he could get to sleep.

The night before midsummer's eve he was sitting in the kitchen having a little celebration. Well, maybe celebration wasn't quite the word. Shut in the kitchen with his own thoughts. Poured himself a drink, talked to himself, drank the drink on his own. Went to bed in the end, tried to sleep. It was as if something was thumping in his chest. Something he hadn't felt since he was a child.

Then he got in the car and tried to pull himself together. He remembers he almost put the car in the ditch when he was reversing out of the yard. And then Nalle came running out in just his underpants. Lars-Gunnar thought he'd fallen asleep hours ago. He was waving and shouting. Lars-Gunnar had to switch off the engine. "You can come with me," he said. "But you need to put some clothes on." "No, no," said Nalle, refusing to let go of the car door. "It's okay, I'm not going anywhere. Go and put something on."

There's a kind of fog in his head when he tries to remember. He wanted to talk to her. She was going to fucking listen to him. Nalle fell asleep in the passenger seat.

He remembers hitting her. Thinking: That's enough. That's enough now.

She wouldn't stop making a noise. However much he hit her. Rattling and squeaking. Breathing. He dragged off her shoes and socks. Shoved her socks in her mouth.

He was still furious when he carried her up to the church. Hung her up by the chain in front of the organ pipes. As he stood up there in the gallery he thought it didn't matter if anybody came, if anybody had seen him.

Then Nalle came in. He'd woken up and came stumbling into the church. Suddenly he was standing down there in the aisle gazing up at Lars-Gunnar and Mildred with huge eyes. He didn't say a word.

Lars-Gunnar sobered up at once. He was angry with Nalle. And suddenly terrified. He remembers that very clearly. Remembers dragging Nalle to the car. Driving away. And they didn't speak. Nalle didn't say anything.

Every day Lars-Gunnar was expecting them to come. But nobody came. Well, they came and asked if he'd seen anything, of course. Or knew anything. Asked him the same questions they were asking everybody else.

He remembered he'd put his work gloves on. They'd been in the trunk of the car. He hadn't done it intentionally. Hadn't been thinking about fingerprints or anything. It had just been automatic. If you're using a tool like a crowbar, you put your gloves on. Pure luck. Pure luck.

And then everything carried on as usual. Nalle didn't seem to remember anything. He was just the same as always. Lars-Gunnar had been just the same as always too. He slept well at night.

*   *   *

I was lying there like a wounded animal, he thinks now, as he stands there with this woman at his feet. Like an animal that lies down in a hollow, but it's only a matter of time before the huntsman catches up with it.

When Stefan Wikström rang he could hear it in his voice. That he knew. Just the fact that he was ringing Lars-Gunnar, why would he do that? They saw each other when they were hunting, but he didn't have anything to do with that milksop of a priest otherwise. And now he was ringing up. Telling him the parish priest seemed to be changing his mind about the future of the hunting team. Bertil Stensson might suggest to the church council that it was time to revoke the lease. And he talked about the elk hunt as if . . . as if he had something quite different to say about the whole thing.

And when Stefan rang, the fog in Lars-Gunnar's head cleared. He remembers standing by the jetty waiting for Mildred. His pulse throbbing like a jackhammer. He looked up at the priest's house. And somebody was standing at the upstairs window. He didn't remember that until Stefan Wikström rang.

What did he want with me? he thinks now. He wanted power over me. Like Mildred.

Lars-Gunnar and Stefan Wikström are sitting in the car on the way to the lake. Lars-Gunnar has said he's going to lift the boat out of the water for the winter and chain down the oars.

Stefan Wikström is whining about Bertil Stensson like a baby. Lars-Gunnar is listening with only half an ear. It's all about the hunting permit and the fact that Bertil doesn't appreciate the work Stefan does as a priest. And then Lars-Gunnar has to listen to his unbearable infantile babble about hunting. As if he understood anything about it. The little boy who got his place on the team as a present from the parish priest.

The constant babbling is confusing Lars-Gunnar. What does he want, the priest? It feels as if Stefan is holding the parish priest up to Lars-Gunnar as a small child holds up its arm when it's fallen over. Kiss it better.

He has no intention of being under the thumb of this little runt. He's prepared to pay the price for his actions. But that price is not going to be paid to Stefan Wikström. Never.

Stefan Wikström keeps his eyes on the section of the road that can be seen in the headlights. He gets carsick really easily. Has to keep looking ahead.

A sense of fear is beginning to steal over him. He can feel it writhing in his stomach like a slender snake.

They talk about all kinds of things. Not about Mildred. But her presence is tangible. It's almost as if she were sitting in the backseat.

Stefan Wikström thinks about the night before midsummer's eve. How he stood by the bedroom window. He saw somebody standing next to Mildred's boat. Suddenly the person took a few steps. Disappeared behind a little log cabin on the museum's land. He didn't see anything else. But he thought about it afterward, of course. That it was Lars-Gunnar. That he'd had something in his hand.

Even now, he doesn't think it was wrong not to tell the police. He and Lars-Gunnar are among the eighteen members of the hunting team. That makes him Lars-Gunnar's priest. Lars-Gunnar is part of his flock. A priest lives by different laws from normal citizens. As a priest, he couldn't point the finger at Lars-Gunnar. As a priest, he must be there when Lars-Gunnar is ready to talk.

This was another burden laid upon him. And he accepted it. Placed it in God's hands. Prayed: Thy will be done. And added: I cannot feel that thy yoke is gentle, thy burden light.

They've arrived, and get out of the car. He is given the chain to carry. Lars-Gunnar tells him to walk in front.

He sets off along the path in the moonlight.

Mildred is walking behind him. He can feel it. He's reached the lake. Drops the chain on the ground. Looks at it.

Mildred climbs into his ear.

Run! she says inside his head. Run!

But he can't run. He just stands there waiting. Hears Lars-Gunnar coming. Slowly he takes shape in the moonlight. And yes, he is carrying his gun.

*   *   *

Lars-Gunnar looks down at Rebecka Martinsson. After the trip down the stairs she's stopped shaking. But she's still conscious. Staring at him all the time.

* * *

Rebecka Martinsson looks up at the man. She's seen this image before. The man who is an eclipse of the sun. The face in shadow. The sun coming in through the kitchen window. Like a corona around his head. It's Pastor Thomas Söderberg. He is saying: I loved you like my own daughter. Soon she will smash his head.

When the man bends down over her she grabs hold of him. Well, grabs hold is putting it a bit strongly; the forefinger and middle finger of her right hand creep in under the neck band of his sweater. Only the weight of the hand itself draws him closer.

"How can a person live with that?"

He detaches her fingers from his sweater.

Live with what? he wonders. Stefan Wikström? He felt a greater sorrow that time when he shot a female elk over in Paksuniemi. That was over twenty years ago. The second after she fell, two calves emerged from the trees. Then they disappeared into the forest. He thought about his mistake for a long time. First the female. And then the fact that he hadn't reacted in time and shot the calves as well. They must have faced an agonizing death.

He opens the trapdoor in the kitchen that leads down to the cellar. Grabs hold of her and drags her toward the hole.

Nalle's hand is knocking on the kitchen window. His uncomprehending gaze between the plastic pelargoniums.

And now the woman comes to life. When she sees the hole in the floor. She begins to wriggle in his grasp. Grabs the leg of the kitchen table, the whole table is dragged along with her.

"Let go," he says, unclasping her fingers.

She scratches his face. Writhing and lashing out. A silent, jerky struggle.

He lifts her by the collar. Her feet leave the floor. Not a word comes out of her mouth. The scream is in her eyes: No! No!

He hurls her down like a bag of garbage. She falls backwards. A thud and a bang, then silence. He lets the trapdoor fall shut. Then he gets hold of the cupboard that stands over by the southern wall and drags it over the trapdoor with both hands. It weighs a ton, but he has the strength.

* * *

She opens her eyes. It takes a while for her to realize that she'd lost consciousness for a little while. But she can't have been out for long. A few seconds. She can hear Lars-Gunnar dragging something heavy over the trapdoor.

Her eyes are wide open, and she can't see a thing. Pitch dark. She can hear the footsteps and the dragging noise up above. Up onto her knees. Her right arm is dangling uselessly. Instinctively she places her left hand over her right arm at shoulder level and pulls the arm back into joint. It makes a crunching sound. A bolt of pain shoots from her shoulder down her arm and her back. Everything hurts. Apart from her face. She can't feel anything there at all. She touches it with her hand. It's somehow numb. And something is hanging off, loose and wet. Is it her lip? When she swallows she can taste blood.

Down on all fours. Earth beneath her hands. The dampness soaks through the knees of her jeans. It stinks of rat shit.

If she dies here. Then the rats will eat her.

She begins to crawl. Gropes ahead of her with her hand, looking for the staircase. Sticky cobwebs everywhere, winding themselves around the hand as it fumbles its way. Something rustles in the corner. There's the staircase. She's on her knees, with her hands resting on a step a bit higher up. Like a dog, up on its hind legs. She listens. And waits.

* * *

Lars-Gunnar has dragged the cupboard into place. He wipes his brow with the back of his hand.

Nalle's "What?" has stopped. Lars-Gunnar looks out of the window. Nalle is out in the yard, walking round in a circle. Lars-Gunnar recognizes the signs. Whenever Nalle is unhappy and afraid, he starts walking around like that. It can take half an hour to calm him down. It's as if he loses the ability to hear. The first time it happened, Lars-Gunnar felt so frustrated and powerless that he hit him in the end. The blow still burns inside him. He remembers looking at his hand, the one that had delivered the blow, and thinking about his own father. And it didn't make Nalle any better. Just worse. Now he knows you have to have patience. And time.

If only there were time.

He goes out into the yard. Tries, although he knows it won't work: "Nalle!"

But Nalle doesn't hear anything. Round and round he goes.

Lars-Gunnar has thought about this moment a thousand times. But in his thoughts Nalle has been sleeping peacefully. He and Lars-Gunnar have had a wonderful day. Maybe they've been in the forest. Or been on the river on the snow scooter. Lars-Gunnar has sat by Nalle's bed for a while. Nalle has fallen asleep, and then . . .

This is too much. It couldn't be any bloody worse than this. He runs his hand over his cheek. It seems as if he's crying.

And he sees Mildred in front of him. He's been on his way to this point ever since then. He realizes that now. The first blow. At the time he was full of rage toward her. But afterward. Afterward it was his own life he smashed to bits. Hung it up for everyone to see.

To the car. The rifle is there. It's loaded. It has been all summer. He releases the safety catch.

"Nalle," he says thickly.

He still wants to say good-bye. He would have liked to have done that.

"Nalle," he says to his big lad.

Now. Before it gets to the point where he can't hold the gun. He can't be sitting here when they arrive. Can't let them take Nalle away.

He raises the gun to his shoulder. Takes aim. Fires. The first bullet in the back. Nalle falls forward. The second bullet in the head.

Then he goes in.

What he'd like to do most of all is to open the trapdoor and kill her. What is she? Nothing.

But the way he feels at the moment, he hasn't the strength to shift the cupboard.

He slumps down on the kitchen sofa.

Then he gets up. Opens the door of the wall clock and stops the pendulum with his hand.

Sits down again.

The barrel in his mouth. It's been torture for as long as he can remember. This will be a relief. It will be over at last.

*   *   *

Down in the darkness she hears the shots. They come from outside. Two shots. Then the outside door slams. She hears footsteps across the kitchen floor. Then the final shot.

Something old wakes up inside her. Something from times past.

She scrambles up the steps to get away. Bangs her head on the trapdoor. Almost falls back down, but grabs hold of something.

It's impossible to shift the trapdoor. She bangs on it with her fists. Her knuckles are torn open. She rips off her nails.

Anna-Maria Mella drives into Lars-Gunnar Vinsa's yard at half past three in the afternoon. Sven-Erik is sitting beside her in the car. They haven't spoken all the way down to Poikkijärvi. It isn't a nice feeling, knowing that you're going to have to tell a former colleague that you're seizing his gun and taking it in for testing.

Anna-Maria is driving slightly too fast as usual, and she very nearly runs over the body lying on the gravel.

Sven-Erik curses. Anna-Maria slams the brakes on and they jump out of the car. Sven-Erik is already on his knees, feeling the side of the neck with his hand. A black swarm of heavy flies lifts from the bloody back of the head. He shakes his head in reply to Anna-Maria's unspoken question.

"It's Lars-Gunnar's boy," he says.

Anna-Maria looks toward the house. She hasn't got her gun with her. Shit.

"Don't you even think about doing anything stupid," Sven-Erik warns her. "Get in the car and we'll call for backup."

*   *   *

It'll take forever before the others get here, thinks Anna-Maria.

"Thirteen minutes," says Sven-Erik, checking the time.

It's Fred Olsson and Tommy Rantakyrö in an unmarked car. And four colleagues in bulletproof vests and black overalls.

Tommy Rantakyrö and Fred Olsson park up on the ridge and come running down to Lars-Gunnar's yard, crouching as they run. Sven-Erik has reversed Anna-Maria's car out of firing range of the house.

The second police car pulls up in the yard. They shelter behind it.

Sven-Erik Stålnacke picks up a megaphone.

"Hello!" he shouts. "Lars-Gunnar! If you're in there, come on out so we can have a chat."

No response.

Anna-Maria meets Sven-Erik's eyes and shakes her head. Nothing to wait for.

The four men in bulletproof vests go in. Two through the outside door. One first, the other right behind him. Two get in through a window at the back.

There isn't a sound, apart from the noise of breaking glass from the back of the house. The others wait. One minute. Two.

Then one of them comes out onto the porch and waves. Okay to come in.

Lars-Gunnar's body is lying on the floor in front of the kitchen sofa. The wall behind the sofa is spattered with his blood.

Sven-Erik and Tommy Rantakyrö push aside the cupboard that's standing in the middle of the floor on top of the trapdoor.

"There's somebody down here!" shouts Tommy Rantakyrö.

"Come on," he says, reaching down a hand.

But the person who's down there doesn't come. In the end Tommy climbs down. The others can hear him.

"Shit! Okay, take it easy. Can you stand up?"

She comes up through the trapdoor. It takes a long time. The others help her. Support her under the arms. That makes her whimper a little.

It takes a fraction of a second before Anna-Maria recognizes Rebecka Martinsson.

* * *

Half of Rebecka's face is swollen and black and blue. She has a large wound on her forehead and her upper lip is hanging off, held only by a flap of skin. "Looked like a pizza with everything on it," Tommy Rantakyrö will say much later.

Anna-Maria is thinking mainly of her teeth. They're clenched so tightly, as if her jaws have locked together.

"Rebecka," says Anna-Maria. "What . . ."

But Rebecka waves her away. Anna-Maria sees her glance at the body on the kitchen floor before she walks stiffly out through the door.

Anna-Maria Mella, Sven-Erik Stålnacke and Tommy Rantakyrö follow her out.

Outside the sky has turned gray. The clouds are hanging low, heavy with rain.

Fred Olsson is standing out in the yard.

Not a word passes his lips when he catches sight of Rebecka. But his mouth opens around the unspoken words, and his eyes are staring.

Anna-Maria is watching Rebecka Martinsson. She's standing like a statue in front of Nalle's dead body. There's something in her eyes. They all sense instinctively that this is not the time to touch her. She's in a place of her own.

"Where the hell are the paramedics?" asks Anna-Maria.

"On the way," someone replies.

Anna-Maria glances upward. It's starting to spit with rain. They need to get something over the body lying outside. A tarpaulin or something.

Rebecka takes a step backwards. She waves her hand in front of her face as if there were something there she was trying to shoo away.

Then she begins to walk. First of all she staggers toward the house. Then she sways and walks toward the river instead. It's as if she were blindfolded, doesn't seem to know where she is or where she's going.

The rain comes. Anna-Maria feels the chill of autumn like a torrent of cold air. It sweeps across the yard. Heavy, cold rain. A thousand icy needles. Anna-Maria pulls up the zip of her blue jacket, her chin disappears into the neckline. She needs to sort out that tarpaulin for the body.

"Keep an eye on her," she shouts to Tommy Rantakyrö, pointing at Rebecka Martinsson who is still tottering away. "Keep her away from the gun in there, and from yours too. And don't let her go down to the river."

*   *   *

Rebecka Martinsson makes her way across the yard. There's a big dead dead dead boy lying on the gravel. Not long ago he was sitting in the cellar with a biscuit in his hand, feeding a mouse.

It's windy. The wind is roaring down inside her ears.

The sky is filled with black scratch marks, deep gouges that in their turn are filled with black ink. Is it raining? Has it started raining? She raises her hands tentatively toward the sky to see if they get wet. Her sleeves fall back, exposing the thin, bare wrists, the hands like naked birch trees. She drops her scarf on the grass.

*   *   *

Tommy Rantakyrö catches up with Rebecka Martinsson.

"Listen," he says. "Don't go down to the river. There'll be an ambulance here in a minute, and then . . ."

She isn't listening. Staggers on toward the riverbank. Now he thinks this is unpleasant. She's unpleasant. Horrible staring eyes in that raw meat face. He doesn't want to be alone with her.

"Sorry," he says, grabbing hold of her arm. "I can't . . . You just can't go down there."

*   *   *

Now the world splits open like a rotten fruit. Somebody's got hold of her arm. It's Pastor Vesa Larsson. He no longer has a face. A brown dog's head is sitting on his shoulders. The black doggy eyes are looking accusingly at her. He had children. And dogs, who can't weep.

"What do you want from me?" she screams.

Pastor Thomas Söderberg is standing there too. He is lifting dead babies out of the well. Bending down and lifting them out, one after the other. Holding them upside down, by the heel or by their little feet. They are naked and white. Their skin is loose, they've been in the water for a long time. He throws them onto a great big pile. It grows and grows in front of him.

When she quickly turns away, she's standing face to face with her mother. She's so clean and smart.

"Don't you touch me," she says to Rebecka. "Do you understand? Do you understand what you've done?"

*   *   *

Anna-Maria Mella has got hold of a rug. She's going to put it over Lars-Gunnar's son. It's not so easy to know what the scene of crime technicians will want her to do. She also needs to set up some kind of barricade before the whole village starts turning up. And the press. Why did it have to bloody rain? In the middle of everything, when she's shouting about barricades and half-running with the rug, she longs for Robert. For this evening, when she'll be able to sob in his arms. Because everything is so pointless and so unbearable.

Tommy Rantakyrö calls out to her and she turns.

"I can't hold her," he shouts.

He's wrestling with Rebecka Martinsson in the grass. Her arms are flailing, hitting out wildly. She breaks free and begins to run down to the river.

Sven-Erik Stålnacke and Fred Olsson set off after her. Anna-Maria hardly has time to react before Sven-Erik has almost caught up with her. Fred Olsson is right behind him. They grab hold of Rebecka. She's like a snake in Sven-Erik's arms.

"It's okay," says Sven-Erik loudly. "It's okay, it's okay."

Tommy Rantakyrö is holding his hand under his nose. A trickle of blood is seeping through his fingers. Anna-Maria always has paper tissues in her pockets. Gustav always needs something wiped off his face. Ice cream, banana, snot. She passes the tissue to Tommy.

"Get her down on the ground," shouts Fred Olsson. "We need to cuff her."

"Like hell we do," answers Sven-Erik sharply. "Is the ambulance coming soon?"

The last remark is shouted to Anna-Maria. She makes a movement with her head to indicate that she doesn't know. Sven-Erik and Fred Olsson are now each holding on to one of Rebecka Martinsson's arms. She's on her knees between them, lurching from side to side.

At that very moment the ambulance finally arrives. Closely followed by another radio car. Flashing lights and sirens slicing through the hard gray rain. There's a hell of a noise.

And right through the middle of it all Anna-Maria can hear Rebecka Martinsson screaming.

*   *   *

Rebecka Martinsson is screaming. She's screaming like someone who's lost her mind. She can't stop.

YELLOW LEGS

He's as black as Satan. Comes racing through a sea of brownish pink fireweed that's gone to seed. The white, woolly seed heads whirl like snow in the autumn sunshine. He stops dead. A hundred meters away from her.

*   *   *

His chest is broad. So is his head. Long, coarse black bristles around his neck. He isn't handsome. But he's big. Just like her.

He remains stock-still as she approaches him. She's been listening to him ever since yesterday. She's enticed him, called him. Sung for him. Told him in the darkness that she's all alone. And he's come. At last he's come.

Happiness is prickling in her paws. She trots straight up to him. Her admiration is totally unconditional. She draws her ears together and places herself in the courtship position. Arches her neck. Her long back like a sinuous S. His tail makes long, slow, sweeping movements.

Nose to nose. Nose to genitals. Nose under the tail. And then nose to nose once again. Chest puffed out, neck extended. The whole thing is unbearably ceremonious. Yellow Legs places all she has before him. If you want me, you can have me, she says clearly.

And then he gives her the sign. He places one of his front paws on her shoulder. Then he springs forward skittishly.

And she can't hold back any longer. The sense of playfulness she'd forgotten she possessed returns with full force. She leaps away from him. Hurtles away, the soil spraying up behind her. Accelerates, does a U-turn, races back and soars over him with a long leap. Turns around. Lowers her head, wrinkles her nose and shows her teeth. And off again.

He races after her and they tumble over and over together when he catches her.

They're full of it. Playing like mad things. Afterward they lie in a heap, panting.

She stretches her neck lazily and licks his jaws.

The sun is sinking among the pine trees. Their legs are tired and contented.

Everything is now.

AUTHOR'S ACKNOWLEDGMENTS

Rebecka Martinsson will get back on her feet, I believe in that little girl in her red Wellington boots. And remember: in my story I'm God. The characters might make a fuss about their free will from time to time, but I invented them. The places in the book are also mostly invented. There is a village called Poikkijärvi by the river Torne, but that's where any resemblance ends, there's no gravel track, no bar, no priest's house.

Many people have helped me and I would like to thank some of them here: jur. kand. Karina Lundström, who sniffs out interesting characters within the police authorities. Senior doctor Jan Lindberg who helped me with my dead bodies. PhD candidate Catharina Durling and deputy judge Viktoria Edelman, who always checks the statute book for me when I don't understand something or I've run out of energy. Dog handler Peter Holmström, who told me about Clinton the superdog.

Any errors in the book are mine. I forget to ask, misunderstand, or make things up against my better judgment.

Thanks also to: publisher Gunnar Nirstedt for his opinions. Elisabeth Ohlson Wallin and John Eyre for the cover. Lisa Berg and Hans-Olov Öberg who read and had opinions. My mother and Eva Jensen, who always manage to press the repeat button and say wonderful! Really! My father, who sorts out maps and can answer just about any question and who saw a wolf when he was seventeen and laying nets beneath the ice.

And finally: Per, for absolutely everything.

ABOUT THE AUTHOR

ÅSA LARSSON was born in Kiruna, Sweden, in 1966. She studied in Uppsala and lived for some years in Stockholm but now prefers the rural life. A former tax lawyer, she now writes full-time and is the author of *Sun Storm*, winner of Sweden's Best First Crime Novel Award, and of *The Black Path*.

If you enjoyed Åsa Larsson's *THE BLOOD SPILT,* you will want to read all of the work of this exciting new Swedish crime writer. Look for her debut crime novel, *SUN STORM,* available in trade paperback from Delta.

And read on for an early look at Åsa Larsson's marvelous new suspense novel, coming soon from Delta. . . .

THE BLACK PATH

by

Åsa Larsson

On sale August 2008

THE BLACK PATH

TRANSLATED
BY MARLAINE DELARGY

A NOVEL

ÅSA LARSSON

AWARD-WINNING AUTHOR OF *THE BLOOD SPILT*

THE BLACK PATH

On sale August 2008

EXTRACT FROM CASE NOTES 12 SEPTEMBER 2003
REGARDING PATIENT REBECKA MARTINSSON

Reason for contact: Patient admitted to Kiruna hospital with facial injuries after a fall & trauma to head. On admission found to be in acute state of psychosis. Surgical treatment of facial injuries necessary; patient therefore sedated. On waking, clear psychotic symptoms still present. Decision made to section patient under 3 § LPT. Transferred to psychiatric clinic at St. Göran's hospital, Stockholm – secure unit. Preliminary diagnosis: psychosis UNS. Treatment: Risperdal mix 8 mg/day plus Sobril 50 mg/day.

This is the last time.

Behold, he comes with the clouds, and every eye shall see him.

This is the final hour.

This is the time of the fiery steed. She who comes with the long sword, so that men shall slay one another.

And here! They seize me by the arms! They will not listen! Stubbornly they refuse to turn their eyes to the heavens, opening up before them.

This is the time of the pale steed.

And he paws the ground with his sharp hooves. He kicks earth out of his way.

There came a huge earthquake, and the earth turned as black as ink, and the whole of the moon was the color of blood.

And I remained behind. Many of us were left behind. We fall to our knees before our journey into the darkness, and we empty our bowels through fear. On the way to the lake burning with fire and sulfur, and this is the second death. Only a few minutes remain. We must grab hold of whatever we can. Hold fast to what is closest to us.

I can hear the voice of the seven storms. At last the words are clear.

It says. The time. Is up.

But no one here will listen!

EXTRACT FROM CASE NOTES 27 SEPTEMBER 2003 REGARDING PATIENT REBECKA MARTINSSON

Patient responsive, answers when spoken to, able to give an account of events which triggered depressive psychosis. Displays vital signs of depression: weight loss, listlessness, disturbed sleep pattern, waking early. High risk of suicide. ECT treatments to continue. Cipramil in tablet form 40 mg/day.

One of the nurses (I have nurses, imagine that) is called Johan. Or is it Jonas? Jonny? He takes me out for a walk. I'm not allowed out on my own. We don't go far. It still makes me incredibly tired. Perhaps he notices as we're walking back. He doesn't show it, though. Keeps talking the whole time. That's good, it means I don't have to bother.

He's talking about Muhammad Ali's title fight against George Foreman in 1974 in Zaire.

"He took so much punishment! Leaned against the ropes and just let Foreman keep hitting him. Foreman, well, he was cruel. We're talking heavyweights here, and most people have probably forgotten, but people were worried about Ali before the match. Thought Foreman might actually kill him. And then Ali just stood there like a bloody . . . stone! And took the punishment for seven rounds. Completely psyched Foreman out. In the seventh he leaned against Foreman's shoulder and whispered, "Is that all you got, George?" And it was! Then in the eighth, Foreman could hardly keep his guard up any longer, and then the opening came. Ali just went: bam! (he made a right hook in the air). Foreman goes down like a pine tree! Crrrash!"

I walk in silence. Notice that the trees are starting to smell of autumn. And he's talking Rumble in the Jungle. I am the greatest. Thrilla in Manilla.

Or he talks about the Second World War (is he supposed to do that with me, I wonder quietly to myself, aren't I sensitive, sort of fragile, what would the consultant say?)

"The Japanese, now they're real warriors. You know, when their fighter pilots ran out of juice in the middle of the Pacific, if there was an American aircraft carrier within range they flew straight into it. Pow! Or they did an elegant belly landing on the surface of the water, just to show what incredibly skillful fliers they were. Then when they were sitting there having survived, they jumped in the water and stabbed themselves. Wouldn't let themselves be taken alive by the enemy. Same thing when they were fighting at Guadalcanal. They jumped off the cliffs like lemmings when they realized they were beaten. The Americans were standing there with their megaphones telling them to give themselves up."

When we get back to the ward I'm suddenly afraid that he'll ask me if I enjoyed the walk. If I liked it? If I'd like to do it again tomorrow?

I can't manage to answer "yes" or "that would be nice." It feels like it did when I was little. When some of the older ladies in the village bought you an ice cream or a drink. They always had to ask: "Was that nice?" Despite the fact that they could see. You were sitting there devouring it, in silent bliss. But you had to give them something. Pay the price. "Yes," and preferably "thank you" from the little girl, the poor little soul with the crazy mother. I have nothing to give now. Not even a squeak. If he asks me I'll have to say no. Although it was so good to breathe the air. The ward smells of medication sweated out through every pore, smoke, dirt, hospital, the cleaning fluid they use on the vinyl floor.

But he doesn't ask. Takes me for a stroll the following day too.

Extract from epicrisis October 30 re patient
Rebecka Martinsson

Patient has responded well to treatment. Suicide risk no longer regarded as likely. For the past two weeks has been nursed according to HSL. Low, but not seriously depressed. Transfer to residence in Kurravaara, village outside Kiruna, where patient grew up. To keep in contact with clinic in Kiruna. Continued medication Cipramil 40 mg/day.

The consultant asks me how I'm feeling. I reply: fine.

He looks at me in silence. Almost smiling. Knowing. He can keep quiet for as long as it takes. He's an expert at it. Silences don't provoke him. In the end I say: not too bad. That's the right answer. He nods.

I'm not allowed to stay here. I've taken up a place for long enough. There are women who need it more than me. The kind who set fire to their hair. Who come onto the ward and swallow pieces of broken mirror in the toilets, and have to be rushed into the emergency department all the time. I can talk, answer questions, get up in the mornings and brush my teeth.

I hate him because he won't force me to stay here forever and ever. Because he isn't God.

Then I'm sitting on the train traveling north. The landscape hurtles past in a series of snapshots. First there are the big deciduous trees in tones of red and yellow. Autumn sunshine and lots of houses. People living their lives in every single one. Getting by somehow.

After Bastuträsk there's snow. And then at last: forest, forest, forest. I'm on the way home. The birch trees shrink, standing black and spindly against the white background.

I press my forehead and my nose against the window.

I feel fine, I say to myself. This is what it's like to feel fine.

SATURDAY MARCH 15

An early spring evening, Torneträsk. The ice was thick, more than a meter. All along the lake, some seventy kilometers long, lay arks, small cabins on runners, four square meters in size. At this time of year the inhabitants of Kiruna made their pilgrimage up to Torneträsk. They came up on snowmobiles, towing the ark behind them.

Inside the ark there was a hole in the floor. You drilled a hole through the thick ice. A plastic pipe linked the hole in the ice to the hole in the floor, and that prevented the icy wind from getting into the ark from below. And then you sat inside fishing through the hole in the ice.

Leif Pudas was sitting in his ark in just his pants, fishing. It was eight-thirty in the evening. He'd cracked open a few beers, it was Saturday night after all. The Calor gas stove was hissing and whistling. It was lovely and warm, almost eighty degrees. And he'd caught some fish too, fifteen mountain char, only small, but still. And he'd saved a few sprats for his sister's cat.

When it was time for a pee it felt like a kind of liberation, he was much too hot, it would be nice to get outside and cool down a bit. He pulled on his boots and clambered out into the cold and dark in just his pants.

As soon as he opened the door, the wind seized hold of it.

During the day it had been sunny and calm, with no wind. But in the mountains the weather changes constantly. Now the storm was tugging and snapping at the door like a rabid dog. One moment there was hardly any wind at all, it was as if it were lying there growling and gathering its strength, then it was pulling at the door for all it was worth. Would the hinges hold? Leif Pudas got hold of the door with both hands and closed it behind him. Maybe he should have put some clothes on. Oh, what the hell, it only took a minute to have a pee.

The gusts of wind carried loose snow with them. Not soft, fine fresh snow, but sharp diamond slivers of compacted snow. It whirled across the ground like a white cat-o'-nine-tails, flaying his skin with a slow, evil rhythm.

Leif Pudas ran around the ark to shelter from the wind and got ready to pee. He might be sheltered from the wind, but it was cold so far up north. His scrotum contracted to a rock-hard ball. But at least he managed to pee. He almost expected it to freeze on its way through the air. To be transformed into a yellow arc of ice.

Just as he finished, he heard a kind of bellowing through the wind, and all of a sudden the ark was at his back. It almost knocked him over, and the next second it was gone.

It took a little while for him to understand. The storm had taken the ark. He could see the window, the square of warm light in the darkness, traveling away from him.

He ran a little way in the darkness, but now its mooring had come loose, the ark was gathering speed. He hadn't a chance of catching up with it, it was hurtling away on its runners.

First of all he thought only about the ark. He'd built it himself of plywood, then insulated it and covered it with aluminum. Tomorrow morning when he found it, it would be firewood. All he could do was hope it didn't cause any damage. That could lead to difficulties.

All of a sudden there came a powerful squall. It almost knocked him to the ground. Then he realized he was in danger. And he had all that beer inside him, it was as if his blood was just beneath the surface of the skin. If he didn't manage to get inside somewhere very soon, he'd freeze to death in no time.

He looked around. It had to be at least a kilometer up to Abisko tourist station, he'd never make it, it was a question of minutes now. Where was the closest ark? The whirling snow and the storm meant he couldn't see the lights of any other arks.

Think, he said to himself. You don't take one single bloody step until you've used your head. Which direction are you facing now?

He used his head for three seconds, felt his hands starting to stiffen, and tucked them under his arms. He took four steps from where he was standing and managed to walk straight into the snowmobile. The key was in the disappearing ark, but he had a little toolbox under the seat, and he got it out.

Then he prayed to someone up there that he was going the right way, and set off in the direction of his closest neighboring ark. It was no more than twenty meters, but he wanted to weep with every step. He was so afraid of missing it. And if he did, he was a dead man.

He searched for Persson's fiberglass ark. The wet snow covered his eyes; he tried to peer through, but it was as if a slush kept forming over his eyes and he had to wipe it away. It was impossible to see anything, darkness and snow.

He thought about his sister. And he thought about his ex-partner, about the fact that things had been good between them in many ways.

He'd almost walked straight into Persson's ark before he saw it. Nobody home, the windows dark. He took the hammer out of his toolbox, had to use his left hand, the right one was completely useless, pain shooting through it after holding the cold steel of the toolbox handle. He fumbled his way through the darkness to the small Plexiglas window and smashed it.

The fear made him strong, and he heaved his entire bulk of over two hundred pounds in through the window. Swore when he scraped his stomach on the sharp metal frame. But what did that matter. Death had never been quite so close before, breathing down his neck.

Once he was inside, he had to do something about getting some heat going. Even if he was protected from the wind, it was bitterly cold inside the ark.

He rummaged in the drawers and found some matches. How can you hold something so small when the cold has made your hands completely useless? He pushed his fingers into his mouth to warm them until they were working well enough to allow him to light the lamp and the stove. His entire body wanted to do nothing but shiver and shake, never in his life had he felt this cold. Frozen through to his bones.

"Bloody hell it's cold, fuck me it's cold," he kept saying to himself over and over again. He spoke out loud, it somehow kept the panic at bay, as if he were keeping himself company.

The wind howled through the window like a malevolent god; he grabbed a big cushion that was leaning against the wall and managed to wedge it fast between the curtain pole and the wall.

He looked around and found a red padded jacket, probably one of Mrs. Persson's. He also found a drawer full of underwear, pulled on two pairs of long johns, one on his legs and one on his head.

The warmth came slowly, he held his limbs out toward the stove, pain shooting through his body; it was agonizing. He had no feeling at all in one cheek and ear, which wasn't a good sign.

There was a heap of blankets on the bunk bed. They were ice cold, of course, but he could wrap himself up in them anyway, they'd provide some sort of insulation.

I've survived, he said to himself. What does it matter if I lose an ear?

He yanked a blanket off the bed. It was covered in big flowers in different shades of blue, a relic of the seventies.

And underneath it lay a woman. Her eyes were open and had frozen to ice, so they were completely white, like frosted glass. Something that looked like porridge, or maybe it was vomit, on her chin and hands. She was wearing sports clothes. There was a red mark on her top.

He didn't scream. He didn't even feel surprised. It was as if his emotions had been completely wiped out by what he'd been through.

"What the fuck," was all he said.

And the feeling that washed over him was like the feeling you get when your new puppy pees in the house for the hundredth time. Exhaustion in the face of how crap everything is.

He resisted the impulse to simply put the blanket back and forget about her.

Then he sat down to think. What on earth should he do now? He had to get to the tourist station, of course. He wasn't too keen on going up there in the dark. But he had no choice, did he? And he didn't much like the idea of sitting here thawing out with her.

But he needed to sit here for a little while longer. Until he wasn't so damned cold.

It was like a kind of companionship between them. She kept him company as he sat there for an hour, tortured by the pain in various parts of his body as the warmth brought the feeling back. He held his hands out to the stove.

He didn't say a word. And neither did she.

Inspector Anna-Maria Mella and her colleague Sven-Erik Stålnacke reached the scene at quarter to midnight on Saturday. The police had borrowed two snowmobiles from Abisko tourist station. One of them had a sledge. One of the mountain guides had offered to help out, and he drove them both down. Storms and darkness.

Leif Pudas, who had found the body, was sitting in Abisko tourist station and had already been questioned by the squad car unit who had been first on the scene.

When Leif Pudas arrived at the tourist station, the reception desk was closed. It had taken a while before the staff in the bar took him seriously. It was Saturday night after all, and they were more than used to unconventional dress at the tourist station; people would take off their snowmobile overalls and sit there drinking beer in their underwear and all sorts. But Leif Pudas had come stumbling in dressed in a ladies' padded jacket that only reached just below his navel, with a pair of long johns wound round his head like a turban.

It wasn't until he burst into tears that they understood something serious had happened. They had listened, then treated him somewhat warily while they contacted the police.

He'd found a dead woman, he said. He'd repeated several times that it wasn't his ark. They'd still thought it was probably a matter of a guy who'd killed his wife. Nobody had wanted to look him in the eye. He'd been sitting there all alone and weeping, disturbing no one, when the police arrived.

It had proved impossible to seal off the area around the ark; the wind had simply snatched the police tape away. Instead they had tied the black and yellow tape around the ark, wrapping it up like a parcel. The tape was flapping angrily in the wind. The technicians had arrived, and were working on the small surface area in the beam of the spotlights and the muted Calor gas light afforded by the ark itself.

There just wasn't room for more than two people inside the ark. While the technicians were working, Anna-Maria Mella and Sven-Erik Stålnacke stood outside and tried to keep moving.

It was more or less impossible to hear each other through the storm and their thick hats. Even Sven-Erik was wearing a hat with ear flaps; he didn't normally wear anything on his head, even in the middle of winter. They yelled at each other and moved about like fat Michelin men in their snowmobile overalls.

"Look," shouted Anna-Maria. "This is ridiculous."

She spread out her arms, standing like a sail against the wind. She was a small woman and didn't weigh a great deal. Besides which, the snow had melted during the day, then frozen again in the evening and turned shiny and icy, so when she positioned herself like that the wind got hold of her and she began to glide slowly away.

Sven-Erik laughed and pretended to hurry over to catch her before she slid off to the opposite side of the lake.

The technicians emerged from the ark.

"She wasn't murdered here, at any rate," one of them bawled at Anna-Maria. "Looks like she was stabbed. But like I said, not here. You can take the body. We'll carry on here in the morning when we can see what we're doing."

"And when we're not freezing our asses off," yelled his colleague, who wasn't dressed nearly warmly enough.

The technicians climbed onto the sledge and were driven off to the tourist station.

Anna-Maria Mella and Sven-Erik Stålnacke went into the ark.

It was cold and cramped.

"But at least we're out of that bloody wind," said Sven-Erik as he closed the door. "That's better, we can talk normally."

The small folding table attached to the wall was covered in a wood-patterned material. Four white plastic chairs were stacked on top of one another. There was a small hotplate and a place to wash the dishes. A red and white checked café curtain and a vase of artificial flowers were lying on the floor beneath the Plexiglas window. A big cushion fixed in front of the window provided a reasonable amount of protection against the wind, which was desperate to get in.

Sven-Erik opened the wardrobe. The equipment necessary for distilling alcohol was inside. He closed the door.

"We didn't see that," was all he said.

Anna-Maria looked at the woman on the bed.

"One seventy-five?" she asked.

Sven-Erik nodded, snapping small icicles from his moustache.

Anna-Maria took the tape recorder out of her pocket. She fought with it for a while, because the batteries had got cold and it didn't want to work.

"Oh, come on," she said, holding it close to the stove, which was doing its best to warm up the inside of the ark despite the broken window and the many gaps in the door.

When she got it going, she put the description in first.

"Female, blonde bob, in her forties . . . She's attractive, isn't she?"

Sven-Erik mumbled something.

"Well, I think she's attractive anyway. About one meter seventy-five, slim, large breasts. No rings on her fingers. Eye color difficult to establish in the present circumstances, maybe the pathologist . . . Light-colored track suit top, looks windproof, stains on it which are probably blood, but we'll find that out soon enough, matching track suit bottoms, running shoes."

Anna-Maria leaned over the woman.

"And she's wearing make-up—lipstick, eye shadow and mascara," she continued into the tape recorder. "Isn't that a bit odd, when you're going out to exercise? And why hasn't she got a hat?"

"It's been a lovely day, really warm, and yesterday was the same," said Sven-Erik. "Just as long as you don't get that wind . . ."

"It's winter! You're the only person who never wears a hat. At any rate, her clothes don't look cheap, and neither does she. She's kind of elegant, somehow."

Anna-Maria switched off the tape recorder.

"We'll start knocking on doors tonight. The tourist station and the eastern side of Abisko. And we'll ask the shop owners if it's anybody they know. You'd think somebody would have reported her missing."

"I've got the feeling there's something familiar about her," said Sven-Erik thoughtfully.

Anna-Maria nodded.

"Maybe she lives in Kiruna, then. Think about it. Maybe you've seen her somewhere? Dentist? Behind the counter in a shop? In the bank?"

Sven-Erik shook his head.

"Leave it," he said. "It'll come to me if it wants to."

"We need to go round the other arks as well," said Anna-Maria.

"I know. And in this bloody storm."

"All the same."

"Right."

They looked at each other for a while.

Sven-Erik looked tired, Anna-Maria thought. Tired and depressed. Dead women often had that effect on him. And the murders were usually so tragic. They lay there dead in the kitchen, the husband in floods of tears in the bedroom, and you just had to be grateful if there were no small children who'd seen it all happen.

It never really affected her that much, unless it involved children of course. Children and animals, you never got used to that. But a murder like this one. Not that it made her happy. Or that she thought it was a good thing somebody had been murdered, nothing like that. But a murder like this . . . it gave you something to get your teeth into, somehow. She needed that.

She smiled inwardly at Sven-Erik's big wet moustache. It looked like road kill. Recently it had been more or less growing wild. She wondered how lonely he really was. His daughter lived in Luleå with her family. They probably didn't get together very often.

And then about eighteen months ago that cat of his had disappeared. Anna-Maria had tried to persuade him to get another one, but Sven-Erik refused. "They're nothing but trouble," he said. "They're such a tie." She knew exactly what that meant. He wanted to protect himself from the anguish. God knows he'd worried about Manne and pondered over what might have happened to him, until in the end he'd given up hope and stopped talking about him.

It was such a shame, thought Anna-Maria. Sven-Erik was a good man. He'd make a fine husband for someone. And a good master for any animal. He and Anna-Maria got on well, but it would never occur to them to spend their leisure time together. It wasn't just that he was much older than her. They simply didn't have that much in common. If they met by chance in town or in a shop when they weren't working, it was always so difficult to make conversation. But at work they'd chat away and get on really well.

Sven-Erik looked at Anna-Maria. She really was a little woman, no more than one meter fifty, she almost disappeared inside the big snow-mobile overalls. Her long blonde hair flattened by the hat. Not that she cared. She wasn't one for make-up and that sort of thing. Probably didn't have the time either. Four kids and a husband who didn't seem to do all that much at home. Apart from that, there was nothing wrong with Robert, things seemed to be good between him and Anna-Maria, he was just so lazy.

Although how much had he actually done at home when he and Hjördis had been married? He didn't really remember, but he did remember not being used to cooking when he was first living on his own.

"Okay," said Anna-Maria. "What if you and I fight our way through the snowstorm and go round the arks, while the others take the village and the tourist station?"

Sven-Erik grinned.

"Might as well, Saturday night's ruined anyway."

It wasn't really ruined. What would he have been doing otherwise? Watching TV and maybe taking a sauna with his neighbor. Always the same old routine.

"True," replied Anna-Maria, zipping up her overalls.

Although she didn't really feel like that. This wasn't a ruined Saturday night. A knight can't just stay at home nestling in the bosom of his family, he'll go mad. He needs to get out there and draw his sword. To come home, tired and sated with adventures, to the family who have no doubt left their empty pizza boxes and fizzy drinks bottles in a heap on the living room table, but it didn't matter. This was life at its best. Knocking on doors out on the ice in the darkness.

"Hope she didn't have kids," said Anna-Maria before they went out into the storm.

Sven-Erik didn't reply. He was a little ashamed. He hadn't even thought about children. The only thing he'd thought was that he hoped there wasn't a cat shut in an apartment somewhere, waiting for his mistress.